PRAISE FOR *A WOMAN IN TIME*

"*A Woman in Time* by Bobi Conn is a rich novel that transports readers into the mountains of Prohibition-era Appalachia and into the lives of an incredible family of female healers. An unflinching look at the struggles and suffering that came with being a woman in early twentieth-century Kentucky, *A Woman in Time* is a truly unique journey into a time and place that are too often overlooked in American history. Bobi Conn proves herself to be a powerful voice for Appalachia."

—Stephanie Storey, bestselling author of *Oil and Marble: A Novel of Leonardo and Michelangelo*

"The grace and lyricism of Conn's prose stuns and sustains the reader through this lush tale of women's strength, creativity, and will to love in Depression-era Eastern Kentucky. Conn's poise and confidence as a storyteller hold the reader in a loving embrace through many a well-wrought and gut-wrenching episode, then bring us out the other side more awake to the preciousness of life and what it means to be accountable to one another across a span of generations. Bobi Conn's *A Woman in Time* is an inspiration."

—Robert Gipe, author of *Pop: An Illustrated Novel*

T0059015

A
WOMAN
IN
TIME

ALSO BY BOBI CONN

In the Shadow of the Valley: A Memoir

A
WOMAN
IN
TIME

A NOVEL

BOBI CONN

Text copyright © 2022 by Bobi Conn
All rights reserved.

Published by Little A, New York

www.apub.com

Amazon, the Amazon logo, and Little A are trademarks of Amazon.com, Inc., or its affiliates.

ISBN-13: 9781542031813 (hardcover)
ISBN-10: 1542031818 (hardcover)

ISBN-13: 9781542031806 (paperback)
ISBN-10: 154203180X (paperback)

Cover design by Faceout Studio, Molly von Borstel

Cover illustrated by Alexandria Neonakis

Printed in the United States of America

First edition

To my children—
Being your mother is the best. Thank you for being you.

AUTHOR'S NOTE

Long before I read stories about Zeus or King Arthur, I heard about my great-grandfather, the moonshiner who worked with famous gangsters in Chicago during the Depression. My father recounted endless adventures and exchanges that painted a portrait of a man who died just before I was born, but whose choices helped shape the world I was born into, the world that played an outsize role in shaping *me*.

When I decided to write the story of my upbringing in Appalachia and all the beauty and pain I have witnessed, I spent a lot of time thinking about my ancestors and what they passed down to me, for better or for worse. I thought I should write more about my great-grandfather and his exploits—I could research and construct a coherent narrative to unify the jumbled stories from childhood memories. But I soon realized that my great-grandmother's story is the one I should aspire to tell. Hers is a story not defined by prison terms, not marked by notches on a belt or pistol. Like many women before her and those who came after, her legacy persists in the children she bore and the life they shared, or did not.

I can't gather her history now—that window closed before I could fathom its significance. And so, I tell another story—*this* story—to honor, explore, and give voice to generations of women whose lives have so often been confined to the margins.

PROLOGUE

*T*he human life unfolds: a series of moments, breaths uncounted, bird-songs flitting in memories lost to the waking mind. Days or decades pass and we look back to discover a narrative, as if it was there all along—joys, triumphs, losses, and sorrows, one following the other, each a story within a story.

A girl is born, bound to the time and place that claim her. She loves and grieves and weaves the future in her body, bringing into the world not just life, but history. And though her body passes, her life forms an endless thread aching for the elusive past, reaching into possibilities not yet born.

Before Granny was the family matriarch possessing all the power a woman could in her day, she was first a daughter, and then a mother. Her love and suffering formed new bodies who carried her testimony inside them—living stories, breathing memory. Strength, failure, wisdom, and heartache flowed through her from women past, to her daughters and grand-daughters, into the new era.

Chapter 1

SUMMER, 1899

Bessie hummed one of Granny McKenzie's medicine songs as she picked clusters of elderberries at the edge of the hayfield. She was only twelve years old, but she knew the names of all the plants they could use, and she could find them quicker than any of the adults could. She gathered the fruit with care, eating her fill as she went. When the purple berry juice began to seep through her white cotton sack, she walked into the woods to look for the coneflowers that grew in her favorite spot, an open space with trees that welcomed her.

She ran her finger across the sharp spines of the flower cone, then carefully moved the palm of her hand against it to feel the light scratch. Bessie sat on a thick tree root that had grown up from the ground, exposed but strong, and played with the flower petals absentmindedly—still gentle, even though she knew they weren't medicine—thinking about the crisp January day earlier this year, when Granny brought her here to dig a root for Mama.

Just a couple, Granny had said. *We take what we need but no more.*

When they took them back to the house, Mama snatched one from Granny's hands, both still covered in dirt. Bessie's brother lay on the feather bed they had set beside the fireplace to keep him warm. Mama washed the root as quickly as she could and took it to Benjamin, who was so pale, Bessie would have sworn she saw the blood in his veins.

Chew this, chew it now. Swallow the juices. Don't spit it out, Mama commanded in a tone Bessie had never heard before. She wondered how awful it must have been, as Benjamin shuddered and cried even though he was seven years old and already knew how to work the farm as good as any man. His eyes pleaded with Mama to spare him the medicine and the sickness both, but Mama only gazed back with a steady determination. Granny walked around the living room singing a song that could have been a church hymn but wasn't quite.

The next day, Benjamin's cough was gone, and the color had come back to his cheeks. Mama and Granny cleaned the rest of the roots and set them in a jar of moonshine. Over the next few months, Bessie checked on it every day to marvel at how the liquid transformed, the presence of the root turning corn liquor into something new. Bessie startled from her memory and left the woods, turning back to bid the forest goodnight.

After supper, as the evening sun set into the darkening sky, their father noticed Bessie cleaning up the dishes. "You'll make a fine wife for someone," he told her with all the warmth she would ever feel from him. Bessie looked to her granny, sitting in a worn rocking chair next to the fireplace. Granny met her eyes before turning back to her sewing.

"Thank you, Papa," Bessie murmured, as she looked back to the dirty plate in front of her. Somehow, Bessie knew she would never be a wife, and she knew Granny shared that secret with her.

Bessie had one sister and one brother who had lived past the age of three. Mama gave birth to twins after she had Mary Ann, and neither one lived for more than a few hours. After that, Granny told her it wasn't safe to have any more babies. Mary Ann was seven years younger and the prettier of the two sisters. Bessie used to watch from their shared bed while Mary Ann brushed her hair by candlelight and peered into the small oval mirror hanging on the hewn log wall. The long, patient strokes kept her light-brown hair shiny and soft. Bessie liked to watch her younger sister lost in reverie, humming songs their mother and grandmothers taught them, but she found her own reverie in the forest, where she was at home.

When they were just fifteen, John Conner found Bessie out in the woods that surrounded both their farms, singing a song to herself as she picked buttercup flowers.

"That's a sweet song you sing, Bessie. Pretty words for a pretty girl."

Bessie stopped but didn't turn around.

"I think you're lovely, you know. Even with your songs and your spells." As he said those words, he wondered if they were true—his father always said the McKenzie women were stranger than most, and Bessie was turning out just like her granny. Granny had not been a woman to be messed with in her younger days, so even as she grew old, no man wanted to argue with her. But no matter how odd or difficult he might have thought Granny McKenzie was, John's father still brought his babies to her anytime one of them had the croup. Everybody knew she was a better healer than the town doctor, who was a good three hours from their farms on horseback. Some people liked to tell the story of her husband's death as if Granny played a part in the horse kicking him in the head, but nobody really believed it. Either way, all the menfolk brought her cured meat or quart Mason jars of their whiskey to trade for her healing, and she used most of the amber liquid to make more medicine but saved a nip or two for herself.

Bessie recognized the kindness in John's voice and felt a passing ache for the life she could have with him. For a moment, she lost sight of the elderberry trees around her and the sunshine-yellow flowers at her feet. She saw the children they could bear and the days in her garden, a daughter beside her as they sang the old songs together. She saw herself putting breakfast on the table, nursing her babies, rocking them and singing, and then finally, sewing their shrouds. She nearly lost her balance and John reached out to her.

"It's alright," she said. "I'm fine. Just a bit faint from the heat." He looked at her and she looked away. "I thank you for your kind words. Granny's waitin' for me."

She rushed to the house with the flowers Granny had requested, and when she walked in, Granny looked up from her chair, full of knowing. Granny understood Bessie as well as she knew her own self, a fact that spared Bessie from a loneliness that would have been too heavy to bear. They didn't talk about it, but Granny could give her a look that held all the reassurance Bessie ever needed. She had always felt *different*, and each time she found herself around other girls and women, she grew more convinced that her life could not look like theirs, bound to serving fathers and husbands. Bessie sank into her grandmother's lap and let herself cry for only a minute. They both knew when to fix themselves, dabbing the tears from their eyes and setting their faces in case someone walked in. Bessie hung the flowers to dry while Granny returned to her sewing and whispered a quiet prayer.

❀

Mary Ann was content to help pick flowers and herbs when the women told her to, but she was happiest in the house, where it seemed her presence alone was enough to light a room. She had a knack for arranging things, and the family's simple home radiated comfort after she tidied up and added her flourishes—usually, a bouquet of wildflowers in a

Mason jar and a whimsical arrangement of the prettiest rocks Benjamin brought from the creek.

She learned to cook like Mama when she was seven years old, standing on a wooden chair to stir the pots on the wood-fired cookstove. She possessed a sense of delicacy that didn't wane when she pulled feathers out of a chicken Mama had just killed, and when they all filled canning jars with peaches, tomatoes, or the rare stew to put up for the winter, her jars looked the prettiest. Bessie always thought Mary Ann was the one who would make a fine wife for somebody, even if she did seem to be daydreaming much of the time.

The night after Bessie ran from John in the woods and cried in Granny's lap over things she could see and feel, but didn't understand, she offered to brush Mary Ann's hair. Mary Ann was surprised—Bessie didn't usually trouble herself to fix her own hair. While she often invented new braid patterns, Bessie saved those for the plants she wove and dried. Mary Ann watched her sister in the little mirror as Bessie hummed one of her favorite songs, a song Granny had taught them both, and brushed Mary Ann's hair with the same care she gave to her plants and tonics.

"Bessie, do you think I'll live on this farm forever?"

Bessie stopped brushing for a moment but didn't look up. "No, little sister," she said as she resumed the long, steady strokes. "I think you will move away, but not too far away, so we can see each other whenever we want."

Mary Ann smiled. "Will you come tend to my babies? Bring us your elderberry tonics in the wintertime?"

"Yes, and buttercups whenever you need them." Bessie caught Mary Ann's eye in the tarnished mirror.

Mary Ann pulled Bessie's free hand to her, kissing the back of it. "I'm sure I'll never need those! I want to have lots of babies."

Bessie kissed the top of her head and pulled her hair gently taut. "Of course you will," she said with a smile. "I have a new way to plait your hair. Let's try it."

❋

By the time Mary Ann married John Conner, everybody knew Bessie was going to be a spinster. She was twenty-two years old and had turned away Jacob Smith and Mary Ann's John, the only boys who lived close enough to court her. While Mary Ann went to live on the neighboring farm a half-hour's ride from her parents, Bessie stayed home and learned just about everything Granny could teach her. Most women were grandmothers by the time they turned forty, and they didn't live much longer than that. But Granny's presence filled any room she was in, though her skin was weathered from working in the wind and sun and cold, and everyone who knew her figured she would live forever.

Bessie often thought about thanking Granny for all the times she had brushed aside Papa's suggestions that she needed to find her a good husband. "I can't let her run off just yet," Granny would tell him. "I need her help tendin' all these sick folks showin' up on my doorstep every day. Don't you worry—I'll set her a fine match when I'm good and ready." Papa walked away each time, shaking his head but knowing he had lost the argument, and Granny would wink at Bessie, who was right where she wanted to be.

Not long before Mary Ann moved away, Benjamin met a girl in town while helping his father pick up the month's supplies at the general store. He made every excuse to go back to town from then on, and his father grumbled about the wear and tear on the horses' hooves but smiled as his son rode away. Before long, Benjamin proposed. They lived with his wife's parents for a little while, visiting the farm at least once a week. But soon, he decided he wanted something more than being a farmer.

When he told their father he was moving to the city so he could get an education and maybe even become a doctor, Papa just stared at the wood grain in the kitchen table. Mama smiled and told him how great it would be to have a doctor in the family, though everyone knew it was an act—they wanted him to stay home and take care of the farm, like he had been raised to do. Benjamin and his pretty wife visited the farm a few times but never came home again after the night Granny's heart seized.

Granny had awoken from a nightmare, covered in sweat and filled with dread. She lit the oil lamp that sat next to her bed and walked toward the front door of the house to see if the specter in her dream was indeed just outside, waiting to come in. Halfway through the kitchen, she stopped and tried to lower herself to the floor, setting the oil lamp down as her vision blurred. Before she could settle herself and let go of the lamp, all feeling left her body, and she crumpled to the floor with a quiet thud that awoke no one and knocked the lamp on its side. Oil poured out and snaked across the kitchen floor before the flame caught it and licked the dry wooden floorboards.

Granny tried to speak, but the rest of her words remained locked inside. Only Bessie smelled the smoke before the fire engulfed the house. She threw open her bedroom window, pushing herself through it as it tried to close, unable to tell whether the screams she heard were her own, or those of her parents who had also awoken, but too late.

❦

People came from miles around to sift through the smoldering ashes and carry the bones they found to a shared grave, lest someone be separated from part of themselves for eternity. Even the men shed tears, and from the salt and shared grief, a grove of dogwood trees sprang up. Long after the wooden crosses rotted to the ground, the land was known as hallowed. But Granny's and Mama's stories ended, and those endings became part of Mary Ann and Bessie. That loss wove itself into them, a grief entwined like the roots reaching through Granny's bones, silent in the earth, and into Bessie, into Mary Ann. All that the women had known and felt would pass to the children who followed, though memories would fade and time itself would change. The roots reached farther, invisible, binding the generations to come, waiting for the ones who could be both bound and free at once.

Chapter 2

Autumn, 1910

Before he became a man and started his own family, John noticed the subtle changes in his father's house, though he couldn't put them into words. They returned from town one time to find his mother hanging plants to dry around the kitchen, as she had all his life, but his father pulled down the plant she had hung over the doorway and tossed it onto the table, next to the new Bible he had just brought home.

"Don't be hanging stuff in the doorways, Irene," Haman told his wife. "All this superstition ain't godly."

Irene started to respond, but then thought better of it, and she whisked the plant away before her husband could say anything else. After that, she stopped singing and praying aloud as often as she had done, and the house took on a more ordered feeling.

Mary Ann had married John right after she turned fifteen. John had been working on his family farm since he was twelve, but he learned to read and write before he left school for good. Mary Ann knew they were a natural fit long before their parents held a series of conversations about the potential match. She moved her cedar chest and dresses to a simple house John built for them at the west end of his family farm, and his father gave John a hundred acres, bounded by a creek that meandered between the two plots of land. There was a dirt road you could take to get from one farm to the other, but it skirted the edge of the property and a neighboring farm, so the ride on horseback took at least half a day each way. Most of the time, John and his father traveled along a trail to each other's farms, which took about half an hour to traverse, if the ground wasn't muddy and the creek wasn't too high. If it had come a good rain, you might be better off just to go back home.

When they first married, John and Mary Ann went to his parents' house every Sunday to read the Bible and sing hymns together, the way the Conners had done all John's life. Afterward, they ate dinner and visited for the afternoon. Mary Ann had hoped Irene would be like a mother to her, to ease the grief that tormented her for months after the fire. It wrought a sinister pain, one that whispered to Mary Ann and Bessie—and to Benjamin, too, though his sisters would never know it—about what they could have done that night, how their own deaths would have been more bearable. The heartache gnawed at them like a rat in the corncrib, until they each found a way to pretend it did not.

If Irene knew what Mary Ann wanted from her or how her daughter-in-law suffered, she did not say. They often rocked in chairs on the porch in silence as John and Haman drank a little homemade whiskey or moonshine and ambled around the farm, talking about the work they would do together. Mary Ann had also hoped her father-in-law would show the same affection her father had shown her—reserved but warm. After only a few visits, though, she found herself unsettled by his gaze, as his blue eyes seemed to reach too far inside her, and for too long. In those moments, she looked to her new husband, who didn't seem to notice, and then to Irene, who turned away each time, her thoughts a mystery.

Soon after John and Mary Ann wed, the menfolk built a few barns, and John set out to raise cattle and hogs to sell in town and the horses he needed to run the farm. Like his father, he grew enough hay to feed his animals and enough field corn to make a bit of whiskey. And there was tobacco, of course—enough for them to use what they wanted and sell a little in town or sell a little more if prices were up.

Bessie moved in with her sister and John after the fire, though John was never entirely comfortable with her presence. Since John's encounter with Bessie as teenagers in the woods, he and his father had heard preachers in town talk about the sin of women healing, and how the threat of witchery still made its way into the houses of God-fearing men if they weren't careful. Traveling preachers didn't often make it to their farms, but there was always at least one in town, standing on the corner giving a sermon while John and Haman sold their animals.

John wondered about the disorder Mary Ann brought into their marital home, with plants and rocks here and there, as if the outside and inside weren't all that different, but her sweetness made it clear she meant no harm and would bring no witchcraft into his home, on purpose or otherwise. Still, he told Mary Ann to take down the herbs she was drying anytime his father came to the farm, and she hung them back up only when Haman was well on his way home.

Bessie was a different story. She was always singing or talking to herself or to someone John couldn't see, always weaving plants and hanging them in every corner of his house, and the house itself seemed to respond to her, as if she somehow brought it to life. So, a few months after the cruel night Bessie's granny and parents died, John built Bessie a little house of her own, on a few acres Benjamin agreed to let her have when he sold off the rest of their family's land. Her house sat next to the banks of the Licking River and commanded such a view, John hoped it would keep her away from her sister and his house. Still, Bessie showed up nearly every day to help Mary Ann and, in John's mind, to maintain her influence over their home.

Mary Ann took to her new role as wife and planted the garden with seeds her mama had given her before their house and all the land around it was scorched by fire and heartache. Despite her sorrow, Mary

Ann was pregnant within the first month of their awkward embraces in the dark. Before he was even born, they named the first boy John Jr.

Mary Ann screamed when her sister finally pulled him out, and her delicate body tore in places that were both numb from pain and burning with the fire of new life. Bessie didn't tell her the boy's body was stuck and his face was starting to turn blue from being half in, half out for too long. Mary Ann's blood rushed out after him and pooled around her left foot when she held her newborn son, shaking as she put him to her breast. Bessie quickly squeezed a dropper full of yarrow tincture into Mary Ann's mouth and threaded the needle to stitch her back together with a gentleness the town midwife never showed.

One night after the baby's birth, John watched Mary Ann in the candlelight as she put her nightgown back on.

"You're a beauty, Mary Ann. I couldn't have picked a better wife."

"You couldn't have picked many wives, could you?" she teased. "How many women are there to pick from in Bath County? You'd have been hard pressed to find another." She turned to him with laughter in her eyes.

"Well, there's your sister. I could have kept with the same family." John tried to say the words as a joke, but they fell flat as the truth hung in the air between them. The laughter stole from Mary Ann's eyes.

John broke his gaze from hers. "I just thought she was pretty, that's all. I told her once when she was out picking flowers in the woods. She wasn't the one for me—you were. I just didn't know it yet."

Mary Ann laughed again but for reasons hidden from John, as she realized he had never known either one of them. All at once, she felt a great sorrow for herself and for him—two strangers, really. They were adults but still children in some ways, clinging to childhood daydreams about who they were and who they could be. She looked at her son, and the possible lives to follow his flashed through her mind like a squirrel in the trees.

Worlds of possibility unfolded within her, and she smiled.

"That's no matter now. You're right. I was the one best suited for you." And for several years, she enjoyed a closeness with her husband that would have made most women jealous, though she knew she could not tell him all of her thoughts, like she could with Bessie.

She would be relieved when each of her pregnancies, and then the demands of her babies, made it easy for her to avoid the horse ride to Haman's house and to spend less time with her father-in-law. For her part, Irene claimed she needed most of her days to keep up with the farm and house, so she visited only when Mary Ann needed help with the boys, or when they canned the garden's harvest together. Mary Ann found ways to stay busy when Haman came to their house, and when his visits overlapped a mealtime, she tended the babies instead of sitting to eat with him and John.

A year after John Jr. was born, John added another bedroom to their house with the help of a couple of men from the neighboring farms. He insisted on the new room in case the next child was a girl, despite Mary Ann's certainty it was a boy. Mary Ann went into labor as the sun rose. Sitting in the corner of the kitchen, Bessie wove a St. Brigid's cross from some of the flax she had grown and waited for the woodstove to heat the water to boiling. John glanced at her on his way out, just as the contractions found their rhythm and pulled Mary Ann into the dreamworld between life and darkness.

Bessie saw the disapproval on John's face as he walked out that day, and she told him with a quick smile, "It's a Catholic cross," as she continued weaving. John didn't know any Catholics, and he didn't know enough about their ways to say whether or not she was telling the truth. He kept on walking, though, and told Bessie he would be back before nightfall.

Bessie spoke her prayers in a low voice after John shut the door behind him. Mary Ann moaned, her voice no longer lilting and light, but deep and guttural as she joined the chorus of mothers who had suffered and sweated and broken open for the sake of giving life.

Bessie moved the water away from the hottest part of the cookstove and went to Mary Ann's side. Mary Ann would have this baby in the same living room where she'd had John Jr., and Bessie had already swept the corners with her hand broom and sprinkled salt along the walls for protection, as Granny had always done. Bessie saw the shadow on the day of John Jr.'s birth, the way it stole toward Mary Ann right after the baby came out, before her spilled blood even had time to cool. In the cold sunlight, Bessie had prayed silently for the shadow to let the mother and baby be, and it finally slid away from the light of the house. But she knew she had to be more careful at the next birth.

Matthew was at least eight pounds, just like his brother had been, and also had to be pulled out with some force, but Mary Ann did not have to be stitched with this one. He was born a year and five days after his brother.

Mary Ann loved the boys with a matter-of-fact air. John was quietly grateful she took to motherhood so quickly and did not seem to mind she became a mother right after becoming a wife. She was dutiful and affectionate without doting. John knew she would never make the boys weak, and they grew into rambunctious toddlers with the same determined force with which their grandmother had kept their uncle Benjamin alive through the fever that racked him at the age of seven.

Chapter 3

Winter, 1915

The last time she survived childbirth, Mary Ann secretly prayed to have a daughter. She promised if her prayer was answered, it would be the last selfish thing she ever asked for. Mary Ann kept her word, and never asked for mercy from anything that followed.

As her third baby grew and exerted its own force throughout Mary Ann's body, Bessie told her she would have a girl this time. Mary Ann would only respond, "We'll be thankful for a healthy baby." But she already loved the dark-eyed daughter she was sure she would have, and she knew the baby's name, but didn't tell John.

Over the years, he had sought out some of the traveling preachers on purpose, and sometimes gathered his family in the evening to tell them what he had learned that day, not seeming to notice that some of the lessons contradicted each other, and that different preachers interpreted the same Bible verses in different ways. Mary Ann loaded up the children and went to town with him a few times a year to get supplies, and she found an excuse each time to pull John away from the red-faced men who spat as they roared about the fires of hell and sweated as if they had been there.

Still, John had grown more suspicious of superstition and anything he didn't understand, and he even seemed displeased anytime Mary Ann or Bessie talked about their dreams and what they might mean. He didn't talk about the Bible much, but he always responded to the women's talk when he overheard it, reminding them God had only revealed his will to the prophets. Mary Ann would agree with a conciliatory smile while Bessie looked away, distracted by some piece of handiwork to be finished.

Rosalee's birth was the easiest for Mary Ann. She was smaller than the first two boys—she couldn't have been more than seven pounds—and Mary Ann labored with her in a different way than the others. She felt the force of each contraction as if it was the undercurrent of an ocean no one had ever seen, pushing and pulling her into a space outside of time. Through the pain, she noticed the smell of cedar and rosemary from a bouquet Bessie had woven together and wrapped in twine. Dust motes were dancing in the sunlight that streamed through the window and into the living room. Mary Ann could see the pattern in their movement and how each swirled around the other in time with her contractions, her tight belly now a drum for the entire listening world.

She heard their cow at the fence, chewing bites of grass over and over, filling up with milk John would bring in before the sun rose for Mary Ann to drink. She heard John out there, too, ruminating over questions that couldn't be answered, over thoughts that wouldn't be swept away. Her sons played in the barn alongside him, not knowing what gnawed at him but absorbing it anyway as they made games of their chores. As the baby came fully out and into Bessie's waiting hands, Mary Ann heard its heartbeat and then its cries, and she heard a story in that sound, a story with no ending and no beginning, and she took her baby from Bessie with a sob that leapt from her throat as if she had waited to say something to this new daughter for an entire lifetime. She looked into the endless, dark night of Rosalee's eyes and fell in love.

Later, after John and the boys met the baby, Bessie held Rosalee while Mary Ann slept for a short time. When no one was looking, Bessie whispered secrets to the newborn, telling her the meaning of the whippoorwill song and what happens when crickets sing in unison and then diverge, only to come together again, over and over, across the waiting night.

Not long after their daughter was born, John realized that in some ways, he had lost his wife. Mary Ann's love for Rosalee grew fiercely in the days and months that followed. Rosalee was, for her part, independent and headstrong, even as an infant. She almost held her head steady without help on the night she was born, as Bessie picked her up to look into her eyes. Rosalee looked back intently and hardly cried. Family came to visit, and they all remarked that the baby had Mary Ann's temperament, but both she and Bessie knew this girl was different from anyone who had come before her.

Rosalee grew into a serious child who always appeared to be listening to something no one around her could hear. Her older brothers fished in the evening and brought home a few bass to eat, which Mary Ann prepared along with squash and beans from the garden. John's cows produced plenty of milk, and he sold a few off each fall and butchered one to share with his parents for the winter. Mary Ann spent hours combing and braiding Rosalee's hair, and John noticed she sang new songs to the girl just about every night. He tried to ask her sometimes what she was singing and where she learned it, but Mary Ann just smiled at him like he had discovered something private that only women talk about, so he stopped asking. The more distant she grew, the harder he worked, so the farm thrived as Mary Ann drew deeper into a world he knew he was not part of.

After Granny died, Bessie not only became the local healer, but people from around the county also fetched her to help when it was time for a new baby to come along. She rode all over the dirt roads and forest trails on her sturdy horse, never speaking of her own pain that had first inflamed the marrow of her bones as a child. She had been sick for weeks during her tenth winter, sweating and shivering in a delirium, but Granny watched over her day and night, pouring love and herbs into the girl's body, until they all thought the sickness was gone. Instead, it hid itself, burrowing into her nerves, growing too strong for any treatment yet known by mountain women or city doctors.

Unsettled by the pain she had long ignored but that now grew more crippling by the day, Bessie came around Mary Ann's house more often than not, unsure of when the invisible disease would take her legs. While Mary Ann tended the boys and her chores, still feeding chickens and washing dishes with practiced devotion, Bessie taught Rosalee how to make prayer dolls and infuse them with her most important wishes. They walked along the perimeter of the farm, Bessie's gait growing less steady as Rosalee learned the landscape and its treasures in a way not even her adventuresome brothers had discovered. To John's dismay, the bedroom he had built for a daughter sat empty until Rosalee reached the age of four, and, at his insistence, stopped sleeping in her mother's arms.

There was a small spring northwest of the cow pasture, just a few yards into the forest that surrounded the farm on three sides. Hidden under a rock outcropping, the spring never went dry, even in the droughts to come. After Granny and Mama passed, no one else besides Mary Ann and Bessie knew about the spring. They went to it at least once a week, and each took a long drink without speaking, as if they were in church. Bessie took Rosalee there even more often, pulling the young girl away from the house as much as she could.

Bessie showed Rosalee where the most important plants grew throughout the year and how to identify their leaves, how to dig a single plant so its sisters would continue to grow, and what other plants to look for nearby. Rosalee brought cedar and mugwort home, which she wrapped into small bundles with woven patterns she invented herself. But Bessie took most of the plants to her home, where she dried them or made tinctures for the folks who traveled from other counties for her medicine.

John contented himself with knowing Mary Ann provided well for their children, even if the tenderness between the two of them had faded away. He told himself it was natural for a mother to bond with her daughter and he could respect the closeness they shared, even if it meant his wife's affection for him had diminished. Mary Ann had a vague sense she had grown less interested in her husband over the years, but she was so devoted to her daughter, it didn't occur to her anything was lacking in their family. The boys needed little from her other than the meals she prepared, the laundry she scrubbed, and the intangible net of safety and warmth that permeated the household, despite her obvious and unrivaled affection for Rosalee.

The Depression wouldn't come for the rest of the country for years, but in Bath County, Kentucky, life had always been hard, and just after Rosalee was sent to sleep in her own bed, the cows stopped selling like they used to. The men and boys in the family still hunted and fished, though, and only John worried about the change for a while. As the days wore on, he slaughtered more of his herd to make up for the food they couldn't buy or trade for. He rode the trail from his farm to his father's more often and spent his evenings sitting in the living room at their house, talking as the candles burned into sorrowful puddles and his mother, Irene, cast worried glances at the two men.

Irene sensed the distance between John and Mary Ann, and she knew her son came to his childhood home for a comfort that could not be given. She wondered what would become of them all as father and son debated the benefits of adding more livestock or reducing their costs over profits and actual food they could put away for hard winters. She brought them coffee by the fireplace, and before she could sit, a shadow caught her eye as it crept from the corner of their living room that once had felt just right but now was too large, too open. She held her breath as the shadow withdrew, but not before wrapping a tendril around her husband, whose bones ached and longed to be free of the cold Kentucky winter.

Chapter 4

Spring, 1920

As she grew more sure of the world around her and her place in it, Rosalee spent much of her days wandering around the farm, picking flowers and weeds while she whispered to herself. Her brothers worked like young men alongside their father from sunrise to sunset. They grew, and the fun they once found in farm chores soured as they realized their play had turned to duty. Though the sisters didn't go to school, Mary Ann and Bessie's mother had insisted their father teach them to read, something Mary Ann would look back on with wonder and pride. She or John worked with the boys by lamplight after the day's work was done, but the boys couldn't focus, so they learned to write their names and little else.

The Conners didn't get much news from the outside world, other than the newspaper John picked up on his monthly trips to town. Sometimes, a neighbor or relative visited and brought a stack of old newspapers to exchange. They used the oldest in the outhouse first, saving the latest editions to satiate their curiosity about the outside world.

There was a revival in Owingsville every year, always at the beginning of the growing season, and all the families in the county who lived too far from a church to go on Sundays would come for as many nights as they could manage. Most of the women took the opportunity to barter their extra quilts or jars of food and catch up on all the news they otherwise could only hear when they managed to see each other in town. And since they couldn't always accompany their husbands on those trips, reports of a pregnancy or marital problems often arrived long after the onset. The kids begged for pieces of penny candy, and sometimes they got to take home an old catalog from the general store, filled with line drawings of dolls and wagons and factory-made clothes. Bessie used to laugh when Granny McKenzie refused to go to revivals with the family, calling the preacher "a mindless heathern"—never mind it was almost always a different preacher every year. Not long after the fire, Bessie refused to go to any more revivals herself.

Every year, John and Mary Ann went to the revival, taking the kids with them in a horse-drawn wagon normally used for carrying piglets to the market and bags of flour home. When they were little, the children spent as much time as they could running around outside the revival tent, laughing, chasing, and being chased by the other kids they only saw a few times a year, at best. John always made his children sit still during the sermon, and while preachers warned and threatened them, Rosalee would imagine the world beyond Owingsville, overrun by sinners and lawlessness. Yet certain things confused her. Some of the preachers railed against drinking whiskey, though most of the men sitting in the revival tent drank it, and plenty of them made it. Some years, the preacher talked about Prohibition being the Lord's work, and in other years, he could be seen taking liberal sips from a bottle shared by the locals behind the tent, just before or after he hollered at the crowd for the night. Other times, when the preacher railed against witchcraft, Rosalee noticed her father stiffen and sit up straighter, while an odd look crossed her mother's face. Even as a child, Rosalee wondered why the preacher was so angry.

She asked Bessie about it once, out of earshot of her father, and Bessie scoffed. "Witchcraft is a word men use when they're scared of women. Don't you pay no mind to those old fools," she told Rosalee, "but take care they don't see you doing things that scare them." Rosalee nodded as if she understood what Bessie meant, and Bessie went on to rail against another word, one Rosalee hadn't heard but John surely had: *pagan*. As far as the young girl could tell, the men were deciding what could and couldn't be considered Christian, and most of what couldn't was the healing and praying they didn't take part in.

❧

Even when Rosalee was too little to understand, Bessie had repeated Granny's line about the preacher enough so the girl had her doubts about him before he opened his mouth. But during the sermon, Mary Ann and John exchanged looks as the preacher warned of hard times ahead, pounding his fist and insisting they all deserved punishment for the godlessness overtaking the land. While the grown-ups around her said *Amen* and *Lord, tell it*—as if the preacher needed any encouragement—Rosalee's vision went dark, and the red-faced preacher and his pulpit faded into a new landscape. Rosalee saw the vast countryside she had only heard about, with its endless acres of wheat and wild horses, and no hills as far as the eye could see. The plants withered and finally blew in the wind like ash, and the horses cried for water until the heat of the air reached into their throats and silenced them. With a flash visible only to her, the light greens and deep yellows gave way to a single hue, the gray of thirst and bone.

Rosalee startled when Matthew pinched her arm. "Pay attention," he hissed. "You look like you're soft in the head!" Rosalee glared at her brother but tried to compose herself, willing the vision to leave her alone, even though the smell of death lingered in her nostrils.

John's father died the day Mary Ann became pregnant with their fourth child, another boy. They hadn't touched each other for months, but John was seized by a loneliness in the days leading up to his father's

death, and he reached out to his wife, who responded out of both compassion and duty. The women's unspoken control of the household was
set in stone, while John's authority in his own home all but disappeared.
When Mary Ann told Rosalee and Bessie that John's father had passed,
the three shared a secret relief that they would never again have to
avoid the old man and his blue eyes, which inspected the body of every
woman and girl he encountered, kin or not.

After Rosalee's fifth birthday, they went to the yearly revival, and
Rosalee had no way of knowing this would be her last. Mary Ann rested
her hand on her belly the whole way to town, queasy from bouncing
along the dirt road for hours, but she hoped the trip would bring her
some of the cheer that had stolen from their home.

Rumors of dying crops spread from neighboring counties, and the
preacher assured them pestilence was heading this way, spreading like
the sin that preceded it. This is what he had warned them of for so long,
and Rosalee worried over what it meant that she had seen a vision of this
ruin before any of the adults around her. Worse than any drought they
could imagine, there would be swarms of locusts and rivers of blood.
Babies would die at their mothers' breasts and men would burn where
they stood, unrepentant to their last breath. It sounded to Rosalee like
the hardship was both the Devil's work and the Lord's work, the way
the preacher talked about it. He was almost gleeful at times, delighted
by the punishment being dealt to fornicators and blasphemers and even
to farmers who mostly stayed at home and had a sip of whiskey in the
evening.

Still, the adults shook their heads over the thought. They uttered
appeals to God's mercy when they ran out of things to say, and the children tried to forget these new worries and the preacher's insistence that
they would all go to hell when the world ended, if not sooner. After the
sermon ended, the preacher called for the sinners to *Come forth and beg
for forgiveness!* Rosalee recognized some of the same adults who went to
the makeshift altar every year, and she wondered whether they needed

saving or just liked to do it every chance they got, for good measure. When it was finally over, everyone went outside and had quiet conversations, and only the preacher seemed encouraged by what had just happened inside the tent. The men decided which of them would help mend a fence or add a room to someone else's house, while the women traded seeds for their gardens. Despite making plans for the future, an uneasy feeling followed everyone home.

For a brief time, John and Mary Ann seemed united in unspoken worry. Despite her prayers, Mary Ann's pregnant belly hardly grew. Spring turned to summer and there wasn't enough food to go around, even though everyone tried to make sure she ate her fill before they did. John brought her milk as often as he could, but the dairy cows had less to eat than ever, as a drought took hold of Eastern Kentucky.

Rosalee noticed the looks they exchanged, and when any of the children complained of being hungry, John was quick to snap at them, "We have what we need. There'll be more to eat tomorrow." But as the streams dried up, John Jr. and Matthew couldn't catch enough fish for a whole meal. One time, when there was no meat to eat for a week, the brothers threw as many crawdads as they could find into their bucket and brought them to Mary Ann. They all worried it might be a sin to eat them, no matter what the New Testament said, but John decided they would eat and pray for forgiveness, just in case. The water in the well got so low you could see the rocks that lined the bottom, but it never ran dry, which John took as a sign he was doing something right. As long as there was water to go around, the women kept the secret of the spring in the woods, the only place in the world that seemed fully theirs.

One time, Matthew caught two unfortunate frogs and brought them home for supper. John remembered with a wry smile something he had read long ago about the Cajuns in Louisiana, how he had thought they were crazy to eat frogs' legs, and suddenly the entire world seemed so big, and he so small.

Another change came over Mary Ann during this pregnancy. While she had been distracted by her camaraderie with Rosalee, and Bessie's incantations, she now grew melancholy. She abandoned her housekeeping and the shadows took over, helping themselves to every bright corner of the home that had been tidy and cheerful. Even John, who was determined never to believe in anything he couldn't see or read about, began to worry over invisible things.

They had slaughtered all but the last of their animals. As summer wore on and killed everything in the garden, Bessie foraged mushrooms and plants from the forest, the only place that remembered the taste of rain. Rosalee helped her aunt, and they brought their findings back to Mary Ann, who cooked whatever they collected and tried to find ways to put a little food away for the cold nights to come.

Chapter 5

Autumn, 1920

One afternoon, Bessie walked into the house to find Mary Ann bent over the table, her face pale. It was too soon for the baby to come, but blood was running down her legs and darkening the wooden floor. Bessie dropped the basket of food she had brought from the forest and grabbed Mary Ann's arm to steady her. By the time she eased onto the makeshift bed in the living room, Mary Ann dreaded the hours she knew lay before her. She sent Rosalee to her room. "Wait for me there," she told her daughter. "Bessie will find you when it's over."

Rosalee retreated, and there she braided herbs and prayed over flaxen dolls she had made with her mother and aunt in the previous months. Some of the prayers were for food and the return of good fortune to the farm. Some were for their own strength to weather the endless, quiet storm they faced. She made a new doll for her mother, whose life suddenly seemed independent from Rosalee's own, for the first time. She listened to Mary Ann moaning into the night.

While her body contracted and cried, Mary Ann's mind drifted. She saw the worry in Bessie's eyes and realized it was loneliness she had always seen in her sister—not just some odd nature, which everyone said she got from Granny. Mary Ann recalled the care Bessie used to take when brushing and braiding her hair when Mary Ann was a child, even though Bessie paid no mind to her own. In that moment, she understood Bessie loved her like she loved Rosalee—without need or want.

Mary Ann looked at John, who came to his child's birth for the first time at Bessie's insistence, leaving the boys to muck the stock barn without him. His face was lined and hardened from the sun and the wind. He was a stranger, despite their days working together and their nights of closeness, which she had once enjoyed more than many wives did. For a brief moment, she wondered how else her life could have unfolded, what more it could have been.

She thought about her mama and her granny. She always knew what they talked to her about was important, even if those conversations didn't have the same weight as the ones they had with Bessie. They taught Mary Ann how long to boil a chicken so its marrow would thicken a soup, how to can the green beans and the tomatoes, and how to tell a hard winter was coming. But there was something soft about those lessons, something gentle. Every song Granny had sung with Bessie had a fierceness to it, an edge that was easy to miss if you weren't paying attention. Mary Ann always heard it and let it retreat into the darkness of her mind, where everything else she had seen and heard wove itself into a never-ending tapestry of memory and history.

Mary Ann realized she had never told her daughter about how life is a quilt, and the world itself turns like a spinning wheel and we are its threads.

As Rosalee was finishing the doll she had infused with prayers for her mother, her hands shivered and a piece of flax pierced her palm, drawing a single drop of blood. With a gasp, she dropped the doll to the floor and it came undone. Rosalee ran to the living room, defying Mary Ann's instruction, and found her mother lying there, eyes open, still. The sheets beneath her were soaked with too much blood, and the light from the oil lamps reflected off the deepest puddles, which were slowly congealing.

John held the new baby, and tears filled his eyes as Bessie whispered over Mary Ann. They looked at Rosalee when she ran in, and she saw a new expression cross her father's face.

"This is your brother, Michael. You'll have to take care of him," he said.

Bessie looked into Rosalee's searching eyes, and the five-year-old girl saw the pain of fresh grief. John thrust the baby boy into Bessie's arms and walked out of the house. Rosalee went to her mother, reached out to touch her, and found Mary Ann's body was just starting to cool. Her face bore a strange expression, as if her mother was on the verge of saying one last thing, but was puzzled to find her voice gone. Michael mewled his thin, empty cries and Rosalee hated him.

Bessie cajoled John to mail a letter to Benjamin the next morning. They would hold the wake for three days to give him time to arrive. On the third day, John loaded Mary Ann's body onto a cart and told Bessie and Rosalee to do as they saw fit. He went into the woods behind the house with a jar of moonshine. The next time John went to town, he stopped at the post office and found Benjamin's letter waiting there—a brief apology and description of how busy his new practice was these days.

At Bessie's insistence, they buried Mary Ann in sight of the spring in the woods, though Rosalee understood her father still didn't know exactly where the spring was, and she wondered whether he would ever visit this place. Bessie chose a spot where the forest canopy had thinned, letting dappled sunlight reach the ground. The older boys, nine and ten now, dug their mother's grave and helped bury her as Bessie sang a song none of them had ever heard before. After she finished singing, Bessie walked a few feet away and picked up a heavy limestone rock that had somehow found its way to the forest. She sat it on the fresh earth to serve as a headstone and whispered something no one could hear. From then until Mary Ann's great-great-granddaughter was born, a carpet of wild ginger, with its heart-shaped leaves, grew but didn't flower where she was buried.

Bessie and Rosalee held hands as they walked out of the woods, Michael secured to Bessie's chest with a long piece of cloth, and all of them cried without making a sound. The boys stopped once they cleared the tree line and looked back to where they had just come from, but their vision was blurred by tears, and the path they thought they had just taken was not there. They thought to visit their mother's grave again later but couldn't find the opening to enter that part of the forest. Each time they started to ask their aunt or sister to show them the path, the words dried in their throats and the question was lost, until the burial became part of a dream they could not remember.

The slow decay of the farm and family flooded all around John. The corn they once sold now crumbled in the slightest breeze for lack of rain. The older brothers went to live with family in Pike County, where some of John's people promised they could work in the coal mines and get enough to eat. They might even be able to send money back now and then. The cows had stopped giving birth, and John wondered if he was cursed because of something he had allowed Bessie to mutter in his home, but he quickly pushed the thought aside each time it crept in. They ate most of the chickens, which had stopped laying, and the rooster died with no male chicks to grow up and take his place. John's sorrow and anger bound themselves to one another, hardening him against the weakness, the doubt, he had once harbored.

Irene came to the house on Sundays to pray and sing with John, and Bessie had to go to her own house every time they held their informal service, though John wouldn't let her take Rosalee with her. He would still go to revivals but knew Bessie wouldn't go, so he couldn't take Michael for a while yet. Taking Rosalee seemed like a chore, so she was spared any more sermons from strangers, but John brought the teachings home with him more often than ever. John had his mother watch over Rosalee while Bessie was gone, but instead of stories and songs, Irene subjected the young girl to chores and silence, which Rosalee bore only because she could look forward to her aunt's return. Several days a week, John visited his mother or she visited his home, each of them haunted, bound by memories of a shared past that had slipped out of reach, never to return.

One night, as the sun began to set, he took a jar of whiskey out to the woods behind their house and didn't come back until daybreak. Rosalee awoke to find him sobbing at the kitchen table, his forehead resting on his arms next to the whiskey jar, now empty.

"Daddy?" She waited for him to hear her, and when she reached out and touched his arm, his head flew up.

"Mary Ann?" he asked. Rosalee saw his eyes were red and glassy from crying—who knows for how long—and from the whiskey. Rosalee stared at him, trying to find the right words, but before she could, John's eyes narrowed and he sat up straight.

"I been out there praying all night," he told her, standing up and pushing the chair back as he did. "And it's too late, but I know I'm being punished for what I let go on in this house, with your aunt and all her . . ." Rosalee waited for him to say the word she knew he wanted to say: *witchcraft*. "All her carryin' on," he said instead. "I should have listened to the preacher, but things are gonna change around here, make no mistake."

Rosalee held her breath and waited to find out what he would say or do next. John stared at her until his eyes saw something else, and then they filled with tears that threatened to spill once again. He walked away from the table, steadying himself on the furniture along the way, made his way to his bedroom, and shut the door. When he came outside later to do his chores—few as they were, with the farm nearly dead—he had shaven his face and combed his hair, and Rosalee couldn't detect any anger in his eyes. She couldn't pinpoint exactly what *was* in his eyes, and she waited to see if he would bring up their conversation, but he never did, and she wondered whether he remembered it.

John rode to Bessie's house one morning, and soon after that, he took a wagon over and brought Bessie back with all her belongings. From then on, anytime she mentioned the move, Rosalee saw a flicker of anger and defiance in Bessie's eyes, but Bessie wouldn't talk about what she and John discussed before he loaded her belongings. Rosalee knew, though, that Bessie and John were both unhappy about living with each other. Bessie's lonesome house by the Licking River sat empty until some strangers claimed it for themselves. Rosalee and Michael needed someone to look after them, John knew, and even though she wasn't suited to be a mother, Bessie would have to do. Rosalee made the bed in the boys' room for her aunt, and Michael slept in there, too, until he outgrew his crib and Bessie moved into Rosalee's room.

As days were lost into years, people came to the farm for Bessie's healing, and John allowed it only because of the fathers and husbands who pulled him aside to thank him for the children and wives Bessie saved. They spoke about how she did the Lord's work, and John wondered whether Bessie could be used for good, like some of the Bible stories where even the worst among us end up serving God's purpose. These were questions he could not answer, so he read the Bible to the family at night. During the day Bessie told Rosalee other stories, the ones John didn't know or understand, while Michael played nearby. Bessie watched Rosalee grow from a child into an adolescent, and Michael somehow survived infancy by drinking the mixture of cow's milk, bread, and sugar Bessie gave him.

Rosalee and Bessie told and retold stories of Mary Ann to each other and to the boy, who knew his mother as a saint with infinite patience and warmth. For his part, Michael missed the sweet touch of a mother, but thought himself lucky to have her stories. He told them to the animals he learned to care for, and the last of their chickens clucked their sympathy and the cows exhaled in shared sorrow.

✿

Over time, Bessie sank into a torpor, thinking of the shadows she had seen through the years and what she had done to repel them. How she could have done more. She dreamt of the fire every night and heard her granny's and mama's screams when a crow cawed. In the well water and in the wash basin, she saw her father's eyes reflected back to her, desperate and helpless in the end.

One day, the family from two farms over brought their little girl for healing.

"She's burnin' like she's on fire," Delphia Caudill told Bessie.

Bessie felt the girl's forehead with the back of her hand and then with her cheek. She looked at the girl's eyes and listened to her racing heart.

"I'll give her a feverfew tincture—that will cool her off and she'll be fine tomorrow." But Rosalee noticed Bessie pulled down the jar of jimsonweed from her high shelf instead of the feverfew.

"Aunt Bessie, are you sure that's what you meant to get?" Though Rosalee wanted to spare her aunt the embarrassment, Bessie flushed when she looked at the jar she was holding.

"Of course," she said. "The light's playing tricks on me."

Rosalee started watching with extra care as her aunt measured medicines that were so often just half a teaspoon from being poison. They didn't speak of it, but Bessie knew and was glad to have her niece's watchful eyes, as her own vision grew dark and clouded. Bessie couldn't see enough in the dim oval mirror to know her simple beauty had faded, but she felt it. She never told anyone that the world she could see had narrowed sharply, and she didn't speak of the pain that now seemed to be melting her bones from the inside. Bessie had spent so much of her life safeguarding her secrets, it never occurred to her there were other possibilities.

At almost forty years old, Bessie hadn't completely stopped bleeding each month, but she felt the light within her fading before Rosalee noticed the change in her. And yet, even with the fever that lay hidden in her bones most of her life, she could have kept going, like Granny and Irene had, like the other mountain women who, through stubbornness or fate, outlived their children. Bessie knew she could bend her will to it, but she was tired, too tired to fight. She knew her sister's children could make it without her, and it eased her mind to think they had survived the hardest years.

Still, for a little longer, she held on to savor the memory of her sister, of the babies she had helped bring into the world, and of the countless hours she had spent in the forest. She recalled her best days, the days of chasing shadows, and relished knowing her life of servitude had been unlike those of the women she loved before her. And there was Rosalee, who carried a light in herself, and Bessie whiled away her hours thinking of how Mary Ann tried to hide her impudent love of her daughter.

Rosalee walked her around the farm as long as Bessie could manage with her halting, uncertain steps. Bessie tried new combinations of herbs in an attempt to maintain her strength until the end, to lessen the burden on Rosalee, but Bessie did not know it was a mushroom her body needed, the one they called tinderbox, too tough for eating. It grew plentifully on the beech trees along the Licking River and by the stream that flowed between the two farms, but no one had learned to make tea from it yet, and so Bessie's body succumbed. As her aunt's hands began to shake, Rosalee took over the task of weaving their prayer dolls and crosses, out of sight from her father's watchful eye. Finally, Bessie stopped remembering and no longer whispered the last of her secrets to Rosalee, who locked away everything her aunt had once told her, as if it was the last of an inheritance.

Chapter 6

SUMMER, 1927

O ne June morning after Rosalee turned twelve, Bessie woke up but couldn't get out of bed. She called for her niece, who saw in her eyes that despite Bessie's devotion to her, she was ready to go. Bessie reached out to Rosalee as the sun rose into the sky, hot and relentless. She had dreamt all night of the Christmas when she was four years old, the year she had scarlet fever. Her daddy had carried her to the fireplace when it was time to see the gift Mama had made her, and nothing could hide the worry in Mama's eyes when Bessie was too weak to play with her new ragdoll. They gave her every tincture they could think of, but Bessie burned with fever for a week after that, until Granny found the right prayer to whisper over her.

When she woke up for the last time, Bessie felt the same fire, though less hot, finally retreating from her bones. She looked up at Rosalee and thought of all the things she had forgotten to tell her.

"You take care now."

Rosalee let her tears fall freely as she placed bundles of herbs around Bessie's body, each of them a prayer. Bessie lay there, and then was gone.

John brought Irene to the house to hold the wake and to help with the children. Irene did not offer any comfort, and as Rosalee's tears dried, anger took the place of the sorrow she had carried since her mother's death. Irene's quiet practicality grated on Rosalee as visitors filled the house like never before, all coming to bid Bessie farewell and give the family a loaf of fresh bread or a few jars from their pantries. The men drank on the porch until the sun had passed overhead and then began to talk about the work they had to get back to.

The Caudill twins—older brothers to the little girl Bessie had almost given jimsonweed to—volunteered to dig Bessie's grave, and the other men were relieved that they no longer had to come up with a good excuse to leave.

"You all sure you can handle it?" John asked them.

"Yessir," one of them answered.

"Mama couldn't make it here today, but she said not to come back if we didn't help Bessie," the other added. "She said we wouldn't be here, and Mama neither, if it weren't for Bessie bein' there when we was born."

John nodded. "I'll leave you all to it, then." As the other men gathered their families and left, he went to work on his moonshine still, away from his house and the women. Irene started to cook supper and clean up the dishes strewn about from dinner.

The young men followed Rosalee into the woods, pulling Bessie's body on the cart behind them, and buried her next to Mary Ann while Rosalee sang a song and Michael stood there, solemn. As they walked away, a white willow sprang from the ground above Bessie and sent invisible tendrils into the air, weaving protection around the hallowed space. The young men left the forest and the farm to head back to town, neither of them able to remember exactly where they had buried Bessie, or even what she looked like when she was alive, treating their every illness.

The next morning, Rosalee woke up crying, and all day long she wept as she did her chores. For three days, Irene said little, but her presence loomed like a piece of furniture that doesn't fit in the room.

When she went home, Rosalee breathed a sigh of relief. She looked at her brother and steeled herself to take on the yoke of woman of the house, and to be as much of a mother to him as she could. Though Michael had a weak constitution, he could work hard and took care of the farm alongside his father. Rosalee decided the farm would be okay, though she couldn't imagine life without Bessie.

Every day since Bessie's death, Michael had picked wildflower bouquets to cheer Rosalee. The day after Irene left, Rosalee woke up and saw the bouquet he had put in her room, and she smiled. A wave of shame washed over her as she thought about how little love she once held for him. She realized he had not only lost his mother at birth, but had now lost the only other woman who might have felt like a mother to him. Rosalee was lucky, she realized, to have spent the years she had with Bessie and to be grown enough to remember so much of their time together. Michael had cried only once since Bessie's death, that Rosalee knew of, and she wondered if he felt more than he was showing.

Michael had grown into a solitary child who, even as a toddler, never cried, so they didn't know if he was sick or hungry until they could see the blue veins pulsing quietly through his nearly translucent skin, the signal they had learned to look for, lest the boy disappear altogether. He spent his days with what was left of the cows, two barren females and a sickly bull that didn't even have the energy to charge at anyone anymore. Some days, John thought Michael's company, such as it was, might be the only thing keeping the animals alive.

But most days, John thought about Rosalee and Bessie and how he had allowed the women to dictate too much in his home. He grew old too soon, and he felt in his body a weight he never would have suspected when he was a younger man. He thought about Mary Ann as his wife less and less as time wore on, and when he did think of her, he saw her as a stranger, as if she was something he remembered from one of his own granny's stories. He hid the memory of her away with his memories of happiness, his fondness for idle sunsets and a good meal, his laughter. Weeks, months, and years passed, but a smile never lit his face again.

※

When housework had become hard for Bessie, Rosalee took over the care of the house, and just before Bessie passed away, she managed to chase the last of the stubborn shadows out of it. The house awoke from a nightmare and took on the air of her childish optimism.

Rosalee sent letters to Benjamin in Lexington and to their family in Pike County with news of Bessie's death. Benjamin wrote back once again, lamenting the sorrowful event, but his business had grown so large, he couldn't take the days off to travel back and forth. And besides, they had two children of their own now, and the trip would be hard to make. They were saving up to buy an automobile, though, and would find time to make the drive after life slowed down a little. Rosalee didn't know it yet, but within a couple of years, Benjamin would move his family to California—a place so far away, it couldn't be real—and his children would grow up hearing little about their father's family trying to survive in the hills of Eastern Kentucky.

Rosalee's brothers sent a letter back that someone else wrote for them, which each brother signed with his best attempt at a signature. John Jr. and Matthew were over a hundred miles away, and even if they could get horses good enough to make the journey, they would lose their jobs in the coal mines if they were gone for as long as it would take to ride home and back.

Rosalee began writing weekly letters to her older brothers, sharing the news of a calf's birth or a double-yolked egg, desperate to communicate with someone other than her father and Michael, or the occasional older woman who traveled to the farm with her husband and came to the house to cluck over the widower and *these poor children, Lord help them*. She sent the letters to town with her father, who took them to the post office and picked up the occasional response, which Rosalee devoured.

John would leave the farm to build and repair fences for the few families in town who had any money, staying gone for a couple of weeks out of every month so he could replace the livestock and chickens they had lost. While he was gone, his mother came to stay with Rosalee and Michael, and Rosalee was glad her grandmother mostly left her alone. Irene still had chickens and a garden of her own, but she had sold the livestock after Haman died. Anytime she stayed with them, someone had to go back and forth to put her chickens up and let them out, so the children learned the trail between the two houses, which they had to travel by foot.

John came home one day as Rosalee was walking from the outhouse, where she had emptied the bucket she used as a makeshift chamber pot. She looked just like Mary Ann had looked at her age, poised to become a young woman. She wore her hair like Mary Ann had worn hers, both of them with long, strawberry blond hair that wouldn't stay put in the loose buns they tied up. Rosalee was constantly moving bobby pins from one place to another to catch a stray strand of hair but setting another free, just like Mary Ann had done. Neither of them was particularly vain—they didn't try to imitate the hairstyles of the models they occasionally saw in catalogs and newspaper ads. Rosalee liked to braid her hair, but it reminded her of the times her mother sat behind her, singing made-up songs and laughing with ease, so she would only braid her hair at night, alone in her room, where she could look into the one mirror in the house.

John caught a glimpse of Mary Ann leaving the outhouse and looked away instinctively out of respect for his wife's privacy, but when his eyes snapped back to find it was Rosalee, his bitter loneliness and anger clenched him. He didn't tell anyone he was glad when Bessie passed away in the hot summer, but Rosalee could feel it.

After her death, John once again walked around the house with purpose, as if he was reclaiming his rightful territory. Anytime he found them lying around, John began throwing Rosalee's braided herbs and woven crosses into the fireplace or cookstove, not knowing that most of the herbs were for the teas Rosalee made to keep Michael from being sick year-round. Rosalee began storing everything she made in her mother's cedar chest, which she now kept in her own room, and the cheerful air of the house gave way to a strictness that even surprised John, though he decided not to question himself.

Her father's grip on the farm tightened, and Rosalee took care of the house and her brother with less satisfaction as the carefree days of childhood slipped away. Her body changed, and with it, her under-standing of the passing of time changed, too. The first time she bled, the timelessness of childhood ended. Before that day, her life consisted of feeling, and her true memories stood out as highlights of emotion. After she bled, life was a series of events marked in time, and those events were almost always determined by someone other than herself. Life as a woman would consist of memorable moments, while life as a girl had been flattened into a tranquil landscape.

As a child, she was of little interest to the world; now, she was a possibility, a potential commodity. Her aunt had prepared her for the next stage of life when she was still small, explaining everything she needed to understand about her body and how it would change at the cusp of womanhood, and how it would follow the rhythm of the moon ever after. Rosalee visited Mary Ann's and Bessie's graves often, stopping to pick the flowers growing in the forest and some wild ginger after she drank from the spring, something both women told her would keep her bones strong.

Michael grew less frail under Rosalee's care, but even as a young child, he struck everyone who met him as slightly odd. The men who came by to help John repair a barn or shoe a horse noticed Michael didn't seem to be completely awake, as if some part of him hadn't come into the world with him at birth. The women who visited Irene every couple of months would comment that Michael seemed to prefer the company of the cows to that of people. As he tended to the animals, Rosalee often overheard Michael talking to them, and they listened in turn. Between his conversations with Michael and the rain that eventually fell again, the bull found its strength, and both heifers gave birth in the spring after Rosalee turned fourteen.

When the heifers' milk came in, John took a few gallons of fresh milk to town and came back with a rooster and two laying hens. Soon he took eggs and milk to town and came back with a piglet Michael welcomed into his barnyard. Rosalee found some pleasure in the home that finally recovered from her mother's and aunt's deaths, but John often found her lost in a daydream as she cooked, sewed, and tended the meager garden she grew. He went to town again just after Rosalee's fifteenth birthday, carrying jars of vegetables Rosalee had canned, fresh milk, and sweet breads. He came back with a woman and her two sons and introduced his children to their new mother.

Chapter 7

Winter, 1930

Barbara Carter's husband had gone off to war and gotten himself killed—that's how she put it, anyway. He didn't leave her much except for two boys who didn't seem to notice or care that she talked about their father with contempt. They had lived in Lexington, but when her husband died, Barbara and her sons moved back to Owingsville, where she had grown up, and bought a small farm with the pension from her husband's death. When they arrived, Rosalee felt shy for the first time in her life. She had never met anyone from the city, and their world seemed so different, so sophisticated. All Rosalee knew about the city came from advertisements and newspaper stories, but she was certain they had seen and owned so much more than her family. She thought about Bessie and imagined how her aunt might respond to a bunch of city folk moving to their farm, and Rosalee was ashamed to realize she was glad her aunt wasn't there to comment on it.

Right away, Barbara took over the household duties and put Rosalee to work, and while there was nothing new about the chores she had to do, all of it felt like labor in a way it hadn't before. Rosalee couldn't tell how Michael felt, even though she had grown to understand the subtleties of his emotions more than anyone else ever would. Rosalee sometimes wished Barbara would love him like he was her own. After a while, Barbara's lack of warmth toward Michael inspired tenderness in Rosalee, and she cared for him in a new way, as if she had just begun to understand the power of a mother's love.

Their father now exuded confidence, and Barbara complemented it perfectly with her deference to him in every matter. After she arrived, the family ate John's favorite meals, they consulted him on every decision, and the independence his own children once had was relegated to its proper place, under his watchful rule.

John took to reading the Bible to them in the evenings by the light of an oil lamp, and Rosalee could hardly contain her impatience. Barbara sewed while John read, and her sons whittled. Michael fell asleep next to the fire, lulled by the sound of his father's voice, and it was clear to Rosalee that everyone had something more interesting to do than she did. She found herself wishing for the days when she resented having Mamaw Irene watch them. Her presence had annoyed Rosalee, but she could almost forget her grandmother was there, the woman was so quiet. Not Barbara—her presence commanded the room, even when she wasn't speaking.

Rosalee went to the spring and visited Mary Ann and Bessie only when she was sure nobody was watching, so the strangers could not find their way into her refuge. She stayed as far away from Barbara's sons as she possibly could, acknowledging them solely for the sake of politeness. For a while, she found comfort in the company of the farm animals and thought she could create a new world for herself among them, just as Michael had. She felt sorry for him, as he was relegated to sleeping by the fireplace on the living room floor. Rosalee imagined they would build another room onto the house soon, or the Carter sons would at least sleep on the porch when the nights grew warm.

One Sunday, after eating supper and listening to John read the Bible aloud by the fireplace, Barbara stopped Rosalee from going to her room.

"Rosalee, Samuel. Stay here."

Samuel was the older of Barbara's boys, a good hunter and fisherman who had just turned eighteen. Joseph was two years younger, but in personality, they seemed like twins. Samuel had gone to elementary school long enough to learn to read a little, but he could only write his name. Rosalee sometimes caught him looking at her in a way that made her hurry to finish whatever she was doing so she could escape his gaze. He would usually grin when she noticed him watching her, and he exuded arrogance or confidence—Rosalee couldn't tell which—but either way, it irked her. Still, she tried to sneak looks when he was occupied with something. His eyes changed color depending on his mood. Most of the time they were hazel, but when he was serious or angry, they turned gray. She knew it was natural for her to be drawn to him because of what Bessie had told her about young men, but she also saw a wildness in him that reminded her of how she felt when she went into the woods beyond the ever-flowing spring.

"You are both of age," John said. "And while you have been made family in the eyes of the law, you are strangers in the eyes of God. It's time for both of you to marry."

The meaning behind his words sank in and Rosalee's heartbeat quickened. She could no longer hear what he said but saw Samuel nodding in agreement.

I won't, she thought. *They can't make me. They can't do this. I'll never be his wife.*

John turned from Samuel. "Rosalee, do you understand? You will marry Samuel in a fortnight. Your mamaw is moving into this house and giving her house to Samuel. He'll farm a piece of the land and take care of you." John turned to Barbara and explained, "We've had some tenant farmers on the north side of the farm since Daddy died. They keep that part of the farm cleared, but Mama hasn't wanted to keep much going around her house." Barbara nodded as if it was exactly what she expected to hear, and Rosalee's thoughts ran wild.

Her mind scrambled to find her mother, to return to hair braiding and easy laughter, to Bessie and their walks, their endless conversations about the plants and animals and stars. She thought of her dolls and prayers she hadn't yet thrown into the fire—what fire would be hers now? She looked at Samuel, who was watching her face and smiling. She didn't recognize his expression and wondered if he had been looking at her this whole time.

"It's an honor, sir," he said to John, extending his hand. John nodded as they shook, and Rosalee wanted to scream at her father, but she knew despite how little violence she had experienced from him in her lifetime, lashing out would be met with punishment. As if he could read her thoughts, he looked at her and added, "When you get married, you vow to God you will obey your husband. Best you keep that in mind."

Rosalee's throat caught with words she could not say, and Samuel looked from her back to John. "Don't worry, sir. I'm sure she'll make a fine wife, won't you?" He turned to her and winked, and Rosalee nodded, holding back tears of rage and sorrow, and went to her room as soon as she could.

Rosalee sobbed herself to sleep that night. She knew her father had wanted to find a solution to the problem she presented to him. She was a girl, and now that he had a woman to take care of the house, she had nothing to offer except another mouth to feed. She had hoped he would be satisfied with Barbara's control over the house and pay Rosalee little mind, as long as she did what she was told. It had never occurred to her that he would marry her off, sending her like they sent the cows to the bull, with no concern for what she wanted.

They held a simple wedding in March, not quite two months after the Carters first arrived. John had arranged for the new preacher in town to ride to Irene's house and perform the ceremony at noon. Joseph stood as the best man. They had enough witnesses to make it legal, so no one else was invited to attend, and John didn't think it worth sending a letter to Pike County for that news alone. Rosalee made her own dress, modest and simple. When the preacher turned to her, asking her to recite her vows, Rosalee's face flashed with anger for an instant, but she recited the words she knew she had to speak. In her mind, she ran to the woods. There, she found her mama and Aunt Bessie watching, the wildflowers beckoning, the great oaks welcoming. In the forest—her true home—Rosalee was safe, shielded from the world's whims and desires, protected by women and wilderness.

Samuel's gaze pulled Rosalee back to the ceremony. Ever since John announced they were to marry, she found Samuel watching her every time she looked up from her chores or her meal. His self-assurance was at once impressive and grating. He bore more confidence than her father ever did, and Rosalee wondered what made Samuel so sure of himself, when he had so little experience in life. As the preacher pronounced them man and wife, Rosalee tried to assume an expression of indifference, and Samuel looked at Rosalee with what the small audience thought was approval of his new bride.

Rosalee swore to herself she would never let Samuel touch her, and she spent their wedding night wearing a gown she had sewn with so many ties and buttons, her new husband gave up on his advances quickly. He rose from the bed and picked up the oil lamp, shining its light toward Rosalee, winked at her, and walked out. Rosalee fumed at his petulance and wrapped herself tightly in the quilt Irene had left behind.

Samuel was gone to work on the farm before sunup, and Rosalee went into the kitchen to light the cookstove. Like so many other aspects of her new life, Rosalee found it both irritating and interesting that she was swapping places with her grandmother Irene, a woman she had spent time around as a child, but whose eyes didn't light up when she looked at Rosalee—this grandmother shuffled about quietly, never smiling, and was nothing like the women Rosalee grew up with, who were full of life and wisdom.

Rosalee put on the coffee and started a pot of water to simmer chicken bones left over from the wedding meal. She planned her day around the meals Bessie had taught her to make: biscuits in the morning with some butter and jam, dumplings in the chicken broth for dinner, then cook down whatever vegetables she had on hand in the last of the dumpling gravy and add fresh meat. After she set the pan of biscuits out to cool, she wandered around the house to see what her grandmother had left behind and to get to know the place she would now call home.

Handmade curtains hung in the windows, so rich with detail that Rosalee wondered if her grandmother could have really been the person to sew them. A bouquet sat in a Mason jar on the kitchen table. Someone had picked a few twigs of redbud and some lush mountain laurel leaves—those trees wouldn't bloom for a couple of months yet. At first, Rosalee thought her grandmother must have put the bouquet there for her, but she realized they weren't there on her wedding night, so Samuel must have picked them this morning. The realization incensed her. She didn't want him to act like they were a couple, just because they were married. It was a legal arrangement, and in her young mind, she thought there might be a way to bear it without thinking of him as her husband.

Trying to calm herself, she examined the rest of her grandparents' home. A simple desk sat beneath the window of a small room adjoining the living room. Rosalee knew the desk was made from a walnut tree her grandfather had cut down, and her father had helped build it, but she had never noticed the depth of color before, nor the intricate pattern of the resilient wood. She tried to open the desk's one drawer by its small brass knob, but the drawer was stuck. After tugging on it a few times, she realized it was locked, and though she searched the house, she found no key.

"What are you looking for?" Samuel had come back in without making a sound.

Rosalee rolled her eyes before turning around.

"Nothing much," she responded. She smiled at him, knowing he would know her obedient wife act was just that—an act. "Biscuits are on the table and the coffee's hot."

Samuel tore open a biscuit and slathered it with yellow butter churned from the milk of Michael's favorite cow. He sat at the kitchen table and looked out the window. Rosalee wanted to go back to exploring the house alone and tried to ask about his day without revealing her impatience with his presence.

"How's things going out there? You real busy today?"

Samuel knew right away what she was getting at. "Sure am, sweet bride. I'll be out of here soon." He winked at her, his eyes twinkling with good-natured amusement.

Rosalee bristled, but she set her face as the women in her life had taught her. "Oh husband, I'll be countin' the hours 'til you come back. I'll be cooking all day for you, and I sure hope to please you." As the words left her lips, she realized their implication and blushed, turning her attention to an invisible mess to clean up. The sweetness of her speech would have fooled anyone except Samuel—he heard the rebellion behind her placating words and grinned as if he were in on the joke.

He responded as if playing the dozens. "I'm sure you will, darlin'." He paused for a moment to let her know he had caught her accidental flirtation. "But don't you worry—I'll be ready to eat a boiled possum here soon."

Rosalee startled for a moment at what sounded like an insult, even if it was a joke. But she remembered to smile as she told him, "Glad to know your standards aren't too high for a new bride like me. If we ever run out of chicken, I'll remember you're not picky about your meat."

Samuel stood up and finished his cup of coffee before giving Rosalee a look, and she fought the urge to throw something at him for being so unbothered. He turned around and walked out of the house, whistling the tune "Meet Me in St. Louis, Louis," though Rosalee didn't know what it was. She only knew she wanted him gone, and she hated every minute of this new life.

They went on like that for weeks, Rosalee lobbing veiled insults, Samuel enjoying the banter, neither sure if they cared whether the other one broke first. John and Barbara came to the house several times in the first few weeks, bringing farm animals and supplies Samuel needed to get started. They heard the contempt in Rosalee's voice and the playfulness in Samuel's. "They've got a hard row to hoe," the parents told each other. "She'll have to give up that sharp tongue before he loses his patience with her." They nodded and turned back to their routines. The daily life on a farm stretched out before them.

Rosalee longed for the flowing spring and the forest that wrapped itself around her like a veil each time she entered there. It wasn't so far away, but keeping the house and farm took most of her day, and she could no longer steal away, unseen, to visit the swaying flowers and bowing oaks that bore whispers from Bessie and Mary Ann to Rosalee's listening heart. She wondered when her longing would disappear, and sometimes told herself it would be better this way—to leave every bit of her childhood behind her, at her father's house, no longer home.

Rosalee found a fresh bouquet of flowers in a Mason jar on the kitchen table almost every day, and while she refused to look at him if she didn't have to, she was touched by the gesture. If he walked in while she was changing clothes, he ducked back out of the room, averting his eyes and apologizing, "Sorry about that, beautiful." Rosalee's cheeks burned out of embarrassment when he caught glimpses of her uncovered skin, but a thought began to tug at her mind: *He's such a gentleman.*

One evening, Samuel stumbled into the house well after sundown. Rosalee was looking through an old newspaper Irene had left behind, reading stories about outlaws and looking at every advertisement, fascinated by the fashions and gadgets that she never could have imagined and that still didn't seem real. She folded the newspaper and laid it on the chair when she stood up to greet Samuel.

Nearly two months had passed and they still hadn't touched in an intimate way, and Rosalee's smug satisfaction had started to give way to boredom. Samuel slumped into a kitchen chair as she brought him his dinner, which she had kept warm on the cookstove without wondering where he could be. She set it in front of him and smelled perfume, a bold fragrance, both feminine and overpowering. Samuel looked up at her with a drunken smile. "There's my pretty bride."

Rosalee felt the blood rise to her face, and she turned away sharply. "Where've you been?" she asked, angry with herself for wanting to know.

"Oh, that's an interesting question," Samuel told her with mock surprise. "I had to go to town—working, of course. How was your day, dear wife? You been missing me?"

"You can sleep in the living room tonight," she responded in a clipped voice. "I don't feel good."

With that, Rosalee went to the bedroom and put on the gown from her wedding night, in case Samuel found his way through the door. She lay in bed, nearly overcome with rage as she listened to him fumbling in the kitchen and then in the living room. The smell of perfume lingered in her nose, and she discovered she hated it more than she had ever hated anything in her life—more than the look her father used to give her when he found her weaving herbs, more than the lonesome feeling of the farm when everything seemed ready to die, maybe more than finding her mother's body cool to the touch.

She fell asleep saying prayers she had never said before, asking for the kind of help she had never wanted nor needed. Her dreams were troubled with images of her mother and Bessie, both trying to tell her something, but their voices were muffled. Rosalee felt like she dreamt all night, but the details of the dreams flitted from her mind moments after she awoke. She startled at the sound of Samuel opening and then shutting the front door behind him, and she lay in bed with her eyes open for a good while longer.

Chapter 8

Summer, 1930

The weeks dragged on, and Rosalee's outrage gave way to confusion. Their standoff had entered a stalemate, and Rosalee had a
nagging feeling something wasn't right, beyond her dislike of her husband. Samuel brought home metal crates filled with Mason jars, which
themselves were filled with liquids of different hues: some amber, some
deep brown, and others with no color at all. He brought in a crate or
two at a time, usually a couple of times a month, and winked at Rosalee
as he set them in the kitchen. "You can use this for medicine and your
little potions, but be sure not to use it all."

She hardly looked at Samuel, and he had stopped flirting with her.
Sometimes, she thought she smelled a perfume on the wind. Sometimes
it was the sharp smell of magnolia flowers, and the woman who wore
it taunted her from some faraway place. Other times, a light, woody
scent drifted along the breeze, and Rosalee inhaled deeply, captivated
by the beauty it implied until the image of a woman appeared in her
mind—the kind of woman who would wear such a perfume.

By the time summer eased itself into the hills of Kentucky, Rosalee
was exhausted. In the garden, she fought against the heat and the wet
summer air. The pond teemed with life, but mostly flies and mosquitoes

that Rosalee fought to keep out of the house. She fell into drudgery, each day marked by another encounter with the world she needed to tame to survive. And then there was her husband—gone when he wanted to be, home when he pleased. Sometimes she rode Bonnie, her favorite horse, back home under the pretense of borrowing a bit of flour or to drop off some extra biscuits, but Barbara offered no warmth, and only Michael's face lit up with excitement to see her. When she could, she explored the woods around her new home, not ready to venture too far without knowing where the invisible boundaries lay, and still too angry with them both to ask her father or husband to tell her.

Rosalee never knew whether Samuel would be at her father's or if her father and Joseph might show up at their farm. They all worked together, at least much of the time, planting more field corn than all of the previous crops John had grown when Mary Ann was alive. They made most of the moonshine and whiskey at John's. Rosalee understood there was a bigger still there now, maybe even two, but Samuel had built his own in the woods behind their house, and he made his own liquor on the side. He bragged to Rosalee about how he had known the farm would be the perfect place to start a real moonshine operation and had bought up plenty of field corn before moving there, so they could get started without having to wait for the first crop. "And I ain't talkin' about the little operation your daddy's used to," he told her. "I found caves on this land and set up in one of those, so we can make whiskey all year long." He waited for Rosalee to respond, and she smiled.

"Sounds like you got big plans. I just hope there's no trouble."

Samuel laughed. "Ain't no trouble comin' to me unless I make it," he said before going back outside.

From then on, Rosalee sometimes caught the scent of the sour mash he fermented in the cave wafting along the wind, and her stomach heaved in revolt each time.

Rosalee worried and wondered at first why her father had given up on restoring his farm to what it once was, but she often overheard

Samuel talking about how much money a man could make from whiskey and moonshine these days. The Carter brothers convinced John to put the money he made in town toward building stills and to grow field corn to make liquor, instead of raising more animals or even tobacco. Rosalee could wonder all she wanted, but she would never understand the change John went through when Mary Ann died, nor the impact of having Bessie around, and how his calculations of what it meant to be a man had changed in the last ten years. For his part, John couldn't have explained why he let his stepsons talk him into this illegal business venture, which would soon change everything.

More often than not, Samuel took his shirt off while he was working, and Rosalee caught glimpses of him outside, his skin wet with sweat and his lean muscles taut. He washed himself outside at the end of the day, his clothes in a pile on the porch, and walked past Rosalee wearing nothing but a smile as he went to their bedroom for clean clothes. Rosalee busied herself each time, unable to hide her red cheeks or to will away her growing attraction toward him. And then, Rosalee could no longer tell whether he smelled like another woman or he carried the scent of the entire teeming world, overflowing with pollen and nectar and honey.

Inside the henhouse one morning, she remembered the smell of magnolias that had overpowered his usual scent—the sweat, dirt, and salt that were uniquely his. She reached beneath her favorite hen, a black one she had named, though she wouldn't have admitted to anyone the chickens were her closest confidants, even if there had been someone to admit such a thing to. There were three eggs beneath the hen, and Rosalee placed them into her basket with care. She could hear her mama's and Bessie's voices and what they said to her when they taught her how to handle the hens and how to tell when the eggs had chicks inside them. But hatred for the magnolia perfume mixed with the heartaches she had named and those she did not yet understand. She stared at the eggs and began to sob.

She tried to stop crying when she heard the henhouse door open, but she swung around to find Samuel standing there, staring at her before she could assume the cold look of indifference she had mastered around him. Frustration made her cry even harder, and she sank to the dirt floor on her knees as the chickens looked on. Samuel knelt beside her and put his arm around her, and Rosalee was infuriated but exhausted. She kept crying as he stood up, not knowing whether she should throw something at him or scream or lie down on the henhouse floor and weep for an eternity like she felt like doing.

"Come here, pretty bride," he commanded, and he picked her up like a child, with a strength that surprised her. He reached down for the basket of eggs and took them all into the house. He set the basket on the butcher block and carried Rosalee into the bedroom, laying her on the bed with a gentleness Rosalee had not felt since she was a child.

Rosalee wore a handmade flower-print dress she often threw on in the morning when she went to gather eggs or sit on the porch alone, drinking her cup of coffee and watching the sky change as it was lit by the waking sun. She looked at her legs and noticed the streaks of dirt marking where she had knelt in the henhouse. When she looked up, Samuel met her eyes, and Rosalee trembled as she pulled the dress over her head, revealing her full body in front of him.

She thought she would recoil from his touch, but when his large, callused hands met her skin, she leaned toward him, surprising herself. They made love and Rosalee's body shook with a pleasure that sent her mind into forests and springs she hadn't seen before, but there were no words in her mind or between them. A slow, easy smile broke across her face for the first time in front of Samuel, and she opened her eyes to find him watching her, still moving inside her.

A pang of jealousy nearly overtook her as she thought of the perfume, but she decided then and there she would never again care about another woman's perfume or share her man with some faceless competitor. She pulled him to her with a ferocity that caught Samuel off guard, and to which he happily gave himself.

After their first intimate encounter, they frolicked in the bedroom as often as possible, leaving cups of coffee to grow cold on the kitchen table in the mornings, at times abandoning their dinnertime routines as Samuel chased Rosalee toward their bed, both of them laughing with delight. Sometimes, Rosalee caught herself staring at his naked back in bed next to her, as she wondered how this stranger had become her friend and lover. As if he could sense her questioning mind, Samuel would roll toward her, his sharp eyes cutting to the quick of everything Rosalee wanted to leave unspoken. They both knew they had crossed a necessary bridge, and for a time, it seemed like they were bound by love, finally.

Rosalee awoke on a sticky August morning as Samuel hurried to get dressed in the dim light of sunrise.

"Where are you off to in such a hurry?" she asked, coaxing him to return to bed.

"Got some business with your father today." He leaned over and kissed her hair.

"Can you get some things while you're in town?" she asked, imagining her father and husband selling livestock or making plans for a fall slaughter with some of the other men.

Samuel laughed. "I don't know what kind of time I'll have for that, but we'll see." He looked at her and saw the questions in her eyes. "The law's been crackin' down on us that's making whiskey and moonshine, you know." Rosalee nodded. She had overheard her father and Samuel talking about it, and Samuel had brought a newspaper home not long ago with stories about tax evasion and Prohibition. "And with the drought going on, lots of farms can't produce the corn to make it," he continued. "It's a great time to be a moonshiner, and we're about to make some real money at it." He waited for Rosalee to acknowledge how great a plan it was.

She thought about the jars of whiskey Bessie always had around and what her parents kept for sipping and medicine. Listening to the revival preachers rail against drinking had always been laughable. Just about everybody in the audience had some liquor at home, and nobody thought much of it except when they shook their heads over stories of drunk men who wouldn't take care of their families. Unease crept in. *How could they sell all they've been making?* Rosalee asked herself. *What if they get caught?* She started to speak her concern, but before she could, Samuel went on.

"Don't worry, I'll be back before nightfall. Save a kiss for me, pretty bride." He grinned with the same brazen look that used to drive her mad with indignation, but now it lit something inside her, a rushing sensation that made her feel like the whole world was coming toward her at once, filling her mouth with a sweetness never tasted before.

"I'll look forward to it," she told him with a smile, and he left.

Rosalee moved through the day with the smile still on her face, reaching down to touch her belly each time she thought of the baby growing within her. The monotony of her housework and garden chores disappeared in the pleasure she now reveled in, and she wondered how life had felt so heavy just a couple of months ago. Her questions about whiskey and moonshine fell away, too, as she picked tomatoes with a languid joy and cut them into thick slices to eat with the sourdough bread she made for supper. At the end of the day, she set quart jars full of tomatoes into the water bath for canning, certain they would have plenty to eat in the winter, and she calculated what else they would need while she recovered after childbirth. She started wondering what time Samuel would come home just before the sun began to set.

With a dish towel to protect her from the hot lids, Rosalee pulled the jars out of the washtub once the lids popped to form a seal. As she pulled the last one from the water, a cardinal flew into the kitchen window with a smack and she spun around, dropping the jar.

Hot tomato pulp splattered onto the floor, and shards of glass mixed with the juices that stung her legs. She glanced back at the window before turning to clean up the mess and found the bird sitting on a tree branch, unharmed from its collision. She wondered who it could be—a red bird was always the spirit of someone who had passed over to the other side. Bessie or her mama seemed most likely, and Rosalee laughed at how startled she was by the unexpected visit.

"You must be coming to see me and the new baby," she whispered as she poured water onto the wood floor and swept up the last shards of glass and tomato seeds. She looked up at the window and the cardinal was gone.

Rosalee went out to the porch as the sun sank in earnest behind the steep hills all around her. She sat in the rocking chair her grandmother had left at the house as she mused over the differences between Irene and herself. Rosalee felt lucky to have a husband she loved and wanted to be close to, even if it took some time to get there. Bessie had warned her a husband might demand things of her even if she didn't want to give them, and wrong as that arrangement might be, a woman must suffer it. Rosalee thought of the time that had passed since she first met Samuel—just over half a year now—and how everything had changed. With the last of the fading light, she looked over the buttercups, coneflowers, and lemon balm her grandmother had planted in front of the porch, and Rosalee thought about which plants to harvest, which to leave alone.

With the last of the sunset behind her, Rosalee walked into the house and lit several oil lamps. Samuel liked the light, even if it was wasteful to have more of them burning than they needed. A smile stole across her face as she remembered what he said about seeing her body in the lamplight.

She cooked dinner and waited to eat with Samuel, but the baby's hunger overpowered her will to wait, and she kept everything else warm for Samuel as the night settled in. She busied herself by tidying up around the house, dusting corners that were left neglected. She stoked the fire in the cookstove just as the air began to cool, thinking she might keep the coals hot for the next morning's coffee and breakfast without heating the house. She put the clothes iron into the belly of the stove, letting it warm to red-hot before she pulled it out, a thick glove covering the pale skin of her hand. Rosalee ironed the freshly laundered clothes first and then the nightgowns she didn't usually iron. The stillness in the air grew thicker as moisture settled onto the grass for the night, and the crickets sang their practiced song. The shadows crept closer to Rosalee, whose mind turned to empty birthing beds and hungry mouths.

The lamplight flickered low just as Samuel burst through the door, startling Rosalee from her thoughts.

"Wife!" he nearly shouted. "I missed you. It's so good to be home."

He stumbled a little as he made his way toward the kitchen table where Rosalee sat.

"Where've you been?" she asked, caution in her voice.

Samuel looked at her and laughed a little. "Don't worry, little wife. I've been taking care of us. Me and your father have it all worked out."

Rosalee smelled the whiskey on him, the same biting scent from tinctures and the swigs Granny once took for herself. A powerful wave of nausea swept over her, and she closed her eyes, trying to will it away. When she opened them, Samuel was looking at her. "You might not like it now, but you will. I've got a good thing started with your daddy, and now it's gonna make us rich."

Samuel sometimes came home with whiskey on his breath, and Rosalee knew he sipped it with her father after working on their farms together. But she hadn't seen him drunk since the night he came home smelling of flowers. He sat out on the porch most nights after supper, drinking a little out of a pint Mason jar. It was the only time he looked serious, and Rosalee sometimes wondered why his expression was always the most sober when he was drinking.

"Hey darlin'," Samuel drawled, and Rosalee snapped to attention. "Don't worry now. I told you, it's gonna work out great. You'll see. You'll be wearing the prettiest dresses, prettier than any woman in town."

Rosalee's mind snagged on those words—*woman in town*—and she touched her belly. Most of the women in stylish dresses she had seen were at the revivals, but some of them dressed up to go to the general store, and Rosalee had seen them in there "all gussied up," as Bessie would have said. Rosalee had never considered whether she would like to look like those women, other than her casual daydreaming over the mail-order catalog. But the thought of Samuel noticing them and the thought of her own homemade dresses made her stomach drop. She fought the panic creeping into her throat, pushing it down along with the news of their baby she was waiting to share with him, once she was sure it wouldn't be lost. She forced a smile and replied, "I can't wait. I'm so glad to have a man like you."

Samuel smiled to himself as he fumbled toward their bedroom, undressing as he went. Rosalee put the food away, still warm. She turned off most of the lamps and walked into the bedroom to find Samuel on the bed, asleep and snoring just a little. He hadn't managed to pull his pants fully off, so she wrestled them down and over his ankles, then folded them and set them on the chair in the corner. She sat on the bed, pulling the quilt over her legs, and in the dim lamplight, she watched as something crossed his face—a flickering shadow from the lamplight, like a bird's wing trying to find the wind. Maybe it was a smirk in response to something real or imagined. Rosalee watched his face as shadows flew, and she saw him age, saw his sharp features sink into weathered skin and remorse. She shivered and the real Samuel returned, strong and full of youth and vigor.

The fear of what was yet to come tried to overtake Rosalee, and she steeled herself against it. The world around her grew less certain, but there was nothing she could do, other than to blow out the lamp and go to sleep.

Chapter 9

Rosalee's sleep was fitful for the rest of the pregnancy. She blamed it on the hunger and nausea, and Samuel rubbed her belly each time she paused to fight back a wave of sickness. "My boy's already raising hell," he would say. "Don't worry, little wife, he'll take care of you later, even if he's trouble now. Us Carter boys are always tough from the start!"

But Rosalee worried over the changes all around her. Samuel came home after dark in the waning summer nights, not hungry for the supper she had made and that sat cooling for hours before he arrived. For a while, he told her he'd be home in time for supper tomorrow, but he finally stopped saying it. Rosalee's appetite was unpredictable anyway, between the heat and the pregnancy. She ate whenever she felt like it, often in the rocker on the front porch, staring at the Queen Anne's lace growing wild at the edges of the fields, a pale and perfect tapestry.

At first, Samuel still pulled her close to him, interrupting her as she washed dishes in the sink or pulled laundry off the line, and Rosalee let herself relax into his arms, all sweetness and holy lust. Some nights, though, Samuel stumbled into the house after being gone all day and grabbed Rosalee with a roughness that caught her off guard. The first time it happened, she admonished him with a smile, an *Easy there*, but his eyes were empty, nothing but fragments of thought and blurred vision. He fumbled to take his pants off, then heaved himself onto her.

Whiskey oozed from his pores and filled her nostrils, and Rosalee was too shocked by his carelessness to understand it. By September, he was coming home like that more often than not, and in the mornings, he either rushed out to vomit in the grass or scowled over his coffee until the headache eased.

When he wasn't around, Rosalee searched herself for the sweet and wild longing she had felt for him—briefly—but it had withered, and in its place was something stony, something she told herself could break open and flower once more. Knowing it was the easiest way to buy herself time to sort out her confusion over what her husband was becoming and what that meant for her, Rosalee told him they had to be careful of the baby. Eventually, Samuel stopped reaching for her. The thought occurred to her that he might seek satisfaction elsewhere, and Rosalee braced herself to smell the magnolia perfume once more. The thought hurt, to her surprise. She expected the familiar anger, but another kind of sorrow was taking hold.

Samuel started spending nights away from home when Rosalee was just three months along, her skin taut around the growing baby. He warned her the first time he would be gone overnight: "Your father and I have business in town. I'll be home tomorrow." With a quick kiss, he left. Rosalee knew how to use the shotgun, so she didn't worry. Sometimes he spent two nights away, but Rosalee never smelled the sharp perfume on him when he returned, so she stopped imagining where he might be and thought instead about what to name the baby.

Alone, Rosalee looked through the growing stack of catalogs Samuel brought home to her, hungry for something other than housework and the garden to occupy her mind. She visited Barbara a time or two, mostly to see Michael, but the older woman warned her riding on a horse could hurt the baby after it got a little bigger. Rosalee didn't have anyone else to ask, so she stopped taking the trail back home to her father's house. While Samuel was gone, Rosalee found new ways to braid her hair and picked bouquets of flowers to brighten the house. She sewed baby clothes and imagined how she would play with a child of her own, how much they would love one another.

By the middle of September, Samuel was bringing Rosalee gifts from town after selling liquor to the local farmers there. At first, it was a pretty dress that wasn't homemade from feed sacks or reams of plain cotton, like all of Rosalee's clothing. Next, he brought her a large, shiny mirror and propped it on their dresser with a wooden holder made especially for it. The gifts took her breath each time—they never had anything so pristine in her childhood home. But without fail, after a few days, the excitement of the gift waned, and Samuel's presence reminded Rosalee of the invisible price she paid for each thing he brought home. When he was gone at night, she sat brushing her hair in front of the mirror, staring at the face reflected back to her, hoping her mother's face would appear and take her back to the childhood she had loved and did not want to leave.

One evening when Rosalee was alone, she watched as the sky darkened low to the horizon, the sun still high enough to ignite the edges of the billowing white clouds standing out in stark relief. A distant rumble of thunder confirmed her suspicions, and as the moisture in the air grew thick, Rosalee could taste the storm. She put up the chickens early and called for the cows to come across the field and into their barn, carefully locking the doors so they wouldn't blow open in the wind. Samuel had ridden their spirited horse, Billy, into town, leaving Bonnie at the farm, and Rosalee tried to calm her with a gentle touch and a sugar cube. She whinnied restlessly, but Rosalee's reassurance took hold, and all of the farm relaxed, expectant but ready. The pigs had settled into their shed and grunted at Rosalee when she stopped to look in on them.

She closed the wooden shutters on the house and picked some flowers that were ready, putting the rowdy bouquet into one of the innumerable quart Mason jars Samuel left lying around the house, the porch, and even in the barns after drinking the whiskey or moonshine in them. Satisfied she had secured everything she could, Rosalee poured one of her teas into a jar.

Flower water, Samuel liked to call them with a laugh. Rosalee had spent a lot of her pregnancy to that point in solitude, picking flowers and leaves and sometimes roots to prepare for the birth. The flowers and leaves went into teas she steeped for hours, and Samuel decided not to try them again after finding how bitter they could be. "Something so pretty really should taste better," he said, grimacing. Rosalee had just smiled, not bothering to explain how the clear, green-tinged liquid would strengthen her uterus for labor.

As the sky darkened toward her, Rosalee realized she should pick everything from the garden tonight, instead of waiting for the morning like she had planned to. There was a bumper crop of cucumbers and squash to harvest, and she planned to pickle most of them, already imagining winter nights next to the cookstove, a skillet of cornbread slathered with melting butter and the bright taste of cucumber and squash to counter the cold and dreary Kentucky nights. She had survived on less at times but was determined her child would come into a world where there was food on the table even when little was growing and much less could flourish.

She rushed into the house and set her jar of tea on the table, then grabbed her favorite basket for picking from the garden. She stepped into the raucous rows, overflowing with vivid hues that almost glowed in the strange light of the sun as it gave way to the purple-black clouds now covering the sky. She reached down to grab the first cucumber when a deafening crack jolted her, and she dropped the basket. Lightning raced across the clouds and bolted down to a tree in the cow field, and Rosalee watched as the tree split and then smoldered. Looking back to the sky, she watched the lightning race side to side again, and the hairs stood on her arms.

She ran from the garden, casting a worried glance to the chicken coop as she made her way into the house, slamming the door shut behind her. She peeked through a crack in a shutter to see the lightning strike another tree in the field. Hail hit the tin roof in tiny pings that grew louder and angrier until Rosalee was sure the roof would cave and crush her there, alone but not alone. The shutters strained against their metal hooks and slammed into the windows after every great heave. Rosalee looked up to see glass cracking, a spider web etched into the clear pane nearest the kitchen sink, and she said a quick prayer for the rest.

The cows were bellowing but then the wind howled louder and louder, until she couldn't tell where any sound was coming from. Then she realized a sound was coming from her, too. Overwhelmed by fears she had not named, she sank to her knees in the dim light of a single oil lamp, both knowing and not knowing what she wept for. The storm howled as tears of anger and fear flowed from her until she ran dry, exhausted. She took herself to bed as the winds quieted down and she could once again hear the leaves rustling outside. *Sounds like Mama and Bessie,* she thought, as the urgent whispers tried to tell her something, but she could not stay awake long enough to hear.

In the morning, she woke up and went outside, at first happy to find the storm hadn't ruined her flowers. She opened the chicken coop and barns, and none of the animals seemed at all bothered by what had happened the night before. *What a relief,* she thought, before walking to the garden.

Rosalee stepped onto a sodden row, a cloud of uneasy thoughts looming just beyond her consciousness. She discovered most of the cucumber plants had been destroyed, and slugs were feasting on what was left, some of them still lounging in their slimy trails, unable to escape after eating their fill. The wind had torn down the little fence she put up to keep animals out, destroying the bean plants and a good many squash. As she walked up and down the rows, rabbits scurried from their newly acquired bounty. Tears stung her eyes and would have fallen, but her anger contained them.

Almost as an afterthought, she walked down the onion rows, just to find the tops eaten. She pulled a couple of bulbs out of the ground, and they were sodden and yellow with rot. She threw an onion back at the row and started to walk into the house, her jaw set. Something in the garden row caught her eye, glimmering in the sunlight that belied the destruction all around her. Wedged beneath a half-uprooted onion was a small brass key. Rosalee picked it up, brushed the dirt off, and put it in her dress pocket without thinking what it might unlock.

Instead, she thought of the winter, and her mind scrambled to replace the foods she couldn't put away to eat during the rest of her pregnancy or for when the baby was born on the cusp of spring, before the garden was planted. Her father and Barbara would surely spare a little for the new grandchild, if their garden hadn't been ruined, too. And she could forage from the forest if need be. She would pick more wild blackberries and blueberries and make jellies to barter. She knew where the hickories and chestnuts grew on this farm, as well as her father's farm; she would begin picking stores of both as soon as possible.

When Samuel came home that night, just a little drunk, he sat down to the table and ate a piece of cornbread. "Whad'ya think about the storm last night? Hope you wasn't too scared. I wish I'd been here for you, but I know you're tough." He grabbed Rosalee's hand and kissed the back of it, a gesture that awoke her affection toward him.

Sitting across the table from him, Rosalee broke the news. "We lost a good bit of the garden last night. There's time to plant a little more to put up for winter, but I'll forage from the forest, and I've got some ideas for how to make up for what we lost. The baby will be well fed. I'm not sure about the field corn, though—I didn't go down that way."

She rested her hand on her belly and smiled, waiting for her husband to respond.

Samuel waved his hand in dismissal. "We planted so much field corn, we could flood the whole county with whiskey by the time we're done making it. We planted a bunch where it wouldn't get wiped out by a storm, anyway." He grinned, and it dawned on Rosalee that they could have planted the garden in a safer place, but Samuel didn't care about it. "You don't need to worry about all that no more. We don't need no garden and my wife won't be digging roots in the woods like some country bumpkin! We'll buy what we need. Don't worry," he said with a wide smile. "Everything's gonna be different now. Me and your dad have a good thing going on, bigger than you know. I'm gonna take care of you and the little one, don't you worry. We don't need a damn garden," he said, laughing.

Rosalee wanted to believe him, that there was nothing to worry about. But she was certain he was right about one thing, though not in the way he meant it: everything was about to be different. She searched her mind for some wisdom Bessie had bestowed or even a faint lesson from her mother to help her understand and navigate these uncharted waters. She saw the locked desk in her mind and thought of the key in her pocket, and she tried to hide how eager she was to be finished with the conversation.

"I'm glad to hear it," she told him, while Samuel pushed back from the table. He poured himself a generous drink of whiskey into a pint jar and winked at Rosalee, who smiled back with a practiced expression. He walked out to the front porch and sat in the rocker, where she knew he would remain for a good hour or two.

Rosalee went to the room with the desk, and she perched on the dainty chair, pulling the key from her pocket. The lock clicked open and the smell of rose rushed out, thrusting her into a memory of somewhere she had been before, though she couldn't remember where. Rosalee's breath caught in her throat and her eyes moistened with tears for the place that was lost to waking memory but not to her senses. She looked back to the open drawer and reached for the yellowed papers lying inside it. Laboring over the faded letters by lamplight, she discovered the world of her father's mother, Irene.

There were eleven letters in all. Eight of them were from some of her sisters or her brothers' wives. Some had moved into neighboring counties, but Rosalee recognized a few names and remembered meeting them at the revivals or at occasional family gatherings. The other three letters were from Irene's own mother, Rosalee's great-grandmother. They were dated around the Civil War, when her grandmother Irene would have married and started having babies, Rosalee realized.

The letters mostly shared important family news: updates on the children who had been born, who all had died, and who had gotten married. The letters fed a part of Rosalee's mind that she never realized was there, hungry for stories and ideas. There was trivial news about how the gardens and livestock were doing, and who had added another room to their house with the help of family and neighbors. But in the letters between Irene and her mother, Rosalee noticed a reference to *the child*.

At first, she thought it was like a reference to any other child, maybe one that was sicklier than the others or more difficult to manage. But in the faint and labored handwriting from Irene's mother, Rosalee read confessions and fears the mother and daughter must have planned to keep secret, and Rosalee thought about the key being lost in the garden, when it would have been dropped there, and why.

She couldn't cipher much from the letters, though—only that there was a child who wasn't Irene's, and when the war ended, the child and its mother went away. The third letter from Irene's mother was not exactly comforting but held a cautious lamentation for her daughter. *You must forgive him,* it read. *We don't think like they do, but we move on.*

For the first time she could remember, Rosalee wanted to see Irene, and she began to think of how she could get back to her father's farm, to the grandmother she never really knew, and to the forest still calling her name.

Chapter 10

Autumn, 1930

Samuel was up at dawn and Rosalee with him. "I want to see my daddy," she told him as he pulled a shirt over his head. "And my brother," she added for good measure. But as she said it, she saw the spring and the patch of coneflowers in the forest, and she wondered if Samuel would be able to tell there was more to her desire to go back home.

He paused to look at her. "What about the baby?"

"I was thinking if we go slow and you're with me, we can take the trail and it'll be fine," she said with a hopeful air.

Samuel's face flashed with confidence, and in a paternal voice, he told her, "I know how to take care of my woman. We'll go see that daddy of yours. I need to talk to him anyhow."

"I can ride Bonnie in front so you can keep an eye on me, make sure I'm safe." She beamed with a sweetness he couldn't see past, and he grunted an agreement as he finished getting dressed.

As they started on the trail to her father's house, Rosalee let herself imagine visiting her mama and aunt, and she could taste the sweet spring water, but then she wondered how she would get away from Samuel and everyone else, to be alone. She would wait until he was distracted by talk of whiskey, or in the woods behind the house, looking at the still.

Samuel's voice pierced her daydream. "What's on your mind, Rosie?"

Rosalee startled, then tried to find the right words in a fluster. "I's just thinking about the baby," she lied. "What we'll name him."

Samuel raised his eyebrows, and a smile broke over his face. "Well, we're gonna name him after my daddy, of course. Jabez."

Rosalee grimaced before she could stop herself, and Samuel noticed.

"Something wrong with that name? Not good enough for you?" Rosalee paused at the cold edge in his voice.

"Not at all," she responded with a quick glance and conciliatory smile. "Was just remembering Jabez from the Bible."

Samuel weighed the truth of what she said before accepting it. "It's a family name," he explained. "All our first-born sons are named Jabez, but my oldest brother died when we were little, so that's why you didn't know." He rode up next to her as the trail widened, so she could look at him.

Rosalee took in his interest and softened. "It's a good name," she said, and meant it.

Samuel smiled and fell back behind her. Rosalee relaxed into the swaying heft of Bonnie's power. Their life would be good, she knew, and she'd have to forget the things that bothered her now and then. He was happy about the baby, and happy to have children with her. He would be good to all of them. She could almost see Bessie roll her eyes at her next thought: she would have to be patient with this man, but it would be worth it. Rosalee didn't yet know about the different ways a woman can be safe, and how to tell them apart. At that moment, the safety of his approval and sense of certainty seemed like enough.

"We're gonna have so many babies," she heard him say.

They rode onward, and Rosalee saw why Samuel was so confident about all the corn they had planted. Downhill from their house, on either side of the trail to John's, corn grew as tall as she was in every open space and flourished like weeds. Slightly lower than the farm itself, the area they had plowed and planted wasn't as susceptible to the wind. They rode through woods and over the creeks for a while before reaching the open land around John's farm, all of which was devoted to growing corn, other than a field of hay and the pasture. She still couldn't comprehend how much whiskey and moonshine they were making, but thought Samuel might not be exaggerating when he said they would be able to flood the county with it.

Irene was sitting on the front porch when they arrived, rocking in Granny's old rocking chair to a heartbeat rhythm no one heard, but everyone felt. Mamaw Irene's hair was pulled back in a bun like most of the old women at the revivals wore, but thick pieces of hair hung down to her shoulders with a surprising youthful air. Hints of the black hair she'd had as a young woman still peeked through the light silver glinting in the midday sun. She met Rosalee's eyes for a moment and looked back to her knitting.

As they dismounted from the horses, Michael walked up from the stock barn, smelling of pigs. He nodded at Samuel, who nodded back, and then smiled an easy smile toward Rosalee.

"What've you been eating, Rosalee? Looks like that belly of yours done grown a bit since I last saw you."

Rosalee wanted to throw her arms around Michael—she hadn't realized how much she missed him. "Come here, little brother. You smell like pigs." She feigned a look of disgust. "Have you been feeding them or playing with them?" She still could see so much of his blood through his skin, she was half-afraid she would crush him. She pulled him toward her in a gentle hug.

"What have *you* been eating? You're thin as a rail."

She meant the last comment to tease him, but Barbara had walked within earshot and heard it. "We feed him as well as we can, but the boy won't hardly eat. If you reckon you can do better, feel free."

Rosalee recognized the look on Barbara's face and didn't have to be told what it meant, though she hadn't argued with her stepmother before.

"He looks good," Rosalee said with a smile toward Michael. "You're just built like a stick. It's hard to believe you're almost ten."

Michael grinned at her and showed off his biceps, as if he had muscles.

Barbara exhaled loudly and turned back toward the house. "You'll be hungry for dinner. We ain't got much but you all should come on in. I've got to feed my first grandchild, don't I?"

Irene rocked in the rocking chair and knitted without acknowledging any of the exchange.

Rosalee and Samuel sat down at the table where Rosalee used to eat every meal. She looked around and wondered at the familiarity rushing back to her. Light streamed through the windows where she and her mother used to dry herbs. The simple walnut shelves of the pantry were filled with canned beans and tomatoes, but no dark liquids stewed there, no medicine brewed.

Michael sat next to her, and Rosalee noticed how his serious air made him seem older than he was. She stole looks at him now and then, and each time he was also looking at her with a knowing in his eyes. A wave of sadness washed over her as she wished she could go back and hold the baby he had once been, but this time without resentment or scorn. Instead, she passed him the pot of soup beans, leaving the biggest piece of ham right on top so he would see it and take it for himself. He scooped it out and laid it into her bowl without looking at her, and when she started to protest, he said, "For the baby."

The fact of her pregnancy hit her anew. *The baby*—no longer her little brother, who she could tend to with whatever love came naturally to her, and no longer herself, having her hair brushed by Mama or being led to the forest by Bessie. It was *her* baby now, and the child she had been would soon be a dimming memory, the matter of stories to be told or forgotten.

She could see the child she used to be, the little girl playing with a handmade doll by the fireplace where Mama sewed and told stories. The daughter in the kitchen, learning to clean a chicken and make biscuits next to the women. The young woman next to Bessie, preparing herbs and watching over her aunt's remedies. It was so easy to picture those scenes, but she could no longer *feel* them. It was as if she was watching the life of someone else, looking from the outside in, and both familiarity and home were a thing of the past. She realized life sometimes shifts like that, pulling us down a pathway, and we follow like children rushing after breadcrumbs along some forest trail, until we find ourselves somewhere different, and we find our *selves* are different as well, as if by magic.

She realized Samuel was staring at her, bemused. Her father sat down with a nod to her husband, and Rosalee wondered if there had ever been any humor in his eyes at all.

"Time to bless the meal," Barbara said, and Rosalee lowered her eyes, staring at the table as her father said a prayer. He asked the good Lord to bless the family, and then the corn harvest, and finally, the new baby on its way. Rosalee sneaked a glance at Samuel, daring to open her eyes during prayer, and she found his eyes were closed while a familiar smile played at the corners of his lips. She thought his smile must be a happy one, from the baby or their marriage or both.

"When's the baby coming?" her father asked without looking up from his plate.

"About mid-March, I reckon," Rosalee told him.

"Barbara will come tend you when it's time," John responded.

Barbara looked at Rosalee. "The doctor came when it was my time, but I know what to do."

Rosalee shifted on the wooden chair. "I was thinking Mamaw Irene might help out." She ignored Barbara's pointed look and turned to her father. "I don't want to be a bother to Barbara, and she has so much work here already. If she don't mind."

Everyone looked to John's mother, who, for the first time in Rosalee's life, seemed fully material and not a floating presence who observed without affecting. Then, she spoke more than Rosalee had ever heard from her in one day: "I tended plenty of births. I can help Rosalee with the little one. How about I come before you're ready and we'll make sure you've got enough to eat? It'll be hard to cook much yourself for a few days."

Samuel responded before Rosalee had a chance. "We'll have plenty of food, don't you worry. You can come but I'll make sure my family's taken care of."

Rosalee flushed at his arrogance, but Mamaw Irene's face didn't change. Barbara answered before Rosalee could. "It will be good for Irene to go stay with you all for a while. She can help plant the garden when Rosalee's too big to bend over." At this thought, Barbara smiled and her sons laughed. Michael and Irene looked at Rosalee with the same hint of sympathy on both their faces. John just looked at his beans and cornbread, and then out the kitchen window toward his solitary thoughts.

Rosalee mustered a smile. "It's settled, then."

"Me and Rosalee will wash up," Irene told Barbara. The men had gone to the field to look over the corn. The women cleared everyone's dishes from the table, and Michael surprised Rosalee with a quick hug after he brought his own to the sink. He ran out to feed scraps to the chickens and return to the company of his farm animals. Barbara said something about the never-ending laundry she had to wash for a house full of men and went out to the porch to labor over the washboard and tub. Rosalee thought to ask her how the garden was doing but decided to look at it herself rather than risk aggravating the woman—just about every question from anyone but John or her boys seemed to aggravate her.

Rosalee looked out the kitchen window as she dried each plate Irene handed her. "How are you two getting along?" Irene asked. The concern in her voice surprised Rosalee.

"We're fine," she said, wondering if it was true. "We had a rough start but now we're about to be a real family."

Irene washed a bowl without looking at Rosalee. "He's good to you?"

The memory of a stranger's perfume crept into her thoughts, and Rosalee shook it away. "He's a good man," she said. "He'll be a good daddy." In that moment, though, she realized she didn't know what kind of father he would be.

"Does he hit you?"

Rosalee glanced at Irene before shaking her head. "No."

"You're lucky, then," Irene told her without looking up from the wash basin. "Of course, some of you McKenzie women like to fight back, so maybe he's scared."

They shared a look and Rosalee laughed.

"Who you talking about? Not my mama—she wouldn't hurt a fly. Not that Daddy ever hit her," Rosalee rushed to add.

"He wouldn't have dared," Irene told her. "Your Granny McKenzie was meaner'n any man I knew. She whipped her husband the one and only time he dared raise a hand to her, and your daddy knew she would be quick to step in if anyone hurt her daughters. Marrying into the McKenzies ain't for the faint of heart."

Rosalee noticed a twinkle in her grandmother's eye and remembered what she was there for.

"Mamaw Irene, do you care to visit Mama's grave with me?"

Irene wrung out the threadbare rag she had used to wash the dishes and hung it to dry on a line of twine strung above the basin.

"I'll be happy to. We need to see if Barbara wants to come along."

Rosalee hesitated, and she knew her grandmother could feel her resistance, but she also knew there was no way to refuse. They walked outside to find Barbara hanging wash on the line, muttering something to herself.

"You want some help?" Irene asked her.

"I can manage," Barbara responded without looking. "Been doin' this my whole life."

"We're going to Mary Ann's grave, if you care to come," Irene told her.

Barbara looked at them, then nodded to the basket of wet clothes on the ground next to her. "Gotta finish this, or I would."

Rosalee suspected it wasn't the truth, that Barbara didn't want to visit the grave at all, but she was relieved her stepmother wasn't coming with them.

"Next time," she told Barbara with a smile.

"Mm-hmm," Barbara responded, and Rosalee walked off with her grandmother. As they made their way, Rosalee saw the farm much like she had seen the inside of the house, at once both familiar and foreign. The corn almost looked like a fortress wall around a portion of the farm, but otherwise, nothing was really different, other than a few new animals here and there. Still, the place felt like it was all now Barbara's, as if Rosalee was a visitor and maybe even intruding. She wondered how it could have ever felt like her home, or her mother's. Their lives there might as well have been a dream, rendered in the pastel hues of memory. The men were out by the cornfield, Samuel looking animated as he explained something to John and Joseph. He caught Rosalee's eye before she could turn away, and she worried he would try to talk to her, but he gave an absentminded wave, and the women continued walking.

They arrived at the foot-worn path leading into the forest and paused before stepping inside. Most of the tree leaves were still green, but tired. The occasional red or yellow maple leaf flashed here and there, a promise of one more display of beauty and brilliance before the forest, done with her show of effusive life-bearing, would withdraw inward and downward, near silent for the winter to come.

Rosalee spotted the same coneflowers Bessie also used to run her hand along, and she walked to them, trying to control her pace. It was childish, she thought, to want to touch the flowers and feel them scratch her palm as she had felt so many times before. She didn't want Irene to think her silly, so she tried to feign disinterest as she rested her hand on one of the flowers standing like a sentinel to welcome her.

"Do you have any of them made into medicine?" Irene's question startled Rosalee.

"I've got a bit left. Half a pint maybe."

"I'll come dig some root before the baby comes and make more, just in case. It never hurts."

Rosalee looked at her in surprise—Irene never spoke about having the passion for healing Bessie and Granny had. Rosalee realized she didn't really know what her grandmother might have been passionate about at one time. With a tinge of shame, she understood how unfair it was to have judged this woman as she had, as if Irene could have been and done everything she ever wanted in life. She didn't know what to say, though, so Rosalee smiled a thank-you, and they walked to Mary Ann's grave, marked by the limestone rock and the thick, dark green carpet of wild ginger leaves that had proliferated in the dappled sunlight on the forest floor. Rosalee laid a trio of purple-pink coneflowers on top of the millstone. Both women closed their eyes for a moment, saying silent prayers.

Rosalee opened her eyes and looked to the white willow where Bessie was buried. She marveled at how it had grown and walked to it, careful not to tread over her aunt's body. Not quite as tall as Michael, the tree had sent out a few limbs that year, and its delicate leaves still hung on, soft to Rosalee's careful touch. She thought of the medicine she would make from the tree as it matured, then turned to Irene.

She hesitated before asking, "Care to go to the spring? I need a good drink."

Irene nodded. "It'll be good for you and the baby," she said as she set off toward it. Rosalee wondered how Irene knew where it was—she thought it was known only to her, Mary Ann, and Bessie. They arrived at the spring and crouched down next to it. Irene picked up the simple tin cup that had always stayed perched between two rock ledges, safe from the rain. She gave it a rinse in the spring water and handed it to Rosalee. "You first."

Rosalee filled the cup and drank it down, thirsty in a way she had never been before. She looked to Irene, who told her, "Get you another."

Something inside her relaxed, and Rosalee realized she had been holding herself tight inside for a long time now, at least since she moved in with Samuel. There was no need to talk for a while. She took her time with the second cup of water, thinking of her mother and aunt, and of the grandmother she had known as a child. She thought of her own child, who would soon stir within her. She finished the cup and handed it to Irene as her imagination drifted through images of newborn faces and children toddling around her kitchen. She saw little girls there with her and boys in the fields with their father, talking. They weren't plowing or coaxing the cows but peering into a sea of field corn towering above them, and she started, then glanced at Irene.

Irene looked out at the forest as she took her time drinking from the cup. She filled it again, dipping into the stream running over a moss-covered rock. For now, the stream flowed easy, taking its time. In the heart of winter and the bone-dry summer, it would slow to a trickle. Spring, though, would see its exuberant return, and the water would splash from the cup as the spring poured onto itself, eager to be consumed.

"I left my desk at the house," Irene told Rosalee, still gazing at something in the forest. "Did you find the key?"

Rosalee was surprised at how easy this was, as if her grandmother knew why she'd brought her here.

"I did," she responded. "And the letters. I read them, but I couldn't ken some of it."

Irene sat quiet for a moment. "I couldn't either. But I thought you ought to know. And being I'm the last of the women in your family, I'm likely the only one to tell you."

She took a breath and continued, "Your papaw stepped out on me. We got married right before he left for the war, and I kept livin' with my folks and waitin' for him to come home. He set out from Virginia with five other Union soldiers after the war was over. Half of them didn't make it back, and they didn't know whether any of them would. They got caught in a blizzard after getting into Kentucky and found a house where a young widow lived. Her husband probably went to war as soon as they got married. The men stayed there for a week and made themselves at home." Irene looked straight at Rosalee. "He finally came back to me, and we built the house you're living in and got started making a family. About the time I was pregnant with your daddy, a woman came to the house with a baby girl. It was a pretty thing, with the same blue eyes as my husband." Irene turned to look into the forest once again.

"She said she didn't want it, said my husband had forced himself on her and she couldn't stand to look at it. My blood ran cold, listening to her. I hated that baby, and I hated the woman standing there. I sent her away and told her never set foot on my doorstep again. I told her I'd bury her in the woods myself if she ever came back." Irene's voice wavered. "And she never did. She couldn't have been sixteen years old—hardly older'n you now—but I held on to my hate for as long as I could. By the time I realized I was in the wrong, she was long gone. And neither of us was girls no more."

Rosalee sat in silence as the spring spilled into its cold pool.

"Your life is about to change. Just try to remember what's important." With those words, Irene stood up and walked away, and Rosalee hastened to follow.

Chapter 11

Time stopped moving like it used to for Rosalee. Her days dragged on, the tedium of housework blurring into the routine of feeding chickens and coaxing cows back to the barn. One October morning, she awoke to find her breasts were larger than they had ever been—or were they? She looked at herself in the mirror, trying to measure something for which she had no real point of reference, other than the knowing of her body and its dimensions she had always taken for granted. It wasn't long before she felt a flutter inside her, and though she knew it was this new thing, this new life that was at once part of her own and still apart, she decided it could have been her imagination and didn't tell her husband. So little was hers now. Even her body was home to someone else, and in the eyes of the law, it belonged to her husband, too. But Rosalee could have secrets, even if they didn't amount to much, and at least those were hers alone.

October rushed in and subdued the last of the summer garden that had survived or sprung back after the storm. Rosalee was surprised and a little ashamed to realize she was glad for frosty mornings that killed the cucumber and tomato plants that lingered, producing the occasional fruit that she felt obligated to pick and eat long after she had her fill of both. She could have left some to wither, but anytime she thought to do so, she heard Bessie's voice tell her, *Waste not, want not,* and she tried to be grateful there was still food to eat, tired of it as she was.

Samuel came and went without warning, and Rosalee learned to savor her evenings alone on the porch, watching as the sun began to set. She fixed herself teas from red raspberry leaves and wild mint, often letting them steep for a day or two at a time, and sipped them as she listened to the nocturnal world awaken. But when she laid her head down some nights, images flooded in and sat in the pit of her stomach. She closed her eyes and saw Samuel's wide smile standing in sharp relief to the blurred faces of women all around him, but the music and lights and money were beyond Rosalee's imagination. Her jealousy filled her with shame, and she prayed for both to leave her be. In the morning, the farm and forest were real, the cruel visions just a nightmare, gone now, and her days belonged to the beauty around her.

Each time Samuel came home after staying gone for a few nights, he burst into the house without warning, oblivious to the tranquility he disrupted, but always bringing something exotic from Owingsville or Salt Lick, besides the necessary food supplies and fabric. Rosalee's collection of store-bought dresses grew, but they were all made for a body that wasn't pregnant, a body that did not spend its days working on a farm. She folded and stacked each new one on top of the others in a cedar chest, trying to imagine her belly ever fitting into such a thing. When she realized she was wistful to wear them—and for a reason to wear such a pretty thing—she chastised herself, remembering neither Mary Ann nor Bessie ever had fine clothes, and they didn't go to town for dances or picture shows.

But still, the dresses filled Rosalee with a certain pride, and she sometimes took them out of the chest when Samuel was gone, when it was just her and her thoughts alone in the house. She would lay them on the bed in the order of when she would wear them, given the chance. The rose patterns were her favorite—delicate pinks and light greens set against cream or dusty blue. Sometimes, she sat in front of the large mirror he had brought her, braiding her hair and inventing new styles.

One evening, just as the sun was setting, she twisted her hair into swooping curls that framed her face just so, the back of her hair pulled taut and tidy near the nape of her neck. Her cheeks were rosy from pinching them—a beauty trick no one taught her, but she figured out on her own. She pinched her lips just a little, wondering if that would make them redder, like she was wearing lipstick, but quickly decided it wasn't worth it.

She held her favorite dress up to her body and swayed back and forth, like she imagined she would do at a dance. She had never been to a dance, but sometimes the people at revivals would get taken over by the Holy Spirit, and they shook and jumped and swayed and cried in the aisles formed between rows of hard wooden chairs. Rosalee figured a real dance would be more graceful, more elegant, but she wasn't sure exactly what it would look like, so she kept her movements more controlled than some of the churchgoers did.

The other women will be jealous, she caught herself thinking. Her cheeks flushed in earnest, though no one was there to reprimand her for her sinful thoughts. She folded the dress in a hurry, still careful to match each shoulder and sleeve cuff together, and placed them back into the chest. She unpinned her hair and plaited it into a simple braid that hung between her shoulder blades, unassuming but beautiful still.

Rosalee went to the kitchen and lit the oil lamp and a couple of candles. She eyed a quart jar of clear liquid Samuel kept in the pantry, then decided to pour herself a drink. She added it to a cup of red raspberry tea and sat on the porch as the sun finished setting. Her granny had always said a little liquor could soothe the nerves, but too much during pregnancy could make a child soft in the head. The thought of whether Samuel would disapprove flitted through her mind, not because she was pregnant, but because she was helping herself to his liquor, and some men didn't like it when a woman drank. She decided it didn't matter what he thought that night, while he was in town or God knows where, drinking to his heart's content, and she was there alone, too big to fit into her lovely dresses and trying to ignore the fears creeping into her mind: How would she take care of the house and the farm with a baby? Would Irene stay, or would Samuel come home more often? Would Irene keep her safe when the baby came? Or would she die like her mother did, and would it be this first baby or the next, and how many would she have to have?

Her tears finally fell, and she was thankful to be alone on the porch, crying without worrying that anyone would hear her, aching for comfort from her mother.

Barbara's sons slaughtered a pig and a cow and then hung them in John's meat house to cure as the days grew shorter. The chickens laid fewer eggs in the chilly weather, and Samuel noticed the worry on Rosalee's face one morning as she set his breakfast before him.

"What's troubling my little bride?" he asked, and then he patted her behind with a smile. "Oh, looks like my boy isn't the only one growing around here! You won't be little for long!"

Rosalee stiffened. "What would you know about that?" she asked, not so much asking but telling.

Samuel turned and looked up at her.

"What's wrong, can't take a joke?" He swatted her backside again. "Don't be hateful. You're still the prettiest girl in Kentucky, and I'll still want to make all those babies with you, don't worry."

"What about what *I* want?" Rosalee shocked herself with the question and realized it was a mistake to speak her mind so freely as soon as the words left her mouth.

The smile stole from Samuel's face, and he eyed her coolly.

"I know you're carryin' my baby and not thinkin' straight all the time. But you best remember yourself."

Waves of anger and fear washed over Rosalee at once, and she set the skillet of biscuits she was holding onto the table in a hurry, burning her fingers on the hot cast iron. The pain broke her will to hold back the tears, and a sob escaped before she could push it back down.

Samuel studied her for a moment and looked back to his breakfast. "Careful there. Ain't nothin' to be worried about. You're alright." He shoveled a bite of biscuit, soaked with the orange liquid of an egg yolk, into his mouth.

Rosalee glanced at him and turned to the basin to pour cool water on her fingers. "I'm fine," she lied.

Samuel finished his breakfast.

❀

Rosalee sewed for her growing body and the baby to come in the long winter nights. It was better when Samuel wasn't there, and she had only herself to talk to. As she sewed, she could hear Mary Ann guide her: *Keep your stitches tight. Like that, yes, good work.* And Rosalee would smile at her mother's words, alone but not truly. She helped herself to a strong tea with a bit of liquor in it when it pleased her, but sometimes it made her head swim, and she wondered what it was that Samuel liked so much about being drunk.

One night, sitting alone by the fireplace, she had a second drink. Samuel wasn't there and the crisp November days left her more tired than before. She had spent the day putting extra bedding in the chicken coop and cowshed. It had snowed but not much yet—the heavy snows would arrive any time. Rosalee struggled to warm herself by the fire, but the corn whiskey soon took hold of her blood, heating her from the inside.

The red oak popped in anger in the fireplace, reminding Rosalee of her anger with Samuel. She let her thoughts linger over the fact she never wanted to marry him, and how her father had sent her off as if she had been a burden, a girl to get rid of, instead of the girl who had helped him and took care of everyone and everything when he was broken. She thought of Samuel's cocky assurance and how he didn't know anything about taking care of a family. Her daddy gave him this house, the farm, even started moonshining with him. Samuel couldn't have made all that happen on his own. But it didn't matter what she thought. She let her tears fall, not sure exactly what she cried for, until the fire settled into deep red embers with no pockets of moisture left in the wood.

Rosalee awoke in the morning, still sitting in the rocking chair next to the fireplace, though the last of the fire was ready to give out. She sat up but found herself battling a wave of nausea unlike what she had seen before in this pregnancy, and sat back into the rocker to catch her breath. The room began to spin, and she wondered whether to stoke the fire before it died or let herself vomit first. While she was still trying to clear her mind enough to decide, the liquor and tea and what little was left of dinner the night before came raring up and onto the floor, just missing the patchwork quilt she had pulled around her shoulders late in the night. She cleaned the mess in a hurry, waves of nausea still threatening to overtake her.

Winter arrived and trudged along in a bleak, lonely parade of gray skies and biting winds that reached through the hewn log walls. Ice covered the surface of the farm pond, and Samuel had to break it with a shovel to give the cows a way to drink.

Christmas came and Samuel brought her another dress from town. Rosalee didn't have to pretend she was pleased—it was the most perfect thing she had ever seen. She pulled it out of the wrapping paper and let the silk fabric unfurl toward the floor. The salmon-pink tailored dress had a belted waist, and its delicate, billowy sleeves stopped at the elbow. A smart bow was tied high at the neck, and white buttons led from the bow to the belted waist. It was the most expensive thing Rosalee had ever held. She looked to Samuel, the question apparent in her eyes.

"I told you, business with your daddy has been good! I want to see you in it after the baby comes. I'm gonna take you to the city and we'll go dancing in Lexington—hell, maybe even Cincinnati!"

His words swirled through Rosalee's mind without finding a place to land.

"That's not all," Samuel told her. "Look what else I got you."

He held out a large paper box, and Rosalee draped the dress onto the back of a chair. She sat with the box in her lap and pulled the lid off with care. She unfolded layers of tissue paper to find a porcelain doll lying there, and Rosalee caught her breath. The doll was so lifelike, she couldn't help but pick it up as if it were a real baby. Her brown eyes were flawless, and her rosy cheeks were framed by dark curls that hung perfectly, never a hair out of place. She had the face of an infant but wore a dress finer than any Rosalee had seen before holding her new silk dress. The doll looked like some of the ones from the catalogs, but more vivid in real life than the drawings could have conveyed.

"You like it?" Samuel interrupted her thoughts.

"She's gorgeous," Rosalee exclaimed. She compared this doll to all the homemade dolls she had played with as a little girl, none of which looked like a real baby. She hadn't wanted a store-bought doll then, but now that she had one, it seemed to fill a hole that she had carried with her but never noticed. She looked at Samuel, excited by the possibilities before them. He had brought her something wonderful, something she never knew to ask for. Maybe he could keep doing that. Maybe this was a new beginning, the kind of life other people had in other places, but one she and her mother and aunt and grandmothers could only struggle to imagine, before now.

"I knew you'd love it," Samuel said, satisfied with himself. "Girls always love dolls." Rosalee stood up and hugged him, pressing her cheek against his broad chest. Samuel squeezed her and then leaned back to look at her face.

"I know I been leaving you a lot, but it will be worth it soon, don't worry. We're gonna live like you never dreamed of. I'm gonna take such good care of you and the baby."

"I know you will," she told him, and in that moment, they both believed it.

They hadn't talked much about the moonshine business, and she never knew any real details about it, other than how it was taking her father and Samuel and his brother out of town more and more, even after the corn was finished for the year. She didn't know how to imagine the kind of life he was talking about, but she couldn't wait to find out.

"I couldn't get you much," she apologized. She stood up and went to the pantry, coming back with two Mason jars. One was loosely packed with blackberries and the other with wild blueberries, Samuel's corn liquor taking up all the space between the colors that were nowhere to be found around the farm at this time of year.

"What's this?" Samuel took a jar and mused for a moment before opening it and taking a drink. "Goddamn, woman—what is this?" At first, Rosalee thought he might be upset.

"I made you something. I tried, I mean. There's more—different kinds I tried to make with the extra liquor sitting around."

"There's more of this? What else did you make?"

Rosalee thrilled at having pleased him. "I've got a bunch for you to try. Some are—probably more medicine than anything." She hesitated. "But some have a good flavor like these."

She went to the pantry and came back with a large basket full of pints and quarts mixed together in a medley of colors that defied the dreary December skies.

"I had to make 'em when the fruits were producing."

Samuel picked up a quart jar of moonshine filled with elderberries, opened it, and took a sip.

"This here is a fine mix." He took a swig before closing it back up. For the rest of the night, he took sips out of each concoction Rosalee had dreamt up, and he indulged in a little more of those that tasted good. None of the jars with roots or leaves were worth drinking for the flavor, but as he put it, "They'll cure a cold or whatever ails you." He was surprised at the variety of the fruit jars Rosalee had made. Besides the wild blueberries, blackberries, and elderberries, there were jars filled with peaches, apples, raspberries, and persimmons. She had started on the jars soon after they were married, and she had worked on them for months, admiring their beauty and wondering what would come of this alchemy. Rosalee knew she hadn't done it just for him, but some part of her wanted him to see what she could do, how she could combine the knowledge her mother and aunt had passed to her with an artistry all her own.

They didn't get to talk about any such thing, though, and Samuel fell asleep curled up on the floor next to the fireplace. She watched him for a while, until the oil lamp flickered and threatened to go out. She put her new dress away, pausing to admire it once more, and then looked for a place to keep the doll. She didn't want to put it in the trunk on top of her dresses, where it would wrinkle them, so she perched it on the chair in their room.

She lay in the bed and pulled the quilt up to her chin, watching the doll in the last bit of light glowing from the fireplace. "Goodnight," she whispered. She wondered if it was crazy to talk to a doll, but decided she was too tired to worry, and fell asleep.

In the morning, just before the sun rose, Rosalee listened to Samuel retching outside the house onto the frozen grass. She fought off a wave of nausea, then got up and made breakfast. When he came in, he didn't look like he had even been sick.

"You and your potions got me all tore up!" he laughed. He plunked himself onto a kitchen chair and devoured the eggs and biscuits Rosalee had served him. He had two cups of coffee while Rosalee sipped her one cup, surprised and impressed by how good he felt.

"Me and your daddy are going to town for a few days." He saw the look on Rosalee's face. "I don't want to go right after Christmas, but New Year's is a big holiday for those town folk, and we stand to make a lot of money. Don't worry—soon it'll be like Christmas every day around here." He stood up and kissed the top of Rosalee's head while she tried to decide what to say, or whether she should say anything at all. Samuel went outside before she could make up her mind.

The days grew longer, one minute at a time, and winter finally gave up its grasp that had choked nearly all the life out of the land. Rosalee awoke one morning, the smell of new grass in the air. She spent the next weeks basking in the joy of their little farm. The chickens laid eggs like it was their job, while some of her flowers sent green shoots through the dead leaves that had rotted to the ground. Some mornings, she could hear the dew as it sighed from the leaves and blades of grass, slipping down to the earth that drank it in.

Sometime in the spring, the cold relented, and Rosalee thought life might flourish once more. She sensed a different perfume in the air then—the earthy scent of bluebells and bloodroot that made her think of the women she had loved. But a dogwood winter soon descended upon them, and the memories of her maternal ancestors pulled at her with no focal point she could fix upon. When the animals began to calve, Samuel brought Irene to the house to stay. Irene's hair had turned grayer than what it was just last autumn, and a tired look deepened the lines around her mouth and eyes.

Over the next four weeks, Rosalee learned more about grief than she cared to know, listening to Irene's stories about her grandfather, the man who died the same day Michael was conceived and whose life was extinguished by a wisp of shadow, too small to be seen by anyone but Irene. At first, Rosalee was curious to know more about this man, part of her bloodline and yet brutal when it suited him. A father and a grandfather, but also a rapist, and a cheater. Rosalee waited for the story to bring it all together, to create a portrait of a man—good or evil, hero or beast. Instead, Irene recounted his daily habits and notable moments—some of the stories were of passing interest, but most were mundane. He liked his coffee black until his last years, when he added a bit of cream by milking a cow directly over his cup. He wouldn't whip his sons, but he did hit John in the mouth one time for sassing. He didn't change his socks nearly enough. And this could be a man's legacy, Rosalee realized: the tedious details of his day, the women he betrayed, the children he left behind.

Irene recounted her life and even some of those who came before her, as if Rosalee's memory would enshrine the history of her existence. For her part, Rosalee longed for the quiet solitude she had grown accustomed to, and she sometimes asked herself if she had been lonely before. It seemed like Mary Ann and Bessie had walked alongside her even as she cleaned the chicken coop, or called the cows, or drew water from the well. She had never felt alone when Samuel was gone, but now that Irene's stories took up so much room in her mind, she couldn't hear the voices of her mother and aunt telling her *This hen isn't laying much anymore, let some chicks hatch and it will be her time* or *Give the horses an extra apple—they've been scared by the storms.*

Just before her baby was born, Rosalee realized her mother's and aunt's voices had all but disappeared, and they had been replaced by Irene's monologue, a never-ending, lonesome story beginning and ending with a widow who was just a child herself and the blue-eyed baby she brought to Irene's door. About half the time Samuel was gone, Irene slept in the bed next to Rosalee instead of sleeping in her own room, the bedroom once occupied by her son. Rosalee gave thanks that she could enjoy a nip or two from a Mason jar of moonshine at night, when her thoughts could wander or she was spared from thinking at all.

Chapter 12

SPRING, 1931

F inally, the labor pains set in.

Irene knew without Rosalee having to tell her, a fact Rosalee realized in a rush of gratitude and a pang of guilt, as she asked herself whether she had kept her impatience with Irene hidden. Irene told Samuel the baby was coming. He was fixing to leave for the night or maybe longer, but he rode off to tell John they needed to postpone the trip.

While she still could, Rosalee walked around the farm and tended to the animals, smiling when she realized she and some of them might very well labor together. Then she thought of her mother and how the women had told her childbirth was the knife's edge, the place between life and death known by women the world around, since the beginning of time. She reached into her pocket and touched the woven doll she had infused with her prayers for an easy delivery and for them both to survive it. There was nothing more to be done.

Rosalee made her way to the garden, pausing with each contraction. She checked on the sweet peas she had just planted, to see if they looked like they had taken root in the still-cool earth. As the sun began its descent toward the horizon, Rosalee picked a few daffodils growing wild all over the farm, no longer contained in the ringed beds where Irene had planted them so long ago, when she was preparing to become a mother for the first time.

Rosalee dropped the flowers into a jar and filled it with a bit of water. She looked at them and thought about her jars of moonshine and fruit and recalled how Samuel had taken some to town right after Christmas. He had returned full of excitement and insisted Rosalee make as many as she could, and he brought home more moonshine than ever before.

The water looks like moonshine, she thought. *Flower 'shine.* She laughed at the thought and had no way of knowing how seldom she would laugh in the years to come.

A contraction knocked the breath out of her, and she grabbed the back of a kitchen chair for support.

"Are you okay, child?" Irene put her arm around Rosalee's waist. Rosalee nodded, though she wasn't sure.

"I'm okay. Just need to sit."

Irene helped her to one of the armchairs Samuel had brought home. They were from the new furniture store in town, he said, and these chairs had thick, comfortable cushions like the ones Rosalee had seen in catalogs. She labored by the fireplace and wished Samuel would come home.

Irene heated water on the cookstove and readied clean cloths as Rosalee moaned through the later stages of labor. Irene tried to put some beans on to simmer for dinner, but the smell drove Rosalee crazy with nausea, so Irene carefully moved the covered pot to the back porch, hoping they would keep well enough to cook later.

Samuel burst through the door just as Irene lit an oil lamp and the last of daylight vanished. He rushed to Rosalee by the fireplace and put his hands around her face, tilting it up toward his.

"You okay? Do you need anything?"

Rosalee shook her head as another contraction gripped her. She squeezed her eyes shut and grasped his hand, with nothing to do but wait for the pain to pass.

"I'll be outside. Irene, you come get me if you need me but I'm not gonna be in the way. I'll leave you women to it." He kissed the top of Rosalee's head and rushed out before she could catch her breath and tell him to stay.

Irene looked at Rosalee with a sympathy that, at any other time, Rosalee would have found irritating. She tried to find her bearings, but the contractions fell into one another soon after, and all thinking ceased. Between waves of pain, she felt only her breath and the respite from pain. Irene lit the fire and it crackled, casting a low light that threw shadows all over the house. Rosalee could hear the water on the cookstove as it turned to steam, disappearing drop by drop. Outside the living room window, the moon rose into the sky, and Rosalee found its face watching her as she sweated and panted on a new chair that didn't quite belong in a farmhouse.

Suddenly, her water broke and rushed through her clothes and soaked into the chair's fabric, a mess Irene later cleaned so the chair could be salvaged. Rosalee gasped and tried to move, but her waters could not be controlled. A few minutes later, the labor pains tore through her. Her thighs shuddered while her back and belly grew taut, like a deerskin stretched too thin. With a plea in her eyes, she looked to Irene, who helped her onto the floor. There, she rocked on her hands and knees and groaned with each contraction, no space left that wasn't filled with pain, pinned by her own body, no rescue to come.

"I can't do this," she whimpered to Irene. "Make it stop. I can't do it, I don't want to. I shouldn't have come here. I want to go home." Her words trailed off in a whisper and then she sobbed, still planted on the rug next to the fireplace, rocking back and forth.

"You have to," Irene told her with a grave look. "There's no going back."

The need to push overtook Rosalee, and she moved from her hands and knees to perch on the edge of the armchair seat, its cleanliness no longer important. Irene brought clean sheets and cloths to Rosalee's side and coaxed her through the rest of the birth.

Outside, Samuel heard his wife's screams as the baby tore through her, and then heard his son cry as the newborn took his first breath of the cool Kentucky air. Samuel hurried inside to find Rosalee sitting in the ruined chair, cradling Jabez while Irene bound her and cleaned the blood from her legs. Irene waited until the umbilical cord stopped pulsing before she tied and cut it, something the doctor in town would have railed against. She finished cleaning Rosalee and wrapped clean cotton around her to soak up the trickling blood. While Irene worked, Samuel took Jabez from Rosalee and looked into the boy's face with approval.

"We did good," he said to Rosalee before handing the baby back to her. "You two sleep in the bed tonight. I'll sleep in here. I don't mind the floor." Before she could protest, Samuel picked her up while she still held Jabez and carried them both to the bedroom. He laid them on the bed with care and went out to the front porch, where he watched the sun rise as he sipped some whiskey he and John had made last spring. Inside, Rosalee pulled Jabez to her breast and fell into a dreamless sleep, waves of exhaustion and relief washing over her as Mary Ann and Bessie watched and whispered comfort.

Rosalee woke later that morning at the sound of Jabez's cries and found him tucked into the crook of her arm, rooting to find her breast. She shifted him toward her and he latched on, nursing and looking up at her. His eyes were still dark—*like something from a dream,* she thought.

She could hear Samuel outside but didn't know he hadn't slept and had spent most of the night drinking. As day broke, he began feeding the animals and checking the fences around the farm, sobered by the crisp morning air.

For the next couple of days, Rosalee and Jabez floated in their newfound identities, immersed in the cycles of sleeping, eating, and relieving themselves. Irene brought Rosalee meals to eat in bed and helped her shuffle to the outhouse when necessary. She brought clean clothes for Rosalee to change into twice a day and hot water to wash herself with while Irene held Jabez and stared into his eyes, watching the story of his life unfold in their depths.

Irene brought her a tonic each morning. It had an awful lot of bloodroot in it, from what Rosalee could tell. "It'll keep your blood from goin' sour," Irene told her. Rosalee didn't remember Bessie giving this kind of tonic to new mothers she tended, but Bessie wasn't there, so Rosalee took whatever medicine might ward off the fever that took so many women after birth. And though her milk was strong, she drank nettle tea each day, just in case.

Samuel left the day after the baby was born, promising Rosalee he would bring them the best presents ever when he came back. Rosalee was reluctant to see him go, but she was content to lose herself in hours spent holding the baby, rocking in a chair next to the fireplace, and singing songs while he slept and nursed. If it weren't for the farm chores that would soon demand her attention, Rosalee thought she could live like this forever.

But on the third morning after Jabez's birth, Rosalee awoke with a weight inside her. She lay in bed for what felt like hours, watching the sunlight play across the bedroom walls. Jabez stirred and flung his hands into the air, looking for his mother. His squirming turned into a struggle against the nightgown and wet cloth diaper he wore, and his face contorted as he prepared to cry in earnest. The sound reached Rosalee as if from a distance, across acres of farmland and through trees beyond counting. Irene pushed the bedroom door open and paused when she saw Rosalee was awake.

"Good Lord, child, what are you doing just laying here?" Irene picked up Jabez and took him out to change his clothes and diaper. Rosalee turned toward the window and waited for her body to pull itself out of bed. She could hear Jabez crying now, this time out of hunger, she knew. Her breasts ached as they filled with milk to feed her baby. There was something different about the sunlight, though—it was cloudy and dull, like the sound of her son's cries. The budding leaves on the sugar maple outside her window were the same bright green as they ever were, but the green itself was different, its luster gone. The promise of new life, abandoned.

Irene brought Jabez back into the bedroom and put him in Rosalee's arms.

"Are you hungry, child? I'll bring you some breakfast." Irene waited for an answer. "You not feeling well? Are you bleeding again?" She laid the back of her hand on Rosalee's forehead and cheek, then pressed her own cheek against Rosalee's forehead.

"You ain't got a temperature. Maybe you're just wore out. I'll get you a little tonic." Rosalee saw the truth in Irene's eyes—she knew it was something beyond tiredness. As her grandmother walked to the kitchen, Rosalee pulled her baby to her breast and let him nurse. Jabez latched onto her, oblivious to what had changed, and Rosalee lay down to feed him, not realizing she no longer wanted to hold him, musing at the shadows as they played on the wall.

When Samuel returned, he found Irene holding Jabez as she cooked dinner.

"Where's Rosie?" he asked with a lightness that irked Irene through and through.

She nodded toward the bedroom door, casting a glance to him before she looked back to the stove. Samuel paused for a moment and entered the bedroom.

"Are you sick? What happened?"

Rosalee wanted to *want* to answer him, but making her mind and her mouth work together was something she would have to prepare herself to do. Everything was far away now: the sounds of the farm, the sounds of her baby, Irene's concern, and now Samuel's concern, which would soon give way to contempt. That didn't matter, either—they were all so far away. Rosalee was in a forest, but it wasn't the forest where Mama and Aunt Bessie rested beside a never-ending spring or beneath wildflowers and willows. She was lost in the darkness, not tired or sad or wanting, but distant, with no desire to return.

Samuel's voice snapped, pulling her back to the bedroom where she had lain for hours now.

"What the hell is wrong with you, woman? You've got a baby to take care of, and a house." He loomed over the bed, and Rosalee noticed the sunlight no longer played on the walls.

"If you ain't sick, you need to get out of bed. I brought things for you and the baby. Now come on out here."

He left the room, but the threat in his voice hung in the air behind him. Rosalee pulled herself into a sitting position and glanced outside. The sun had peaked and was starting to set. She hadn't eaten since breakfast but still wasn't hungry. She stood up with effort and looked into the mirror. A ghost stared back at her, its eyes dark and vacant, its skin translucent. Her hair was tangled, unbrushed for days now. A look crossed the ghost's face—an expression of emotion, which the ghost hadn't experienced for some time now. What was the emotion? She tried to think of the word for it: *vexed.* And then the face in the mirror went vacant, and Rosalee pulled a brush through her hair. She changed into a housedress before leaving the bedroom, not because she wanted to, but because she knew what Samuel would say if she didn't.

"There's our pretty little mama!" he about yelled when she entered the living room. He was sitting on the clean armchair, Jabez stretched out on his legs and half-asleep. Rosalee paused, taking in Samuel's too-wide smile. She was still searching for words to speak when the fire popped, sending an ember onto Samuel's pants and burning a hole clean through them. He leapt to his feet when the ember hit his skin, sending Jabez onto the floor, where his head hit first, breaking his neck in an instant.

"Rosie!"

Rosalee snapped back to find Samuel sitting in the armchair, watching her with his eyebrows raised. Jabez had drifted off to sleep on his lap, the warmth of the fire lulling him to dream his newborn dreams.

"Where you at, girl?" Samuel asked Rosalee.

She tried to fake a smile. "Right here."

Rosalee sat and opened the presents Samuel had brought them: a couple of store-bought gowns for Jabez and an evening gown for Rosalee. "For when you get your figure back," he told her with a smile. She waited to feel angry at his comment, but there was nothing other than the heaviness she had fought against to join her family. The baby lay asleep, and Irene watched from the kitchen, thinking her own thoughts. Rosalee let her mind wander into a fog where Samuel could not see.

"They're all lovely," she said, and meant it.

Samuel stood up and put Jabez in her arms before pouring himself a drink. Rosalee stared at his infant face, which betrayed no sign of the calamity she had watched unfold just a few minutes ago.

Irene set the table and Rosalee did what she could, pouring water from the pitcher into Samuel's glass and putting his food on the plate while he sat in the kitchen chair and watched. She held Jabez in the crook of her left arm as she ate her dinner, half listening to Samuel as he wolfed down his food and talked about the whiskey operation. Rosalee let her attention drift away but pulled it back as often as she could manage, in case he noticed she wasn't really listening.

"And those Chicago boys, they really like our stuff. Can't get enough of it, I'm telling you. We're gonna make the biggest batch we ever have and head up there next month."

Rosalee met his eyes.

"Where? What do you mean?"

"Chicago—me and your dad are taking the liquor to them. Get this—they're sending a car. A car to drive us to Chicago, Rosie! Then your dad's gonna keep the car as part of his half of the payment. I'm telling you, things are going good. You'll see—everything's about to change."

Chapter 13

Jabez was a few weeks old when Samuel left for Chicago, taking what remained of the fruit and moonshine Rosalee had made as his Christmas gift.

"They're good but men don't like a bunch of fruit with their liquor," he said with a smile. "But you know who might? The girlfriends of these Chicago guys. They've got wives, too, but they like to take their girlfriends to the clubs."

A sharpness flew across Rosalee's face, and he added, "We'll give them some of these to share with their girls, and they'll be even happier to do business with us. I'll bring you back a present."

Something stirred within her—not quite jealousy, she realized, but maybe something akin to it.

"When you coming back?"

Samuel studied her face before answering. "It won't be long. No need to worry. You just take care of my little man while I'm gone." He looked to Irene. "You can stay a while longer, can't you?"

Irene nodded and lifted a basket of laundry to wash. "Long as you need me."

"Alright then." He hoisted a milk crate of Mason jars onto his broad shoulder, the jars full of fruits that could never be seen ripe in Kentucky at the same time. Rosalee flushed with pride as she imagined how all the city people would be impressed by the beauty she had created, how it would be special even to them, because it was something they couldn't buy in a store. But then, she saw a glimpse of who would be drinking it, how they would laugh and dance and flirt while she was at home, in another world. A pang of hurt filled her eyes, and Samuel took it in before he turned around and walked out the door.

Jabez started fussing from his cradle by the fireplace. It was the same one Rosalee had slept in as an infant, listening to songs her mother sang as she sewed by the fire. Rosalee couldn't bring herself to sing very often, and Irene's watchful eyes made her keenly aware of how little warmth she felt for the baby. He was three weeks old, and instead of growing more plump at her breast, he seemed thinner. His skin was pale and paperlike. She thought of Michael as an infant and how she'd had to care for him. Rosalee stared into the fireplace as her son's cries grew louder.

Irene came in from the porch with several diapers still in need of washing. She rushed toward the cradle but stopped in front of the chair Rosalee sat in. Without looking at Rosalee, she asked, "You gonna get your baby?"

Rosalee tried to find the right words, but they were drowning like a gnat in molasses—lost, beyond words and salvation.

Irene swooped up her grandson and thrust the baby into Rosalee's arms with a force that defied her age. "This is your baby now, you hear me? There's nothing to do but keep him alive. You might not like being a mama but that's what you are, and you'd best get used to it."

Rosalee startled and looked down at Jabez. He had worn himself out with crying and now lay quiet in her arms, gazing into her eyes.

"I don't know how," Rosalee whispered to Irene.

"Just nurse him." Irene helped untie the front of Rosalee's shirt and lowered one side past her breast. "You have to hold him as much as possible. If you don't try, this baby won't live."

Rosalee saw the seriousness in Irene's expression.

"I'll try," she said, surprised to find she meant it.

For the next few weeks, Irene hounded Rosalee to hold Jabez all the time. They sat in the rocking chair next to the fireplace as the mornings grew warmer and the fires were left to burn out, no longer warding against frosty spring mornings. Irene slept in the bed with Rosalee and Jabez, the baby between them and often attached to Rosalee's breast for most of the night. As the days quickened, Jabez's cheeks filled out and dimples appeared where he had once been too lean. Rosalee began tying him to her chest with a broad piece of cloth as she moved through the house, cooking breakfast and washing dishes. Irene showed her how to tie him to her back so she could walk to the barn, feed the animals, and gather eggs.

Rosalee drank Irene's tonics throughout the day, and the taste made her gag one morning. "I can't keep drinking this stuff. It's turned bitter and I can't hardly swaller it."

"You need to take it 'til you stop bleeding," Irene told her. "I can't get you to a doctor if your blood turns."

Rosalee went through the motions, often adrift in daydream. She noticed Irene's looks, which shifted from concern to frustration, but Rosalee tended the baby and the farm, and Irene talked less and less about the memories occupying so much space in her waking mind. As much as Rosalee welcomed the respite from Irene's monologue, the growing quiet reminded her of Bessie's last weeks, and so she began to observe Irene more than she had before. Irene had ridden the trail back to John's house twice since the baby was born, each time to get something she needed right away, so it couldn't wait for a trip on the wagon with one of the men. It seemed she had all but moved in with Rosalee and Samuel.

Rosalee sent letters to her brothers in Pike County through Samuel, full of false cheer about her new baby and the farm. Various family members wrote her back with news of her brothers' marriages and children, along with stories of life in a coal company town. The coal bosses were bringing in more hired guns to discourage the workers from organizing, and the women at home grappled with this new worry, this new threat of violence. Still, the letters made it sound as if their lives were bound to one another out of love and not just obligation. Rosalee couldn't help but wonder if that world was the better one.

Barbara visited once during that time, riding a bedraggled horse who probably shouldn't have made the trip, with Michael squeezed between her and the horse's mane. In the house, Michael cooed over Jabez and held the baby, beaming with pride as he supported Jabez's head like Irene told him to. Barbara said little but gave Rosalee a patchwork quilt she had made for Jabez, along with a nightgown for the baby to grow into. When she held Jabez, Barbara looked into the boy's eyes before proclaiming he looked just like his papaw. "Samuel's daddy," she clarified. She handed him back to Rosalee with her eyebrows raised. "This one'll be trouble, guarantee it."

Rosalee didn't know how to respond, so she said, "He's a good baby so far," and Irene nodded, though Barbara wasn't paying attention. Barbara watched Michael climb back on the horse before long and promised another visit, though Rosalee wasn't sure whether she meant it.

The second time she returned from John's, Irene brought several cans of snuff back with her. There was an unscented can, but Irene liked the spearmint flavor. Rosalee told her she liked the rose flavor the best. "Funny," Irene said, "rose for little Rosalee," and they shared a rare laugh.

At the end of the day, they sat on the front porch if it was warm enough, or by the fireplace when the nights grew too cold. After Rosalee fed Jabez for the last time that evening, they each drank a bit of moonshine and pinched snuff with their fingers, pulling it into their nostrils with a quick snort.

One night, looking into the fire and rocking the cradle with her foot, Rosalee finished her drink and told Irene, "This isn't what I wanted. I didn't want to marry him in the first place, but I thought it was getting better there for a minute. But I don't know now. Somethin' just don't feel right. And he's got a mean streak—I've seen it." She turned and looked at Irene, who stared into the fire. "I don't want to stay here no more."

"Look here, little girl." Rosalee bristled at the words, but they also made her ache for her mother.

"Most of us don't get what we want. And it don't matter whether you like it or don't. You're here, your baby's here, and there ain't nowhere else for you. You want to go back to your daddy's house?"

Rosalee shook her head as she fought to hold back tears.

"No, you don't. This is your home now, and unless that man of yours comes home with another woman or his hands get too heavy, you're best off to make peace with it."

Tears streamed down Rosalee's face, which was red from the firelight or the moonshine or maybe even the sorrow breaking loose inside her.

"I don't want this baby," she whispered.

Something flickered in Irene's eyes, and she turned back to the fire. "It's too late for that," she responded.

John drove Samuel straight to the front porch one morning, sending the chickens scattering away from the tires and sending dust onto the laundry Irene had hung out to dry. Samuel hopped out of the car and swaggered up to the steps just as Rosalee walked out, carrying Jabez.

She didn't recognize him at first. He was wearing a striped suit and a fedora, along with black patent leather shoes. But it wasn't just the clothes—he put on an air like he was a different man. He held his head a little higher and whistled as he made his way to the door. Rosalee enjoyed the fleeting thought that maybe he had come to say goodbye before moving to the city forever. She looked past him to the car, a marvel to everyone these days, but even more so for the woman who had never seen one up close. John stepped out of the passenger side and went to the back, where Rosalee couldn't see him. She took in the gleaming headlights and the mass of metal reflecting the sunlight, the very image of newness. It possessed a certain beauty, but she thought of Bonnie, and decided then and there she would rather be with her horse than in such a contraption.

Samuel interrupted her thoughts. "It's a Model A, top of the line. And it's ours—can you believe that?" Rosalee looked at him, a question on her face. "Well, it's your daddy's, I reckon," he went on. "Remember, I told you—he's taking it as half his pay for this load. But between you and me"—he leaned in, as if he was sharing a secret—"I gotta tell you, I'm the better driver."

Rosalee stumbled over how to respond, but before she could say anything, Samuel continued, "Your daddy can drive here now, in a pinch. It'll take an hour or two with the road so rough, and we ain't wastin' gas just to go back and forth. But you'll get to ride in it sometime soon." He beamed. "And hey, I told you I'd bring you back something good, didn't I?" he asked, holding his hands out as if to show he was the something good. "And I sure did. Me and your dad will come inside here in a minute. You go sit down with the baby."

She bristled at his command but decided sitting down and letting him bring her a present was the best idea he had come up with since she met him. Samuel and John came inside, and John paused to look at his grandson.

"He's a good-lookin' little thing," he told Rosalee. "Your brother and Barbara will visit again soon."

"Thanks, Daddy." Rosalee smiled at him as he lingered for a moment longer, and he almost said something else but decided against it.

"Here, give me the baby while you open your present." Irene held her arms out and took Jabez. She and John sat down to watch Rosalee while Samuel stood next to her chair.

The gift was in a large, rectangular box, gleaming white and held shut with a pink satin ribbon tied into a simple bow. Rosalee ran her finger along the ribbon. The color took her away, and she envisioned the pink lady's slipper flowers she once found in the woods with Bessie.

Bessie had led them farther from the house that day, intent on finding something beyond their normal domain within the forest. A pine grove appeared out of nowhere, dark and still, as if the gentle babble and chatter of the forest knew to hush itself in this place.

They stepped across a carpet of dry pine needles, silent beneath their feet, as the sunlight abandoned its search for the forest floor. Pink lady's slippers sprang from the ground, regal in the dimmed luster of the sky. The flower petals hung from the stem like an egg. Rosalee knew it was a pink lady's slipper but had only seen the yellow ones before. Something about the color and shape meant they were mothers, in her mind.

Without thinking, she bent down to pick one. "Don't touch them," Bessie admonished her. "They'll sting you. And besides, they're special. We'll take them only if we need them."

"Can I touch the petals?" Rosalee remained crouched next to the flowers, the sweet scent of their false nectar blending with the pine forest floor, flooding her senses and locking the moment into her memory.

Bessie nodded, and Rosalee touched a deep-pink petal like she would touch a new baby or the family Bible. Just then, Rosalee noticed the flower moving from something inside it, and a bee emerged at the opening formed at the top of the petals, the clever trap formed to lure in the insects that would spread their pollen. It crawled out and onto

Rosalee's finger, and she and Bessie watched as the pollen-laden bee paused there, as if to assess these witnesses to its emergence.

Rosalee shifted on her knees and the bee stung her in an instant.

"Ouch!" She flung her hand and the bee flew away, the venom spreading in her finger, the sanctity of the moment shattered. "Why'd it have to do that?" She looked up at Bessie, who knew the hurt in her voice meant more than the hurt in her finger.

"That's what they do, child. Don't be surprised when something that's meant to hurt you does it. Let's go find some plantain to put on it."

"Where you at, Rosie?" Samuel startled her from the memory. Though he was smiling, Rosalee heard the impatience in his voice. Irene and John were looking at her, and she wondered how long she had been lost in memory.

"It's so beautiful." Rosalee forced a smile. "Can't hardly bear to open it."

She pulled the ribbon and the bow fell apart. Inside the box was a porcelain doll wrapped in delicate layers of white tissue paper. Rosalee lifted each layer with care, unfolding them as if they were as precious as the doll itself. When she pulled it out, she found another replica of a baby girl, just a few months older than her actual child. Her dress was white with pale blue roses, and her eyes were painted the same shade of blue. A matching satin bow adorned the baby's head, and a few locks of painted-on blond hair peeked out from beneath the ribbon.

Rosalee knew she was supposed to feel something, and she struggled to find the words Samuel wanted to hear. A thought crept in—*at least it won't cry*. She looked up at Samuel. "Now I've got another baby to love on, thanks to you." She thought about the first doll he had brought her. It sat on the chair in their bedroom, lifeless, and the pleasure Rosalee once felt seemed locked away inside the doll, a snapshot in time, never changing and never coming to life. Another thought tugged at her: the memory of the ruined garden and the autumn harvest that wasn't replenished. What else could have been bought with the money Samuel spent on this doll?

He grinned at her. "I know how much you love them baby dolls." He shot a look at John. "You might not have had much when you were growin' up, but I'm taking care of you now. We're gonna have the best things money can buy!"

Rosalee's stomach dropped, and she hastened to fix her facial expression so it could not betray her. She glanced at her father, whose stony countenance revealed nothing.

"I'm sure you're right," she managed to respond. She glanced at Irene, whose feelings were also locked away behind a still face.

The air thickened around Rosalee, and thoughts hovered at the edge of her mind over what the doll meant, over what Samuel meant, and over what her father and Irene wouldn't say.

An image of Samuel walking with another woman flashed before Rosalee's eyes. "It's such a pretty doll. Did somebody help you pick it out?" She knew it was a mistake to ask as soon as the words left her lips. Samuel's face darkened, and his pleased look gave way to the cold disdain Rosalee had seen before.

"That's not your business, now is it?" He stood up and walked to the door, and John stood to follow him. "I'm going outside to talk to your daddy and then I want my supper. Make it good. I've got used to eatin' at those city restaurants."

After he walked out, Rosalee and Irene exchanged a look. Irene's face was tired now, and she gave a little shake of her head. Rosalee took the doll to her bedroom. There wasn't room enough on the chair for both of them, so she sat them together on top of her cedar chest. She paused to look at the dolls before she walked out, and they stared back in fixed wonder, unable to help at all.

Chapter 14

A fter John had left, Samuel drank his usual whiskey on the porch while Rosalee drank the last of the tonic Irene said she needed. She and Irene washed dishes and took turns entertaining Jabez. Samuel had brought him a silver rattle with a little bell inside it, and the women waved it for the baby, all of them mesmerized by the gleaming metal and delicate musical chime. By the time he was three months old, Jabez could grasp the rattle for a time, though he would still drop it—sometimes on himself—and howl with frustration at losing his toy.

Rosalee imagined Samuel inside the store where he bought the rattle, and she wondered how big the store was. It must have been a department store, like the ones with advertisements in the paper, large and full of nice clothes, not like the general store she had been to in town where her mama had bought sacks of flour and sometimes let her get a penny candy. She couldn't conjure an image for what such a store would look like, but something else appeared in her vision, just like when she had opened the box with the doll inside—a woman next to Samuel, a *girlfriend*, picking out the rattle, trying on fancy hats with lace veils.

"I'm going to bed now," she told Irene, who was darning socks in the light of an oil lamp. Irene nodded without looking up, and Rosalee realized how much comfort she now took from her company. They had a rhythm in their farm life, dividing up chores and caring for the baby without having to talk much about who would do what. Irene had stopped talking much at all, except the rare occasion when the liquor hit her just right and she remembered to retell the stories from her younger days. Rosalee was often fascinated or horrified by the patchwork of history her grandmother wove—some stories were about days of war between states, others about the wars taking place within her home or heart—but Rosalee absorbed it all the same.

She laid Jabez in his cradle next to the bed and closed her eyes. She could hear the rocking chair on the porch as Samuel rocked in a rhythm that lulled her to sleep. He came into the room after Irene had gone to her bedroom, and the entire house was still, though Rosalee's mind was not.

In her dreams, honeybees buzzed around white bloodroot flowers someone had put in a jar in the kitchen. Rosalee tried to shoo away a bee as it flew toward her, and she knocked over a jar of whiskey, the liquor soaking into the wood grain of the table as she rushed to clean it up. Just as she discovered the glass jar had broken and cut her, she realized she hadn't seen the baby in days.

The whiskey and blood and horror of losing her child threatened to overtake her, and Samuel shut the bedroom door, jarring her awake. Once she realized it had been a dream, she sighed with relief and nestled back into the blankets, the sound of Samuel undressing fading as she fell back to sleep.

He climbed into the bed and soon rolled onto his side, putting his arm around Rosalee. His touch awoke her just enough for her to realize he was there, and she slipped back into her dreams. Samuel caressed her arm at first and then her hip, rousing her from sleep. She realized what he wanted and lay there, unmoving, willing him to fall asleep.

With one hand, he pulled her nightgown up as much as he could, but the weight of her legs secured it beneath her. Rosalee offered no help, pretending to be asleep and thinking he would soon give up. Instead of giving up, Samuel sat up on his knees and pulled Rosalee onto her back, bringing her nightgown up to her waist. He began tugging at her underwear, and Rosalee pushed his hands away.

"What are you doing?" she demanded. "I was sleeping."

Samuel ignored her and grabbed the waistband of her underwear, trying to pull it down, working against the weight of her backside.

"Stop it! What do you think you're doing? Go to sleep," she whispered with as much force as possible, not wanting to wake Jabez.

"Come on, Rosie. It's been enough time since the baby was born. Give me some love." He bent down and pressed his lips against hers, and the warm whiskey on his breath filled her mouth and nostrils. With a shudder, she turned away and pushed herself up toward the headboard to get away from him.

"What's wrong with you," he said, not really asking a question. "We haven't made love since you were pregnant and now you want to push me away?"

"I'm tired," she responded. "It's late and you stink of whiskey." As soon as the words left her lips, she wished she hadn't said them. The back of his hand fell across her mouth with a sting, bringing tears to her eyes.

"You think you're gonna play games again like you did when we got married, but that ain't how it's gonna work now." Samuel pulled her by her hips until she lay flat on the bed again, and he grabbed her underwear and yanked it down, leaving it around her ankles. "I have needs and your job is to take care of them, just like I take care of you." He pushed himself in and lightning coursed through her, all fire and pain. Rosalee writhed and clenched her body, trapped beneath Samuel, unable to catch her breath, unable to speak.

She closed her eyes and saw the spring. Cool and clear, the water would taste as it always did. There was the wild ginger, its blooms hidden but promised. There was the willow tree—radiant, showy, elegant, not like Bessie had lived but perhaps part of who she was, though no one could see it. Between the ginger and willow was a patch of white trout lilies. *Those are new,* Rosalee thought, and she reached out to touch them, but they shrank into the earth.

Rosalee turned her head away from Samuel, tears leaking into her hair and onto the pillow. She stifled her cries well enough so Jabez did not wake, though he whimpered now and then. When Samuel was finished, he put his hand on the side of her face and turned it toward his. "See?" He smiled at her. "That wasn't so bad, was it." He kissed her lips, not tasting the blood on them. He rolled over and fell asleep on his back, his breath heavy and hot, and when Rosalee relieved herself into her bucket next to the bed, the urine stung her torn skin. She eased herself back under the quilt next to her husband and stared at the ceiling, where shadows flew until daybreak.

After the sun rose and Samuel left the room, Rosalee sat in front of her mirror, dabbing comfrey salve on her split lip before she left the bedroom. She stared at her reflection, wondering who this girl was, with vacant eyes and a bottom lip a little too red to be real. She picked up the hairbrush and dragged it through her hair, some of which was still matted against her face where her tears had dried. The bristles scratched her head at first, annoying in their rigidity, but then she dragged the brush against her scalp as the anger welled inside her. The pain reached a crescendo, and tears spilled from her eyes just as Jabez began to stir. Rosalee dried her face and took a deep breath.

"I guess you're still here after all," she whispered as she picked him up. "Ain't we lucky." Jabez looked into her eyes and laid his head against her shoulder, sucking his forefinger. She carried him into the kitchen, where Irene looked at her mouth, looked up to her eyes, and turned away. Samuel sat at the table, drinking coffee.

"There you are," he said. "My little family, up and ready to go."

Rosalee steeled herself before speaking to him. "Go? We're going somewhere?"

"We're going to town to buy supplies. Wear one of the good dresses I bought you. I want everybody to see how pretty you look in them."

"Samuel, I-I can't take the baby to town yet. He might need to nurse while we're gone and I'm still not ready for a long ride. I sure wish I could go," she hastened to add, "especially if it meant I could wear one of them dresses."

"Alright then." Samuel looked at her and nodded. "I'll take you to your daddy's house so you can visit with Mama and she can see the baby. I promised her I'd bring him to see her soon. I'll pick you all up after I'm done in town." Rosalee saw her day was set for her, no matter how little she wanted to spend it with Barbara.

Rosalee turned to Irene. "Are you coming with us?" Irene shook her head. "Got too many chores here," she said. "But Samuel, pick me up some snuff, will you? Spearmint." She looked at Rosalee. "Get us a couple of them rose-flavored ones, too, if you don't mind." Samuel nodded and went outside to ready the horses and wagon.

Rosalee gathered the baby's blanket and an extra gown for him in case he needed it later. It was the first time either of them was leaving the house since he was born, and Rosalee wasn't sure how to prepare to be away with a three-month-old. She paused next to the wardrobe Samuel had bought from the furniture store in town for hanging his new clothes and Rosalee's dresses. She opened one of the cabinet doors and looked at the dresses hanging there, unworn. She imagined wearing one into town and remembered thinking the other women would be jealous to see her wearing it. *They won't be jealous. They'd think I was crazy to wear that in town.* A wry smile crossed her face and disappeared when she wondered next, *Where would I ever wear these things?*

Any dance in Owingsville or Salt Lick would be a square dance, not something to get dressed up for. *They'd laugh me out of town for wearing such a thing,* she thought. They'd have to go all the way to

Lexington at least, to go to a dance and dinner where people wore those kinds of clothes. When would she be able to leave her baby for that long, and who would she leave him with? Irene was only getting older, and she doubted Barbara would be willing to watch him much. Rosalee looked in the mirror and, with an empty laugh, asked herself if any of the women at those dances ever showed up with a bloody lip anyway.

"Rosie, let's go!" she heard Samuel call from outside. Rosalee shut the door of the wardrobe and wondered if she would ever truly need to open it.

She picked up Jabez from his cradle, grabbed the basket she had filled with his clothing, and hurried outside where Samuel had the horses hitched to the wagon. They took the dirt road to John and Barbara's house, winding around the property where Rosalee had hardly ever traveled.

By the time they got to her old home, Rosalee's stomach ached with hunger. She realized she hadn't eaten anything before they left and hoped Barbara would have some breakfast to offer her. Samuel helped her down from the wagon and sauntered to the front door, which he flung open as if he was still at his own house. Rosalee followed him inside and found Barbara sitting in a chair, sewing something that looked like it was meant for the baby. Something about that image startled Rosalee, and she realized she had half expected to see her mother sitting in the chair. A new hurt filled her, and the coldness in the house reminded her that the women who had loved her most were gone forever.

Barbara spoke to them as she kept her eyes on her sewing. "John and Joseph's in the horse barn. Go on out there and John'll tell you what we need from town. Joseph might come with you. Y'all work it out but don't stay gone all day. There's work to be done here." She cast her eyes toward Rosalee. "I don't ken where your brother is. I never know about that boy." She noticed Jabez and put her sewing aside. "Bring me the baby," she told Rosalee, as Samuel ambled back out the door.

Rosalee laid Jabez in Barbara's arms and stepped back, watching for a tender look to cross Barbara's face, but her face didn't change as she examined the baby, peering into his eyes.

"You feeding him enough?" she asked Rosalee. Before she could answer, Barbara continued, "And are you eatin' enough yourself?" She looked at the young mother. "You gotta eat to feed a baby. There's biscuits on the table if you're hungry."

Rosalee mumbled her thanks and walked to the kitchen table. From her chair, Barbara added, "Careful not to eat too much neither. You can't keep a man's interest if you lose your shape."

Rosalee stood at the table, a pat of butter sliding off the butter knife as she recalled the night before: she didn't want much of Samuel's interest. She moved the biscuit under the knife just in time to catch the falling butter and turned around to look at Barbara as she ate.

"Lord, child, have you a seat. You ain't gotta stand there like it's time to sing a hymn. What happened to your lip?"

The biscuit turned to sawdust in Rosalee's mouth as she struggled to find the right words. She wasn't sure whether Barbara would feel for her, or if she would see the truth as an insult to her son. Worst of all, she might tell Samuel, and Rosalee didn't know how he would react. "I ran into the door frame in the middle of the night," she lied. "I was just so tired but had to get up with the baby."

Barbara watched Rosalee's face and must have discovered something Rosalee didn't even know a person could find. "Believe me, you wouldn't like what happens when a man loses interest in his wife. You've got years ahead of you. Try to make the best of them, because they'll be gone before you know it."

Rosalee tried to feign interest in what Barbara had to say.

"You're right, Mother. Samuel's a good provider, and it's my duty to be a good wife to him." Rosalee thought of Bessie and how her aunt would have rolled her eyes, hearing such a thing.

Barbara stared at her for a moment and turned back to Jabez, apparently satisfied with Rosalee's response. "Well, you all made a good baby, that's one thing for sure."

"He's an angel," Rosalee heard herself say. "I couldn't ask for a better child."

Chapter 15

Rosalee waited until the men had gone to get some bottles of moonshine from near the still that was hidden in the woods so they could take some to town with them. Once they were out of sight, she decided to look for her brother. "You mind to watch Jabez for a minute while I look for Michael?" she asked Barbara.

"Me and this baby are fine," Barbara told her without looking up, and Rosalee wondered for a moment at her uncheerful tenderness, but decided it was best to accept whatever Barbara had to offer.

Rosalee found Michael right away at the stock barn where the cows were kept. Her brother's smile lit up his face quicker than ever before when he saw Rosalee.

"There's the new mama! Did you bring the little man out here to work?" Rosalee laughed and threw her arms around his neck.

"You've got your work cut out for you here, little brother."

"What happened to your lip there, sister?"

Rosalee took a step backward and touched her lip. A little blood stained her finger—it must have split open again when she smiled. "It's nothing," she told him. "Ran into something in the dark is all."

Michael looked down at the ground and smiled. "With Daddy and Joseph running off to the still and the cornfields with that husband of yours all the time, I'm 'bout overrun with these animals. I sure wish you was here."

"Me too." The words stuck in her throat, and Rosalee hurried to wipe a tear before it could fall.

"Well, where's my nephew?"

"He's in there with Barbara. You want to go in?"

"If that's what it takes to see the baby." Michael sighed. "Elsewise, I might just live in one of these barns."

Rosalee noticed the twinkle in Michael's eyes, and their easy laughter made her ache for the time before she had become a mother, or a wife, or even a stepdaughter. She followed her memories backward, saw herself standing next to the barn in all the different incarnations of who she had been, and snagged on an image of her mother before Michael was born.

"Let's go inside," she told him.

Barbara was still sitting in the same chair, Jabez sleeping on her lap with his head toward her knees as she continued her sewing. "I'm making him some bigger clothes," she told them without looking up. "Your mama teach you much sewing?" She shifted her gaze to Rosalee.

"I can sew," Rosalee told her. "I spent more time cooking and learning medicine."

Barbara let out a laugh. "Medicine's for doctors. A woman needs to know how to take care of her family. Samuel can't buy everything the baby needs."

Rosalee bristled inside, but a glance from Michael helped her control her tongue. "It's a good thing I've got you to teach me, and Jabez has you for a granny." Barbara glanced at Rosalee, her eyebrows raised. She must have been satisfied with Rosalee's response because she looked back to her sewing and nodded.

Jabez shifted and began to fuss. "Go ahead and get him," Barbara told Rosalee, who hadn't been sure how she would pick him up without touching Barbara. Touching her seemed impossible, Rosalee realized. It was as if Barbara had built an invisible fence around herself, and no one could get through it. They wouldn't even *want* to get through it.

Barbara shot her a look. "You gettin' the baby or not?" Flushed, Rosalee pulled him from Barbara's lap and turned to Michael.

"You want to hold him?" Michael grinned, and Rosalee could tell he knew just how flustered she felt inside. "Sure, sis. Let me see that boy."

When Jabez's fussing grew to throaty cries, Michael handed him back to Rosalee and went outside. "Come see me before you leave," he said, and Rosalee promised she would. She sat in a rocking chair with Jabez, nursing him while Barbara sewed in silence. Jabez drifted back to sleep, a dribble of milk leaking from the corner of his lips, which twitched with a smile born of infant dreams.

"His daddy had a heavy hand sometimes, too."

Barbara's words broke the hush and hung in the air. Rosalee's mind stumbled around them, kenned what they meant, and then fumbled for the right words to say back. Before she could say anything, Barbara continued. "I learned to keep my mouth shut and read his moods. They're not bad men, but the Carters have got a temper. You just have to learn how to work around it."

Rosalee couldn't have responded if she'd wanted to. Anger flashed in her eyes, but a cry threatened to escape her throat if she spoke. She thought about what Samuel had done the night before and pushed it back out of her mind so she wouldn't cry right then and there.

Barbara glanced up at her but still appeared consumed by her work. Finally, Rosalee cleared her throat. "I'd like to go see my mama's grave while the baby sleeps. That okay with you? He won't need to eat for a good while now."

"Go ahead, then." Barbara lifted the baby's gown and studied a hem. "We'll start supper when you get back."

Rosalee thought about asking Michael to join her but decided she wanted to be alone when she visited Mary Ann and Bessie.

The forest closed itself around her like a protective veil, and by the time she reached the spring, sobs were rising up from her throat. She sat between the white willow and the wild ginger, closed her eyes, and let herself cry, knowing no one would hear her. She realized she could still feel Samuel—his weight on top of her, his breath on her face. And inside her. His touch was different from before, when she had felt safe, and she wondered whether her father had ever done that to her mother. *Surely not,* she thought, believing she could never again bear any affection for Samuel. Her mother would not have been happy ever again, either.

When it seemed all of her tears had fallen, she went to the spring and drank from the tin cup, and then held her hands under the water and splashed it on her face. She pushed up her sleeves and cupped her hands under the spring again, brushing her wet hands down the length of her arms. She wet her hands again and patted her face, cleaning the salt that had dried there.

She walked back to Mary Ann's and Bessie's graves and sat once again. The warm darkness of the forest surrounded them, but the willow bathed in sunlight without oaks and maples to crowd it. Trout lilies sprouted out of the ground around her, bowing to the forest floor that had taken in Rosalee's tears, that was listening still, waiting to hear what she needed.

"What else didn't you tell me?" she whispered. "I didn't know it would be this hard." She thought of Jabez and the endless days ahead, how much he would want and need from her. "Help me."

Her tears fell again, this time without a sound. She thought of Samuel and his moods that changed in an instant. He was a stranger, made over again and again. And she was his.

A sound caught her attention and pulled her mind back from the darkness. Rosalee scrambled to her feet and strained to hear a child's voice carrying from somewhere in the woods. She walked in the direction of the pine grove she and Bessie had once stumbled upon and found it once again full of pink lady's slippers. Rosalee smiled at the memory and kept following the voice—a girl's, she thought—now singing. She reached the edge of the pines and stood still, awed by the mountain laurels sprawling along the forest hillside. Their pink-and-white blooms lit the landscape, luminous against the greens and browns of the late-May forest.

Through many dangers, toils and snares, I've already come, hmm hmm hmm hmmm . . .

Rosalee turned to find a little girl, maybe six or seven years old, picking wild blueberries that grew alongside the mountain laurel. Her long hair hung in braids on both sides of her head, each braid adorned with a blue bow at the end. The little girl noticed Rosalee and stopped singing, her basket of berries in hand, and Rosalee noticed the girl's eyes matched the ribbons in her hair.

Samuel and Rosalee got back to their house just after the sun went down. Rosalee had hugged Michael as tight as she could before they parted, and she had overheard Samuel telling John they should take Michael with them to Chicago sometime, to show him the big city. "You stay here on this farm," she whispered in his ear, and Michael just smiled in response before breaking the embrace to go call the cows in for the night.

Irene took Jabez from Rosalee's arms and handed her a pint jar with a tonic to drink. "Made you a little extra since you been gone all day," she told Rosalee. Rosalee drank it down with a faint shudder, noticing the bitter taste was even more pronounced than usual. "We're down to the last of it," Irene told her. "It's strongest at the bottom of the jar. But you should be fine 'til your next baby comes along."

Rosalee avoided looking at Samuel, knowing his eyes had probably gleamed in excitement at the idea. She had finally healed but couldn't imagine having another baby. Most families had ten or more children, but the women on her mother's side only had a few. She had never wondered why before, but now it occurred to her that her own mother might have easily had two or three more children if she hadn't died. She could see the embers of the woven doll she had burned the night of Mary Ann's death, and though she loved her brother now, she wished he had not taken her mother away.

"Jabez is sleepin' like a rock," Irene told her. She held out the pint jar, this time half-filled with clear moonshine. "Let's sit and have a pinch of snuff. Looks like Samuel brought back plenty for the both of us."

Samuel was out in one of the barns. *Maybe he'll sleep out there,* Rosalee thought. She and Irene settled into the rocking chairs on the front porch and snorted a bit of their flavored snuff. The shadows of the farm and Irene's dimly lit figure all swam for a brief moment, and as the effect of the snuff faded, Rosalee thought she would rather feel this way all the time. This was the respite she could claim, when she didn't worry about the baby and her own disinterest in holding him or about Samuel and how she detested his touch. She sipped on the moonshine, willing those worries away.

He slid into bed about an hour after she did, drawing her from the edge of sleep. She lay facing the window, away from him. He put his hand on her arm and felt her stiffen. Samuel sighed.

"Don't be like that, Rosie. Why can't you just relax? You take care of me and my needs, and I'll take care of you."

She thought of the brief months during which she had enjoyed him and even wanted him. She saw the girl in the woods who had just looked at her, no longer singing. The moment was fixed in time, and even the birds had ceased their chattering, the leaves their rustling. Rosalee stared into the blue eyes of the girl before her, and the girl peered back into hers. Rosalee smelled the rose scent of letters freed from her grandmother's desk and through the darkness saw a young woman's face—a girl's, really—and the baby she held in her arms.

Her grandfather and what he did with the young girl somehow connected to Samuel, the smell of magnolias Rosalee had grown to hate, and the words he had just spoken. Samuel pulled her arm and rolled her onto her back. She calculated her options, but a fog of confusion overcame her, and she softened.

"You know I never want to hurt you, Rosie," Samuel whispered. "I know I've got this temper, but you make me so happy most of the time." Rosalee met his eyes, illuminated by the moonlight. "There you are, my little wife. Come here."

Samuel eased himself onto her and Rosalee lay silent, obliging him. Samuel's touch was gentle now, nothing like the night before, but she wondered what would happen if she told him to leave her alone. Her thoughts raced and faces flashed in her mind and nothing fit together, so she sent it all away, into a locked room.

Chapter 16

SUMMER, 1931

S everal weeks passed and another Kentucky summer began in earnest. Irene and Rosalee followed the same routine they had established when Samuel was gone. For the most part, he came home and took up his farm chores, and never asked the women who had done them in his absence. Rosalee didn't mind mucking the horse stalls or shoveling animal manure into the old wheelbarrow and carting it to the pile at the edge of the garden, where it would sit for a few months or more before she added it to the soil. She discovered she was grateful, though, that she didn't have to smell as much manure when Samuel was home, and she didn't occasionally find a bit she had accidentally wiped on her clothes or into her hair.

Rosalee awoke one morning to find Samuel sitting on the porch with his coffee, rather than working on the chores like he normally did. She gathered the hens' eggs, and when she brought them back to the house, Samuel told her, "You'll need to milk Daisy. She's probably about to bust." Rosalee started to ask him why he hadn't milked her, but as she was thinking about what to say, he continued: "I'll be heading out soon and can't get in the muck. I'm going over to your daddy's house for the day. We gotta get some whiskey bottled. Cook me up a few eggs after you get the milk in, Rosie."

"Alright," she said, and set the basket of eggs down on the porch. She milked Daisy and brought the milk to the house, where she found Irene had picked up the eggs and cooked Samuel's breakfast. He took his last bite as she poured fresh milk into a jam jar for him, and he drank it in one long swig.

"Ah, you can't beat that!" he exclaimed before wiping his mouth on the back of his hand. "Take good care of everything while I'm gone." He stood, kissed Rosalee on the cheek, and left.

Rosalee thought little of it when Samuel didn't show up before sunset, and she was relieved to go to bed knowing he wasn't home, but hoped he wouldn't wake her in the middle of the night. The next morning, she started to wonder what might have kept him so long. By dinnertime, guilt set in as she thought she should be more concerned. She told Irene she was going to ride over to John and Barbara's to make sure he was okay.

"Feed this baby before you leave," Irene responded, and Rosalee sat to nurse him in the shade of the back porch, where they still sweated together, baby and mother, with no breeze to cool them. Afterward, she took a nip of the latest tonic Irene had made her, which was supposed to keep her milk going strong for the baby. It tasted of roots, and her tongue tingled with a buzz that reminded her of the snuff hitting the inside of her nose in just the right way. Irene saw the surprise on her face and smiled. "It's good stuff, I tell ya. This is what let me nurse my nine babies and made them all strong as an ox." Rosalee nodded as if she could understand the possibility of having nine babies, but a chill ran through her.

Growing up, she had met some of her father's siblings a handful of times. Playing with her cousins had been a treat, but she had overheard the adults' conversations and knew there was some falling out about her grandfather Haman. He had done something most of his children wouldn't forgive, except John, and they wouldn't forgive their mother for it, either. It had something to do with a girl in the county church, and that was why the Conners never went to church except when it was time for a revival. Two boys died in the Great War, and John's other brothers and sisters refused to see their father or mother long before Rosalee was born, despite living in the same county for the rest of their lives.

Samuel had ridden Billy to John's house, leaving Rosalee with Bonnie. She saddled the horse and climbed on, nervous and excited to make the trip alone for the first time. She realized that other than her trip to the spring, it was the first time she had been alone since Irene moved in, but this time, she could stay gone for longer. Jabez didn't need to nurse as often now, and Irene could give him a rag with sugar and lard to suck on if he got hungry before she returned. Rosalee had fashioned a bag from a cotton sack and slung the strap over her head and one arm, letting the sack rest against her hip. She tucked an apple and a bit of cornbread into it, in case she arrived too late to eat dinner at her father's house.

They crossed one of the shallow streams cutting through the middle of the property and reached another surrounded by trees on both sides. Rosalee slowed Bonnie to a careful walk, and they entered the patch of woods. The sun filtered through a thick canopy, sending slivers of light to reach the water, where they danced on the babbling stream. Rosalee smiled—she had never been to this creek at this time of year, and it teemed with life and a mirth that reached into her and kindled a joy she had forgotten. Tears rushed to her eyes and a sob escaped her throat as the sunlight played on her skin and something within her returned to an ease that had long been lost.

The barrage of thoughts and chatter pulling at her mind fell silent. For a moment, Rosalee was at peace.

She thought of Jabez with a twinge of regret, wondering how long she could be gone before he would really need her. But the urgency to find Samuel had diminished, and she hesitated to leave the blissful stream and the solace she found there.

A colorful glimmer caught her eye upstream, a little farther into the forest, and Rosalee coaxed her horse forward, toward a carpet of red flowers that continued to thrive even into early summer. As she rode closer to them, the air cooled and settled onto Rosalee's bare arms, which tingled as her hairs stood on end. She thought about Samuel's offhand statements about more children, and she decided to gather some of the roots she might need for those babies while she had the chance.

As she got ready to dismount from Bonnie, a baby copperhead flashed across the stream toward them, and Rosalee froze. The snake slowed as it reached the rocks where Bonnie stood, just out of the water, and made its way beneath the horse, winding away from the creek and toward the trees, seemingly unaware of Rosalee and uninterested in Bonnie. Rosalee relaxed as the snake slithered toward the dark edge of the forest.

Just then, something shot out of the water and grabbed the copperhead, sliding against one of Bonnie's legs as it traveled beneath her. The unexpected touch startled the mare, and she reared and whinnied, despite Rosalee's attempts to calm her. Rosalee grasped the reins and pressed her legs tight against the saddle as Bonnie kicked in panic, but she reared again and backed toward the water, landing Rosalee onto the creek bed at the water's edge. Bonnie galloped downstream as Rosalee tried to take a breath and force air back into her lungs, which had been emptied by the impact. She struggled to keep her eyes open, but before she passed out, she saw a full-grown cottonmouth had caught the baby copperhead and was eating it. The sunlight glinted off the cottonmouth's eyes, which fixed on Rosalee as she succumbed to darkness.

Chapter 17

When she opened her eyes again, the sun had shifted in the sky, and the light no longer played on the water like it had at midday. She pushed herself up and looked around for Bonnie, hoping against hope the horse had returned. She had not, but Rosalee took some small comfort in finding that the cottonmouth had also left, likely looking for a sunny place to rest and digest its meal.

With a sigh, she stood up and looked in her cotton sack. The cornbread was mostly destroyed, only a few pieces large enough to grab between her forefinger and thumb. She ate those and pulled out the apple, which was also damaged from the fall. She ate what was left of it and dumped the crumbs out of her bag, thinking what an interesting treat they would make for the creek's insects.

Rosalee looked to the birthroot flowers. Mary Ann had called them by their common name, *trillium*. The sunlight could hardly reach them now, and she decided to dig a few before setting out on foot to find Bonnie. The air was still cooler where the flowers unfolded like a thick tapestry reaching deep into the forest. Rosalee rubbed her arms, which were covered in goosebumps, unaccustomed to such a cold temperature in the midst of summer.

She found a good stick and began digging around a flower, watching for the roots of the nearby plants, which grew clustered together. As Bessie had taught her, she only took a couple from each spot and was careful to push the soil back into place after removing them. She brushed the damp soil from the roots as best she could and tucked the plants into her cotton sack as she wandered farther away from the stream to dig again.

Rosalee hummed one of the songs Bessie had taught her for healing, surprised to realize she hadn't sung anything but lullabies for a while now—she hadn't sung her favorite songs since before she married Samuel. She whispered the words at first, but then let her voice loose to sing: *Bring the light to me, where it shall e'er be. A song is sung, a bell is rung, the body is set free.*

The lyrics echoed off the hills in an ethereal voice that Rosalee thought sounded more like her mother's than her own. A twig snapped, shaking her from her reverie. She looked up from the root she had grasped and saw the same girl as before, standing next to an enormous tree. Rosalee startled and looked into the girl's piercing blue eyes, which reminded her so much of her dead grandfather's that she crossed her arms as if she could protect herself. Rosalee realized then how naked she had felt when he stared at her, though she didn't understand that feeling or what it meant when she was a child. Flustered, she asked the girl, "What are you doin' here? This ain't your land, don't you know?" The girl stood still for a moment and then turned around and began to walk away.

Rosalee scrambled to her feet and put the birthroot in her bag. She fixed herself and called out to the girl's back, "Wait! Come back, little girl. I didn't mean anything by it. You startled me, is all."

The girl stopped walking and turned around to look at Rosalee, but still didn't speak.

"You didn't see a horse go by a little bit ago, did you?" she asked. The girl shook her head.

"Alright." Rosalee paused before she went on. "I'm Rosalee. Rosalee McKenzie." She thought for a moment about her last name changing upon marriage, but decided it didn't bear a mention. "My daddy owns this land. I seen you before, over by the—" She started to mention the spring, but decided she didn't want to share her secret with this stranger. "By the willow tree in the woods. You were over there, too, weren't you?" The girl nodded, not breaking her gaze.

Rosalee drew in a deep breath and let it out. "Well. You can't be doin' much harm now, can you? What are you doing out here? Picking mushrooms?" The little girl nodded again. "It's alright to talk. Where do you come from? What's your name?"

The girl paused before speaking, and Rosalee felt each second in the forest surrounded by red flowers turn into an hour, and she knew the day would be gone before she could leave.

"I come from yonder, over the ridge. Mama sends me out to pick in the forest. I'm Anna."

Rosalee smiled. "What a pretty name."

The little girl didn't respond and Rosalee began to repeat herself, but thought better of it. "Well, you best be careful out in the woods alone. Watch for snakes. And don't stay out long. It'll get dark quicker'n you know." The girl just looked at Rosalee, who started to wonder if the child was simple.

"You've got pretty eyes," Rosalee told her. Anna gave the faintest hint of a smile then. "Yes, ma'am," she responded with a nod.

The sound of Samuel's voice came booming from the field beyond the forest: "Rosalee! Where you at, Rosalee?"

She whirled around, though he was still too far away to see her, and realized she should answer him. But before she left, she decided to tell the little girl—*Anna*—not to be picking too many flowers, and certainly none too close together. Rosalee turned back to give the girl a quick talk, but she was gone.

"Rosalee! Where are you, Rosie?" Samuel called again, with impatience in his voice.

Rosalee turned back toward the field and made her way downstream.

"I'm here!" she yelled out as she left the cool forest and entered the hot light of June. Samuel had ridden past the stream, toward their house, and led Bonnie beside him. They turned around and galloped back to Rosalee.

Rosalee smiled as he drew closer, relieved she wouldn't have to walk back home and Bonnie wasn't lost. She was glad to see Samuel, too, and not to have to search for him after all. She shielded her eyes from the sun's glare as Samuel drew closer and found he wasn't smiling at all.

"What the hell are you thinking, woman!" He nearly threw Bonnie's reins at Rosalee. "I been out here searching for you, my horse wandering around, and you left the baby? What do you think you're doing?"

It was then Rosalee noticed his face—one eye was black, and his lip was split and swollen. "What happened to you?" she asked, ignoring his questions. "Where were you?"

For a second, Samuel looked embarrassed, but that look was quickly replaced with defiance.

"I told you, I went to your daddy's house. That's where I've been."

"But who—who did this to you?" she stammered.

Samuel tried to grin and instead grimaced as his cut lip stretched too far. Wiping a little blood onto his hand and then onto his pants, he looked at Rosalee and gave a laugh. "Your dear old daddy, Rosalee. But I got him back, don't worry." He saw the alarm on Rosalee's face and added, "It's what men do, Rosie. We argue and then we come to terms. Sometimes we gotta work it out with our fists. It's our nature. Now get on this horse and let's go. I'm ready to eat something."

Rosalee climbed onto Bonnie. Sitting close to Samuel, both of them on their horses, she could smell the whiskey from his pores. Samuel looked at her and grinned, this time not trying to protect his lip. "You know me, Rosie. I'm always hungry."

He flicked the reins and sent his horse homeward. Rosalee hesitated, thinking about the snake and the little girl, and how she hadn't told Samuel what kept her in the forest for so long. She prodded Bonnie with her heels as they began moving forward, wondering how the sun was still high overhead.

Chapter 18

B ack at the house, Samuel wouldn't say much about what had happened between him and John. "He can throw a good punch," Samuel said with a laugh, but Rosalee noticed a coldness in his eyes that she had seen a few times now. "Don't you worry, Rosie," he told her, though her feelings did not concern him. "I can take a lick as well as I can give one. Me and Joseph learned that young, same as my boys will." He looked pleased with himself at that last thought.

Irene handed the baby to Rosalee with a look bordering on disapproval. "You can't be off gettin' yourself hurt now. How'd you lose the horse?" Rosalee thought for a moment and decided when they were alone, she would tell Irene all about the little girl with blue eyes and they could speculate on where the woman from the letters might have gone.

"Rosie! Get me a drink and start on supper. Get some ham from the smokehouse. That'll bring back my strength," Samuel said. Rosalee put Jabez in his cradle in the bedroom and brought Samuel a jelly jar of whiskey before making his supper, just like he said to.

After he had eaten and poured himself another drink, Samuel started talking about the next trip to Chicago. "We've got them wrapped around our little fingers, I'm telling you. This Prohibition is the best thing that ever happened to us Kentucky boys!" Rosalee tried to smile. An ocean lay between the law that men declared in cities and the lives of her people in the country, and it was impossible to know when those waves would find their way into the Kentucky hillsides.

"Think you'll be gone long?" she asked him, unsure of the answer she wanted to hear.

"Couple weeks, probably. Just long enough for you to start missing me."

She glanced at him before turning back to the stove. "You know I always miss you," she said, and Samuel looked to her sharply but decided he was satisfied with her words.

"By this time next year," he told her, "we'll be rolling in cash like you've never seen."

It wouldn't be hard to come up with more cash than she had ever seen. Rosalee had held a penny or two at once for candy at the store, and she had seen her father give money to the clerk for their monthly goods, but she didn't know how much it was. Most of the farm business took place between the men, away from the conversations of women and children. She had seen a wad of bills sticking out of Samuel's pocket once when he fell asleep on the bed early one night, his pants tossed onto the floor, but she didn't dare touch it or ask what he was doing with it.

He poured another drink, and Rosalee wondered if he would be more cheerful or easier to anger afterward. The moon was full, and soon after sunset, it lit the farm almost like daylight. "I'm going on a walk," he told her with a ragged smile, and she noticed his lip had split open once again, the blood reflecting lamplight like a crescent moon. Rosalee hesitated, but then picked up Jabez and followed Samuel outside. "Do you want me to wait for you?"

Samuel studied her face and turned toward the woods beyond the barns. "No," he said as he walked away. Rosalee watched him disappear into the shadows, beyond the reach of the moonlight. Irene came out to the porch, two jelly jars in hand. The women sat in the rockers, and Rosalee accepted the jar Irene handed her, Jabez on her lap and leaning against her chest. She set the jar on the boards of the porch and repositioned Jabez to nurse him, rocking gently so she wouldn't upset his stomach. His eyes watched her face at first and then closed and opened as the motion and his mother's touch lulled him to sleep. Rosalee watched him, too, mesmerized by the perfection of his every breath. She let him grasp her finger in one hand as the rocker fell into heartbeat rhythm and they both sank into a timeless spell.

A while after he fell asleep, she took him inside and came back out to sit beside Irene, ready to share her story. Irene pulled a tin out of the pocket of her dress and handed it to Rosalee. She took her pinch and picked up the jelly jar half-full of clear liquid shimmering in the moonlight. *It's like the moon's been poured into my cup,* she thought, and a childlike joy rushed through her.

"Mamaw Irene," she said, "you remember those letters I found, how you told me about Papaw and the girl?" Irene turned toward her, and even in the pale light, Rosalee saw her eyes were flashing with emotion. Was it anger? Or sadness? She cleared her throat and continued, "Well, when I was in the woods today—I mean, when Bonnie ran off—I was at a creek in the middle of the farm and there was this girl, a little girl with blue eyes." She realized her heart was racing, and she stumbled over the words. "I-I saw her before, too, over by Daddy's house and I think she, well, do you think maybe . . ."

Her words trailed off as Irene began to laugh.

"Girl, have you lost your mind? What on earth are you talking about? There ain't no girls walking around in the woods, and they sure ain't got nothing to do with your papaw."

Rosalee stiffened, her mind racing to understand why Irene was laughing. What was so hard to believe about her story? And how was it impossible to think the child could be a descendant of her papaw?

"How can you be so sure?" she asked her grandmother.

Irene's laughter subsided and her expression turned to seriousness again as she looked toward the woods and answered, "It don't matter anyway. It's all in the past, and you best let it go." She turned to look at Rosalee. "That's what women have to do sometimes. It's best you learn quick."

Rosalee sipped her drink and thought of Bessie, who would have never told her to let something go instead of trying to understand it. And she sure wouldn't have let a man get away with the things her grandfather had done. She thought of everything Samuel had said and done to her and wondered what Bessie would say about all of it, if she knew. *She'd have probably shot him by now,* Rosalee thought with a chuckle.

Irene looked at her. "You're right to laugh when you can. They ain't always much to laugh about." She sipped her drink as Rosalee started to explain what she had chuckled about but then decided not to. The two women sat silent as the moon climbed into the sky above them, lighting the whole world so Rosalee almost forgot what the darkness ever looked like.

In the morning, Rosalee woke up earlier than usual and found Samuel asleep beside her. She remembered he had woken her in the middle of the night when he came to bed, and she had let him have her body once again. This time, when he had finished and rolled onto his back, he told her, "It wouldn't kill you to pretend you like it, you know." Filled with dread at what that might mean the next time, she tried to assure him: "I do like it. I will."

She sat up and shook her head, willing the memory to fade like a dream, and a wave of nausea hit her. She ran out of the room as quietly as she could and made it to the porch before vomiting onto the weedy yard. She knelt there, waiting for the nausea to fully subside.

She walked back inside to find Samuel and Irene sitting at the kitchen table with freshly poured cups of coffee. Irene gestured toward a third cup. "That one's yours," she told Rosalee.

Rosalee stood there, pondering the smell of coffee as if it was something she had never before encountered.

"You're awfully pale," Samuel told her. "What happened, did you get into too much of my 'shine last night?"

Before she could answer, Irene spoke for her. "Can't you tell?" Samuel gave her a blank look. "Your wife is pregnant. I can see it in her face."

Rosalee's stomach heaved, and the room began to spin. "Go on, don't throw up in here," Irene told her, and Rosalee ran out the door and vomited in the yard again. She could hear Samuel's voice boom with pride at the table. "I told you all, didn't I? We're gonna have all kinds of babies! There'll be a whole pack of Carter boys running around here before you know it." Rosalee squeezed her eyes shut, trying to push away the sound of his laughter.

She knew Irene was right. Something felt different inside her—not exactly like the pregnancy with Jabez, but different in a similar kind of way. She thought about the times Samuel had been inside her, and she shuddered at the thought that she could have gotten pregnant on the night he hit her. She hadn't started bleeding again on a regular basis, probably because she was still nursing Jabez, so she couldn't be sure how far along she was, but it felt early. She opened her eyes and the world stopped spinning long enough for her to get to her feet once more.

She walked back inside, finding Samuel still at the kitchen table and Irene holding Jabez. Irene looked at her with a mix of pity and some other feeling Rosalee couldn't quite pin down. "You'll have your hands full with two little ones soon," her grandmother told her. "Best you enjoy these quiet days while you still can." Her head still swimming from nausea, she avoided Samuel's eyes, knowing she would see a look of pride there that she could hardly stand right now. She took Jabez from Irene and sat down to nurse him.

"I'm heading to town today," Samuel announced. "I'll get supplies to last you while I'm gone up north. Don't worry. I'll make sure you've got everything you need. And I'm sending Michael over to check on you. I'll be gone a couple weeks and don't want you women here alone the whole time."

She wasn't sure whether to be sad or angry he was leaving just when they found out she was pregnant again, so she said nothing. Something about Irene's company was starting to wear on Rosalee. She knew she should be grateful for the older woman's help, and she was, but it was hard to feel like a true adult with Irene around all the time, and it was even harder to feel like she was in her own home, and not a visitor in Irene's. At that thought, Rosalee realized she would probably never again be comforted like she had been as a child, and a sense of loss tore through her like she hadn't felt since Bessie died.

Samuel walked over to Rosalee and put his hands on her shoulders. "You'll be okay, little wife. I'll take good care of you, like I said. You just take care of my babies." He kissed her on the forehead, touched the baby's cheek, and got ready to leave. "I'll be back in a while." Rosalee nodded, hiding her doubt.

He came back in the evening with the usual supplies: coffee, sugar, flour, salt, a ream of cotton, and some shotgun shells. There were a few newspapers for Rosalee to read, but he also brought a box of food in metal cans that Rosalee had only seen in newspaper advertisements. There were cans of beef, tomatoes, and peaches, as well as other foods Rosalee had never tasted, like tuna, which was nothing like the bluegill and bass she had grown up eating. Samuel grinned when he saw the shock on her face.

He reached into his pocket and pulled out a stack of cash held together with some kind of clip. Samuel told her it was called a "money clip" and talked about some of the food he had brought as if he was a teacher patiently educating a young child. Rosalee bristled as he began talking but realized she didn't know the things he was explaining and decided to let go of her indignation. "Now don't get me wrong, Rosie, you're a good cook. But this is what the rest of the world is eating. It's modern times and we don't have to kill or grow everything we eat these days. You should keep up the garden, and we'll keep raisin' animals as long as I see fit, but I told you I'm making a better life for us and I meant it."

She could tell he was waiting for a response, so she forced a smile and told him, "Can't wait to try them all, thank you."

He took most of the cash out of the clip and showed it to her, a mix of twenties, fifties, and hundred-dollar bills. "I'm putting this under the loose floorboard in our bedroom. You don't need it, but I want you to know where it is in case I ever need you to get it for me. Don't go tellin' anybody about it, now. We don't want nobody snooping where they shouldn't be."

Rosalee smiled a genuine smile. "Who am I gonna tell? The baby don't care much for money yet, and Mamaw Irene ain't goin' anywhere."

A shadow flitted across Samuel's face and settled into his eyes.

"Nobody, Rosalee. Not now or ever." Taken aback by his seriousness, Rosalee heard the words he wasn't saying: *don't tell your father.*

She nodded in agreement, and Samuel grabbed an empty coffee can and took it to the bedroom, along with the money. Rosalee heard him pry the loose board in their bedroom and then bang the nail back down with a hammer. When he came back into the kitchen, his familiar smirk had returned.

"Just you wait, Rosie. You won't know what's happened when you see all the money I'm gonna make." He looked at her from the corners of his eyes. "All because I know how to make the best corn liquor anybody's ever tasted."

Chapter 19

After a few weeks in Chicago, Samuel came home. When John dropped him off at the house, he put more money in the coffee can under the floorboard and brought more presents for Rosalee and Jabez. There were two new dolls, both wearing the latest fashions, according to Samuel. The layers of tissue paper and overdressed babies struck Rosalee as wasteful now. Some of the barns and outbuildings would need to be repaired soon, and they'd have to pay someone else to do it if Samuel wasn't going to be around or interested enough to fix them himself. She said the words he wanted to hear, but Rosalee wondered when he would realize she was too old for dolls, and her needs were far beyond the imaginary world they occupied.

He also gave Rosalee another dress, all silk and lace this time—again, she thought, something she would never wear at the farm and might never get to wear at all. But it was beautiful. Morning sickness had pulled her into a chasm where she felt at war with her own body, and the summer heat had stretched her days into a cycle marked by sweat, milk, wet diapers, and baby spit-up. To imagine herself in something fine, something clean, was a welcome and brief respite.

After all the other gifts were opened, Samuel brought Rosalee a large, heavy box wrapped in yellow-and-white-striped paper, tied with a white ribbon. She pulled on the ribbon and let it fall across her lap, then lifted the lid off the box. Inside was a silver tea service gleaming with newness. Rosalee gasped and looked to Samuel, who smiled at her.

"It's just like some of them fancy restaurants have up in Chicago. And look—I brought you this." He handed her a Sears and Roebuck catalog. As a child, Rosalee had heard kids in town talk about circling their Christmas wish list in the catalog, but she had never seen one herself. This one was the newest edition and featured housewares and women's clothing on the glossy front cover, which was itself tantalizing.

A rush of giddy excitement filled Rosalee as she looked through the pages of jewelry, clothing, and furniture. On a page featuring women's hats, she startled at the drawing of a woman who looked just like her mother, with an elegance Mary Ann had achieved in her homemade dresses and simple braids. Shame washed over Rosalee as she realized neither her mother nor Bessie ever cared for frilly dresses and other things they didn't need. Memories of braiding herbs and gathering plants for food and medicine flooded into her mind, and she saw the faces of the women who had taught her how to survive. It all seemed so far away now, an impossible dream of a life surrounded by women who would protect her, love her, and guide her through a world that was just as nurturing as they were.

"Don't get your heart set on everything in it just because you've got it. Go through it and I'll get you something nice from the city when I can."

Rosalee looked at Samuel, who was smiling to himself, looking at the pages of the catalog as she turned them. She wondered what it was he liked so much about what he saw in those pages, which led her to wonder what he saw when he went to the city. He had returned home wearing new clothes himself, clothes clearly not meant to get dirty on a farm. He walked around the house with a kind of swagger Irene had noted with raised eyebrows, before looking back to her sewing. He had also taken to wearing a pistol on his hip, and Rosalee wanted to ask what it was for, but the combination of Samuel's quiet brooding and irritating confidence made it seem like he was always putting on a show—for who, she wasn't sure, but she was pretty certain it wasn't for her.

At supper that night, Samuel told Rosalee he was setting up a new still behind their house. "This way, I can make twice as much whiskey as I'm doin' on my own, and I'll make the recipe even better. There's plenty of corn for it." His eyes flashed for a second and he explained, "Your daddy doesn't want to change things up, but I'm gonna show him I know what I'm talking about. He ain't the only man around here that's been making whiskey all his life. I learned it from my papaw, and he was the best moonshiner around."

Rosalee nodded in agreement, but a sense of dread took hold as she again heard the words he wasn't saying. She imagined the conversations her father and husband must be having at the still and in the shack where they bottled their spirits. John's unyielding commitment to what he knew and Samuel's unchallenged self-assurance could not always work well together. She thought about Joseph, his little brother who seemed so much like him, and wondered whether the brothers argued with her father. Her own brother Michael was not quite like John, but his steady temperament had always complemented John's steadfast command of the farm. The Carter boys, she realized, were now men with their own ideas, and her father had brought Barbara and them into their lives without knowing what his choice would mean, how it would alter their paths.

As the summer months wore on, Samuel spent more and more time in the woods somewhere behind the house, where he set up his stills. The sheriff had never been to their house, and as far as Rosalee knew, no kind of law had ever been to the farm at all. She was glad, though, that Samuel had the sense to set up his operation away from their home, hidden from plain sight. For years now, there was at least one story about an illegal liquor operation in every newspaper Rosalee got to read, some of them ending in arrests, others in bloodshed.

One morning, Samuel rode to John's and returned with Joseph and Michael on horseback alongside him. Michael hopped off his horse and Rosalee threw her arms around her little brother. She eyed Joseph, who had somehow grown wilder than Samuel, and he exuded a palpable arrogance. He wore a pistol on his hip, too, and Rosalee amused herself thinking the Carter brothers were expecting a shoot-out at any minute. She caught him looking at her more than once, eyeing her breasts. Samuel noticed his brother staring and hit him on the arm. "Knock it off, little brother. I'd hate to have to whip your ass in front of my wife."

Joseph smirked, and when Samuel looked away, he winked at Rosalee. "Didn't mean no harm, you know. There ain't a lot of ladies around the farm." Rosalee's cheeks flushed, and she went to tend Jabez without responding.

Michael took her aside after supper. "Tell me how you're doing, sister." Rosalee was surprised by the concern in his voice.

"I'm fine, I reckon." She rubbed her swollen belly and gave a wry laugh. "Didn't expect to be pregnant all my life after I left Daddy's house. Why, you worried about me?" she asked with a smile.

Michael didn't smile back. "I don't much like this liquor business, but Daddy don't ask my opinion." He motioned in the direction of the still, where Samuel and Joseph had gone to work. "They argue with him all the time now. And I don't know what they're gettin' into up north, but it ain't small-time no more. I think they're gettin' mixed up with some serious business. To hear them talk of it"—Michael looked toward the door—"up north they've got guns and money like you wouldn't believe, and they like to fight. It ain't like around here."

Rosalee took one of his hands in both of hers. "You just stay away from it, you hear me," she told him in a maternal voice. "Stay on the farm where you belong, and don't get involved any more'n you have to."

Michael looked away, worry evident in his face. "Daddy's looking older. He's tired and none of them are doing much with the farm now, other than growing field corn. I'm doing what I can, and Barbara helps some, but their minds"—he nodded toward the still—"their minds are somewhere else. They think they're gonna be famous like those gangsters they're selling to."

Rosalee's mind caught on that word—*gangsters*—and she tried to imagine what it must mean. Michael saw she was puzzling over it and explained, "There's some powerful families up there, and they like to fight each other. Always trying to take control of the liquor business and . . ." His voice trailed off and he cleared his throat. "And other business."

"Well, it's a shame, I know, but people around here quarrel, too," Rosalee mused. "People lose their minds over a cow or little bit of land, and some of them go on fightin' each other's families 'til nobody remembers what they're fightin' over."

Michael looked at her with a tender smile. "You're right, Rosalee. But it's different, I think. From what Daddy says, and listening to them all talk about what they do in Chicago, there's just something different. Maybe it's all them cars and lights everywhere. I think it makes 'em wild, but not the good kind."

Rosalee smiled back. "As long as they keep the city up there where it belongs, it don't matter much down here." She thought of the creek and Anna among the birthroot. "Sounds like they've all gone crazy."

Later that evening, they all ate supper together and afterward, Irene went to bed. The young men went back into the woods for a while longer, along with Michael, leaving Rosalee with her thoughts and her baby. They returned after sunset, the two brothers bickering while Michael avoided looking at anyone. Samuel burst into the house, arguing with Joseph about corn mash and how much sugar should be in it.

The sound woke Jabez, who had fallen asleep reluctantly in Rosalee's arms by the fireplace. She had sighed with relief when his eyelids flickered from the dreams he was having, and she groaned when he opened his eyes and cried, flailing his arms. Samuel and Joseph pushed the kitchen chairs back from the table and dropped into them with a clatter. Michael cast a concerned look toward Rosalee, who glowered at the men as she put Jabez to her breast, hoping to nurse him back to sleep.

"Hey," Michael said to whoever might listen, "the baby's tryin' to sleep."

Both Samuel and Joseph looked at him with surprise and then laughed.

"Don't you worry about that, little man. I'm takin' care of my family, and Rosie knows what she has to do around here. Sit down and have yourself a drink."

Joseph laughed and poured three generous shots of whiskey. Michael sat down, careful to lift his chair a bit so the legs wouldn't scrape the wooden floor.

"Come on, Michael. We'll show you how the Carter men like to do things."

From her chair, Rosalee could see the hint of a threat in Samuel's eyes.

"In our family, the men make the decisions and the women know what's best for them, don't they, Rosie?"

Samuel and Joseph looked at Rosalee, but Michael turned away, embarrassed for her. Rosalee considered her response for a moment and replied, "You know what's best."

Samuel and Joseph looked at each other. "You've got her trained," Joseph told him. "That's what you have to do, and I heard those McKenzie women were hard ones to teach."

Samuel smiled and nodded. "Yeah, they're stubborn ones alright. But she's learning and starting to be a real good wife." He looked at Rosalee. "I think I'll keep her."

Rosalee knew he expected a smile, and she did her best to give him one, though she wasn't sure her face could comply with such a demand. She seethed with anger at what he was saying and wanted to tell him how little she thought of him then. But she remembered the back of his hand against her lip, and how he had pressed her against their mattress with so little care. She didn't want Jabez around such a thing again, even if he couldn't understand it when he was so little, and she had to think of the one inside her, too. She wasn't sure, but she had her doubts that Samuel would spare her a punishment, even while pregnant.

She looked down at Jabez's face, the spitting image of his father. Would he think like his father, too? Would he learn to hit, and would he hit only as a way to protect his family, or to control them? She thought about the baby inside her, if it would be a boy, and she wondered whether she could survive what was yet to come.

She took a drink of blackberry moonshine and rocked Jabez with little affection.

The days turned into months, and time seemed to stand still and disappear, all at once. Christmas was a fractured dream, and the arrival of a new year did little to brighten the dark winter. Rosalee sometimes quilted with Irene, and they made several new patchwork quilts from Samuel's old clothes. The women sewed a few gowns for the new baby and made some shirts for Jabez, but Samuel brought knickers, long socks, and even a little hat from the city, telling Rosalee his sons would have good clothes like everyone else and would not look like ragged bumpkins all their lives. Rosalee didn't understand why it mattered to Samuel what Jabez wore—there was no one there to see him—but one night, she noticed he had filled the coffee can under the floor and started hiding money in another can next to it. She had nowhere to spend money, but something about knowing it was there comforted her.

Jabez began walking early, at ten months old. He was into everything, and Irene constantly rebuked Rosalee for not spanking him more often. "That boy's gotta learn," Irene would tell her, and Rosalee would pull him away from the cabinet or whatever he had opened and put everything back in its place. Irene thought Rosalee was sparing the child because she wanted to spoil him, but Rosalee secretly worried that if she spanked him at all, she would open some floodgate holding back all of her anger, and she wouldn't be able to control it any longer. And so, she pulled her apathy tight around her, ignoring any chance to correct or teach Jabez.

For his part, Samuel laughed each time he saw his son pulling food out of a cupboard or knocking a jar to the floor. "He's got Carter blood for sure—you can't control a Carter boy!" He would beam with pride and then tell Rosalee, "You've got your hands full, Rosie. Good thing you've got the patience of a saint." She would smile back at him each time, knowing he didn't understand the true nature of her patience.

Jabez had a couple of toys, blocks with the alphabet on them and a wooden train set Samuel had ordered for the past Christmas. Samuel promised he would bring something else soon, as an early birthday gift. Rosalee started bringing the dolls out for Jabez to play with when his father wasn't home. Samuel wouldn't like it, but Rosalee thought it made sense to use them, and not just look at them all the time.

Sitting in the chair and creating characters for Jabez, Rosalee invented voices for each doll and told stories about their lives and adventures, ideas she stitched together from the Sears and Roebuck catalog, the Bible, and her trips to town when she was younger. Irene sat and watched, too, and soon, the three of them shared story time after supper, just before Jabez went to sleep for the night. Afterward, Rosalee and Irene would sit by the fireplace with a bit of sewing and a drink, taking pinches of snuff when it suited them.

Before long, Rosalee and Irene were both sure the new baby would be a boy—she carried it high and the morning sickness wore off, leaving her only with a dread she often mistook for nausea. She tied Jabez to her back so she could do her farm chores, but he grew into a restless child who squirmed when Rosalee wrapped him onto her back. If

Rosalee bent over to pull weeds or tie up a tomato plant, he lunged in the opposite direction, threatening to knock her off balance. He never fell asleep but fussed and whined in her ear, pulling on her hair, and sometimes Rosalee thought about untying the cloth that held him to her and letting him fall to the ground.

She lived as if in a dream, watching herself do the things she somehow knew she was supposed to do. At night, she let Samuel please himself with her body and didn't try to stop him even as her pregnant belly grew bigger. In the mornings, she rose out of bed and picked up Jabez, who looked more and more like his father each day. In rare moments, Rosalee looked into Jabez's eyes and saw his innocence, the part of his self that had nothing to do with Samuel, and her dark dream was penetrated by a needle prick of guilt. In those moments, she saw how she punished the child for his father's transgressions. Her own needs then threatened to overwhelm her, to force tears from her eyes and onto the baby whose eyes searched hers and onto her swollen belly containing a mystery, an untold story, but Rosalee could find no hope for how her own story might end. Only then did she understand everything she had lost when they buried Mary Ann and Bessie close to the spring, and her mind searched through memories and feelings, trying to make sense of her life unfolding as it had.

But it did not make sense, and there was no story she could tell herself about why she had lost the women who loved her and now lived to serve a man with shadows in his eyes and the babies he would force upon her. Jabez cried or the animals called or the laundry beckoned her to the washboard, and she pushed her thoughts aside.

Chapter 20

Irene's age began to slow her down, and she no longer wanted to walk around in the cold. "My bones is hurtin'," she would tell Rosalee, and she simmered cinnamon sticks and black peppercorns on the stove to add to her evening whiskey.

Rosalee felt the first contraction in March, a month before Jabez's first birthday, while sitting in the same chair her water had broken onto, next to the fireplace with Irene. Rosalee pressed her hand to her stomach and told her grandmother, "I think the baby's coming soon."

In the firelight, the lines on Irene's face were drawn so deeply, her features cast shadows that made Rosalee catch her breath. "Best he come on," Irene told her. "If you're wantin' my help to get him out, it better happen soon. And get off that chair this time."

Rosalee understood but wasn't sure how to feel about what Irene meant. Her grandmother had withdrawn into herself, nearly crippled now by the pain in her bones. Rosalee had thought it would get better when the weather turned warm again. Now she began to understand the change was permanent, but her grandmother's ability to withstand it was temporary. Irene had grown thinner, too, and her gray hair had lost its luster and now hung like dried corn silk from her head. She looked like the old women Rosalee had sometimes seen in town and at revivals, an image both severe and impressive. She had often thought there was no way her mother could have looked so old, and she wondered if she could ever look like an old woman herself. Samuel had gone to Owingsville with his brother that morning but said he would be back in a day or two. Michael was coming to check on them just about every day now, even when Samuel was home, riding his pony back to the farm to let Barbara know if she was needed. Rosalee felt her belly tighten once again and wished someone else was there with her and Irene. She wasn't sure her grandmother was in good enough shape to help her if there was any trouble during labor, and though her hands were steady, Irene's strength was failing. She might not be able to tend Rosalee, care for Jabez, and help with the newborn baby once it came.

Contractions tightened Rosalee's belly once every couple of hours or so, and she knew there was a while yet to go. She decided to make a prayer doll that night—something she hadn't done since marrying Samuel. She wrapped a scrap of fabric around willow twigs, humming a song as the light from the fireplace danced on her face. Irene stopped sewing for a moment to watch Rosalee and then spoke. "You gotta be careful doing that kind of thing, you know."

Rosalee hummed the rest of the line of her song and asked Irene, "What do you mean?"

"I mean that husband of yours. He wouldn't understand. Your daddy don't neither. It's something for women, and you best keep it to yourself." Irene looked back to the patchwork quilt she was making for the new baby. "I learned that the hard way, and I'm trying to save you some trouble."

Rosalee looked into the fire and let Irene's words work through her mind. "He doesn't understand much of anything," she said with an edge to her voice.

Irene kept sewing. "Might be, but I'm telling you, some things a man don't understand make him feel helpless, and that makes some men mad. This is one of those things." She looked into Rosalee's eyes. "I know a lot makes your man mad. But he won't like your prayer dolls, just like he wouldn't like your boy playing with dolls."

Rosalee sighed. "You're right." She thought about asking Irene right then and there how it was fair that she was married to this man and expected to obey him, and how he had become someone she feared. The little girl with blue eyes darted through her mind, though, and Rosalee wondered how she could ask about her once again. She took a sip of whiskey and cleared her throat.

"You're right, Mamaw. And I thank you for saying it. I've had a lot to learn, and I've got more to learn if I'm gonna make it as a mother and wife."

Irene nodded toward her sewing.

"Mamaw, can I ask you something?"

Irene nodded again, in assent.

"The girl that brought her baby to your house—the one you said Papaw was with." Rosalee saw Irene stiffen, her hands clutching the baby's quilt. "Does Daddy know?"

"Of course he doesn't," Irene shot at her. "Why would anyone tell a child about such a thing?" She tried to resume her sewing, but Rosalee could see her hands were shaking and she could hardly sew a stitch.

"That baby would be his sister . . ." Rosalee's voice trailed off as she realized what she was saying. How many people had her grandfather hurt? How many women, and how many children? Her stomach turned as she considered her grandfather's cruel legacy and the families who were broken for it.

Irene's eyes went cold. "It doesn't matter anymore." Rosalee noticed her grandmother's skin had turned translucent, and the blood crept through her veins now. She sat quiet for a moment and then asked, "Should we have Michael tell Daddy to come here, so you can see him?" *One last time,* she thought to herself.

Irene pushed the needle through the quilt and tied off the thread. "It's finished now. And as for your daddy, we'll see whether there's time after the baby comes."

Chapter 21

The newborn boy arrived two days later, after hours of hard labor that ended early in the afternoon. Samuel had returned before the labor began, and he spent the time checking on the animals and his still as Rosalee and Jabez both wailed inside the house, each for reasons of their own. Irene put Jabez down only to help the laboring mother move into different positions as she tried to find comfort, which redefined her understanding of futility.

Rosalee had made and burned two prayer dolls—one at the beginning of her labor and the other as it intensified. Her first prayer was for a safe birth, and she threw the prayer doll into the embers still smoldering in the fireplace before anyone else awoke, as the sun lit the morning horizon. Several hours later, with Samuel safely out of the house, she knelt at the fireplace and prayed for a gentle son—something she wished she had known to pray for the first time.

As the baby worked his way closer to the world and Rosalee's mind and body edged closer to death, she noticed Irene watching her. Irene's face was lost in a flight of shadows, and Rosalee could no longer see her expression but only the sorrow and anger that had shaped her, sustained her, and were now leaving her a broken woman.

After it was over, Irene handed her the newborn in a warm quilt, cleaned Rosalee as best she could, put Jabez in the bed next to Rosalee, and went to her own bed.

Samuel came in to look at his new son, holding him up as if examining a piglet for sale. "He looks pretty good, Rosie. He looks like me. That's good." He looked at her and without humor told her, "I'd hate to find out you'd stepped out on me."

Rosalee was too exhausted to be angry or alarmed by his comment. She fell asleep with the newborn nursing at her breast and Jabez napping alongside them, the eldest frustrated he could no longer nurse as well. Rosalee dreamt and saw somber forest gardens where she and Bessie sat, weaving willow baskets. The wind lifted Mary Ann's laughter toward them and she was there, a buttercup behind her ear, smiling at Rosalee.

When Rosalee awoke, both children were crying and she had bled through the cotton cloth she wrapped around herself after the baby was born. She called for Irene, but there was no answer. She lay in bed for a while longer, willing the blood to clean itself, wishing she was not covered in sweat from the hours of her newborn's skin being pressed against her. Jabez was sitting up, playing with a loose string he had pulled from the quilt, making it dance in the sunbeams that floated through the air, lazy and careless, as if three lives did not rest on the bed, all of them vulnerable.

Finally, Samuel came back inside the house and ladled some soup beans Irene had left on the stove at dinner. Rosalee listened to him moving around the kitchen, scraping chair legs on the floor as he pulled it out, dropping his full weight onto the chair, clinking the spoon and bowl and water glass. He pushed away from the table, leaving his dishes where they sat. He came into the bedroom and Rosalee asked, "Can you check on Mamaw? She's been too quiet."

Samuel glanced at the children and walked out of the bedroom. Rosalee forced herself onto her feet. She put the new baby in the cradle and patted Jabez, who had been lulled into a light sleep full of dreams. She wondered how she would clean her birthing clothes and tend to the babies if Irene couldn't help her, and she somehow knew she would have to learn soon.

"Rosie!" Samuel called. "You need to come here."

She knew he didn't understand what he was asking of her, but in that instant, Rosalee also knew Irene was dead. By the time she made her way to Irene's bed, careful not to tear her own body back open, Samuel had closed Irene's eyes and folded her hands upon her chest. Rosalee looked for some sign from the woman's face, their conversations flooding her mind along with a wave of shame over how she had grown tired of listening to the old woman's stories. There was only silence. A few days later, when Rosalee had the strength to walk around, she opened the drawer to her grandmother's desk and the scent of rose flew up, carrying Irene's bitter farewell. She searched for the letters, but they were gone.

John brought Barbara and Michael to meet the baby and bury his mother, taking a horse-drawn wagon along the road. They brought supper and ate with Rosalee, and Joseph and Samuel arrived a couple of hours later on horses they rode from John's. The young men dug a grave next to John's father and buried Irene, both of them resting not far from a sycamore tree. John said he would get a headstone made for her in town, but for the time being, he brought an old millstone to mark where it should go. Rosalee watched her father as he lingered at his mother's grave, and when he turned to walk into the house, she saw him wipe a tear from the corner of his eye, though she couldn't know whether he was mourning for his mother or for the loss of the last person who had known him as a child.

For a couple of hours afterward, they did what they had all grown accustomed to: the men went outside and drank, Samuel and Joseph taking the opportunity to drink too much and raise their voices as they debated one thing or another. Barbara held the baby and Michael played with Jabez when he wasn't bringing Rosalee a drink of water or kissing the baby's head. Rosalee tried to find ways to be comfortable, lost in a haze of pain that persisted long after their visitors left. That pain etched itself into the letter she wrote her brothers about Irene's death and the baby's birth, and the women who read it aloud for them felt her pain and wrote back to Rosalee with tidings of sorrow and joy.

Rosalee suggested they name the baby Ezra, which she remembered was a book in the Bible. Samuel nodded without responding, and she decided the baby's middle name would be John, after her father. A few days after Ezra's birth, Samuel found her in bed long after the sun had risen, lying with her eyes open as both boys napped beside her. She had awoken early in the morning and tended the babies, but the same weight that had descended upon her after Jabez's birth had returned. She wanted to ask herself whether it was grief for Irene or a function of childbirth, but the thoughts in her mind had become like gnats in molasses again, and there was no piecing her words together to form a question.

"Rosalee."

She turned to see Samuel standing in the doorway of their bedroom, and some corner of her mind registered surprise that he didn't call her Rosie this time.

"I'm going to get my mother to look after you for a few days. I've got work to do and can't tend to all this." He gestured toward her and the children on the bed. "I'll be back in a few hours."

Rosalee just nodded, though she wished she could tell him not to bring Barbara. She couldn't imagine the woman would be warm or a good caretaker, and she knew Barbara would judge her for any weakness. But weak she was, and there was no way to refuse the help.

They arrived in the afternoon to find Rosalee still in bed, Jabez pulling at her hair and exploring his little brother's hands and feet with curiosity. Barbara went to work, changing Jabez's diaper and setting him in a corner of the room with a sugar rag to chew on. She changed Ezra's diaper, swaddled him, and placed him in the cradle. She turned to Rosalee.

"Girl, you look pitiful."

Rosalee didn't know whether she meant it as a kindness or an insult and didn't have the energy to determine which it was. Her clothes and bedsheets were dirty, her hair tangled, and she smelled of sour milk.

Barbara went to the kitchen and came back with a kettle of hot water, which she poured into a washbowl on the vanity. "It's gonna get harder before it gets any easier," Barbara said as she pulled Rosalee's clothes off her. She dipped a rag into the hot water and cleaned Rosalee's breasts first, and then her thighs. Rosalee could sense something like embarrassment within herself, but she succumbed to Barbara's care. Barbara dressed her in clean clothes and sat her in front of the mirror, brushing her hair and untangling the knots more gently than Rosalee expected her to.

Barbara glanced at Rosalee, reflected in the mirror. "This happens to some girls after giving birth. My mama was like this, and I had to take care of her when she had my littlest brothers and sisters." She brushed Rosalee's hair in long, smooth strokes now. "I'll stay 'til you're back on your feet. But you're gonna have to learn to take care of all three of you now, whether you feel like it or not. I'll make you a tonic that'll help."

Rosalee met her eyes in the mirror, surprised Barbara was speaking of tonics. Her mother-in-law gave a little laugh. "You McKenzies ain't the only women in the world who know how to make a good tea, you know." She braided Rosalee's hair into a single plait that hung down her back. "Keep your hair in a braid or bun while you're wrangling these two little ones," Barbara told her. "It will make your life easier and give them less to pull on."

She left Rosalee sitting on the chair in front of the mirror for a few minutes while she stripped the bed and brought clean sheets in.

Barbara had placed a makeshift cushion on the hard chair, forming a circle from rolled cloth so Rosalee could sit without putting pressure where it would hurt the most. "I'll wash these, but you can't let 'em get so bad, hear me? You ain't never gonna feel better by laying around in your own mess." Rosalee nodded and tears sprang to her eyes. She felt like a child herself, though she had turned seventeen before Ezra was born. Rosalee was struck by a longing for her mother to hold her, sing to her, and smile at her as only Mary Ann had done.

Barbara picked up Ezra after finishing the bed and held him close. She smiled and her face softened into an expression Rosalee hadn't seen on Barbara's face before. For a moment, Rosalee thought Barbara would turn that same warmth toward her as well. But after gazing at Ezra, Barbara kissed his forehead and her expression returned to normal, lacking any emotion except perhaps a firm determination. She laid Ezra back in the cradle, picked up Jabez, and turned toward the door. "I'm gonna start supper. You take a minute if you need to, but come in here and sit by the fire."

Barbara and Samuel ate supper at the kitchen table, Barbara holding Jabez and feeding him from her plate. Rosalee sat in the chair next to the fire, holding Ezra until Barbara could take him and bring her a plate. She brought a drink for Rosalee as well, and the bitter taste was almost more than Rosalee could stomach. There was something in it similar to Irene's tonic, but this one seemed stronger. "You best drink it," Barbara told her when she noticed the young mother's look of disgust. "You need to be back on your feet, and this'll help you heal." Barbara offered her a teaspoon of amber liquid. "I got a bit of honey with me. Put it in your mouth after you finish your tonic."

Rosalee did as she was told, and the sweetness of the honey contrasted with the bitterness lingering on her tongue. She hadn't tasted anything so sweet in such a long time, it almost felt painful. As the flavor of liquid sunshine dissipated and eased across her taste buds, she forgot the acrid taste of the tonic.

Barbara stayed with them until Rosalee stopped bleeding, a full six weeks after Ezra was born. Rosalee came to realize her mother-in-law was much like Irene, with their grim countenances occasionally interrupted by moments of warmth. Both took care of her and the babies out of a clear sense of duty, something Rosalee hadn't detected in her mother or aunt, who instead had cared for her as if it brought them joy.

She realized she wasn't likely to feel maternal joy herself, and she hoped she could muster the will to love her children out of obligation, if nothing else.

Chapter 22

SPRING, 1932

Before Barbara left, she made several gallon jars of tonic for Rosalee, telling the young mother she'd need to keep her strength up if she was going to handle two boys. Rosalee drank it without fail, thinking Barbara's medicine was the reason she could get out of bed and fulfill her role as a wife and mother.

"You can go visit her if you like," Barbara told her one day. "Best do it now, before I leave. I'll watch the young'uns if you want to walk over there."

Rosalee knew she meant Irene's grave, which had a headstone now. John had bought one for his father's grave at the same time, so the two now sat next to each other. Rosalee thought sometimes it would have been better just to have Irene's alone.

She nodded to Barbara and made her way there after feeding Ezra. The earth above Irene's body had settled, and Rosalee realized nothing but weeds would grow where she lay—no forest flowers or willows— but in the fall, broad sycamore leaves would scatter over what was left of her body and memory.

Rosalee knew it would be difficult to get back to Irene's grave alone for a while, and for most of her trips anywhere, she'd be carrying an infant and coaxing a one-year-old to follow. She stared at the head-stone above Irene and tried to think of something to say. She cleared her throat and began, "You taught me so much . . ." But she trailed off, hearing a rustling close by, in the woods at the edge of the field. She strained to listen, wondering if Samuel was walking in this part of the woods for some reason. Her thoughts rushed to Joseph. As if a pond had stilled, revealing that which it reflected in a clear picture, she recognized the hungry look he had sometimes given her when no one was looking. She hadn't registered it when he was at the house right after Ezra was born, she had been so distracted by grief and pain, but she remembered finding him watching her several times, his lust unmasked. She imagined he was close by, and her pulse quickened with a new kind of fear.

The rustling in the woods stopped, and Rosalee tried to push her fear away. *Probably just squirrels,* she thought, though she listened for a few minutes longer before she turned her attention back to Irene's grave. She realized she didn't know what to say to the woman. Rosalee had needed her, and she was there. And yet, Rosalee needed something more that Irene wouldn't, or couldn't, give. *You can't really blame her,* Rosalee thought. *She wasn't Mama. Or Bessie. Nobody is.* She thought of the letters, her last connection to Irene and family she had never met, and she knew Irene must have moved them before her death. Rosalee thought of the places she could search in Irene's bedroom—under the mattress, or maybe at the bottom of a cedar chest—but in her mind's eye, she saw Irene throw them into the fireplace one night and watch the pages curl, then catch flame, the last of her own mother's wisdom gone to ashes.

A twig snapped in the forest, jerking Rosalee from her vision. "Who's there?" she demanded. She saw a flash of white disappear into the shadows of the trees, and her heart pounded, pulsing in her ears so she could no longer hear the world around her. She knew she would be too scared to walk to the house with her back to whatever she had glimpsed, so she crept toward the forest, listening.

"Who's there?" she said again, this time unable to pretend she felt brave. Questions overtook her mind of who could be out there and why, and she realized her body would not hold up well if she ran, and she wouldn't be able to outrun another person or an animal, even if she tried. The thought of her children came to mind, and she wondered with a rush of guilt whether someone else would mother them if something happened to her.

The rustling sounds retreated, and Rosalee's heartbeat slowed almost to normal. Her relief gave way to anger, though. This land was her father's, and would be her husband's, and then it would belong to her sons—no one had a right to make her feel afraid at her own home. She trembled with fury entangled in fear. Easing closer to the woods, Rosalee was emboldened by the idea that Samuel would shoot anyone who hurt her, and she pushed aside the nagging thought of his ability to hurt her himself.

She stepped into the forest, scanning the sea of browns and greens for a fleeting white form. Her eyes landed on a slight figure crouched next to a tree trunk: it was Anna in a white dress, the same blue ribbons tied to her braids to match her eyes. She was singing and humming the song Rosalee had heard from her before: *T'was Grace that brought me safe thus far and Grace will lead me home.*

"Anna!" Rosalee exclaimed, both relieved and irritated to find it was just a child who had frightened her. "You scared me," she said. Curiosity subdued her irritation, and she relaxed into the safety she had always known in the forest. "What are you doing out here?"

Anna returned Rosalee's questioning look, as if she was deciding whether or not to answer.

"I'm picking mushrooms and some plant medicine for Granny."

Rosalee caught her breath. "I see," she said, nodding toward Anna's basket, and she noticed Anna had brought a ragdoll along this time.

"But, what I mean is, how did you get so far over here? Last I saw you, you was near my daddy's house, and this is a good ways away from there. You're over by my house now."

Anna picked up her basket and moved as if to leave.

"Wait—don't go," Rosalee implored her. "I see you've got a doll with you. What's her name?"

"It's Jerusha," Anna replied, "from the Bible."

"I remember her," Rosalee said, thinking back to a street-corner sermon her father had recounted for them at home: *Jerusha gave birth to a son who became a great king,* John told them. *He served the Lord well, despite his own father not being so good.* John looked away for a minute, and then turned to Rosalee. *It's a great honor to be the mother of such a man. Even though she was one of the king's many wives, she got recognized because of that. She's remembered through the ages because she got married and had a child.*

Rosalee shifted on her feet, suddenly aware her body was not used to walking or standing for so long since giving birth, and she felt as if the earth itself was pulling her down into it. A weariness overcame her as she tried to say something more to the girl, who was walking farther into the forest, her white dress disappearing as the trees enveloped her, and Rosalee sank to the ground, resting her face against the cool forest floor.

She fell asleep and knew she was dreaming, but could not free herself from the weight of the fragmented images. Mary Ann and Bessie were trying to warn her about something, and Anna appeared at their graves, her basket full of trillium flowers. Rosalee opened her mouth to ask Anna a question, but a young version of her grandmother Irene took the little girl's place, and Rosalee watched as her grandmother transformed from a young beauty into a shriveled crone. Her face twisted from an expression of haughty pride into anger, and she whispered curses while casting something into a fire. Just as the old woman looked at Rosalee, Samuel's voice pierced the fog of her mind and woke her.

"Rosalee!" He knelt by her side. "What in Christ's name are you doing out here? Mama said you came to see Irene, not to wander off in the woods by yourself." He picked her up with a gentleness that surprised her. "You can't be doing this again," he commanded. "You've got babies to tend to, you know." He carried her back to the house, and Rosalee was overcome with a desire to sink into him, to keep her head against his chest and let him wrap her in his protection.

But once inside, he laid her on the bed and told her, "I'm serious, Rosie. Don't pull that again." His eyes were cold and empty, and Rosalee knew that whatever gentleness she thought she had felt in his touch was not something she could have whenever she wanted it. As he walked out of the room, he told her she could rest for a little while longer, but it was almost suppertime. Rosalee felt the pillow turn wet beneath her face as the world spun around her, a carousel of women and girls she wanted to pull toward her but could not reach.

While Barbara was packing up to leave, she told Rosalee, "Michael will come check on you. Send for me if you need me, but I've got a house and a husband to tend to. I can't be running over here every time you're too tired to take care of this brood you've started." She nodded toward the babies, and then looked at Rosalee with a hint of softness. "But you don't got your own mother, so I know you might need some help sometimes. And Samuel—" Barbara took in a deep breath. "He's a lot like his daddy. They ain't always easy men." With that, she left and Rosalee was surprised to find she wished Barbara would stay.

She wanted more time to tell Barbara about Anna, and about how she might be related to Rosalee, maybe the granddaughter of the woman Irene turned away from her door so long ago. She wanted to ask Barbara more about her late husband and find out how to live with

Samuel and maybe even feel happy some of the time. She worried about what Michael had told her about their business, and the apparent fight Samuel and her father had gotten into those months ago. But Ezra began to cry, and Jabez toddled into the living room with a wet diaper, so Rosalee turned her attention to them instead.

Chapter 23

SUMMER, 1932

Samuel spent the next couple of months close to the farm, and Rosalee was relieved he took on most of the barn chores again, when he wasn't tending the corn. She tried to keep up with the garden, but every time she mentioned the weeds were taking over or the tomatoes couldn't handle much more of the summer heat, he brushed off her concerns with a wave of his hand. "We don't need a garden like you're used to, Rosie. I'll pick up more food in town and we'll have plenty for winter. Put up what you can, but we'll be fine. You've got your hands full with those boys," he said with a laugh.

Rosalee wanted to believe they would be fine, but she couldn't remember a year when her mama and aunt hadn't planted a big garden, making sure there was more than enough in case a crop failed or a neighbor needed help. Samuel was buying more packaged food from town, and sometimes Rosalee was relieved to cook some meals with short notice, but she thought the food didn't taste as good as homegrown.

She still struggled to get out of bed each morning, and sometimes she had visions of Ezra wriggling out of her hands and onto the floor, neck broken, his delicate skull fractured beyond saving. She often dreamt she couldn't find Jabez and would begin searching the house, panic filling her throat. Then, in her dream, she made her way outside to find him at the well, peering in, and he would fall just as she reached out to grab him.

She startled from her visions and woke up gasping from her nightmares, and if Samuel was around, he would ask, "You alright?" with a strange expression. Rosalee would nod, willing her heart to stop racing, pushing the images from her mind. Since her first vision of Jabez falling from Samuel's lap, she refused to think about why she imagined such a thing and what it meant. She had hoped the visions would go away after Ezra was born, as if maybe his birth would fix whatever the first one had broken inside her.

Rosalee ran out of Barbara's tonic a few weeks after Barbara left and picked herself some raspberry leaves and rose hips to make one of her own. She hummed as she strained the tea after it sat for a day and held up the jar of clear green liquid to eye it as the sun shone into the kitchen. Something about it seemed so light, so airy after the tonic Barbara had made, and Rosalee felt oddly happy not to have to drink the other woman's concoction anymore.

The next morning, Rosalee woke up and realized she wasn't tired, and she didn't want to lie there until Ezra's cries grew too persistent to ignore. She went into the bedroom where the boys now slept, Ezra in a new crib Samuel had brought from town, Jabez in Irene's old bed. Ezra was sitting up and peering out the window toward the sugar maple whose leaves were streaked with the lightest yellow, a hint of the golden display yet to come. Jabez was still asleep, and it struck Rosalee that she couldn't remember the last time her morning began in peace.

For the next couple of weeks, she marveled at how good she felt, and she sometimes hummed a song when she sat on the porch at the end of the day, a jelly jar in hand. Her baby turned eight months old and her visions of him being hurt faded like a nightmare that no longer felt important. Samuel noticed Rosalee's improvement and made more trips to her father's house, carrying a Mason jar of whiskey with him to sip along the way. Sometimes he came back jovial and half-drunk, still smelling of liquor and smoke from the fire he tended at the still with his brother or John. But most nights, he returned home with a defiant set to his jaw, brooding, which Rosalee dreaded because he liked to slam doors and drop things carelessly rather than setting them down in their place. Once, she pointed out that his noise had awoken both of the babies just after she got them to sleep.

"What of it?" he growled at her. "You don't get to tell me what to do, Rosalee. Put 'em back to sleep and don't bother me over no baby crying."

Rosalee fumed, but knew that to say anything else would only provoke him more, and he probably wouldn't hesitate to turn his anger more fully toward her. She hid her emotion behind the mask she had perfected, and rocked the babies back to sleep.

Samuel rushed into the house one night, eager to tell Rosalee what he had discussed with her father.

"Rosie, listen to this—we've got these connections in Chicago, you know, they've been buyin' our liquor and going crazy for it. Well, we're meeting with the big man next time we go there!"

Rosie looked at him, puzzled. "What big man?" she asked.

Samuel laughed. "*The* big man, Rosie—the boss of every drop of liquor that gets bought or sold in that city. Hell, maybe even the whole state! This guy just took over the business, and it's gonna be good for us." He poured himself a drink. "You don't get it, Rosie—this is the big time. You and your daddy'll see."

Rosalee's stomach sank. She had a murky idea of who Samuel was talking about. She had seen stories about him in the newspapers Samuel brought from his trips to town, and she knew if a man in

Chicago made it to the Owingsville paper for trouble with the law, he must be a bad man.

"My daddy wants to get involved in all that?"

Samuel eyed her coolly. "*We* know it's good business, and *we* are getting somewhere because some of us have done damn fine work to get us there." He looked in the direction of John's house. "We don't always see eye to eye, your daddy and me, but we can work together. And that's enough for now." He looked at her again and smiled. "I'll be in the woods."

She knew what that meant. He would be drinking and tinkering with his still until long after sunset. She asked him as he walked out, "When are you going back to the city?"

He responded without turning around: "Tomorrow."

Rosalee was struck with an urge to go see her father. Something about what Samuel had said—*You and your daddy'll see*—made her worry about what it was Samuel wanted to prove to her father, and why. She thought of the fistfight they had gotten into and wondered how her father felt about this man he had married his daughter to.

That night, after putting the boys to sleep in their room, Rosalee lay awake for longer than usual, waiting for Samuel to come to bed. She finally heard him enter the house, but it sounded like he was going to make another drink and go back out to the porch. Rosalee knew Samuel wouldn't want her to go with him tomorrow—bringing her and the babies would just add more time and trouble to his trip. They would have to take the wagon and she would have to drive it back without him, all for a few minutes to see her father before he left for Chicago. She would have to convince Samuel to let her do what she wanted, and she knew the best time to suggest it would be when he was satisfied. Though she hadn't turned him away since she healed from Ezra's birth, she never reached for him anymore. She was sure it would work, but she would have to convince him she was sincere.

Rosalee got out of the bed and went to the mirror, where she saw her reflection in the dim moonlight. She brushed her hair and untied the ribbon at the top of her nightgown, then practiced a smile and what she hoped was a come-hither look. Samuel stood in the kitchen with his back to her, preparing his drink. Rosalee walked up behind him and whispered his name as she got close, so she wouldn't startle him.

"What is it, Rosie?" Samuel asked without turning around.

Rosalee put her arms around his waist. "I've missed you."

Samuel turned to look at her over his shoulder. "Rosie, what's gotten into you? Did you have an extra drink tonight?" He laughed at his joke.

"No, I've just been missing you." She put her hands on his waist, and he turned to face her.

"Rosie, you never act like this." His forehead furrowed in suspicion, and Rosalee knew she had to make him forget his doubt. She couldn't think of anything seductive to say, so she leaned up and kissed him, putting her arms around his neck and pulling him toward her.

Samuel fumbled for a moment and then leaned into the kiss. He picked Rosalee up and carried her to the bedroom, his drink forgotten. Rosalee rushed to pull his shirt off him and pushed him onto the bed, surprising herself with how passionate she could appear to be. Samuel watched as she pulled his shoes off and then unbuttoned his pants and pulled them down. Rosalee smiled back at him and managed to push away the thought of him hitting her, and how her blood had tasted on her lip. She stretched herself over his body, and in a deft move, he turned her onto her back. Rosalee tried to relax, knowing it was the easiest way, and she made the sounds she knew he liked.

After he was finished, Rosalee laid her head on Samuel's shoulder, both of them looking up at the ceiling.

"Damn, Rosie—you must have missed me alright. It's good to see you gettin' some fire back."

Rosalee hummed in agreement and leaned over to kiss his chest.

"I'm glad we got to do that before you left," she told Samuel. "I would have really missed you bad if we hadn't."

"I'm glad we did, too," Samuel responded. "A man gets lonely, you know. I'd rather it be my wife who keeps me warm at night than somebody else." He turned to her and smiled, and Rosalee knew what he meant: there were other women who would keep him warm if she wouldn't. She would have to submit to him all the time, anytime he wanted her, or wonder who might be next to him anytime he was away for the rest of her life. She stifled her indignation and made her voice even sweeter and more doting than before.

"You know what would be nice? Me and the babies could go to my daddy's with you tomorrow. I ain't seen him in a long time."

Samuel furrowed his brow in the silver light.

"I'll be in a hurry, Rosie. We need to get on the road and not waste a bunch of the day."

"Oh, I know. You've got a lot to do. It's just, it would mean a lot to me. And if we take the wagon, your mama can come back with me and the babies, if she wants to." Rosalee kissed his chest again. "Whatever you say, of course."

Samuel sighed. "You caught me in a good mood, Rosie. Get the boys ready first thing in the morning and we'll head out." Rosalee smiled at the ceiling, satisfied.

Chapter 24

They loaded up in the morning, Ezra tucked into a basket in the wagon and Jabez sitting on Rosalee's lap. As they rode to John's house, Samuel grinned at Rosalee. "You still got me all worked up, Rosie. I wouldn't mind gettin' used to that!"

Rosalee smiled and feigned a shy look. She didn't want to think about what happened last night, or any other night. She didn't like the feeling of him touching her, but she was surprised it wasn't hard to pretend when she really wanted to. She thought of Mary Ann, and the question of whether her mother had ever pretended darted through her mind. She gave her head a little shake as she pushed the thought away. Surely her mother had never felt the need to lie to her father. Mary Ann had always seemed to love him, even when he was suspicious and moody.

When they parked the wagon at John's, Michael shuffled toward them, his eyes down. "Little brother, you don't look happy to see us," she teased him as he helped her out of the wagon. He didn't respond until Samuel was out of earshot, talking with Joseph.

Michael jerked his head in the direction the brothers had walked, deep in conversation between themselves.

"Just tired of listening to these hotheads. They don't do nothin' but argue."

Rosalee looked at him. Michael was about to turn twelve and already carried the weight of the world on his shoulders. She wondered how hard it would be for him to stay sweet, though, the way things were going. "Don't worry, little brother. Everything is going to be fine. You just take care of those cows and don't pay no mind to them." She glanced in the direction of the men. "We can't let their foolishness bother us too much."

They walked into the house with the babies to find John and Barbara sitting at the kitchen table. John's face had aged, and Rosalee thought his body must have, too. He leaned over a cup of coffee, his arms resting against the table as if it was holding him up. Barbara sat there, expressionless, staring into a crack between two boards or perhaps the woodgrain itself. The tension between them hung in the air, and Rosalee wished she was somewhere else—anywhere else—other than next to them.

Michael cleared his throat. "You need help gettin' the car packed, Daddy?" John stared at his coffee cup before taking a deep breath. "Think I 'bout got it all, son. But you can check it for me."

Michael ran out to the car with purpose, and Rosalee sat at the table with her father and Barbara, wishing for her own way out of that discomfort. She pulled Ezra from his basket and held him facing away from her, toward her father.

"I think Ezra looks a lot like you, Daddy," she told him. "He's got your eyes."

John looked at the baby and then at Rosalee, and he almost smiled, something Rosalee hadn't seen in as long as she could remember. The moment soured as he responded, "Let's hope he's got some sense from our side of the family, too." Barbara stiffened as he stood up from the table, and Rosalee noticed her father wore a pistol on his hip now, just like Samuel.

"Daddy, why you all wearing guns nowadays?" she asked, trying to keep her voice light.

John looked away, and she thought he wasn't going to answer, but he finally spoke. "We've got some competition, and some of the other moonshiners around here don't want to share customers with us. The revenue man and sheriff are sniffing around town, too, trying to find out who all's brewing." Rosalee looked at him in alarm. "It's part of the business, Rosalee. A man can make good money if he's got something everybody wants, and he can make even more money if the government says you ain't allowed to sell it. But there's risks. We're up against the law and the other outlaws." He gave a wry laugh. "Ain't that something."

Barbara got up from the table and cleaned the kitchen, and John went outside. Jabez played on the floor while Rosalee nursed Ezra.

"Barbara," she started, "it'd be a pleasure to have you at the house while the men are gone, if you want to come." She wondered if her mother-in-law would appreciate the invitation or feel put upon, after what she said last time.

Barbara nodded her head and stood facing away from Rosalee, looking out the kitchen window toward the men at the car.

"Is everything okay?" Rosalee asked her, unsure if she really wanted to know the answer.

"No," Barbara snapped as she wheeled around to look at Rosalee. "No, it sure ain't. You heard what your daddy said—that whiskey ain't nothin' but trouble, and I've told 'em all but they don't listen to me. Damn men don't ever listen." She turned back to her dishes and Rosalee sat there, shocked into silence. She had never heard Barbara curse, and her anger unsettled Rosalee.

"What's that mean, the revenue man?"

Barbara gave up on finishing the dishes and sat at the table. "He's the tax man. He goes after anybody making money who ain't paying taxes on it, like your daddy and the boys. I'm sure you know what a sheriff is," she said, surprising Rosalee with her condescension.

"Yes." Rosalee looked into Barbara's eyes.

"I'm sorry, girl." Barbara looked down at the table. "I shouldn't take it out on you."

"Do you want to go back to the house with me and the babies?" Rosalee asked. "It'd be a sight less lonely with you there. Samuel said they'd only be gone two weeks but it's still a long time not having anybody else to talk to."

Barbara nodded again, and Rosalee was relieved she didn't seem to think it was a burden after all. "You don't need to be at the house alone with two little ones neither. I'll keep you company and tell Michael to come check in on us. For his sake, as well as ours. There's no telling who'll be comin' around with your daddy gone."

They rode to the house a couple of hours later, after Barbara assured herself everything in the kitchen was set up so Michael could feed himself while she was gone. "He's skinny as a rail," she told Rosalee, "but I do my best to keep him fed. Maybe he'll put on a little weight if I keep trying." Rosalee was struck by her concern and smiled at the thought that Barbara wanted to take care of her brother, who had never had his own mother. She thought of what Mary Ann might say if she was there, and a bitter sadness filled her. Everything would be different. The Carters would have never moved in, and she wouldn't have married Samuel. Her husband and father wouldn't be getting into fistfights or chasing trouble in Chicago. They would be happy, she thought. She could have stayed with her mother forever.

The first thing Barbara did when they got back to Rosalee's house was to get a tonic brewing for her. "I see you're out," she told Rosalee. "You can't be nursing a baby and chasing a toddler around without something for your strength." Rosalee dreaded the taste, but thanked Barbara and made sure the bedroom was ready for her. She watched Barbara add extra bloodroot to the tonic, and she started to speak up about how Bessie didn't use so much, but she hadn't seen Bessie use it many times, and she was a child then—she couldn't be sure. And besides making the tonic taste bad, she didn't know what could happen if there was more than enough in it. She decided not to say anything to Barbara, certain the woman was set in her ways for a reason.

In the first few days Barbara was there, the women fell into a routine of tending to the babies, feeding the farm animals, and harvesting the last of the crops lingering during the Indian summer. The men had harvested most of the field corn, so even the air grew still, with no cornstalks to whisper on the breeze. Barbara remarked on how little food Rosalee had put up for the winter, and Rosalee tried to explain how Samuel could buy more food from town and they didn't have to work so hard in the garden. "I just about couldn't keep up with it this year, with the little ones. Samuel didn't want me worrying over it too much."

She tried to sound confident, but as she spoke the words, she knew they were hollow, and Barbara would know it, too. Rosalee had heard stories about hard winters, when hunger lasted longer than the food. Mama and Bessie had told stories about times when a person couldn't go to the store and get everything they needed, so they gathered more food from the woods and bartered with far-flung neighbors for what they lacked. There were stories about taking an extra chicken to a family who needed it when times were plenty, and when times were lean, pails of milk or baskets of bread appeared on their porch with nobody claiming credit for the gifts.

Rosalee decided she would be more careful next year, and she would store extra eggs and potatoes away now. They could eat more wild greens and mushrooms to fill their plates in the meantime. *Maybe buy a pig and a cow from Daddy and have them butchered, so we've got 'em if we need 'em,* she thought. Pleased with her good sense, Rosalee started cutting up squash and onions to put up, and the memory of Mary Ann's pickled squash made her mouth water.

Chapter 25

Michael came to see Rosalee and Barbara at the end of the first week and spent the day helping with some of the dirtier farm chores. After supper, he played with the babies and then sat with the women next to the fireplace.

"You're not much bigger than Jabez," Rosalee teased him. "Working like a man on the farm but you're still my baby brother."

Michael grinned at her. "I'm the man of the house while Daddy's gone, you know." Barbara gave him a look. "I mean, when Daddy and Joseph are gone. And probably Samuel, too, even though he lives over here."

"You're growin' up too fast," Rosalee told him. "You don't need to be in too big a hurry." She smiled, though her voice was serious.

"Can't stay little forever." He grinned back at her, and then held up a letter. "I brought this from the house. I remember Daddy said he'd got one from our brothers in Pike County when he went to town. I saw it by the fireplace and thought you'd want to read it."

"Daddy didn't tell me he got a letter! I get letters from them sometimes, and I knew they wrote Daddy some." Rosalee looked at Barbara with a smile. "Why didn't you all tell me? Did you forget?" She didn't wait for the woman to answer, but looked back to the envelope and opened it, smiling. Barbara kept mending the baby gown in her lap, a frown deepening the lines around her mouth.

Rosalee unfolded the letter and started to read it aloud, but stopped as her eyes raced ahead and her smile faded. She looked to Barbara, who finally stopped sewing and looked back at Rosalee.

"What is it?" Michael asked. "What's wrong, Rosalee?"

Tears spilled down her cheeks and dropped onto the letter, smudging the ink as they soaked the paper. She tried to speak but couldn't find the words. Barbara spoke up. "Your brother, John Jr.—he was in an accident in the coal mine." Michael looked at her, waiting to understand. "He's gone," Barbara continued. "He died in the mine."

Rosalee's eyes flashed as she looked to Barbara. "You knew? And Daddy? Why didn't somebody tell me? Or us?" She gestured toward Michael. "Why haven't you told me this whole time?"

Barbara turned her stern gaze back to the gown. "Doesn't make any difference. We can't bury him. The only thing we can do is pray his wife finds another husband real quick to take care of her and the little ones." Rosalee searched her mind for an image of these people, but she had never met her sister-in-law or their babies. She couldn't imagine their faces and could only conjure an outdated version of her brother. She looked at Michael, whose memories of his older brothers were fleeting, at best. She could tell he was sad, but how do you grieve someone you can't remember?

He met her eyes, full of desperation, and turned away. Michael picked up one of Jabez's blocks and traced the letter *A* someone had carved into it, and then he looked at the image of an apple on the other side. "Whatcha think about these blocks, Rosalee? Can you teach me to read with 'em?"

Rosalee stood up and laid the letter on top of the desk so it could dry. Her mind drifted as she stood there, waiting for her hands to stop shaking. She saw another young woman or girl open the drawer some years later—the desk was dusty—and pull the letter from the drawer. The paper had turned brittle and was missing little pieces where the creases met the edges. The writing was smudged and stained in places where saltwater tears had fallen, a record of grief unfolding.

❧

Rosalee awoke in the morning just before dawn. Barbara and Michael were in the kitchen having coffee.

"Glad to see you up, sister." Michael smiled at her. "I didn't know if I should wake you before I left. I've gotta get back to the animals."

Rosalee smiled weakly. "We didn't get too far with your reading, did we?"

"It's alright, Rosalee. I'll come back for lessons as soon as I can."

Outside, Rosalee watched as he prepared his horse and stood on a wooden stool so he could reach to sling his leg over the saddle. She tried to stifle a laugh, but he turned to look at her from atop his horse. "You keep laughing, Rosalee—I'll be bigger than you here soon!"

He rode off, and Rosalee walked back into the house.

She didn't know what to say to Barbara, and she knew there was no real reason to be angry with the woman. After all, her own father didn't bother telling her about John Jr. when he could have. Barbara was waiting when Rosalee entered the house.

"Look here, Rosalee," she said, and Rosalee stopped in the kitchen to listen. "I know you're sore at me for not telling you about John Jr." Barbara took a deep breath. "But it was your daddy's place to tell you, not mine."

Rosalee nodded in agreement as her resentment diminished.

"And something else you need to know," Barbara continued. "Men die all the time. They go and get killed in wars, or in coal mines, or in some barroom brawl." She waved a hand in the direction of her home. "They run off to do what they have to or want to, and we stay here to take care of what's left. You're lucky you've got your daddy and this land, so no matter what happens, you and your babies will have a home."

The color drained from Rosalee's face.

"Your mama would tell you the same thing if she was here," Barbara finished. "Life ain't never been easy, and that ain't gonna change no time soon. It's just the truth."

Rosalee thought about the man her father was, back when her mother was still alive. He had never been one to smile much, but once Mary Ann was gone, it was as if her father disappeared, too, and became a man whose life was shaped by the outside world, no longer influenced by love or sentimentality. Ezra began to cry, and Barbara picked him up to hand him to Rosalee. "Even these boys," Barbara said, trying to be gentle now. "They're yours for a short time, and then they belong to the world."

Rosalee sat by the fireplace to nurse Ezra and watch Jabez suck on the sugar rag Barbara had made for him.

❧

A few days before Samuel was supposed to return, Rosalee said to Barbara, "It's been a couple months since you were here last, and I ain't been able to visit Irene since you left." Rosalee offered with a smile, "I promise I won't have another spell in the woods."

Barbara studied her face for a moment and turned back to the laundry she was washing. "Suit yourself, Rosalee. But don't go wanderin' off where I can't find you in a pinch."

Rosalee concealed her impatience. "Don't worry—I'll be more careful from now on." But she was eager to get back to the woods, and to see if she might find Anna again. She finished her morning chores, and when she sat to nurse Ezra, Barbara brought her tonic in a jelly jar. "Here you go, drink up. Maybe this'll keep you from having another spell out there." Rosalee swallowed the drink and grimaced.

"What, you don't like it?" Barbara asked.

"It's just strong, is all," Rosalee responded as she drank some water, trying to rinse the taste away.

"It ain't supposed to taste like apple pie," Barbara told her.

Rosalee thought back to the tonics and tinctures Bessie had made and wondered what was in Irene's and Barbara's that made them taste bad, with Barbara's being the worst. Rosalee remembered the young mothers who came to Bessie, and she couldn't recall many who needed bloodroot, or anyone who took it every day. But Delphia Caudill came to mind, and Rosalee asked herself what other mistakes Bessie had made back then, and what consequences they had avoided by luck alone. Barbara seemed impatient, as she often did those days, so Rosalee decided not to question her about the ingredients. "I sure appreciate you fixing it, Mother." Rosalee stumbled over that last word but held her gaze steady as she tried to beam daughterly love toward her mother-in-law.

Barbara just waved her hand in dismissal. "Can't have you breaking down and staying in bed all the time. I don't want to have to move here and take care of all of you."

After dinner, Rosalee walked down to Irene's grave and said a quick prayer for her last grandmother. She turned quickly to the woods and walked to the spot where Samuel had found her. That part of the forest floor was clear, but something grew around it in a near-perfect circle. Rosalee crouched down to look closer, and found the circle was formed by small, white mushrooms that looked like some of the mushrooms Bessie had gathered in the forest. Rosalee reached out to pick one.

"Mama says not to touch those," a voice warned her. Rosalee startled and lost her balance, falling backward with a thud into a sitting position. She knew right away her dress must have gotten dirty, and Barbara would know she had been out in the woods after all. She looked up to see Anna, who stood on the other side of the mushrooms.

"It's a fairy ring," Anna went on to say. "The fairies don't like it when we pick them, and they visit your house and make you sick after you fall asleep."

"Your mama sounds like a smart woman," Rosalee said as she stood up and brushed her skirt. "I ain't seen these before."

"Mama also says you don't pick mushrooms you don't know," Anna replied.

Rosalee thought about whether or not to defend her pride, but decided she was more interested in finding out what she could about Anna.

"That's smart. I'll not be picking any mushrooms I don't know from here on." Anna gazed at her, as if she was waiting for Rosalee's true intention. "Well," Rosalee said, clearing her throat. "I see you're out here in the woods again. You pickin' plants for your granny?"

"Mushrooms," Anna responded.

"She's lucky to have you out here gettin' what you all need from the woods," Rosalee told her. "Do you ever get lost?"

"No. I been all over these woods since before I could walk."

"That's good. Where do you live at?"

Anna stood there, looking into Rosalee's eyes as she so often did. The story behind Rosalee's questions passed between them like a morning glory vine climbing, its flowers opening to greet the sun. There was her entire history, laid bare for this strange girl to make of what she would: Mary Ann in the kitchen, Bessie by the spring, Mamaw Irene's rose-scented letters, Samuel and the smell of magnolia, the smell of whiskey too close to Rosalee's face, his weight upon her. Rosalee gasped as the vision unfurled before her, and the little girl with blue eyes finally responded, "Sorry, miss. Mama told me not to tell strangers where I live."

Anna turned around and walked away, deeper into the forest. Rosalee watched the little girl's back retreat into the shadows and disappear.

Chapter 26

S amuel returned home a few days later, as planned. Joseph showed up on a horse alongside his brother, and Samuel dismounted as the women came outside, each carrying one of the children. Joseph smirked at Rosalee, but she ignored him and looked to Samuel. When he finally looked at Rosalee, his eyes were bloodshot, and he smelled like whiskey.

"You alright?" she asked him, and everyone waited for his answer.

"Sure, Rosie," he slurred. "Couldn't be better."

Barbara looked at Joseph. "You all've been drinking all day?"

"Yes, ma'am," her son responded. "We've been celebrating!" He laughed and added, "Some of us might've celebrated too hard."

Barbara went back inside and gathered her things, and Samuel swayed as he walked toward the woods behind the house and urinated into the trees. Rosalee looked away from him to find Joseph watching her. "He sure did miss you, Rosie."

Rosalee bristled to hear him call her by Samuel's nickname. "It's Rosalee," she told him. Joseph looked back at her, grinning, and though she saw the same unfeeling look in his eye Samuel often had, it clashed strangely with his mouth, with one side still curled upward, showing his teeth.

"Sure, Rosalee—whatever you say," Joseph said after a pause. "I'll call you whatever you want. And you can call me whatever you want."

Rosalee's thoughts fumbled over those last words, and before she could say anything else, Samuel walked back to them.

"I'm about ready to starve to death," he exclaimed. "What does my dear wife plan to feed me?"

"Your mama made soup beans," she responded in a rush. "I can fry you some hoecakes if you want."

"Come on, Joseph—you can't pass up a meal. And Rosie'll make you some fine hoecakes, too, won't you, girl?"

Rosalee smiled at Samuel and nodded, reeling as everything inside her rebelled against Joseph coming into her home. They walked in, Samuel and Joseph arguing and laughing. As everyone ate, Joseph gulped a glass of milk, letting thin streams dribble from the corners of his mouth. He slammed the glass down and belched, and Barbara glared at him.

"Act like you've got some sense," she snapped. "This ain't no barroom. Show some respect."

Joseph wiped the back of his hand across his mouth, and a slow smile broke over his face. "Alright, Mama, you're right. I should act better for Rosalee. I'm just not used to being around a young lady, you know." He turned toward Rosalee, who had ended up sitting kitty-corner from him at the table, and pretended to bow. "Forgive me, miss. I forgot my manners," he exclaimed with mock regret. "I'll never do it again." He grabbed Rosalee's hand from the table and kissed the back of it, looking up at her with a taunt in his eyes.

She recoiled and snatched her hand away from him before she could think. "That's fine," she stammered, her heart racing, feeling dirty from his touch.

At the other end of the table, Samuel banged his glass down hard, sloshing some milk over the side. "Enough," he said in a low voice. He glared at Joseph, whose smile hung suspended on his face as he sized up his older brother.

Joseph gave a little laugh. "Don't worry, big brother. I didn't mean no harm." Rosalee looked between the two brothers and wondered which of them was quicker to lose his temper.

"Both of you all best knock it off," Samuel warned, and Rosalee looked at him, sure he couldn't mean what he said. But he looked at her, his eyes red and bleary, his expression nearly hollow except for the simmering anger. He pushed his chair back and stood up, using the table to steady himself as he rose to his feet.

Barbara jumped up and turned to Joseph. "I've got to get home," she told him. "John's gonna need his clothes washed and I've got to start supper. Let's ride on back."

Joseph stood, and Rosalee could feel him looking at her, even though he kept his eyes fixed on Samuel. "Sure, Mama. Let's get you home. I'll see you in a couple days, big brother." He turned to the door, leaving Samuel to sway in the kitchen until he walked to the bedroom and fell down on the bed, fully clothed.

Rosalee kept the babies as quiet as she could in the next room, though she wasn't sure anything could wake Samuel. She never knew him to get so drunk in the daytime, and something about the sight of it sent her stomach into somersaults. When he woke up, he said nothing but went outside with his pistol and shot it over and over, aiming toward a tree but not caring what he hit. Rosalee listened to the gunfire echo and bounce off the hills around them. She thought of Joseph's touch and kiss on her hand, which felt dirty for the rest of the day, no matter how much she washed it. She wondered how Samuel could blame her for what Joseph had done and hoped he might forget everything that happened before his midday sleep.

He spent the evening drinking on the porch, unfazed by the cool air sinking between the Appalachian ridges and settling into the valleys as the sun went down. Rosalee went out to check on him after she put the babies to bed. She cleared her throat as she sat down in the rocking chair.

"Good to have you back," she said, wondering whether it sounded like a lie. "Everything go alright up north?"

Samuel rocked in his rocking chair—just a little too fast, Rosalee thought—and looked at the backs of his hands before he answered.

"We did good, just like I said we would. I brought back a few things for you all," he said, still not looking at her. "You oughta like that." His last words seethed with an unfamiliar anger.

"I'm sure I'll love whatever you brought back," she offered, trying to find the words to soothe him. "You always bring back nice things."

"Well, it's hard to tell around here," Samuel replied, his frustration laid bare. "I don't get no appreciation, and you act like you're too good all the time. You're a little farm girl just like I'm a farm boy, Rosalee, even if I am tryin' to do better for my family." Rosalee didn't know what to be dismayed by first. His little-boy tone was more exaggerated than she had ever heard it, but she thought the accusation was laughable. If he knew what she had suffered at his hands and because of childbirth, he would know better than to say such things. Or maybe he wouldn't, she realized. Maybe he could never care about her feelings as much as he did his own.

She rocked and looked out at the stars, which shone bright alongside the crescent moon. "I know you try hard," she told him, as she decided to ignore his insults. "And I appreciate it. Me and the boys are lucky to have you."

Samuel huffed a little in response and walked to the corner of the porch to relieve himself. Rosalee took the opportunity to go back inside, where she hoped she could go to bed without arousing Samuel's ire. She fell into a dream. Within that world, she found herself in the woods behind her house, running with baby Ezra in her arms. She knew Jabez had fallen behind, but it was too late to go back for him. She had to make it to the still, where Samuel would be, waiting to protect her. But the farther she ran, the farther away everything fell. Exhausted, she looked down and found her arms were empty, and she fell to her knees in the woods with nothing left to hope for.

Samuel came into the bedroom and dropped his boots to the floor, startling Rosalee from her restless dreaming. She sighed, grateful to be rescued from the grief threatening to engulf her.

He struck her with the back of his hand, splitting her lip open. Her hand flew to her face before she could feel the sting, a split second of shock between the event and her realization of what was happening. She scrambled backward toward the headboard, yanked from her drowsiness, and tried to reason with him: "Samuel, I didn't say anything—"

But before she could finish her sentence, he hit her again, his fist closed this time, and said, "You best remember what happens when you act like you're better'n me." Satisfied he had made his point, Samuel changed out of his clothes and lay down.

Rosalee sank into the bed and pulled the blanket up to her chin. Her hands were still trembling, and a sob threatened to escape her throat, but she held it back, determined not to cry. She turned over so the side of her face he had hit would not press against the pillow, and she realized with a grim satisfaction she didn't have to lie facing him. She listened to Samuel fall asleep, and his breath deepened into a drunken snore.

Rosalee awoke the next morning to hear Samuel whistling a tune to himself as he tended to some of the animals. She searched her mind for some bit of wisdom her mama or Aunt Bessie might have shared with her, before she ever imagined herself married, and long before she could comprehend how it would feel to be married to a man like Samuel.

But the only thing she could conjure was the day Irene talked about Granny McKenzie and how she had fought—and beaten—her own husband one time. Though it wasn't her victory, Rosalee flushed with pride to think her great-granny had not allowed a man to mistreat her. She knew she could not defend herself from Samuel with her fists, though. *If only Aunt Bessie had taught me*—the thought brought a smile to the corners of her mouth. The only thing she did have was the shot-gun, or maybe Samuel's pistol, if she got ahold of it after he fell asleep for the night. Guilt flooded her mind then. To kill a man was a sin, and neither the Bible nor Bessie said any different. She would have to suffer this life, like so many other women had done and were doing.

Before she could stop it, a moan escaped her lips as she realized how disappointed Bessie and Mama would be to see her now. She tried not to cry.

The boys grew and by the time he turned two, Ezra was weaned. Rosalee scrubbed the boys' clothes against the washboard one morning as they played with a chicken pecking around the yard and searching for grubs. Jabez led his little brother in all their games, and sometimes was a little too rough. Samuel laughed anytime he saw the older toddler push his brother, who always fell onto his bottom, a quizzical look on his face. Rosalee tried to teach Jabez not to push, but Samuel interrupted, telling her, "They're boys, and someday they'll be men. They have to learn to hold their own."

Rosalee thought the age of two was awfully young to learn how to hold his own, and when Samuel wasn't around, she held Ezra more than she needed to, hoping her affection could somehow make up for everything else.

Though Prohibition had ended, Samuel's customers preferred his liquor over what they could buy legally, so he left for trips to Chicago every couple of months, and sometimes he went to Lexington. Most Kentucky counties stayed dry, and Bath County would refuse to legalize for years to come. "Homemade liquor is booming," he explained to Rosalee. "And now that regular folks know how to make a good livin' off it, the law will have a hard time shutting it back down." Rosalee combined moonshine and fruits from around the farm and forest, but Samuel waved his hand when she asked if he'd like to take some to the city. "We ain't tryin' to impress nobody's girlfriends up there now, and men don't want a bunch of fruit mixed in their liquor." Rosalee enjoyed those jars herself after that, though every time she ate a pawpaw or blueberry soaked with moonshine, the conversation with Samuel came to mind and dulled some of the pleasure.

One night, John dropped Samuel off late, and Samuel stormed into the house, slamming the door shut behind him. He crashed around the kitchen, not realizing he had awoken the boys and they were crying, or that Rosalee stood there on edge, not knowing what had gone wrong. After he poured himself a drink, he turned around and his face changed, as if Rosalee's presence was a complete surprise. "Hi there, Rosie," he slurred. "Wait 'til I tell you what your daddy and them Chicago boys were sayin' this time." He walked into the living room and collapsed into a chair, where he fell right to sleep. The next day, he didn't seem to remember he had a story to tell her, and she was afraid to ask.

Samuel kept bringing packaged food from town, and he wanted Rosalee to try to make meals like he ate in Chicago: pasta and other foods Rosalee had never heard of, much less cooked. Sometimes the meals weren't fit to eat, despite her best efforts. Samuel might laugh, making a joke of the inedible disaster, or storm out of the house and drink on the porch until after sundown, when he would eat whatever Rosalee cooked after the failed meal. Rosalee knew to make him a plate and keep it warm, no matter how long it took him to eat it.

Another time, when Samuel got home from a trip to the city, the scent of a perfume followed him into the house. That night, Samuel didn't try to pull her close to him or tug on her nightgown, his way of telling her to take it off. Instead, he fell asleep and made little sounds of enjoyment, dreaming of someone far away. Rosalee waited for jealousy to follow, but it didn't come, and instead, she prayed someone else would fulfill his desires and draw his interest away from their bedroom.

Rosalee started gathering more leaves and roots for medicine from the woods behind the house, in the direction of Samuel's stills, though it always seemed less special there, somehow, than in the forest by the spring, and she wondered how one part of a forest could be so different from the other.

On one of Michael's visits to check on Rosalee and the boys, he told her how Daddy all of a sudden seemed *old*, and the next day, Rosalee rode over to their house with her sons. Aside from Christmas and Easter dinner, Rosalee had gotten to where she mostly went to her father's when Joseph was with Samuel at her farm, and the two Carter brothers seemed intent on outdoing each other with their acts of bravado. She didn't want to forgive her father for marrying her to Samuel, but drew a sharp breath when she walked into his home and saw how the gray now streaked his hair. His features had grown sharper as his face thinned, and an air of defeat surrounded him.

The quiet scowl Barbara often wore had carved itself into her forehead so she wore a permanent look of disapproval. Like Irene before her, her hands shook when she was sewing, so the heavy, warm quilts she was always making no longer featured the tight, precise stitching that had once set her work apart from all others. Despite how close they lived and how unpleasant Barbara was toward her, Rosalee missed her sometimes and longed for the company of another woman, but settled for her memories of the women who had shaped her in different ways through the years.

Not long after she saw how gaunt her father had grown, Rosalee took the boys to Barbara and asked her to watch them so she could visit her mother's grave. Barbara agreed without warmth, and Rosalee rushed out of the house before she could change her mind. But by the time Rosalee reached the edge of the forest, she was overcome with guilt, thinking about Barbara's shaking hands and the children. She stood at the edge of the forest and tried to imagine how tall Anna would be by now, and how her face might have changed with time, but she could hardly recall any details—only her blue eyes remained fixed in Rosalee's mind.

Chapter 27

SPRING, 1934

S amuel rushed into the house one evening, just before the sun began to set, his eyes frantic.

"Lock this door, Rosalee. Now!" he commanded.

Rosalee hastened to close the two sliding latches Samuel had recently installed, one just above the doorknob and the other higher.

He had been at John's all day, and Rosalee thought they must have fought again. Samuel held a cloth sack pressed against his chest with the crook of his left arm, struggling to keep it from falling open, and his pistol in his right hand. He rushed past Rosalee and the children toward the bedroom, dropping a small cylinder from the bag and muttering to himself. Rosalee could hear him pry the board loose and rummage around with the coffee cans under there, which had multiplied in the past year. She peered at the cylinder on the floor and found it was a roll of twenty-dollar bills, wrapped tightly and held with a rubber band. She whisked it into her dress pocket and went to the bedroom door.

"What's going on?"

Samuel kept talking under his breath, too quiet for Rosalee to understand. She noticed he had set the gun on the floor next to him, and she imagined herself picking it up. She would aim it at his head, back away just a little, and pull the trigger.

"Ran into a little trouble—the sheriff's on his way here."

Rosalee gasped. She saw the sack was still half-full of tight cylinders, more than she could count. Most rolls had a twenty-dollar bill on the outside, but she saw quite a few fifty-dollar bills, too.

"What is that, Samuel? What are you doing with all this money? Did you rob a bank?"

Samuel shoved money into the coffee cans and pushed what couldn't fit into the space around them. He took a second to look up at her with a smirk. "No, Rosie, I made this money off of whiskey and my own smarts. Can't be spending it all—some of it's for other people to keep our business going. And who knows—you might have to come bail me out of jail." He flashed her a smile, but Rosalee could see a worried look in his eye.

"What on earth are you talking about? You can't go to jail. What about me and the babies?"

Samuel put the floorboard back where it belonged. He stood up and stomped on the nails with his heels to push them into the well-worn holes. "You're a tough McKenzie girl, remember? You'll be just fine. Joseph has some of my money to come bail me out. He can check on you while I'm gone."

Rosalee's blood ran cold, and they both heard a heavy knock. She picked up Ezra from where he was playing, and Samuel walked toward the door, his pistol cocked.

"Who's there?" Samuel shouted, and Jabez began to cry.

The sheriff burst through the door, breaking the locks. He pushed Samuel to the floor as Rosalee shrieked, and Ezra began crying along with Jabez. The sheriff and his deputy handcuffed Samuel and pulled him to his feet.

"We've got you, Carter," the sheriff told him. "We know you been making whiskey and selling it in town. Now tell us where your still is, or we'll find it ourselves. If we lose the light tonight, we'll come back tomorrow." The sheriff shot a look toward Rosalee. "You don't want us to trouble your sweet wife over this now, do you?"

Rosalee returned the sheriff's cold gaze. "What's the meaning of this? How can you bust in here like that, scarin' my babies?"

The sheriff looked around the kitchen, noticing the quart jar of moonshine she kept on a shelf, and laughed. "We're doin' the right thing for your babies, ma'am." He nodded toward Ezra in her arms. "You might not know what your husband's been up to, but we do. He's a lawless man." He eyed her for a moment longer, and Rosalee looked away.

The sheriff turned to Samuel and stuck his finger in Samuel's chest. "Tell me, son, and I might go easy on you."

Samuel smiled and held his hands out, as if to show they were empty. "I got no idea what you're talking about. We're just poor farmers here."

"Bring him outside," the sheriff told his deputy. "Let's check the woods out back and see what we can find."

Rosalee shut the door behind them, her heart now pounding so the sound drowned out the children's cries. She put Ezra in his crib and went to her room. She pushed the dolls to the floor, opened her trunk full of unworn fancy dresses, and tucked the roll of cash beneath them.

Later, after the sheriff informed her they had found Samuel's still— not knowing there were two—and he would be spending the night at the county jail, she pried the bedroom floorboard up and took three more rolls of the tightly bound money. She fished the bills out from under her dresses and pushed the trunk aside, and then used a hammer to pry another board loose. She put the four rolls into a Mason jar and put the jar into the floor, pushed the trunk back, and had a drink as she watched the fire.

A few days later, they let Samuel out of jail on bail. He came home and pulled the bedroom floorboard up and put the loose rolls of cash into another coffee can, not noticing several rolls were missing. He took one to town, telling Rosalee before he left, "Gotta take care of the real crooks. The government wants its share or they won't give me no peace."

Somehow, she knew what he meant: he would pay his fines and maybe slip an extra fifty-dollar bill to someone along the way, helping buy a little protection for next time. Joseph showed up in John's car and drove Samuel back to town, bringing a crate of whiskey-filled Mason jars with them. When Samuel came back, he bragged about all the people who did what he wanted, now that he knew how to play their game. She could only hope it would work, and the sheriff would stay away.

Chapter 28

SPRING, 1938

O ver the next few years, she watched as her sons grew into little boys, and she went through the motions of feeding and bathing them as if they were all in a dream. The boys looked into her eyes but saw no expression there. And so, wordless, their lives moved from one day into another as a wheel underwater.

Samuel went to do some work on his still in the cave. "They'll never find this one," he told Rosalee. Joseph helped him and came into the house when they were done, staring at Rosalee each time Samuel turned his attention elsewhere. The men wolfed down dinner afterward and went outside to shoot their pistols into the forest, aiming somewhere away from the new whiskey setup. Rosalee wondered what they might hit as they shot toward the trees, and then realized there was a *who* to think of. *She surely won't be in the woods behind our house,* she thought, and hoped.

Rosalee enjoyed Ezra as much as she could. He was easy to care for, always hugging Rosalee when he came into the room or found her outside, doing chores. He wanted to learn how to do everything she did, but Samuel warned her not to make a little girl out of his son, so she didn't let Ezra help her in the kitchen or with laundry. The boy appeared to understand Rosalee's predicament and whenever she told him no, he responded with sweetness.

When she wasn't doing chores inside the house or around the farm, and if Samuel was away for a while, Rosalee sat and tried to weave the St. Brigid's cross Bessie had taught her, though it was hard to remember the words to the song Bessie sang as she wove. Sometimes, Rosalee tried to recall all the most important songs her mother and aunt used to sing—during a birth, or while straining medicine into jars, or as they threw prayer dolls into the fireplace—but the words jumbled, the melodies faded.

Each time she worked on a prayer doll, she recounted the short list of joys she might hope for—miracles, one might call them—and threw the doll into the fire while her daydreams scattered like ashes onto the floor. But her prayers were not answered, and as she thought about the losses she had endured, she wondered whether they ever had been.

One April morning, nausea hit her as she rose out of bed, and Rosalee knew she was pregnant with another son. She asked herself if maybe this one would be a girl, but the women in her family never had morning sickness when they were pregnant with daughters. Thinking back to the last time she bled, she figured she was just over a month along. She told Samuel at supper, and he bragged to Jabez and Ezra, "You all are gonna be big brothers," before turning to Rosalee. "Look at you, about to be a mama again!"

Rosalee looked down at her plate. "It's a blessing," she said without believing it.

Samuel brought his mother to the house a couple of weeks later. He and John had been more careful about their whiskey business since the sheriff came around. They stopped selling in town and only sold to a handful of people they knew in the county. But their customers in Chicago couldn't get enough, and the stills were running all the time. The men hid jugs full of liquor in their stock barns and cellars, which held less and less of anything they could eat when hard times came.

After Samuel's arrest, Rosalee found out the sheriff had gone to her father's house first. The sheriff and his deputy couldn't find John's still, and both Joseph and Michael acted like they had never seen a drop of whiskey before. For her part, Barbara picked up the Bible and read passages in a quiet voice, but loud enough for the men of the law to hear her. Rosalee thought it was strange to choose between her father and her husband, but she was glad it was Samuel who had gone to jail.

On the day Samuel brought Barbara to check on Rosalee, Joseph came with them. Over dinner, Barbara talked about Joseph courting a girl in town, and how he was going to propose marriage soon. Joseph grinned at Rosalee and said, "I'm about to make her a happy woman," but Rosalee felt Samuel's eyes on her and kept her gaze fixed on the food. "I'll be happy to meet my new sister," she said with a smile, and turned her attention back to Ezra, making sure he ate everything on his plate.

"We'll build their house somewhere close, so they can get to the road when they need to," Samuel told her, and a chill ran through Rosalee as she realized Joseph would live closer to her—maybe within walking distance. *Maybe he'll be too wrapped up with this girl to look at me,* she thought. But each time she looked away from her plate or the children, she felt his eyes on her, and knew he wore the familiar slight smile.

"We'll be busy for a while," Samuel announced to the table. "Everybody's got to pull their weight around here, and you boys have to help your mama anytime she needs it." He looked at Jabez and Ezra, who nodded and waited for his unspoken permission to return to eating their dinners. Rosalee ventured to look at Samuel's face, and expected to see his wide grin. But his youthful arrogance had given way to concerns that lined his forehead.

The Great Depression kept dragging on. The palpable suffering that had taken hold of the country, and even much of the world, had seized the hills of Kentucky first and would stay there longer as an unwelcome guest. Samuel was determined not to become like so many city folk, desperate and uncertain during this time of lack. The Chicago gangsters were the only ones that knew what they were doing, he thought. And he was sure he was smarter than them.

Samuel kept buying food in town, but brought fewer gifts back for the boys and Rosalee. He still came home from each trip wearing a new suit and hat, and shiny shoes that didn't belong in the dirt of the farm. He put fewer rolls of money into his coffee cans than what he took out, emptying all but one that was no longer full.

He moved the coffee can out of the house and buried it in the woods one day, and Rosalee saw him but tried to hide the question in her eyes. "Times are lean, Rosie," Samuel told her after he came back into the house, his hands still dirty from burying the can. "Don't worry—I got it under control." They had never talked about the money, and Rosalee knew it wasn't hers to ask about, so she simply nodded and thought about their garden, smaller than ever, and how much fabric she had to make Jabez some new clothes.

"I'll be heading to the city tomorrow, and we'll be just fine. It's gonna be a big sale this time." Rosalee saw him as an unbothered young man for a fleeting moment, though his excitement did not reach his eyes. "Mama will stay with you for a couple days. I'll tell Michael to come get her. I'll see him tomorrow, when we go get your daddy."

Rosalee shivered and Samuel laughed a little. "You know how your daddy is, Rosie. Hard-headed man." Rosalee tried not to let shock show on her face. Samuel was the most stubborn man she had ever met, and she was sure he was harder to get along with than her father could ever be.

"It's alright," Samuel went on. "I know how to handle him. He don't like being told how to do things, but he's learning that I know this business better than he does."

Rosalee doubted Samuel knew as much as he thought he did, and a pang of sympathy for her father shot through her. John's gray hair and gaunt face suddenly appeared, clear as day. His face was all lines and quiet anger. The image dissolved into shadows but his blue eyes remained, piercing Rosalee's vision and asking a question about the curse Mary Ann and Bessie had invited upon his house.

Chapter 29

The day Samuel left to get John and Joseph and head to Chicago, Rosalee went to Irene's grave. The boys were old enough to leave alone for a while, but she worried Jabez would be too rough with Ezra while she was gone. Barbara would stay a couple more nights, which made Rosalee comfortable enough to ask for the time away. "Go on ahead," Barbara had told her. "But mind yourself." Rosalee knew what she meant: even though it had been years since Samuel found her in the woods, it would always be a concern.

As she stood there, she thought about Mary Ann and Bessie, and how no one had visited their graves for so long. She thought nobody would have touched the cup at the spring either, and even the creeks might feel lonesome by this point, with only the dead to visit them. Maybe Anna would have visited, though—she seemed like the sort of girl who would visit forest graves, even if she didn't know the people there. Rosalee realized with dismay that everything would have changed by now. The plants must have grown tall over her mama and aunt, the cup would have grown dingy from lack of use, and even Anna wouldn't be little anymore.

She turned toward the forest and considered whether she should walk through the woods for a bit. As she walked closer, she heard the trees whispering, inviting her in. The forest air reached out and caressed her arm. It was warm, unlike the air beside Irene's grave, which still ferried the cool spring dew. Stepping into the shadows, she heard a faint song drift from somewhere within the darkness.

"Rosalee!" Michael yelled as he ran through the field. "Rosalee, you've gotta come quick!"

His voice shook Rosalee from the spell, and she took a step away from the forest's edge. Michael stopped running when he reached her and breathless, he told her, "It's Daddy. Something happened." Rosalee could see a problem in Michael's eyes, but she knew he didn't want to speak it, and she wasn't sure she wanted to hear it. They rushed back to the house, passing Jabez and Ezra next to the pigpen, Rosalee aware of her pregnant belly feeling looser, somehow, than it had with the other babies.

Inside the house, Barbara was sitting at the kitchen table, her eyes red from crying. Joseph sat next to her, and the sheriff stood, facing them both. Rosalee stopped when she saw the sheriff and waited to hear what he had to say.

"Well, there you are," he said to her. "I'll let them tell you what happened, but your man will be locked away for longer this time. Good thing you got some family around here." Out of the corner of her eye, Rosalee saw Joseph nod and smile to himself.

"What's going on? Where's Samuel and Daddy?" she asked no one in particular. She looked at Barbara, who stared at the table just beyond her trembling hands. The sheriff walked out and drove away in the Ford he had parked in the yard.

"Your daddy's dead," Joseph told her, his voice flat. "Samuel shot him." Rosalee's stomach confirmed his words, and she thought she might vomit. "We were packing the car up, gettin' ready to leave, and Samuel made some smart-ass comment John didn't like." Joseph sighed. "They started yelling and John swung at him." Rosalee looked at him, waiting, not sure it was the truth.

"They both pulled their guns and Samuel just happened to be the one who made his shot." Joseph looked into her eyes. "Then we saw some cars coming down the road, and me and Samuel had to hide all our whiskey real quick, in case it was the cops. Sure enough," he continued as if telling an everyday story. "They came looking to bust us, but when they saw what Samuel did, they took him in and the sheriff brought us over here to tell Mama. Reckon I'll take one of your horses back."

Rosalee turned to Michael, who stood silent and stone-faced. He was eighteen years old now, and taller than she was. He was still thin, but his work on the farm had shaped him into a strong young man. His fists were clenched, and Rosalee could see him mentally calculating the steps it would take to get to Joseph. She put her hand on Michael's arm. Her thoughts flew too quickly to have one at a time. She searched his eyes and tried to tell him without speaking to *let this go, don't get yourself hurt*. He must have understood, because though his expression did not change, he unclenched his fists.

Rosalee turned to Barbara. "You've got to get Daddy laid out for the wake. Michael can stay here tonight and come get the wagon tomorrow. He'll bring us over so we can say goodbye." She waited for Barbara to respond, but the older woman sat as if she had been turned to stone. "Can you do it? You need help?" Rosalee asked her. Everyone sat in the silence for a moment, until somewhere outside, Jabez shouted and Ezra began to cry. Barbara jerked to her feet and told Joseph, "Take me home."

❀

Rosalee lay in the darkness that night, aware of Samuel's absence in a way she had never felt it before. He was in a jail cell, not in Lexington or Chicago doing things she didn't understand with people she would never meet, in places she might never get to see. Rosalee tried to imagine what a jail cell would feel like, and the thought of him in a cold, dark room made her smile at the moon. But she thought of her growing belly, the little bit of meat hanging in the smokehouse, and the boys, and she shuddered to think what might happen to them, alone.

Rosalee thought of her father and pictured him lying on the dirt behind his car. She imagined a lot of blood next to him, and then wondered if it was less blood, and how much of it had soaked into the earth beneath him before it pooled, drawing the dust upward at the rounded edge of the puddle. The earth would have been light brown, she thought, a spot worn by feet and hooves over the years, and now by wheels as well. He would be scowling, angry at having been outdrawn. And maybe in his last moment, his mind dredged memories of a time when women and girls sang songs and wove crosses and dolls in his house, locking him out of a world they somehow created under his very nose. His spirit would have left in a hurry, his pride wounded for the last time.

The next day, Rosalee and Michael rode horses along the trail back to John's farm. Ezra, holding on to the horse's mane, rode with his mother, while Jabez rode with his uncle, both of them proud to be as big as they were. Joseph had already dug a grave in the meadow, not knowing or caring where John might have wanted to be buried. Rosalee thought of pointing that out, but decided it was better this way—better than dragging them all to her forest haven, and better than having to take Barbara's body to be buried in the woods someday, too.

They spent a couple of hours in the house with John's body, where Barbara had prepared him and kept watch all night. As she and Barbara sang "Amazing Grace," and the boys kept a solemn watch, Rosalee wondered for the first time why her father hadn't insisted on burying her mother himself. She realized it was grief that kept him from asking about Mary Ann's grave, and resentment that kept him from wanting to find Bessie's. She thought about who she should tell where to bury her when the time came and tried to ignore Joseph's look, which he didn't try to hide from his mother.

Finally, Joseph hauled John's body out of the house and onto a cart he wheeled to the fresh grave. He and Michael shoveled dirt onto John's cold body and rolled a chunk of limestone over to serve as a headstone. Rosalee started to mention how they could buy a proper stone, but Barbara's eyes were empty, so she waited. After the burial, they all went inside to eat the soup beans and cornbread Barbara had fixed. She hadn't spoken a word to Rosalee since hearing the news of John's death, and as they sat there eating, Rosalee realized her mother-in-law might grieve more for her father than she could. Rosalee tried to figure out what emotions were churning within herself as she forced small bites of food into her mouth. She didn't eat because she was hungry, or because of the baby, but to give the impression she felt normal inside. Who might care, she wasn't sure. John's presence still lingered at the kitchen table, and Rosalee felt his disapproval of the women who raised her, and all they taught Rosalee, bearing down on her, heavy as ever. And Samuel—he took her father away, and got himself taken away. Neither loss would have caused her much heartache, but with a baby on the way, she needed her father or her husband.

Another thought stole into her mind: since John was dead, Barbara owned the farm. It would be Carter property from now on. Her sons would control it and then pass it along to their sons. Rosalee was a guest. And the quality of her life depended entirely on Barbara and her sons. With Samuel gone, Joseph would have control of the farm. The thought made Rosalee's heart skip, and the full weight of what had befallen her settled into her body. She saw the wild ginger and white willow tree in the forest, and something called her to come, though she was eager to get back to her horse and back to the place she called home.

"I'll be going to check on Samuel tomorrow," Joseph said, interrupting the silence. "I'll let you all know what I find out." Rosalee tried to thank him, but the words stuck in her throat, and she panicked at the thought of him coming to her house afterward, or at any time, with Samuel gone.

"Michael can come in a day or two and tell me the news," she offered, the worry in her voice apparent.

Joseph eyed her and smiled. "We'll figure it out, Rosie," he said. "Your little brother's got plenty to do on this here farm. Hogs to talk to and cows to play with." He laughed at his joke, as Michael stared at his untouched meal. Barbara stood up and took everyone's dishes, whether they had finished their food or not, and emptied the scraps into a bucket for the hogs.

"I'll take you all home now," Michael told her, and Rosalee took Ezra's hand and bade Jabez to follow them, relieved to get away.

Michael drove the wagon along the road, his eyes fixed just above the horse's head, but Rosalee could tell his mind was elsewhere.

"Where you at?" she asked him. She touched his arm, eager for her brother's warm smile, the best good thing she could think of.

Without looking at her, Michael responded, "You know Samuel had it out for Daddy." Rosalee sighed and moved her hand up to Michael's shoulder.

"There's never any telling what Samuel will do," she told him. "It wears me out, trying to figure out what he's gonna do and how he's gonna take things. I'm so glad I've still got you, little brother."

But Michael shrugged his shoulder away from Rosalee's hand.

"You could've tried," he told her. Rosalee paused, shocked by the weight of his words, by the ignorance he was fortunate to have. He knew nothing of what she had tried to do to keep Samuel happy, to manage his temper. He knew nothing of the pain she had endured, all because their father married her to an overgrown boy who thought himself a man.

But then again, she realized, there was no way for Michael to know what she had suffered. She had never told him, and no one else had, either. He was a boy, with much to learn. Rosalee softened, vowing to help him become a better man, somehow.

Rosalee wanted Michael to stay the night at her house and not leave until after Joseph came back from the jail the next day, but her brother insisted he had to get back to the farm. He would hardly look at her, and what was left of his little-boy manner had disappeared over the course of two days.

"I can't control Samuel—you have to know that," she pleaded with him.

"All I know is now I don't have any parents, and it's your husband's fault." Michael drove the wagon back and Rosalee sank into a chair, this new loss compounding with the others in a broken kaleidoscope. The boys chased each other outside, their shouts just noise to Rosalee.

After she got the children to bed, Rosalee sat in a rocking chair on the porch and listened to the spring peepers out at the farm pond. Their song spread as a chorus through the night sky, calls echoed and affirmed in a primordial story of creation. They sang of the coming rain and of salvation blooming, of the sweet, damp earth and her endless affection. The moon rose high and bright, and the air settled onto Rosalee's arms. Along the damp and quiet winds, the love-drunk frogs heard Rosalee's unsung lamentation, and trilled a lonesome hymn just for her.

Chapter 30

Joseph arrived on a warm day in May as Rosalee was hanging the laundry to dry. Jabez was slopping the hogs while Ezra watched, and then the boys went to tend seedlings in the garden. Rosalee tried to ignore the knot that formed in her stomach as Joseph pulled into the yard in John's car, sending small plumes of dust into the air behind it. Rosalee pulled a sheet loose from the clothespins to wash it again.

He hopped out of the car, and Rosalee watched him stride behind the house. He disappeared into the woods for a little while, and when he came back out, he carried a dirty coffee can. He held it up and showed Rosalee. "Found it right where Samuel said it'd be." He walked toward her, and Rosalee busied herself with the laundry. Joseph walked closer and stood a few feet away, silent, with the coffee can hanging by his side. "What, you don't care?" he asked with feigned concern. "Your man's gone to jail and he's probably going to prison." He took a step closer and in a hushed voice, told her, "Who knows how long he'll be gone."

Rosalee moved away from him and hung a flour-sack dress on the line, trying to hide the fact that her hands were shaking as she pinned it. Joseph sidled closer to her with a look that reminded her of Samuel. "I bet you're gonna be lonely while my brother's gone. And my new wife-to-be ain't here for a while yet. Not 'til her birthday." He grasped her arm above the elbow, and Rosalee whirled toward him with fire in her eyes, but said nothing. Joseph smirked. "How about you feed me some dinner," he told her, and walked into the house.

After she finished hanging the laundry and rewashing the dust-covered sheet, Rosalee called the boys to come into the house with her. She fixed plates of fried chicken and greens for everyone, and though the pregnancy had whetted her hunger, she nibbled at her food as the others ate. Joseph lingered at the table after he finished his meal, and told the boys to go finish their chores when they were done eating. The boys went outside and Rosalee bustled around the kitchen, cleaning and hoping Joseph's attention would be pulled elsewhere. He opened the coffee can and counted the money on the table.

"Three thousand dollars, Rosie—how about that!" He looked at her out of the corner of his eye. "This is enough to take care of my brother and have some fun in the meantime." Joseph laughed, and Rosalee pretended not to hear him. He stood up, scraping his chair against the floor, and walked up behind Rosalee at the sink, pressing himself against her. She reached into the soapy water for a knife she knew was in there, not sure whether she could stab him or what would happen if she tried, but certain she couldn't let him do whatever he wanted. She found the handle and almost grasped it, but Joseph grabbed her upper arms, pulling them toward him, and the knife fell out of her hand. "We could have some fun, couldn't we."

Rosalee tried to jerk her arms away, but Joseph tightened his grip and held her where she stood. "Don't try to play with me, Rosie," he told her. "I know you want it." He lifted her skirt up and tugged on her underwear, trying to pull it down, and Rosalee flung around, smacking his face. Joseph touched his cheek where she hit him, and the skin turned bright red. Rosalee braced herself, certain he would hit her, but Joseph smiled and spun her around to face away from him. He tore the seams in her underwear this time and pressed her belly against the sink as he forced his way into her. "Please," she whispered, but there was no telling whether he heard her or not.

She scanned the room around her for anything she could reach—a skillet, a glass—something to help balance the power he had over her. She found nothing, though, and Rosalee sent her mind elsewhere, somewhere in the forest where this was not happening.

Rosalee gave a little cry when she felt him inside her, and as he pushed against her over and over, Rosalee's thoughts darted to her boys, and then to Samuel, before dissolving into an ocean with too much salt. She tried to call out *Mama* but only whimpered, her eyes squeezed shut against what was happening.

When Joseph was finished, he laid his forehead against her shoulder. "You're as good as I thought you'd be," he panted. His sweat left her shirt damp, and Rosalee felt something else trickle down her thighs. When Joseph finally walked outside in satisfaction, she vomited into the sink and onto the dishes she had been washing.

⚜

Her hands shook as she cleaned herself. Rosalee wandered around the house in a daze, trying to find something to do but unable to pick one thing. When the boys came inside, she tried to pretend everything was normal, but Jabez looked at her with reproach, and Ezra with concern, so Rosalee knew she was failing to hide her anguish. Joseph walked into the house whistling, and Rosalee dropped into a chair by the fireplace, where she started to sew a gown for the new baby, her hands too uncertain to thread the needle.

Joseph sat down in the chair next to her, and Rosalee tried to conceal her repulsion. "Rosie, I'm gonna move you and the boys to live with Mama. My brother's gonna be away for a while, even with the payoff I'm deliverin' for him." He patted his bulging pocket, where he had stuffed most of the cash from the coffee can. "There's no sense in building a new house for me and my new wife now." Rosalee understood which words he left unspoken: *now that your father is dead.*

207

"This way, you'll have Mama to help you when the new baby comes. Your boys can help Michael on the farm." He leered at her. Rosalee sat in silence, unsure whether she should speak, or could speak. Joseph didn't wait for her to answer. "I'll be back in a few days to move your stuff over. I'm puttin' boxes on the porch for you to pack in. Get everything ready." He stood up and started to walk away but stopped and looked back at her. Rosalee met his eyes for the first time since she hit him at the sink. "I might be able to get him out in a year with this." Joseph patted his pocket again. "But I'll be holding on to some of it. And don't worry—I plan to take good care of you while he's gone."

With one last grin, Joseph turned and left, tousling the boys' hair as he walked out. They ran into the yard to watch him spin away, throwing clouds of dust onto the clothes hanging on the lines again, and into their hair.

No matter what she did in the next few days, Rosalee felt Joseph inside her, an unwanted guest who had somehow made her body his own. She felt the baby within her, too, though it was still early for him to move. During the day, Rosalee darted from the kitchen to the porch, and then to the garden and the barns, trying to accomplish her chores— any chore—but her thoughts scattered like dandelion seeds flying on the breeze, lost to any purpose. She tried to pack their belongings into the boxes Joseph had brought, and she started several boxes with clear purpose, but abandoned each of them before they were half-full. When the boys weren't looking, she fished her Mason jar out from under the floorboard and stuffed the money into the dress she would wear on the day they moved.

Sometimes, her sons watched her with a closeness unusual for their ages, and Rosalee's breath caught in her throat when she wondered if they somehow knew what had happened. Worse yet, perhaps they blamed her.

She scoured her memory for anything she might have done to invite Joseph toward her, but only recalled turning away to avoid the look in his eyes, which revealed he was helping himself to her, first through his imagination alone. She thought of how she had slapped him—maybe she should have hit him harder. *Could she have hit him harder? Would he have still smiled? What would he have done next?*

It was too much, then, the weight of Joseph's violence, of Samuel's violence. Rosalee wept to think of what was inside her now—too much. For days, she relived it all, a cascade of pain written into her body's memory.

Rosalee made a tea from the buttercups growing beneath her bedroom window and drank it in the morning, one day before Joseph was supposed to return. She tried to think of how much she should drink, reaching back into her memories of conversations between Bessie and other women, but she couldn't find that knowledge, if she ever had it. She drank several cups and said a prayer with each one. By midafternoon, she had to lie down in bed, after running to the outhouse several times. Ezra came to check on her and brought her some water, which she gulped down and then vomited into a bucket next to the bed. Her throat burned, but the feeling of being emptied comforted her—it was the only comfort to be had.

Rosalee fell into a fevered sleep, her dreams vivid and unrelenting as she sweated and soaked the bedclothes. Mary Ann and Bessie appeared before her first, both urgently trying to warn her of something, but no sound came from their lips. Frightened by the panic in their eyes, Rosalee reached out toward them and the dream changed. She was a child again, sitting next to Bessie's rocking chair, playing with a braided doll. *I wish to have a hundred babies,* she said, thinking it would please her aunt, but Bessie looked at her with an expression Rosalee didn't have words for yet: Pity? Concern? Rosalee threw the doll into the fire, and when she looked back to Bessie, Irene sat there instead, watching her with cold disapproval. Suddenly, Irene was at the door, yelling at someone, and she turned back toward her husband inside the house and screamed at him, hit him on the chest over and over, and finally collapsed onto the floor in exhaustion. Rosalee stood next to Irene and tried to figure out how to help her mamaw, but Irene reached up and grasped her arm, and pulled Rosalee down into a new darkness, where Rosalee began to know terror.

She awoke, gasping for breath and soaked with sweat, her clothes and sheets twisted around her. The room tilted and spun, almost alluring in its strangeness. But as her mind returned to the waking world, Rosalee realized she was lying in something sticky, and she turned over onto her hands and knees, not ready to stand. Where she had lain, the bed was soaked crimson with blood. The metallic smell hit her nostrils and she fought the nausea away, frightened the vomiting might make whatever was happening to her even worse.

When she untangled herself from the bedclothes and her clinging dress, Rosalee realized where the blood was coming from. She pulled some flannel and clean underwear from her drawer and cleaned herself as best she could. She folded the bedclothes into a pile and called for Ezra to bring her a clean bucket. He brought it to her and met her panicked look with a solemn expression. As he turned away and shut the door behind him, Rosalee heard the first pattering drops of a spring storm hit the tin roof. She labored in her room as the sky darkened early and thunder rumbled in the distance. Lightning flew across the sky, and Rosalee looked for it when her eyes weren't squeezed shut or blurred by tears or sweat.

A bolt of lightning struck somewhere on the farm, and thunder cracked the sky as Rosalee's body heaved once more, nearly finished now. She heard moaning and a low, guttural sound, like the wailing animals sometimes made as they gave birth or died. As her racing heartbeat slowed and her breath returned to normal, Rosalee realized the sounds were hers, though she couldn't have been inside her body as they happened. She started to clean herself but shook too much to grasp even her clothes, so she lay back down on Samuel's side of the bed, curled herself like an infant, and whimpered until she fell back asleep. One last thought followed her into the darkness: *the boys can feed themselves.*

Rosalee awoke to find the green light of spring pouring through her bedroom window, still saturated with the ardent waters of the retreating storm. She changed out of her clothes once more and sat in front of the mirror. A young woman stared back at her with tired eyes that had deepened in the last eight years. Her innocence had given way to a new understanding—knowledge of a darkness that does not pervade the forest, but the home. Her eyes spoke of a new kind of wildness, not one with tangled roots or vines, or pompous blossoms in the field, daring the rest of the world to drink in their nectar.

Her father's austerity hadn't prepared her for a husband like Samuel, or a man like Joseph, who were all want and arrogance and temper. Her kinship with the whispering woods and sacrificial flowers had not taught her how to suffer and had shown her nothing about the cruelty of men.

But the green light of spring reflected in the mirror as well, streaming into the room behind her as if it could wash away the blood and heartache, and Rosalee believed it was a sign of hope.

Chapter 31

Michael and Joseph arrived with a wagon and loaded Rosalee and Samuel's belongings. Rosalee cringed as Joseph tossed her boxes of dolls and the cedar chest onto the pile without care, but she said nothing, certain he would not handle criticism any better than his brother did.

"How we movin' all the animals?" Michael asked Joseph.

"We're not," he snorted in response. "These'uns will stay here and be *my* farm animals now." Michael and Rosalee exchanged a look. "What, you think you're the only ones who know how to run a farm?" Joseph asked, not waiting for an answer. "It ain't that damn hard, if a little kid and a woman can do it. Don't worry, you can take your horses and I'll bring mine over here." As he walked off to survey his new farm, Rosalee tried to think of a way to take her other favorite animals with her, though it seemed unjust to leave any of them under Joseph's care.

Michael said little as they packed, and Rosalee caught him glowering at Joseph's back sometimes. Joseph hardly looked at Rosalee, but every time he passed by her to load something else on the wagon, she flinched and planned a way to get away from him if he tried to touch her. No one seemed to notice her discomfort, so she was left to grapple with her racing heartbeat without having to explain it away.

"Could you load the desk up next?" she asked Michael, but Joseph stopped him.

"There ain't room on the wagon for that. I might let you have it later, if I don't want it." Rosalee nodded, knowing his word was final. When Michael and Joseph went back outside, Rosalee put the key to the desk next to the wall behind one of the legs, where no one would see it.

She hadn't told anyone about the lost baby, and since her belly hadn't grown to the point of showing through her clothes, no one thought to ask what had changed. Whatever Ezra thought he saw, he never mentioned it again. She couldn't get all of the bedclothes washed before the move, so she had stuffed them into a large basket and placed a clean quilt on top of them, meaning to wash them when she got to her father's house. She rode there in the wagon next to Michael, both of them silent, each preoccupied with their own muddled thoughts. When they arrived, Jabez and Ezra scrambled down, and Michael offered Rosalee his hand to guide her from the wagon.

Inside the house, Barbara sat in a rigid mourning dress, a dim fire glowing in the fireplace as she worked on yet another piece of sewing. The curtains were drawn and an oil lamp flickered on the kitchen table, so shadows now dominated the house, no longer constrained to neglected corners. Even though spring had fully enlivened the outside world, the house embodied Barbara's grief and John's anger. An endless, bitter winter had taken hold within.

Joseph either didn't notice or wasn't bothered by the pain penetrating everyone and everything within the house. He walked in, whistling and dropping boxes in what had been Barbara's bedroom.

"We're moving you to the small bedroom, and the boys will stay in Michael's room. I'm putting Samuel and Rosalee in the big bedroom. I know it's what he'd want." Joseph grinned at his mother, and she nodded without looking at him. Rosalee dreaded being in her father's bedroom, and wished she could take her childhood bedroom instead of Barbara going there, but then Joseph added, "I've had your old bedroom since you and Samuel moved out, Rosalee. Sure am gonna miss it.

I'll sleep in the living room 'til I get moved to my new house, though." He waited to see how Rosalee would respond, and she nodded, knowing he would watch her until he got some kind of reaction.

After he walked out, Rosalee went to her room and unpacked her dolls, setting them back in their place on top of the cedar chest. Though they didn't bring her the same excitement she felt when opening them, they had come to feel like companions, of sorts, almost like her favorite chickens. She could tell them anything.

Rosalee went back into the living room and sat in the chair next to Barbara. She waited for the right moment to speak, but it never came. "I'm glad we'll be here with you," she offered, and she was pleased to find she mostly meant the words as she spoke them. When Barbara looked up, Rosalee saw her expression was more severe than ever before, as if she was fighting against her own sorrow, armed with nothing but helpless anger. Rosalee started to ask herself how this woman could reconcile her son killing her husband, and she wanted to ponder how similar their positions were, but decided those questions would wait for another day, a day when taking her next breath didn't feel like such work.

They ate supper quietly, Rosalee hushing the boys anytime they elbowed each other or started to argue. Michael ate without looking at anyone, but Joseph watched Rosalee when he wasn't looking at his food.

"Me and Bethany will get married in a fortnight," he told the table. He looked at Rosalee. "She don't have as much fight in her as you do, but I expect you'll get along."

Rosalee's face burned and she was grateful the room was poorly lit, though no one but Joseph seemed interested in his unexplained comment. "She sounds lovely," Rosalee said too quickly. She didn't want to respond to his last statement, but couldn't ignore him completely without drawing attention. Joseph kept looking at her, while she pretended to be focused on her next bite of food.

"Us men are gonna be outnumbered for a while." He flashed a grin at Michael, and then nodded to Jabez and Ezra. "I'm gonna have to teach these two how to run a farm while their daddy's in jail." Rosalee stiffened at the thought of Joseph with her sons. Jabez and Ezra smiled back at him, though, and joked around until Rosalee shooed them away from the table to help Michael with the evening chores. Barbara's expression hadn't changed and she had hardly eaten. Michael left the table without acknowledging anyone, and Rosalee tried to stand up and leave right after him, but Joseph reached out and grabbed her wrist before she could.

Her pulse thumped in her ears and her vision blurred as she tried to speak. Joseph beat her to it. "I want you to get my house ready for her," he said. "You can get settled in here first." With that, he let go of her wrist, and Rosalee stood and walked away, flushed again.

When a week had passed, Barbara reminded Rosalee over breakfast that she needed to go help Joseph get the house ready for his new bride. Rosalee nodded in agreement and went outside to find Michael. He spent most of his time with the animals, as he always had, and even slept outside much of the time, so Rosalee hardly saw him, though they were living together again. "The boy's just about gone feral," Barbara said when they tried to find him to come eat. "He won't even talk to anybody but the animals these days." Rosalee thought she could understand why Michael had preferred the company of the animals the past several years, but it stung to realize he wasn't eager for her company, either.

She found him outside the tobacco barn, trying to coax a heifer to come back to the stock barn where she belonged. "Michael!" He pretended not to hear her and continued petting the cow, who had recently given birth to her first calf. Rosalee ignored the pain in her abdomen. She hadn't walked this far since before losing the baby. "Michael?" she asked, her throat filling with the pain of loneliness. "I need you to come back to my old house with me and Joseph." She tried to say it without emotion, but her voice wavered when she spoke her brother-in-law's name.

"I'm too busy here, Rosalee. I'm already behind from helping you move. And another heifer's gonna give birth any day now. I can't leave her." Michael turned around to look at Rosalee. Her face splotched red as she fought back tears, and they hung just at the brim of her eyelids, ready to spill.

"Please," she whispered.

Michael studied her for a moment. "Alright, then," he said as he turned back to the new mother. "I'll be up at the house in a little bit and we can leave right after dinner." Rosalee tried to thank him, but she knew her voice would betray her if she spoke. She turned away and walked back to the house, eyeing the forest where Mary Ann and Bessie slept.

She wanted to find Samuel in his jail cell and punish him. She wanted to make *him* bear a child and watch as his control over his body and life ebbed like an ocean she would never see. She wanted to hurt Joseph for invading her, and she wanted to force both men to see what had come of it all, how their reckless ways brought so much pain.

Surely her mother and aunt had wanted better for her. She saw Mary Ann's eyes, full of tender care and comfort. How would she have responded to a man like Samuel? How would she have survived? Rosalee didn't know.

She saw Bessie's gray eyes, bright as they had been as a young girl. Everyone who met Bessie thought she was haughty or aloof, depending on their own heart's afflictions. But Rosalee had often seen what few others did: the slight smile twitching at the corner of her lips when she was amused by her own thoughts, and how her eyes narrowed when she listened to someone *tell tales*. Bessie chose the life of a spinster, loving only Rosalee as much as she might have loved her own child. *She wouldn't have put up with any of this*, Rosalee thought. *She didn't*. But

Rosalee wasn't given the chance to make Bessie's choice, which had once seemed so lonely but now looked like freedom to Rosalee.

They made the trip to her old house, and Rosalee worked inside while Michael helped Joseph outside. She put away the dishes Joseph had brought from John's house, including some plates Rosalee had eaten from as a child. They were cream colored, with a ring of blue flowers around the edge and a blue bouquet in the center. She thought of the countless meals served on those plates, and the warm conversations that occurred over them. Even John's sullen withdrawal was nostalgic, now that Rosalee had experienced something so different, so aggressive.

She dusted the old desk and retrieved the key from behind the leg, opening it once again. The rose scent lofted to the air, so faded now, and Rosalee knew it was the last time anyone would smell it. Tiny, brittle corners of the lost letters lay decaying in the drawer, nearly impercep-tible. Rosalee stood there looking at the last of those fragments, and then pulled the drawer out and carried it outside, where she held it upside down and brushed the last of the letters away, letting them fall to the ground.

Back inside, Rosalee made her way through every room. She washed the bedclothes and put clean quilts on what had been Jabez and Ezra's bed, as well as the bed Barbara had slept in, and Irene before her, and her own father as a child before that. She lingered at her old bedroom door, thinking about what had just happened inside the room a little over a week ago. She was afraid she would find bloodstains on the wood floorboards, or maybe even a ruined sheet she had forgotten to take with her. But the room was empty of any sign of her suffering.

As Rosalee made the bed, she said a quick prayer for the young woman who would lie there with Joseph. *Maybe he will be gentle with her,* she hoped. Somehow, it seemed possible. After she hung new curtains and swept the floor, Rosalee paused once more in the doorway and thought about everything that had happened there. She recalled her virginal indignation and scoffed to think Samuel had once shown so much patience, or perhaps just so much self-control. She remembered the taste of blood on her lip and touched her mouth instinctively, but there was no blood now—and she had bled so much in that room.

Those memories slipped farther away each day, like a notch on a tree trunk diminishes, its edges growing less defined as the wind and rain soften them, until the mark becomes some lonesome call to the past, an embodiment of intent and force outliving the person who conceived it.

"You missin' your man?" Rosalee jumped at the sound of Joseph's voice in her ear, and she wheeled around to find him so close, she could feel his breath. "I'll take you to go see him soon," he told her with a laugh. "Can't have you heartbroken and pining for my brother, can I?"

Rosalee rushed past him and found Michael outside, where she lingered until it was time to leave. She knew she had to go see Samuel—it was expected of her. But she couldn't be alone with Joseph, not for long. She would have to convince Michael to go with her, yet again.

But two days later, when Joseph showed up with the car and told her they were going to the jail, Michael refused. "I've got too much to do here," he told Rosalee. She knew he sensed her desperation, but maybe he was also filled with a kind of desperation. Maybe he wasn't ready to look at the man who murdered their father. Rosalee wasn't sure she was ready, either, but since he also happened to be her husband, she realized she didn't have much choice.

Rosalee then asked Barbara in the most gentle way she could, whether she would want to go visit her son. Barbara just kept sewing in the dim light of the fireplace she insisted on keeping lit, even though the warmth and light of late spring had permeated the house. Barbara didn't know it was spring outside, or that the Kentucky sun shone all around her, the days lengthening in their steady march to the summer solstice. John had been a good husband. Her shock at his death, and the manner of it, had contorted into an unbearable burden of denial and grief. Her hair had turned fully white within a week, and she said little to anyone, other than to insist they let her fire burn uninterrupted.

"Let's go," Joseph told her, and Rosalee asked if the boys should go with them to see their daddy. Joseph scoffed. "There ain't enough room for them." They went outside to the car, and Rosalee saw the boys join Michael at the pigpen. She took a deep breath and fumbled with the door handle, which she didn't know how to open, until Joseph leaned over and opened it from the inside. She lowered herself onto the passenger seat and started to look around at all the parts.

"Come on, Rosie, I ain't got all day," Joseph chastised her. "Shut the damn door." She pulled the door shut and Joseph sped away from the house, bouncing over rocks and through potholes in the dirt road. She wanted to enjoy riding in the car, but the novelty felt trivial by now, and being confined next to Joseph made it hard for Rosalee to take a full breath.

She was convinced Samuel never planned to let her ride in the car, and maybe meant to never see her leave the farm for any reason. She thought about all the excuses he had made over the years. When the babies were little, she didn't expect to travel. And the one time he asked her to go with him, it wasn't safe. But when they grew older, each time Rosalee had asked to join him on the trip to town for supplies, he made an excuse either then or at the last minute as to why she couldn't come. Most of the time, he would be busy doing business with men in town, and it wasn't right for a woman to be involved. And then there were the dances he had spoken of, trips to Lexington or even Cincinnati, *fancier than you'd ever dream of, Rosie*. As the years passed and the trips never happened, as the dresses went out of fashion, unused and unneeded, Rosalee realized he would never take her on such a trip, and she would never see the bright city lights or its bustle and beauty.

For a moment, her thoughts blurred like the landscape they drove past, and the car seemed to float through the curves as Joseph maneuvered without slowing down. Rosalee looked around in curiosity until she caught Joseph grinning at her, and turned her gaze back to the world outside her window, the barns and farmhouses disappearing behind them. She imagined seeing Samuel, and her heart raced like the car, out of control.

Once they were inside the jail, a deputy showed them to a small room with a table and two chairs, which sat on opposite sides of the table. Joseph motioned for Rosalee to sit in one of the chairs, and he leaned against the wall behind her. The deputy brought Samuel in, looking disheveled and with a light yellow bruise around his right eye, his hands cuffed in front of him. Rosalee gasped as he sat down.

"Don't worry, little wife," he told her. "You should see the other guy. They had to stitch him up pretty good after I was done with him."

"Are you—are you okay?" she asked.

"Good as a man could be, in a place like this," he told her. "How's my mama doing?"

Rosalee stumbled over her words. "She, she's okay, I reckon. I mean, my daddy—" Her heartbeat quickened as Samuel waited to hear what she was going to say, his expression a mixture of amusement and contempt. "I think she misses Daddy," Rosalee finished. She wanted to say more: *How could you do that to my father? What right do you think you have?* But she thought instead of the spring and the forest. She let them pull her attention back to the farm, where her children were helping Michael with the animals, and where she would soon smell the open air, far from this jail.

"Looks like I'll be here for a while," Samuel said, turning his attention to Joseph. "Might not get shipped off to prison, thanks to my little brother." He looked back at Rosalee. "Probably be here for about a year, maybe less if I get good behavior." He laughed and winked his bruised eye. "Ain't likely, though."

Rosalee knew he wanted her to respond. "We'll sure miss you," she said, hoping it sounded sincere. "We'll come visit you when we can."

Samuel shook his head. "You don't need to be traveling in your condition." Rosalee flushed, and he thought it was from her sense of propriety. He continued, "Just take care of my boys and my mama, and I'll be home soon enough. Joseph's got some money to provide for you all while I'm locked up."

Joseph took a couple of steps forward, standing so close to Rosalee's back, she could feel the heat from his body. He chimed in, "I got it all under control, don't you worry. I'm gonna take good care of everybody while you're gone." He put a hand on Rosalee's shoulder and she shuddered. When she looked at Samuel, he was staring at his brother and grinning, his eyes filled with the same expression she had come to recognize as his most dangerous.

"Don't take too good of care, now," he warned. "Seems to me like you all are awfully close. I want my wife to miss me while I'm gone." Joseph moved his hand off of Rosalee and stepped away from her, and though she couldn't see his face, Rosalee heard the mockery in his voice when Joseph replied with a sneer, "Of course, big brother. She pines for you day and night, I swear. She's always missing you something awful."

Samuel turned his attention back to Rosalee. "I bet she is. But you'll be a good wife while I'm gone, won't you, Rosie?" Like a rabbit caught between two hounds, Rosalee wished for a way out, some escape from the two men and their penetrating eyes.

Chapter 32

SUMMER, 1938

O n the day of his wedding, Joseph drove the car into the yard, scattering a flock of chickens. He jumped out with a wide grin and ran to the passenger door, opened it, and scooped up his bride-to-be. Bethany laughed with delight and insisted he put her down so they could walk to the front door of his mama's house like decent people.

Rosalee watched from the kitchen window, and whispered another quick prayer for the girl, who looked to be maybe fifteen years old, at best. The girl still had one foot in her childhood, though she was called a woman now, and Rosalee realized she had also been innocent and naive when she was married off. They were women in one sense alone, and Rosalee began to understand the women who had come before her, how their childhoods ended before any of them were ready. Rosalee greeted them at the door and smiled with as much enthusiasm as she could muster. Bethany curtsied in her handmade dress—it was a hand-me-down, with worn bows at the shoulders. Her shoes looked to be a size too big, but they had been polished and cared for meticulously, and clearly had served as the dress shoes for each girl in her family before reaching her. Rosalee started to ask herself why Joseph hadn't paid for her to have a nice wedding dress and new shoes—surely he had made about as much money as Samuel had—but she suspected he liked his young bride to be aware of how little she brought to the marriage, and how dependent she would be on him for everything.

Rosalee caught her breath when she took in Bethany's face, though. The girl's skin was flawless, and her perfect teeth conveyed a picture of health Rosalee had only seen in catalogs. Sunshine glittered on the lightest strands of Bethany's hair, and for a moment, a halo shimmered around her, the radiance from her smile and the sunlight playing together.

Rosalee showed her in, and Joseph went to set up the chairs with Michael. Some of their family and the preacher would arrive soon for the simple outdoor wedding. Barbara sat next to the fireplace, sewing and moving her lips as if she was talking to someone. Her lips were moving every time Rosalee looked at her these days, but Barbara hardly ever spoke unless spoken to, and sometimes she didn't even speak then.

"Mother, this is Bethany, your new daughter-in-law." Barbara nodded, not looking away from her sewing.

"Pleased to meet you, ma'am," Bethany said as she curtsied again. Rosalee noticed Bethany smiled at Barbara with innocent joy, and she felt a pang of envy that the girl hadn't been there for all the sorrows that had unfolded over the years. *She might have sorrows of her own,* Rosalee realized and ushered the girl to her bedroom, where Rosalee would help her get ready for the wedding. Rosalee shut the door behind them and turned around to find Bethany's eyes glistening with tears.

"You're not supposed to cry on your wedding day," Rosalee told her. "Don't you know it's bad luck?" She said it in a light tone, trying to make a joke, but worried she knew the reason for Bethany's tears. The girl surprised her, though, when she said, "I just wish I had something nice to wear. I'm the youngest girl and Mama passed away before me and Joseph started courtin', and times have been hard. Daddy couldn't afford a new dress." She looked down at her shoes and took a deep breath. "I know Joseph loves me anyway, and I shouldn't be vain. It's one of the worst sins, you know. I just want to look pretty for my wedding." She smiled at Rosalee, who didn't know which of Bethany's statements to respond to first, so she didn't say anything. She felt a duty to warn this girl about what might lie ahead of her, but she brushed the notion aside and decided to focus on the day at hand.

"Where you from?" Rosalee asked, trying to make small talk.

"My people's over in Elliott County," Bethany told her. "I was the baby of the family, so Daddy was glad to finally see me out of the house," she said with a laugh. "But Joseph promised he'd drive me back home as much as I want, so I can see my older sisters and their babies. They all live close to Daddy," she explained.

Rosalee smiled at her happiness, but thought about her years on the farm, and doubted Joseph would ever make an effort to take his wife back home. This girl was at least forty miles away from anyone who knew or loved her, Rosalee realized with a pang.

She opened her wardrobe, where she had hung all of her dresses since moving back to her childhood home. Samuel's dress clothes were still packed in boxes she had pushed under the bed. Bethany gasped. "Look at those! I bet you look like a movie star when you wear them."

Rosalee gave a little smile. "I doubt it. But I've still got my wedding dress in here, and I wasn't much bigger than you when I made it. If it fits and you like it, you're more'n welcome to wear it." She pulled the dress out, and Bethany beamed with pleasure. "It's perfect," she said, touching the fabric. "Are you sure you wouldn't mind?"

Rosalee hesitated, wondering if the dress might bring bad luck, but decided Bethany's happiness wouldn't depend on the dress, and it could at least make this one day a happy one. The dress almost fit Bethany, and Rosalee sewed a few quick stitches to bring it in. "I didn't have no good shoes to wear," Rosalee apologized. "But yours will do just fine."

Bethany threw her arms around Rosalee. "I can tell we're going to be so close. You're already such a good sister to me!" Rosalee stiffened at first, not used to being touched by anyone other than Ezra, who still wanted to be hugged and kissed before bed. She put her arms around Bethany's shoulders, and tears sprang to her eyes as relief washed over her. She hadn't felt that kind of affection for so long—the kind of affection not needing or wanting anything in return—and didn't realize until this moment just how much she missed it. The thought of having a younger sister with whom she could laugh and talk and work—something she had wanted as a young girl with older brothers—thrust her into the sweetness of childhood for an instant, before fluttering back into the deepest reaches of memory.

"I'm sure you're right," Rosalee murmured, and she tried to think only of that possible future while Bethany sat in front of her mirror, letting Rosalee fix her hair.

Everybody left after the wedding supper, and Joseph drove his new bride to their home. They had both smiled the whole day, and Rosalee wondered if Samuel's smile had looked as loving and innocent as Joseph's did on their wedding day. She had been too angry to smile, and Samuel's happiness—if that's what it was—had felt like a mockery to her. She asked herself whether he had loved her, or whether he could love anyone, but pushed those thoughts aside, glad she would not have to look at the deepening malice in his eyes for a while yet.

In the days after the wedding, Joseph drove Bethany back to Rosalee's to ask for a little butter or some lye for the wash. Bethany still beamed with new love, and she blushed anytime Joseph looked at her. She and Rosalee made plans to visit in a week, and as the newlyweds left, Rosalee thought their marriage might truly be favored. Maybe whatever had inspired Joseph's roughness with her couldn't exist with Bethany. Maybe Joseph's nature had changed when he got married and committed himself before the eyes of God and man. Regardless of what might explain it, Rosalee was grateful to think the marriage would be good for everyone.

Over the next couple of weeks, Rosalee fell into a new routine at her childhood home. Her boys helped Michael with farm chores, and he slowly warmed back up to Rosalee. Michael's easygoing nature reminded Rosalee of the boy she still thought him to be, but his eyes revealed he had become a man, and John's death had forever altered his path.

Even though Joseph was supposed to be taking care of the family, he borrowed food and took chickens and pigs to replace what died on his farm, more than he provided anything. Rosalee realized even with the large garden she planted and the healthy livestock Michael raised, winter would be lean without any contribution from Joseph. If the weather turned bad or the animals got sick, they would be lost. She tried to ask him about the moonshine and whiskey business one time, and he responded with such venom, she knew he couldn't have the same success his brother had, but he would never admit it. He complained to no one in particular about how it was just him now, running a three-man show, but with as much time as he spent at the still in the cave and how little whiskey he brought home, Rosalee wondered whether he knew what he was doing. *Maybe he'll drink the stuff you're supposed to throw out and poison himself,* she thought. But he was more likely to go blind and be dependent on them for the rest of his life, so she tried to take back her wish.

She pulled twenty-dollar bills from the hidden Mason jars about twice a month and sent Michael to town for flour, sugar, and some canned goods. Michael was to buy homegrown as much as possible. She hid away the extra food, rotating the purchased jars with her own jars as she put them up. She made Michael swear to tell the storekeeper he made the money selling hogs, so no one in town would wonder where all that money came from, in case they got too curious. Every time she handed him a bill, Michael looked at Rosalee with greater understanding of how she must have gotten that money, until the day she realized the chasm between them had closed, and he trusted her once again.

Barbara still helped with the house chores, though Rosalee noticed the wash wasn't always rinsed before Barbara hung it on the line, and sometimes the food she cooked wasn't quite done or ended up burnt. Rosalee watched and intervened when she could, asking the older woman to help with a different chore so as to never draw attention to her mistakes. She was slow to respond and hardly ever acknowledged when someone spoke to her, so Rosalee thought Barbara might be losing her hearing, if not her wits.

Barbara continued to insist she make Rosalee's pregnancy tonic, though. Rosalee turned away and gave a vague assent each time her mother-in-law reminded her to take it, not sure whether Barbara could see the lie on her face or if she could tell Rosalee's belly and breasts were no longer growing. She figured she would drink the tonic and keep that question at bay for as long as she could, though the question of how she would explain her lost baby began to nag at her. If she kept waiting to tell them the pregnancy was over, it would be past the normal time for such a thing to happen. But for some reason, she wasn't ready to tell anyone. Thinking about the baby conjured up the image of her kitchen sink: how she had gripped it as Joseph pushed her forward, how she vomited into it and there was no one to clean up afterward but her. She shook the question from her mind and again welcomed the warm nights of late May, sitting on the porch and listening for the whippoorwill's first song so she could cast her wish to the sky.

One day, a few weeks after the move, Rosalee was hanging laundry to dry, thinking it was time to go visit her mama and Bessie in the woods. In the distance, the sound of a car engine carried over the wind, and Rosalee watched as it appeared on the road, coming down over a small hill where the land met the sky. It wasn't Joseph's car—or was the car Samuel's, now that John was gone? She expected it to pass the entrance to their farm, but the driver veered left onto the dirt road leading to the house.

She was only a little concerned about who might be in the car. It wasn't the sheriff, and Samuel was already locked up, anyway. The all-black Model T stopped at a respectful distance from the house and the laundry line.

The car door opened and a young man stepped out. He looked to be about twenty-five years old, not much older than Rosalee, and he wore a pinstripe suit and shiny black shoes. He removed his gray-and-black fedora as he walked toward Rosalee, his bright smile gleaming in the midday sun.

"Afternoon, miss." Taken aback by his handsomeness, Rosalee tried not to linger on the man's warm, brown eyes or the dimples in his cheeks. "My name's James Adams. You can call me Jimmy." She tried not to stare at him, but his confidence stood apart from Samuel's or Joseph's, and Rosalee was suddenly aware of her worn homemade dress and how some of her hair had escaped the pins and now fell in damp ringlets onto her shoulders.

"McKenzie," she replied, but then corrected herself. "Carter, I mean. Rosalee Carter. How can I help you?"

His smile steady, the stranger responded, "If your husband's here, I'll speak with him. But you might be interested in what I have for sale, too."

Rosalee felt her cheeks burn, but she wasn't sure what embarrassment was causing it: her husband being in jail or this man speaking to her in such a friendly tone.

"He's not here right now."

"I can come back another time, then," Jimmy Adams offered.

Rosalee studied his face. "It'll be a while yet," she told him and picked up another shirt to hang on the line.

Jimmy walked back to his car and with a pang of regret, Rosalee thought he was going to leave. Instead, he opened the back door and pulled something out of a case. He came back toward Rosalee and opened the tin in his hand.

"Ma'am, I'm a representative of the Rosebud Perfume Company out of Maryland." He held out the bottom half of the tin, which was filled with a waxy substance. "This here is Rosebud Salve, which is the finest product on the market today." Rosalee didn't respond, so Jimmy rubbed his finger around on the hard surface of the salve and massaged it onto the knuckles of his other hand.

"Now I know your hands are still soft and haven't been worked too hard." Rosalee felt herself blush again. "And every young woman wants to keep those hands in good shape—delicate and feminine," he added. "This salve will do the trick, and it is priced at just twenty-five cents a tin. It doesn't matter how much work you're doing—this will keep your hands young and soft your whole life." Jimmy's smile showed all of his teeth, much like Samuel's and Joseph's smiles often did, but Rosalee saw no hint of violence in his eyes. She reached out for the tin.

Jimmy handed it to her, letting his fingers brush against hers as he let go of the tin. Rosalee flinched, not sure how to handle a stranger's touch. Jimmy saw the alarm on her face and held his hands up, as if to show they were empty, with a smile meant to comfort her. A look of surprise crossed his face and he added, "And wait—that's not all. You go ahead and try it out, but I'll be right back."

Rosalee wiped her finger along the surface of the salve and rubbed it onto the backs of her hands, both of which were dry and peeling from washing the laundry. She thought about the money she had left and figured she could buy a couple of tins of the salve.

Jimmy came back with a clear glass bottle filled with a petal-pink liquid. He pulled the cap off and held the bottle out as if to spray Rosalee's arm. The perfume sparkled in the sunlight, reminding Rosalee of the spring and how the sun sometimes reached into the forest, beckoning the water to embrace its hidden nature, surrender to air and light.

Jimmy watched her and waited to interrupt her reverie. "Miss? May I?" Rosalee looked up into his eyes and noticed they, too, played in the light. She nodded, holding out her wrist for him to spray. He misted her arm, the droplets landing cool on her skin. As she raised it to her nose, she knew it would smell like the letters in Mamaw Irene's desk, but more vibrant and fresh. She thrilled at the scent.

"This is a little more expensive than the salve, miss, but I think it suits you awfully well. If you buy a tin of salve from me, I'll give you a bottle of perfume on the house." Rosalee looked up at him, surprised. "It seems like that perfume was just about made for you," Jimmy continued, his face gentler than Rosalee had seen a man's face be.

"I'll get some salve," she declared, and turned to go inside the house, lifting her skirt so she wouldn't trip over it in her hurry.

Barbara looked up as Rosalee burst through the door. "What's going on out there? I thought I heard voices."

"Just a salesman," Rosalee responded, surprised to hear Barbara speak so much at once. She paused outside her bedroom door. "He's got something good for the hands."

When she handed Jimmy a twenty-dollar bill, a look of surprise flashed across Jimmy's face but was quickly replaced with a good-natured grin. "I don't usually get these big bills out in the country," he told her. "Let me get you some change. How many tins did you want to buy?"

"I'll take five," Rosalee told him, not knowing how many a person ought to buy. Jimmy raised his eyebrows and responded, "Anything you say, miss." He came back with Rosalee's change and an awkward stack of tins, which he gripped with ease in one of his large hands. Rosalee put the bills in her dress pocket and accepted the stack of tins with both of her hands, trying to keep them together. When she had them balanced and ready to carry in, Jimmy went to the car and brought back a bottle of perfume, packaged in a white box with an embossed blue ribbon.

"I can help you carry this in," he offered.

Rosalee hesitated. "Alright. You can step in and set it on the table."

Jimmy followed her into the house, and Rosalee's heart pounded at the thought of his presence behind her, watching her as she walked. She scanned the house as she entered, suddenly aware of how Barbara loomed, even while sitting, her sorrow and decline just as palpable as the flowers Rosalee had placed in bouquets around the house. Barbara looked at Jimmy when he stepped into the house, but looked back at her sewing and didn't acknowledge him.

Jimmy set the perfume down. "I thank you for your business, *Miss Carter*," he said with a slight smile. Rosalee followed him out of the house and watched him get into his car. He looked at her once more before backing away, and his smile lingered long after the car disappeared back over the hill, heading toward town.

Chapter 33

B arbara's kin had visited the farm a couple of times since she moved there, and they came by most Sundays to check on her after John's death. They brought loaves of bread and a jar or two of something pickled from last season's harvest, along with news from town and extended family. Rosalee didn't pay much attention to the gossip, but talk of the Depression had started to worry her. It seemed like it might last forever, and if things kept going like this, the hard life they were used to might keep getting harder. Someone had brought five or six recent newspapers with them on one visit and left them behind. Rosalee read them aloud to everyone at night, sitting by the fireplace with a few oil lamps lit after dark, and began teaching the boys how to read on their own.

They learned about other moonshiners and bootleggers who found ways to break the law even after Prohibition ended. Those who got caught were sent to jail or prison, depending on their crimes and how well-connected they were. Rosalee read to them about the Empire State Building in New York, and all of them marveled over the black-and-white photograph of the building the newspaper printed along with the story. Rosalee tried to imagine going to a city—New York or Chicago— and seeing a giant building in person. She hadn't even seen anything close to it, just a couple of two-story houses in town where the rich folks lived when she was little, and wasn't even sure what color such a building would be.

Some of the newspaper stories talked about failed banks and men throwing themselves from windows in New York. Those stories didn't mention the Empire State Building, but Rosalee figured it was the best building to throw a person off of, it being the tallest. And besides, you wouldn't likely die if you jumped from a regular house. You'd get a broken leg or maybe cripple yourself for life, but it would be no quick end. Rosalee didn't understand why a man in a suit would want to kill himself, but then she realized she was glad she couldn't understand the troubles of people who lived in cities.

Rosalee even read the advertisements out loud. The only other thing in the house to read was John's family Bible and a couple of catalogs Rosalee still hadn't sent to the outhouse. Jabez and Ezra pored over the advertisements as Rosalee read descriptions of clothing, gloves, kitchen stoves, and automobiles. All of them shone with the glamour of the unattainable.

The evening after Jimmy Adams sold her the salve and gave her a bottle of perfume, Rosalee noticed an advertisement for the Rosebud Perfume Company, featuring a black-and-white drawing of the very same bottle. She read the description out loud, like she read the others, but took a quick breath when she saw the price: it was worth more than all five tins she had bought put together.

She folded up the newspaper, sent the boys to bed, and spent the rest of her night on the porch with Barbara with their snuff and drinks, thinking about Jimmy and the perfume. After Barbara went to bed, Rosalee took the perfume box from her cedar chest and carefully opened it, not wanting to damage the cardboard edges. She sat in front of her mirror and looked at her reflection for a moment, pulling a few curls from her pinned hair to frame her face. After running her finger along the curves of the bottle, Rosalee spritzed the perfume onto each wrist. She brought one close to her nose, inhaled the bright floral scent, and was once again transported to a rose garden that only existed in Irene's memories, but whose petals and thorns and stems were embedded in

Rosalee's mind, as if she herself was the fertile soil, the dew on the newly formed bud, the glory of the triumphant blossom.

Rosalee slept fitfully, her dreams unmoored by a flood of smiling faces: Joseph, Jimmy, Samuel. Their eyes peered at her, as did the eyes of the children, all bearing some accusation, save Ezra's. What was left of Barbara's face, and the smile she had once possessed but which Rosalee had seldom seen, descended into a well until only her watery eyes remained, telling Rosalee of something yet to come, but without words or pictures—just a feeling Rosalee understood but lost when the sunrise streamed through her bedroom window. Without having rested and unable to sleep, she pulled herself up and into the day.

Rosalee noticed Barbara had begun sewing something different, not a patchwork quilt or clothing for the children, like she normally sewed. Instead, she began embroidering large squares of fabric with intricate flowers, leaves, and vines crawling over them. "It's so pretty," Rosalee exclaimed one evening, but Barbara only nodded. Rosalee thought the squares would make a strange quilt but didn't want to ask why she was sewing it, in case it was for the baby who would never come. *Maybe she thinks it's a girl,* Rosalee thought, and she pushed the thought out of her mind as she went to the kitchen to drink Barbara's tonic.

She gulped down the acrid liquid, and the absurdity of her charade almost made Rosalee laugh. She started to blurt out a confession of the lost pregnancy when Joseph came into the house, and Rosalee's blood went cold.

He looked at Rosalee as he walked past her. "I'm taking Michael over to the house. Gotta get some mash going if any of us are gonna eat this winter." He seemed more sure of himself than ever, and Rosalee didn't know whether that was a good thing or not, but she had a guess.

Michael came into the house, frustration written on his face. "Why can't you just do that over here?" he asked, trying to control his impatience. "I need to be here for the livestock."

Joseph scoffed. "Rosie can take care of some pigs for a few days, can't you, Rosie?" He picked at his teeth and flung something to the floor. "I can't leave Bethany all alone just yet. She wasn't born here and don't know the lay of the land like Rosie does. It'll take us a good while to get everything done, so you'll have to stay at my house tonight. Besides," he said, with a pointed look, "Samuel built a bigger still and it'll be better for making more liquor as fast as we can."

A dark look crossed Michael's face, but he turned to Rosalee. "The boys know how to keep the animals. Just keep an eye on them and make sure they close up the barn doors." Rosalee nodded, and the men walked out, Joseph's arrogance lingering on the air as if to taunt them.

❧

With Samuel in jail, Rosalee decided to plant a bigger garden—late as it would be—than he had let her in the last few years. Joseph kept assuring everyone he would provide for the family while his brother was gone, but Rosalee didn't want to count on him to keep her and the boys fed. She couldn't imagine he would take care of anyone if it didn't suit him in the moment. Joseph never mentioned any money missing from the can buried behind the house, which meant Samuel must have lost count of the money rolls he had thrown under the floorboards, as Rosalee had hoped. She had only spent any of it on the salve and gave some to Michael for supplies, but knowing there was more of it hidden in her cedar chest let her rest easy at night.

As her sons took care of the farm animals in Michael's absence, she hoed the garden rows and cleaned the weeds from around the tender plants planted by Barbara, Michael, or perhaps even her father. *Not Joseph,* she thought. *He wouldn't have planted anything except some damn field corn.* She planted extra beans and peas long after they should have been planted, figuring at worst, her efforts would be wasted. At best, they'd have extra food to sell, trade, or eat if they needed it. She wondered if Bethany had tried to tame the wild and neglected garden Rosalee had left behind, and decided she would talk to the girl soon about how to handle the rabbits that loved to gorge themselves in it.

She tried to think of what she could trade for some extra chickens. She would send Michael to town with some jellies and breads, food she could make that was easy to replace. Even though she might be able to sell her jars of moonshine and fruit, she couldn't take the chance of anything catching the law's attention. But Jimmy's chestnut-brown eyes kept peering into hers, distracting her from the garden and thoughts of survival. The more she struggled to focus, the more persistent his gaze, until Rosalee nearly wept with frustration and exhaustion.

She realized almost two months had passed since her father's death, and she still hadn't visited her mother and Bessie in the woods. Rosalee put the hoe in the tool shed and left the weeds for another day. "The Lord's got this garden or the Devil will take it," she whispered in resignation. She walked up to the house, opened the door, and announced to Barbara, "I'm going to visit Mama. Tell the boys to eat some leftover biscuits if I'm not back by suppertime." She could see Barbara nod ever so slightly, and Rosalee hesitated before she turned around. The boys would be safe with her, though, and she knew she would be back before dark.

As she walked along the edge of the farm toward the forest, the scent of last night's rose perfume wafted to her nose, lifted into the air by tiny beads of sweat forming in the late-day sun. Her worries about Samuel and his lost baby seemed far away. As she drew closer to the forest, the creeping fear of hunger and the burden of her many fears faded like a bad dream, a monster's teeth and nails revealed as a lie, a child's tale meant to frighten. Nothing was more real than the trees inviting her into their sanctuary, and the trickling spring with its promise of eternal life.

Rosalee gasped with surprise when she made her way to Mary Ann's and Bessie's resting places. The white willow reached fifty feet into the sky and had spread out just as wide, a singular presence in the perpetual dusk of an oak-rich forest. Light filtered through the canopy elsewhere, struggling to reach the forest floor, but it streamed onto the willow and through her sweeping limbs, which glided over a carpet of pale and blushing blooms.

Tears filled her eyes and streamed down her cheeks. Rosalee parted the leafy limbs and hastened into the willow's embrace, collapsing against the sturdy trunk. When her tears ceased, Rosalee examined the flowers all around her, expecting to find Mary Ann's ginger had spread wherever the willow had reached, but these blossoms were unlike anything Rosalee had seen before. She rubbed her fingers on each side of a milky petal, careful not to press too hard and damage the delicate structure. Their scent lifted from the earth and filled Rosalee's senses. Overcome with exhaustion, she laid her head on the ground and fell asleep.

❀

Several hours melted into one another while Rosalee dozed, her dreams pulling her back into the earth over and over, defying her will to awaken whenever she nearly regained consciousness. Rosalee's dreams carried her through sagas, lifetimes, and strange faces rolling along the Licking River, women's mouths full of urgency, and men's eyes with insatiable need. Finally, in her half-conscious state, driven by panic that she might lose the light and struggle to find her way home in the dark, Rosalee freed herself from the dreamworld undercurrent and opened her eyes.

Something rustled in the woods beyond the willow tree. She held her breath, not wanting whatever it was to see her first. Black bears and wildcats roamed the woods, though they tended to run away if they heard humans. Still, Bessie had always told her she didn't want to catch certain animals off guard—they might attack if they felt threatened. Over the sound of her own heartbeat, Rosalee heard a faint melody from beyond the tree branches, and she dared to rise to her knees and peer out from behind the veil of willow limbs.

She didn't have a clear line of sight, but watched as someone dipped the cup in the spring and took a drink from it. The intruder was hidden in the shadows cast by towering oaks, but Rosalee could see the outline of a slender arm and decided to reveal herself. She stepped out from behind the willow branches, moving them about so the other person would hear her and perhaps not be as startled.

Anna looked at Rosalee with Haman's blue eyes. She had hardly changed since Rosalee saw her last, and Rosalee had begun to think she might have only dreamt the child.

Chapter 34

Why, Anna, I ain't seen you in so long!" Rosalee exclaimed. "I thought you were a stranger out here. Lord, you haven't changed a bit." Rosalee realized the child should have grown at least a little by now and tried to reassure her. "I mean, you're still just as pretty as ever."

"Thank you, ma'am," Anna replied, her face betraying no emotion. Rosalee started to throw her arms out to hug the girl but thought better of it and wrapped her arms around herself instead.

"I'm glad you're here, glad you come to get a drink at the spring. I'm the only one of my family left now who comes here. At least that I know of," Rosalee rushed. "My mama and aunt used to bring me here, and we picked plants for medicine and food, just like you. They're gone now. Well, not gone—they're right over yonder." Rosalee gestured toward the willow tree, and Anna nodded in understanding.

"You been takin' care of yourself? Any news since I seen you last?" Rosalee asked.

"No." Anna shook her head. "Nothin' much changes around here."

Rosalee thought about saying Anna hadn't changed herself, but decided not to mention it again, in case it hurt the girl's feelings. She might not get enough to eat, and since she was out in the woods so much to forage food, Rosalee decided that must be the case.

"Well, my boys are getting big. They can be a handful sometimes, especially the older one. You might know what it's like if you've got any older brothers or sisters." Rosalee smiled, waiting for Anna to respond, but the girl just looked at her, as if she expected Rosalee to say more. The silence between them grew and Rosalee searched for something else to add, to fill the expectant pause. "And I'm gonna have another baby." Rosalee blurted out the words and a wave of shame washed over her. She looked to the ground as if it might show her how to reconcile her words with the truth.

"Not yet, though," Anna said, and Rosalee looked up with a question in her eyes. Anna looked at Rosalee's belly and nodded. "You don't have a baby just yet."

Rosalee smiled, and the shame ran like rivulets down the flower stem of her body and into the thirsty ground. "You're right. Sometime soon, I'm sure." She decided to change the subject and get away from the look in Anna's eyes, which were at once full of pity and compassion. "We live yonder." She pointed in the direction of the house. "Maybe you could visit sometime."

Anna didn't respond. Her steady gaze drew Rosalee into the pools of her blue eyes, and Rosalee's mind began to swim. The forest enclosed around her and the world darkened. When she awoke, the sun had sunk near the horizon and panic seized Rosalee's throat. She had just enough time to make her way back to the farm before dark, but the walk through the forest seemed so long ago, and the day had passed as if she was dreaming. She tried to replay it in her mind but found it made no sense, Anna's appearance made no sense, her eyes made no sense. A foreboding settled over Rosalee, and her chest tightened with dread.

She stumbled a little as she crossed the invisible threshold marking the forest's hallowed boundary, but righted herself and inhaled the spring air, the scent of new blooms and animal manure sinking all around her as the dew settled onto the wild clover. As she drew closer to the house, a car appeared in the distance, its headlights piercing the dusk. She glanced up at them as she walked, expecting the lights to disappear behind the hill beyond their farm, but the car turned down the driveway and she hastened toward the house.

The car stopped at a courteous distance and Jimmy Adams stepped out. At the same time, Jabez and Ezra burst out of the house to see who had arrived, and Rosalee reached the porch. Jimmy tipped his hat.

"Evenin', miss. Forgive me. I'm having car trouble and my engine started sputtering. I was driving by and I remembered you all to be a friendly household. If it's not too much trouble, could I work on my car here, and I'll be on my way? I'm sorry for the intrusion, truly." He smiled at Rosalee as the boys ventured closer to his car.

Rosalee nodded, still trying to get her bearings. "Get away from there," Rosalee chided the boys, but Jimmy dismissed her concerns. "Not a problem at all. Let them check it out." He went around to the passenger side and opened the door. "You all climb on in and take a look around. Just don't go driving off on me, alright?" He grinned at the boys as they clambered into the car and then turned to Rosalee.

"Is Mr. Carter here? I hate to interrupt anybody's supper, but this will go a lot quicker if I can get a little help."

Rosalee's cheeks burned as she started to answer, and she gave a little thanks that the evening light might conceal her emotions. "He's gone for the night." She considered telling a lie about where Samuel was, and she thought about telling Jimmy the truth but decided not to say anything either way. Michael could have helped if he wasn't at Joseph's house, but it was a relief that Joseph wasn't here.

"Well, I sure hope he won't mind me being here. I'll do my best to get this car fixed up and be on my way. I always carry tools and extra parts with me, so it shouldn't take long."

Rosalee nodded. "I'm going in to fix a bite to eat. Come inside, boys." Jabez and Ezra protested, saying they were plenty full, and Jimmy told her it was fine, the boys could stay and help him if she didn't mind.

"One more thing, miss? I'm going to have to get on the ground to work on this car and don't want to get my suit dirty. Could I change in your barn, if you don't mind?" Unable to respond, Rosalee nodded and turned around, her stomach fluttering as she felt Jimmy watch her walk into the house.

Inside, she found Barbara dozing by the fireplace, smoldering ashes languishing. Rosalee shook her head and decided she would have to hide the flint from Barbara so the old woman wouldn't build fires all spring and summer long. She found a pot of greens on the cookstove, though, and a few slices of smoked ham Barbara had apparently left out for Rosalee, along with a couple of biscuits the boys hadn't finished. There was plenty for a second plate, but she hesitated. Jimmy was a stranger and she didn't even want to think about what Samuel would do if he knew another man was at his house. Joseph, too. She thought about how the boys would talk about Jimmy's car and dreaded explaining it to Joseph. But everything she had read in the Bible said it was good to take in a stranger, and angels disguised themselves as strangers all the time. It was better to offer him some food, she thought, and not risk offending one of God's own messengers.

She guided Barbara to bed, first, not wanting Jimmy's unfamiliar presence to startle her. And though it didn't make a whole lot of sense, other thoughts flitted through Rosalee's mind: Maybe it would be better if Barbara didn't know Jimmy was there at all. Maybe the boys would forget, and Rosalee would never have to explain to anyone, her eyes surely betraying her, unable to deny the thrill of Jimmy's smile, even as it faded to memory.

She walked onto the porch just as Jimmy slid out from underneath the car. The boys ran around in their efforts to explore the car and help fix it, bringing Jimmy tools as he requested them. Jimmy was wearing a sleeveless undershirt and some blue jeans, and she could tell he was more muscular than Samuel, though the rising crescent moon cast little light on them, and the sun finished sinking into the horizon.

Jimmy walked toward her, dusting off his clothes and shaking his head. "I can't get it tonight, I'm sorry to say. I lost the light." He looked at Rosalee. "I didn't mean to cause you any trouble."

Rosalee tried to look interested in what her sons were doing. "Well, come in and get you a bite of supper. Ain't no sense trying to work in the dark if you can't see what you're doing."

"Thank you kindly, but I can't trouble you to feed me. I'll sleep in the barn if you'll let me and be out of your hair by morning."

"We've got extra," she replied in a rush and tried to slow her next words. "I mean, if you're hungry. It's no trouble."

"Just show me where to clean up, and I'll be happy to join you, if you're sure." Rosalee showed him to the washtub and poured some fresh water for him. She went inside to get him a clean towel to dry himself with and nearly ran into him in the doorway. Water dripped from his hair and face onto the seam of his undershirt, and droplets splashed onto Rosalee's face as they both stopped themselves from walking into one another.

Jimmy laughed. It was a carefree laugh, light and free of any malice. She smiled and realized he was the only other person to make her smile, aside from Anna.

The boys ran inside the house, asking Jimmy questions about his car and his job as the grown-ups ate their supper, glancing at each other now and then. He told stories about all the places he traveled to: little towns where he had to drive around cows in the middle of the road, big cities where the lights flashed like a lightning storm that never ended and music played on every corner. The boys bombarded him with question after question, and Rosalee had questions of her own but didn't ask.

A while after they finished eating, the boys started rubbing their eyes, and Rosalee told them it was time for bed.

"I'll show myself to the barn," Jimmy told her, and Rosalee paused as the boys shuffled to their bedroom.

243

"Okay," she responded. "My brother's got a place in the loft of the stock barn. I'll bring you a warm blanket before you go out there."

After she got the boys tucked into bed, Rosalee went to her room and picked out one of the new quilts Barbara had made. No one had ever used it, and Rosalee breathed in the clean scent of cedar permeating the fabric. She carried it and a lantern to the porch, where Jimmy stood watching the stars.

Rosalee cleared her throat. "I brought you a quilt." Jimmy took a few steps toward her, his face beaming warmth. "If you go up the ladder, you'll find the place where my brother likes to sleep. He swears it's nice." She smiled again, and Jimmy took the quilt and lantern, his fingers once again brushing hers, but so lightly, she couldn't think it was on purpose.

"Goodnight, Miss McKenzie—I'm sorry, *Mrs. Carter*," Jimmy said with a smile, and he walked away before Rosalee could respond. She watched him disappear into the barn, his body outlined by the dim lantern and soft moonlight. Rosalee thought to go to bed, but she knew she would lie awake for hours, so she poured herself a drink and found a tin of snuff. She sat in a rocking chair on the porch, her thoughts unfettered like bats flying through the night.

Just as she decided to go to bed, Rosalee saw the barn door open and Jimmy walk out, heading toward the porch. She rocked in the rocking chair, making sure the wooden boards creaked beneath her, and he looked her way.

"Mr. Adams, are you having trouble falling asleep?"

Even in the near dark, she could see his smile.

"Somewhat, miss. And I'm awfully sorry to bother you. I've just been driving a lot for the past week and haven't really got to relax much. I thought I'd step outside and watch the stars for a bit. Don't let me bother you, though. I can go back inside the barn if you need some privacy."

"It's no bother. I was just about to go inside." Rosalee stood up and picked up her glass jar. "I can get you a drink if you want. We've got plenty." She saw the look on Jimmy's face and realized she shouldn't have mentioned liquor. It wouldn't come in a bottle, so he would know it was homemade and might even suspect they sold it.

"Sure," he replied with a serious expression, though the scant moonlight revealed laughter in his eyes. "I would love a good drink. And don't worry—I don't pay no mind to what people do in their homes. I'm just a traveling salesman and I see all kinds of things."

When she came back out with a jelly jar for him, Jimmy was sitting in the rocking chair next to hers. She handed him the drink and stood for a moment, unsure of what to do.

"Would you care to sit for a minute?" he asked, and Rosalee sat in her rocker. She ran a hand along her hair, checking to see whether it was disheveled and unkempt, as it often was by the end of the day. Most days, nobody but her family saw her, and it wasn't until she went to her bedroom, alone, that she discovered her hair had flown loose from the bun she now wore, or her face was smudged with dirt from gardening and farming. These days, when she sat in front of the mirror in her room, she noticed the faint lines forming around her mouth and at the corners of her eyes, as well as the sadness within them. For so long, she hadn't wanted Samuel or Joseph to notice her, and being seen by Jimmy unnerved her in a way she could not have prepared for—it was as if he had found her hiding place.

Jimmy didn't seem bothered by any such thoughts, rocking in the chair and sipping his drink. He surveyed the farm and listened to the crickets and spring peepers, sinking into the tranquility until finally, Rosalee relaxed. Jimmy shared the story of his trip to Bath County from Louisville and how he had gone to the Kentucky Derby just a few days before he sold her the salve. He described men in suits and their cigars, and women with their corsages and elbow-length gloves, and the smell of the horses blending with cigars and whiskey. The thundering hooves, the roar of the frenzied crowd, the din of laughter and chatter—it was a different world, one Rosalee had never before imagined, but as he described it, she saw herself there. She was wearing a beautiful dress and a modest hat, unbothered by life on the farm, her arm hooked with the arm of a respectable man. Her hair was neatly pinned, her lips perfectly stained.

Rosalee tittered, amused by the idea of herself so far away, and Jimmy grinned at her. "You think you'd like such a place?" he asked. "Or does it sound ridiculous?"

Rosalee looked at him, curious he asked for her opinion. "It sounds grand," she replied. "But it's just a dream for a farm girl. I'll never see such a thing." As she said them, the weight of her words hit Rosalee, and her smile waned. She thought of the dresses hanging in her wardrobe. With Samuel in jail, the idea that she would ever get to wear her lovely dresses and hats faded farther out of reach by the day. She never would have wanted to go to the city and wear city-people clothes if Samuel hadn't put the idea in her head.

"What's the matter?"

Rosalee realized her feelings must have been showing on her face, and she forced a smile. "It's nothing. Just thinking about some old daydream."

She could see in Jimmy's face he knew she was hiding something important to her, and Rosalee wanted to tell him everything she had come to understand since her childhood ended more than eight years ago. Nearly a decade had passed since she married Samuel, and she knew now that either her body or her mind—if not both—would age beyond recognition before she felt like she was in control of her own life again. The days of tending a house and taking care of her brother had carried their own burdens, but in comparison, that time in her life was an endless summer filled with simple joy.

"Tell me your daydream," Jimmy said in a low voice. Rosalee looked into his dark eyes and turned away.

"It's silly. Nothing worth talking about." But she imagined putting on an evening gown for him, dancing with him first in the kitchen and then in a ballroom somewhere. He probably knew the best places to go dancing. There would be other women but he wouldn't look at them, and he would never smell like their perfume. He would never hit her or violate her or leave her alone on a farm to be watched over by a worse man. He wouldn't get involved with outlaws in Chicago or even her own father, who he never would have hit or argued with, or killed. No, he would be good to her in every way, in all the ways she now knew a man could *not* be good, and those she hadn't yet discovered.

Jimmy's hand found hers. This time, his fingers didn't brush or hint at touch, but rested with surety, as if they had known each other forever, as if he had always been there. His touch carried no threat and promised no suffering. The moon continued its odyssey across the starlit sky, and the last of her defenses gave themselves over to a sweetness pouring like wildflower honey into the hills and streams.

Chapter 35

The day after Jimmy came to the farm with his car trouble, Michael came back from Joseph's house. His irritation gave way to fascination when he saw the car and Jimmy told him all about the engine, gesturing to parts and saying words none of them had heard before, but Michael and the younger boys nodded as if they could confirm every word was true.

They all sat down to eat dinner, which was filled with questions and talk of cars and which car each boy would have someday. Rosalee pushed away the thought that life could be like this all the time, and a family could be happy. Jimmy winked at Rosalee once while the boys weren't looking, and soon after he finished his plate, he stood up to leave. Rosalee walked out with him, the boys running ahead to look at the car one last time. After checking to see the boys were distracted, Jimmy kissed Rosalee's hand and gave a little bow. He told her he'd stop by as soon as he could, but something told her it would be a while down the road, and she wondered if Samuel would be out before Jimmy returned. For the next few days, whenever the occasional car engine sputtered or roared in the distance, she watched to see if it would turn down the farm road and return him to her, but the cars passed on, and Rosalee knew he was gone.

At first, she daydreamed of him as she worked in the garden, as she cooked supper, as she lay in bed at night, her eyes open to drink in the moonlight that had illuminated Jimmy's eyes and smile, the same moonlight that had cloaked them in silver and witnessed love on the farm once more. She recalled every word he had said, and how he whispered her name with such tenderness that it seemed men like Samuel and Joseph couldn't exist in the same world. The weight of his body stayed with Rosalee long after he was gone, a reminder of the specific pleasure that comes only when a person feels safe and which restored some of her fearlessness, her unharmed—unmarried—natural state.

But the sleepless nights were too quiet, and turning from one side to the other all night long, she tried to imagine where Jimmy Adams slept in different towns, until other women's faces appeared in her mind, taunting her while Jimmy kissed their necks and was covered in the scent of their rose perfume. She tried to pull the sweet memory of their night back to her, but the harder she grasped, the more it faded like an elusive dream.

Rosalee hid the torment of longing and fear of having lost him forever, but she pulled up tomato plants along with weeds and dropped dishes as she washed them. Every sound the boys made grated on her nerves. Weeks passed and her body ached with hunger, but she could not eat for the knot in her stomach. Exhausted, she willed herself to forget him.

She once again found comfort in routine and in the daily tasks before her, which divided each day into different kinds of work. Amid the monotony of laundry and kitchen tasks, Rosalee savored the few markers of progress in her life: a new quilt bound for the baby Anna had predicted, a shelf lined with bright jellies, births and hatchings around the farm. Each time Jimmy's face rose into her mind, she pushed it away with bittersweet resolve.

On a damp July morning, Barbara reminded Rosalee to take her tonic. Rosalee poured just a sip, but as Barbara watched, she gulped it as if she was drinking a hearty amount. This batch was even more bitter than any of the previous tonics Barbara had made, and Rosalee noticed a sweet, earthy flavor she had never tasted before. Her sense of taste had changed, and she didn't want to drink anything but water and fresh milk anymore. Worried Barbara would notice something wasn't right, Rosalee told her one day, "This baby sure is doing strange things to me. I barely grew there for a while, and now nothing sits well on my stomach." Barbara looked at her and pressed her lips together. The haze in her eyes lifted for a moment and she told Rosalee, "I wouldn't trouble yourself over it."

Her belly grew like the food in her garden: tomatoes and cucumbers filling with water and soft flesh, carrots and potatoes slumbering beneath the ground, absorbing the embrace of the quiet, cool earth. Her sons played and worked with Michael, whose sullen silence had disappeared, giving way to comfort with Rosalee and the kids. Barbara's presence anchored them all in her physicality, a surprising comfort, as her bodily elements sought to return to their source: the copper and iron of her blood, the carbon in her limbs, even the mercury of her once-intrepid spirit.

Since moving to the farm, Bethany had only come by the house a handful of times, to Rosalee's disappointment. Most of the time, Joseph came with her, and if he didn't, Bethany was in a rush to get back to her place, but not for the same reasons she was eager to go home on her wedding day. Since that day, her friendliness had given way to nervousness, and though she still smiled at everything Rosalee said, Bethany averted her eyes and was quick to startle during their visits. As soon as she delivered the news Joseph sent her with, or borrowed a tool or a bit of food he wanted, Bethany hugged Rosalee and hurried to her horse.

One hot August morning, Bethany rode up and dismounted while Rosalee hung laundry on the line, her belly starting to swell.

"I'm out here, sister!" Rosalee called to her, thinking Bethany hadn't seen her. But her sister-in-law disappeared into the house without pausing. Rosalee finished pinning a shirt to the line and went toward the house, and Bethany came rushing out with a cotton sack she had put some food into. She pressed past Rosalee, her face turned away.

"Why, Bethany! What is going on? Where are you off to in such a hurry?"

Bethany didn't answer her, but struggled to get onto her horse and manage the bulky cotton sack with one hand. Rosalee ran to her as Bethany rested her forehead against the horse, unable to hoist herself up.

"Are you okay?" Rosalee asked as she placed her hand on Bethany's arm. She felt her flinch, and Rosalee knew what she would see when Bethany turned to look at her.

"Let me see your face, sweet girl."

Bethany hesitated but then turned to Rosalee, her head bowed. She lifted it and Rosalee gasped. Bethany's right eye was swollen nearly shut, and the skin around it was the purple-red of an unripe blackberry.

Rosalee tried to ask what had happened and who had done this to her, but anger seized her throat; she knew the answers.

Tears rolled from both women's eyes. Bethany winced and Rosalee could see that the salt stung her broken skin.

"Come here, sister." Rosalee pulled Bethany to her and wrapped her arms around the young bride. Bethany's body relaxed into the embrace and then shook with sobs, though silent. Rosalee held the girl and thought of her own younger self, who would have collapsed with relief into another woman's arms after Samuel first hit her. She had desired her mother's comfort, but as she comforted Bethany, Rosalee gave thanks her mother hadn't seen her suffer, and she resolved to help Bethany as Irene and Barbara had not done for her.

"I'm not going to let him do this to you," Rosalee whispered, but Bethany jerked away.

"You can't say anything to him. Please—you can't." She fumbled with the cotton sack and made as if to mount her horse. "I've got to go—I've got to get back."

"Okay. It's okay," Rosalee told her. "I won't say anything. We'll figure this out, okay?" Bethany nodded, her eyes filling once again and threatening to spill over.

They heard Michael and the boys approach, and Bethany wiped her eyes and tried to look busy.

"The hens laid a bunch of extra eggs," Michael told them. He held out a sack. "Figured Bethany might want to take these to their house. I wrapped each one but you still gotta be careful."

Rosalee took the sack from Michael and smiled. "I'll take it for her. I'm riding over to the house with her, and I'll be back later on." She surprised herself with those words. She never wanted to see Joseph if she didn't have to, but once it was loosed, the idea made sense. Michael looked back and forth between the two women, and when Bethany looked at him, he blinked, taking in the sight.

He cleared his throat. "Is everything okay?"

Rosalee tried to put on an air of confidence. "It's okay, Michael. Everything is going to be just fine." Michael stared at Bethany's face for a moment longer before shaking his head. "I don't know," he said with a frown. "This ain't no good at all."

"Could you bring Bonnie to me?" Rosalee asked. "And keep an eye on the boys 'til I get back." Michael went to the barn and came back with the mare and handed the reins to Rosalee before turning to Bethany.

"It ain't right for him to be hittin' her." Bethany's face flushed bright red, and Rosalee stumbled over her words in her hurry to soothe Michael's anger.

"You don't have to worry about it," she told him. "We'll get this taken care of and it won't happen again." Michael and Bethany both looked at her with doubt in their eyes, and Rosalee herself wondered where the words were coming from. She knew she never wanted to see another mark on Bethany's face. She wouldn't be able to stop him from hurting Bethany, and speaking up about it would probably provoke him even further. As she mounted Bonnie, she wished she could feel the courage and certainty her words had carried.

Michael helped Bethany onto her horse and handed the sack of food to her after she was situated. He kept his hand on the mare's neck, looking toward Joseph's house, and with a sigh, walked away.

Rosalee waited for Bethany to speak first as they rode, making their way through the fields and streams. The birds who flew overhead saw lined creeks and clean field edges, bounded by forests whose trees did not venture to escape. But the young women navigated around sink-holes and yellow jacket nests buried in the fields, and they guided their horses over shallow streams and through patches of forest transecting the vast farm.

"Maybe one day we'll drive the car back and forth, instead of having to ride these horses all the time," Rosalee joked. Bethany laughed. "That'll be the day. I can't hardly stand to be in it, the way Joseph drives." They both fell quiet.

"He drinks all the time," Bethany said after they had ridden for ten minutes. "He's always out in the woods at his still or sitting on the porch, drinking his whiskey. He won't do much around the farm and gets mad when I don't do something right." She looked over at Rosalee, meeting her eyes. "I burned his breakfast this morning. He says I can't cook worth a lick. That's why I had to come see if you had some biscuits

I could take back to him." She patted the cotton sack. "Lucky for me you made extra." She tried to smile at Rosalee, then turned to look ahead.

"I'm sorry," Rosalee told her. "I know how he can be." Bethany again looked at her, alarm visible in her one open eye. "I mean, Samuel's like that, too. But maybe Joseph's worse." Rosalee's voice trailed off as a vision of the years to come flashed before her. Barbara would soon be gone, but her presence probably didn't matter anymore, anyway. A mother couldn't deter those men from what they wanted to do, what they were determined to be. Michael wouldn't be able to protect anyone, not even himself. All of their lives rested in the hands of two men who would love none of them. It would get even harder as they taught the boys to act like they did—the defiance in Jabez would grow, and a pang hit her as she imagined sweet Ezra turning sour toward her, too.

And this new baby—it would be a girl, and how would Samuel treat her? Would he believe it was his, born a couple of months late? It wasn't unheard of, but then again, she wasn't sure how much Samuel knew about pregnancy. She could tell him she had figured up the time-line wrong, but that would buy her a month, no more. It was not fear or sadness that filled her then, but a protective rage she had never even felt in defense of her own vulnerable body. Rosalee sucked in her breath as she imagined Samuel lifting his hand toward a daughter who didn't yet exist, and the vision of what happened next filled her eyes, blinding her to everything else.

But the horse swayed beneath her, her easy gait a reminder much was not lost, and the land beneath her sure feet knew Rosalee better than anyone living could claim to. The rich earth had absorbed her tears and blood, it had consumed her grief. It wrapped her in vines of trumpet honeysuckle and cooled her cry-torn throat with spring water that had trickled through limestone, carrying the strength of ageless rock into her bones as if the very heart of time itself was imbued into the stream. The earth had always heard and responded to her calls: spring frogs and whippoorwills with their night songs, the whispering wind rustling through the trees, the Licking River rushing and overtopping its banks, the snorts of white-tailed deer at the edge of the field.

Rosalee breathed in the history of the world and thought she understood what must be done.

Chapter 36

Joseph was nowhere to be found when the women arrived at the house. Rosalee hopped down from her horse and took the sack from Bethany so she could dismount.

"He's always off in the woods at that still, like I told you," she said in a low voice, as if he might hear. "Which gives me a break while he's gone, but if he doesn't come home drunk, he gets drunk right quick." Her visible eye filled with tears again, and Rosalee put her arms around Bethany.

"Shhh, don't fret now. We're gonna get everything worked out. I'll make sure of it."

Bethany looked into Rosalee's face with a hopeful, searching expression, and Rosalee saw the face of a child who needed a mother just as Rosalee needed one at Bethany's age, in her place.

"Just try not to draw his attention to you for now, okay?" she said. Bethany nodded, and they heard Joseph rustling through the forest behind the house.

"Dammit," he cursed as he dropped something. He emerged from the trees, his arms full of whiskey bottles. "Come get these," he hollered at Bethany, who scurried to him. They loaded the bottles into her skirt, which she held out like an apron. Some of them dripped caramel liquid from the loose corks, soaking her skirt like pawpaw flowers, whose reproduction depends not on lazy bumblebees or elegant butterflies, but on the flies and beetles who feed on death. "Get those inside and don't break anything."

Bethany nodded and shuffled through the door, and Rosalee knew the girl was afraid to say goodbye to her. Joseph turned to Rosalee with suspicion in his eyes. "What are you doing here?"

His position as a patriarch—small as his kingdom was—had magnified the worst in him. A sneer rested at the corners of his mouth, and his eyes wandered over Rosalee's body, as if to determine whether he wanted anything for himself. Joseph had also dulled in ways. He drank throughout the day and experimented with whiskey recipes, unwilling to admit his brother was the better moonshiner. His swollen stomach told of late nights and meals he couldn't remember. His eyes had grown bleary and bloodshot, and shadows danced across his face, sometimes darkening his visage, sometimes twisting it into a fearsome haint. His handsome face was aging and softening before his time, his body betraying the truth of his ill fate.

Rosalee shuddered inside but smiled and kept her gaze steady. "I was wondering if you'd take me to see Samuel again soon. The baby's growing, and I sure do miss him," she lied, resting her hands on her own slightly rounded belly.

Joseph grunted. "Samuel said you didn't need to be going there anymore while you're carrying." He nodded toward Rosalee's baby. "I reckon I can take you one more time. It'll be a while before he gets out." He smiled, his mouth twisting to show his yellowed teeth.

"How about tomorrow?" Rosalee asked.

"Nah, let's go today. I'm ready." Joseph stumbled as he walked to the porch steps and yelled inside to Bethany, telling her he was leaving and would be back later. Rosalee heard her call back with fake cheer, and Joseph stood on a step for a moment, as if he was waiting for something, but decided to get into the car. The drive to town inspired a new level of morning sickness, as Joseph swerved around curves and swayed along the straight stretches of road. The car floated above the road like a leaf on a stream, borne along the waves by unseen forces, and Rosalee breathed deeply through her nose, careful not to let Joseph notice as she fought waves of nausea.

The same deputy brought Samuel into the visiting room again, seating him and Rosalee at the same wooden table as before, where two wooden chairs sat facing each other. This time, he didn't have any bruises on his face, and he laughed when Rosalee looked over his skin for signs of fighting. "Don't worry, Rosie, I've been on my best behavior. And they're taking pretty good care of me now." He jerked his head toward the deputy. "We've got an understanding. It turns out some of them are pretty thirsty. I get a little more freedom around here, and they'll be getting a special delivery in a few months." He winked at Joseph, who stood beside Rosalee and stared out of the small window.

"Brother, whatcha enjoying out there?"

Joseph swung his head to look at Samuel. "Oh, nothing. Just wore out from working."

"And your new little wife, I bet," Samuel laughed. "She still keeping you up all night?"

Joseph smirked and Rosalee felt her cheeks burn, though she wasn't sure whether it was from embarrassment or anger. Whatever it was, she pushed it away and smiled at Samuel.

"We had to come here before I get too far along with the baby and can't travel." She looked to Joseph, who was once again staring out the window. "Your brother has taken good care of us all. He's really been a godsend." She patted her belly and looked away from Samuel to the floor, and then to Joseph.

"Oh yeah? Is that right?"

Rosalee flashed a smile at Samuel and again looked back to the floor. "Yes, everything's been great. The boys miss you, though," she rushed to add. "I mean, all of us do. We all miss you." She looked up at Samuel, eyes wide and blinking.

Samuel stared at Rosalee, and then at Joseph, who didn't seem aware anyone was in the room, much less talking about him. Samuel cleared his throat. "How's my baby?" He nodded toward Rosalee's belly. "It don't look like you've gotten much bigger than last time I saw you."

"Oh, um, it's great," Rosalee stammered, casting a glance at Joseph and jerking her head back to Samuel. "I'm sure he's growing just fine. I eat enough for all three of us!" She laughed and corrected herself: "Two of us—I meant two." She looked back at Joseph again before turning her eyes to the floor, smiling like she used to smile when Samuel came up behind her, interrupting her from her chores.

Samuel grunted. "Well, I reckon my brother is taking really good care of my wife," he said as impatience overtook the confusion in his eyes. "I reckon that's what he promised. Just make sure you all remember who's head of the family now. Sound good, Joseph?"

"What? Oh yeah, everything's great." Joseph turned from the window and faced Samuel. "I got everything under control." He placed a hand on Rosalee's shoulder, and she smiled up at him, though Joseph didn't see it.

Rosalee made a show out of taking Joseph's hand to help her out of the chair. "We best get back home, so I can help Mother with supper," she told Samuel. "It's been so good to see you."

Joseph nodded and turned to leave, his hand on Rosalee's elbow. Samuel watched as they left, darkness filling his eyes.

As soon as they walked out of the jail, Rosalee pulled her arm away from Joseph and veered toward the passenger door of the car. As they drove home, Joseph warned her, "I don't mind you and Bethany visiting each other some. She needs to learn how to keep house and take care of me, but don't you be filling her head with any McKenzie nonsense, you hear? I'm the man of the house and I'll be deciding what she thinks. Don't need some woman in my business."

Rosalee nodded and looked out of the window, the swaying car and her body inside it no longer drifting according to the whims of nature, but now thrust along a path of her making, one that could not be altered.

❧

Rosalee thought hard about what must be done and how to do it. She bore the August heat with all the dignity a woman could have in a Kentucky holler, fighting against the sweat and sticky air that rendered each sweet smell sickening, every odor putrid. As September arrived with the promise of cool air, she thought about Anna and the unspeakable beauty that would now be flourishing around Mary Ann and Bessie.

She started to walk to the woods one day, but something pulled her back, and she turned around as soon as she reached the forest's edge. When she got to the stock barn, Rosalee found the boys working with Michael to mend a fence. The boys didn't notice her return, and Rosalee took the opportunity to watch them. Jabez swung his hammer and missed often, but Michael showed him how to steady his aim and meet his mark. The boy's frustration cooled under Michael's calm direction, and Rosalee thought perhaps her oldest son would not become his father after all. Ezra watched, absorbing everything.

Inside the house, Barbara sat next to the fireplace as usual, her eyes fixed on cold ghost fires from days past. Spectral firelight flickered in her eyes, and in the dancing reflections, Rosalee saw Barbara as a young beauty, as a new mother, then as a widow once, and yet again. Through Barbara's memories, Rosalee revisited the joy of childhood—not so distant from her own memories yet—and witnessed the decline of joy, day by day, and sometimes in sudden descents.

Rosalee gasped and in that moment realized what Barbara was sewing. "Can I get you anything, Mother?" Rosalee asked. Barbara rocked and embroidered intricate flowers, her silence as good as an answer.

After the boys went to bed, Rosalee walked Barbara out to the front porch. Though she hardly spoke, Barbara could still take her snuff and sip a glass of whiskey. The hot summer air had sunk to the ground and formed a mist that swooned around the grassy fields, weaving and swaying to the last drunken waltz of the evening.

Rosalee took a nip of moonshine and a snort of snuff, her eyes watering at the sting of the tobacco. As the tears fell away, everything sharpened around her, and she knew Barbara would die soon.

"I'm going to tell you some things, Barbara. I don't expect you to say anything, but speak your piece if you want." She looked at Barbara, who didn't respond or look at Rosalee, but she began rocking her chair and Rosalee knew she was listening.

"Samuel's been awful to me. And to you. He killed Daddy." Rosalee took a deep breath. "And he's hurt me. Hit me and—and worse." Rosalee and Barbara both took sips of their drinks and rocked their chairs, nearly in unison. "But it's Joseph I'm worried about." Rosalee stopped rocking and looked at Barbara. "He's hitting Bethany, and she's just a girl—"

Rosalee's voice broke as she thought about her own self at fifteen, and how she must have also been a child in so many ways, so unprepared for life with a man like Samuel, who would force her to hide so much of herself, just to survive.

"I'm not going to stand by and watch him hurt her. He's been rough with me, too, when Samuel wasn't around. I ain't raising my baby like this." Rosalee rested a hand on her growing belly. "I might not be able to fix it all right now, but I'm figuring it out." She stole a look at Barbara from the corner of her eye. The old woman's face was wet with tears glittering in the moonlight.

"I'm sorry, Barbara," Rosalee told her in a low voice. "It's the truth, and it ain't right."

Chapter 37

Autumn, 1938

Barbara's body shriveled and thinned until Rosalee could see through her to the pattern on the cushion beneath her. Though a piece of unfinished sewing almost always rested on her lap, Barbara no longer bothered to thread a needle. She slept in the chair by the fireplace, hardly moving throughout the day. Rosalee brought a bucket into the room to serve as her mother-in-law's toilet and offered to help her squat over it after Barbara nibbled at her meals.

Each time she walked past, Rosalee paused to see whether the older woman was still breathing. And until one day in late September, Barbara's chest would rise a little as Rosalee watched, or Rosalee would see the blood pulsing through Barbara's neck with all the strength of a newborn kitten.

The morning before Barbara took her last breath, she told Rosalee to look in the corner of the pantry, behind two crates of lard stacked on top of each other. There, Rosalee found a quart Mason jar and opened it, thinking it must be another pregnancy tonic, but the smell inside was like nothing else Barbara had given her. It was again both sweet and earthy, but the color of ripe strawberries, and Rosalee hesitated to taste the elixir, alluring as it was. She brought the jar to her lips and tilted it toward her mouth, but the smell made her gag right away.

Barbara made a sound from her chair, and Rosalee put the jar down, thankful to walk away from it. She went and sat in the chair next to Barbara's. "Can I get you something, Mother?" Barbara just looked into the fireplace, seeing things beyond the veil of Rosalee's vision. "I see you made me another tonic. You didn't have to do that." She tried to sound cheerful.

Barbara turned toward Rosalee and met her eyes for the first time in months. "Not for you," Barbara whispered before turning back to stare into the fireplace.

"Who's it for?" Rosalee asked, and in Barbara's silence, she heard the answer. A breeze blew through the house, carrying a warning of winter to come. Rosalee shivered and thought of how she should respond, but the right words would not come. "Let me build you a little fire," she said instead. "To knock off the chill." After starting the fire, she arranged a light blanket on Barbara's lap, tucking it around her feet and placing her hands and sewing on top of it.

Barbara looked into her eyes again, and Rosalee could see a smile, though it could not reach the dying woman's face. Through all that passed between them, Rosalee realized the great and insatiable need bookending a person's life, and the gift hidden within loving one who is helpless. She cried and laid her head on Barbara's lap, the two women finally, and fully, steeped in understanding.

❧

They buried Barbara next to John in the shroud she had sewn in the months leading to her death, a masterpiece of intricate wild lilies against a creamy linen. White satin ribbons served as the ties, and two ornate white lilies were situated above Barbara's closed eyes once the shroud was cinched around her. Joseph dragged another chunk of limestone to mark where her head would be and told no one in particular he would get her a nice headstone before long.

Joseph had driven to the jail to tell Samuel about Barbara's passing, and the sheriff agreed to let Samuel go home for the funeral. The sheriff and Samuel arrived the next day, and Samuel went into the house, rummaged around in the pantry, and brought out two jars of whiskey. He handed one to the sheriff and opened the other for himself. He pulled Joseph aside, and the three of them stood there talking in low voices, Samuel and Joseph passing the jar back and forth. The three of them soon went to the old tobacco barn and came back out, each carrying a crate of quart jars, some filled with whiskey and some with moonshine. They loaded them into the trunk of the sheriff's car, and he shut it, shook Samuel's hand, and took a seat in a rocking chair on the porch, where he would spend the day watching over Samuel, when he wasn't napping.

Some of Barbara's relatives showed up for the simple funeral, and Rosalee spent most of the day cooking for everyone, glad she did not have to be alone with her husband and brother-in-law. She took plates of food out to the sheriff and brought him milk or water to drink when he needed a break from the potent whiskey in his jar. Samuel beckoned her into the bedroom at one point and tried to pull her dress off.

"We can't," she told him, but Samuel didn't stop. "Please, it's the baby," she lied. "I bled a little the other day and it's got me worried. I've got to be careful." Samuel huffed and left the room, leaving her to fix her dress. She walked out of the bedroom, glad to see he had gone back to the porch.

Bethany came to help Rosalee in the kitchen, and Joseph walked into the house to check on them, telling Rosalee, "She ain't figured out how to cook yet, but maybe you can teach her a thing or two." Rosalee tried to smile and waited for him to leave before turning to Bethany for a full assessment. Bethany stared at the floor, her arms hanging limply beside her. Though her natural beauty was still evident, fear had etched itself into the young girl's face and dulled her eyes.

Something else was different, too, and Rosalee pulled the girl to her. They both cried for a few minutes, knowing anyone who walked in would think they were weeping for Barbara. This one time, they would not have to hide any sorrow.

When they ran out of tears, Rosalee let go of Bethany and pulled a kitchen chair out for her to sit on. She poured them both some mint tea that tasted like summer, as if in defiance of the bitter cold to come.

"How far along?" she asked.

"Just about two months, I reckon," Bethany responded, staring into her teacup. "I just realized it myself."

"You'll be alright," Rosalee soothed. "I'll be here for you. I'll teach you everything you need to know."

Bethany looked up and tears streamed down her face once more, though her voice held steady.

"He's a monster. What kind of baby could come from such a man?" she whispered. "It'll probably try to kill me when it's time to have it."

Rosalee choked on her tea and coughed for a few minutes, trying to clear her throat. "Don't talk like that, Bethany. It ain't the baby's fault." She took in all of the heartache pouring from Bethany's eyes. "And it's early. Lots of babies don't make it to birth. You just need to pray for the right thing to happen."

"It don't matter if this baby comes or not. He'll get me pregnant again and one of them will be the death of me, I know it." She took in a ragged breath. "At least he'll leave me alone for a little while when I'm pregnant."

Rosalee reached out and took Bethany's hand. "I don't know what to tell you, sweet sister. I pray neither of us has to suffer these fools much longer." Bethany raised her eyebrows and started to ask a question, but Rosalee stood up and walked to the sink. "Come on now," she said. "Let's wash up. Folks will be getting ready to leave here soon."

Just before they buried Barbara, as everyone began to chat and announce their plans to head home, Rosalee tossed a prayer doll of woven flax into the grave. Samuel gave her a look, which she pretended not to notice. The visiting relatives sang church hymns and wailed over the woman they had hardly seen in the past decade. Barbara's sons stood silent, and Bethany stared into the grave as if it called her name. Rosalee hummed an old song and watched as her mother and aunt guided Barbara to their forest garden, where she was welcomed, to Rosalee's surprise.

Back at the house, the boys played outside with their distant cousins while the adults ate supper and drank pot after pot of coffee. Samuel and Joseph had poured liberal sips of whiskey into their coffee throughout the day, and as evening approached, the relatives wandered back to their homes in wagons and the occasional automobile, leaving as the brothers slurred their goodbyes and the sheriff watched from his chair.

Samuel and Joseph joined the sheriff on the porch and talked for a while, drinking their whiskey straight now, and Rosalee thought of excuses to keep Bethany at the house with her. When he finished putting the animals up for the night, Michael walked toward the house, but Samuel called out to him. "How's your pigs doing tonight, Mike? Did you get you a girlfriend at the barn this time?" They laughed as he stood there, rooted to the ground, his face red as the rooster's comb.

"Bet you like the milk cow best, don't you? Yeah, that's the only girl you'll ever get to touch!" Joseph taunted him.

Rosalee heard them guffawing and looked outside. Michael's face had turned to stone, and it felt like just a matter of time before something bad happened.

"Michael, could you help me inside?" she called out the door to him. He didn't look at her, but after a moment, continued walking toward the house.

"That's right—go help in the kitchen!" Joseph shouted, half turning his head toward the door. He and Samuel laughed again, and the sheriff chuckled along with them. Michael started to turn to the brothers but caught himself, and only Rosalee saw it.

"Michael, I can't get this kindling split," she lied. "Help me get a fire going before the sun goes down."

He looked at her and saw the deceit for what it was but walked into the house anyway. He split the kindling with ease and lit a fire in the fireplace as Jabez and Ezra watched, jostling each other for a closer view of their uncle's magic. Rosalee sent Bethany to sit by the fire and warm her bloodless skin while Rosalee finished cleaning the kitchen. For a while, the men's voices outside fell so low, they didn't intrude upon the home. Michael told stories to the boys, who sat on the floor and listened with rapture. When Rosalee joined the others next to the fire, contentment spread across them like a blanket Barbara had sewn.

But as the day waned, frustration rose in the voices on the porch and tainted the peace inside the house. Rosalee looked to Bethany, who had been listening to Michael's stories and relaxing in a chair, at ease for the first time since her wedding day. Rosalee saw the alarm in Bethany's eyes as Samuel and Joseph grew louder.

"You need to wait for me to get out. Don't go messing around with the stills or talking to customers. I'll handle it."

"I can do it myself," they heard Joseph reply. "I been taking care of the family while you're gone, and I can handle the family business just fine." Michael snorted, and Rosalee shot him a look. She stood up and went outside, where the cool air reflected the brothers' moods. The sun was falling immeasurably toward the hills Rosalee knew like the arms of her own mother. She noticed the sheriff was still sitting where he had been all day and realized he didn't care what laws the Carter brothers were breaking, as long as it benefited him.

"It's about time to head back, Carter," the sheriff told Samuel. "Don't want to drive in the dark too much."

Samuel grunted a reply, and Rosalee walked over to their rockers and stood between the brothers. She looked at Joseph and then to Samuel, laying a hand on his arm. "Is there anything I can get you all?"

Samuel raised his eyebrows and looked over at Joseph, then away. The familiar steel returned to his eyes, though he refused to look at Rosalee and instead stared out toward the farm. "Reckon I've got everything a man could want. How about you, little brother?" Joseph shifted in his chair and looked at the fields and trees separating him from his own house.

Rosalee waited for him to respond, but both men were lost in their swimming thoughts, or perhaps just fragments of thoughts seeking the right pieces to make them whole. She smiled at Joseph. "You just let me know if there's anything you want," she told him, and flashed a look toward Samuel before moving away from them. Samuel's hand shot out and grabbed her arm.

"You worry about our kids and the baby," he told her. "Joseph can take care of himself." Rosalee nodded and glanced at Joseph, who still peered into the distance, as if his future lay somewhere out there. "Of course," she replied, her voice wavering.

"Shouldn't you be bigger by now?" he demanded. "Don't get me wrong—I'm not asking you to get too big, now. I like 'em skinny!" The men laughed, and Rosalee kept her voice steady when she replied, "It's the morning sickness with this one. I can't eat much. But it'll pass and I'm sure the baby'll be just fine."

Samuel looked at her for a moment, a question lingering behind his eyes, and then loosened his grip. Rosalee pulled free, returning to the comfort inside. The boys had fallen asleep on the floor listening to Michael as he told them old stories about white bears and a woman who fell in love with the wrong man. Bethany stared into the fire, fighting sleep and the fresh terrors accompanying it. Michael carried the boys into their room and sat back down in the living room. He kept his eyes toward the fire as well, knowing as Rosalee did that everything was changing.

The sheriff and Samuel came inside and told Rosalee it was time to leave. She stood up and walked toward them. Samuel reached out to Rosalee. "Better give me a kiss before I leave," he told her. "They can't let me go too early, so you're gonna have to wait a while longer before I'm home." He pulled her close to him, his hot breath rousing a wave of nausea, and she fought back her disgust as he mashed his lips against hers. The sheriff laughed, swaying a little by the door, just as red-faced as Samuel. Rosalee's cheeks burned at the thought of him watching this spectacle, but she kept her eyes on Samuel and forced a smile to her face.

They walked out of the house, and Rosalee stood in the doorway and watched the car's taillights disappear into the distance. Joseph drank on the porch until he began snoring, his sleep fitful and haunted by ghosts of women he had never known. Rosalee welcomed them all.

Bethany fell asleep in Rosalee's bed as Rosalee hummed a song and stroked the girl's hair, thinking of her own daughter, who would arrive soon with warm, brown eyes full of knowing. She heard Joseph moan in his sleep and shiver from some chill reaching into his bones. She put her arm around Bethany and laid her head on the pillow, and the two women slept better than they had since before their wedding nights.

Chapter 38

Joseph rushed off with Bethany in the morning, his face a portrait of anger and confusion. Bethany and Rosalee embraced by the car, and as they drove away, Bethany cast a look toward the barn where Michael stood, ready to tend the animals. He smiled at Bethany, who looked away, her mind at war, torn between resistance and resignation. Michael watched them drive into the distance for a few minutes, and Rosalee watched him. When Bethany was beyond shouting distance, he went into the barn and began his daily chores.

Rosalee went inside and wove a prayer doll by the fire, whispering the words to protect Bethany from Joseph's heavy hands and careless heart. A moving shadow kept catching her eye as it flitted around Barbara's chair, and Rosalee nearly told Barbara to go rest now, but held her tongue. When she threw the doll into the ash-covered embers from the night before, blue flames leapt into the air and devoured the doll, consuming Rosalee's words and intention.

October rolled through their lonesome holler with a promise of endless color: sugar maples glowed yellow and orange before they flamed bright red, a last proud display before death. The silver maples that once waved from field edges like sunlight on rippling waves surrendered to the laws of nature and behaved like other trees, golden in their final triumphant hour. The proud and mighty oaks bade farewell with an obligatory show, reserved and majestic in their rich browns and reds.

Thoughts of Jimmy Adams pursued Rosalee all month long, like a dream that won't leave the sleepless to rest. She thought she heard his engine several times a day and looked to the road over and over just to see a turkey buzzard lift off from the ground, wings outstretched toward a dark and empty flight. The sound of Jimmy's voice called to her throughout the days, but she looked up each time to find a horse looking back at her with curiosity, or a mourning dove perched close by, calling for his mate. She saw his face in the well as she drew water, a loving specter that transformed into shadows and reflections of trees when Rosalee's bucket broke the surface.

Her belly grew even though she had no appetite for food, the unborn child thriving in amniotic alchemy. Rosalee tried to hide her torment from Michael and the boys by working around the house and cleaning the tired garden, but she could not conceal the near-constant waves of anticipation and defeat that washed through her, swimming through her eyes and pulling at her face as she yearned for Jimmy's return. She put the rosebud salve on her hands, feeling Jimmy's touch, and sprayed the perfume on herself each morning, the scent its own exquisite torture now. She could see Michael no longer believed her attempts at carefree smiles, and he was beginning to worry.

On the first day of November, the sun climbed into the sky and warmed the world as if it were spring, confusing the chickens and red-bud trees alike, one last gift from autumn in Kentucky. Rosalee told Michael she was going to gather medicine in the forest and walked toward Mary Ann's and Bessie's graves with new urgency.

She thrust herself into the forest this time, rather than savoring her entrance into that kingdom as she usually did. She half walked, half stumbled to Bessie's tree and found it unchanged in the forest, verdant as if the sun and sky had not transformed, as if winter was nothing to fear. Rosalee curled herself at the trunk of the tree and laid her head on the impossible white petals that had bloomed since May, their fragrance saturating the air beyond reason and time.

As she waited for Anna to appear, Rosalee let her mind wander through the brambles of her thoughts she had pushed away all month, and maybe for the entire pregnancy. What she had done with Jimmy was a sin, she knew. And maybe childbirth would kill her as punishment, but she didn't think this baby would bring her any harm. She loved her boys but could not fully separate their beings from the pain Samuel inflicted, which had killed the desire and love she once felt for him. Rosalee thought of Bethany and her unborn child, and wondered how a child could be birthed with love if it was conceived in pain.

Rosalee fell asleep, and when Jimmy Adams appeared before her, she hesitated before stepping into his open arms. When she finally relaxed to his touch, she opened her eyes and found Samuel instead, at first charming and lively in his youth, but soon his face changed and his eyes turned gray, cold, and lifeless. She backed away, but he reached out and pulled her to him, looking down at her swollen belly. She looked down at it herself and understood the sentence, the lifelong commitment she had agreed to when she was still a child. When she looked back up, though, it was Joseph who grinned at her, his breath reeking of whiskey and his eyes ever hungry. She stepped back in horror and fell to the ground, Joseph looming over her with too much power.

Rosalee awoke when her head thunked against the tree root, as if some maternal ancestor was reaching from beyond to awaken her, too urgent to be gentle.

Anna stood there, watching Rosalee from beneath the willow branches as if everyone was exactly where they were supposed to be: Rosalee, her leafy willow, and the flowers thriving beneath it, an island of life in a forest moving toward its annual sleeping death.

"I was hoping you'd come." Rosalee smiled at the girl, not bothering to sit up and present herself well.

Anna set her basket on the carpet of flowers and sat across from Rosalee, tucking her skirt underneath her legs in such a prim fashion, Rosalee realized the young girl was showing more decorum than she was. Rosalee sat up and tried to smooth her hair, knowing she must look wild.

"What are you out here gathering today?" She nodded toward Anna's basket. "Seems like you're always in the forest, gathering something for your family." Rosalee smiled at Anna, who seemed not like a stranger she sometimes encountered, or even like a child she vaguely knew, but like her own flesh and blood. Anna didn't realize it, but she had known Rosalee for going on ten years now. In her hunts for roots and mushrooms, Anna somehow became part of Rosalee's refuge, a space where no one could intrude.

As she often did, Anna looked at Rosalee and didn't answer her question, but tilted the basket so Rosalee could see her bounty: wild grapes, persimmons, sassafras roots, and hickory nuts.

"I want to eat what you're eating," Rosalee said with a laugh. Anna pulled out a couple of clusters of grapes and handed them to Rosalee. She hesitated, but accepted them and popped one into her mouth. "I haven't had frost grapes in I don't know how long," she said with a sigh, closing her eyes to savor the flavor. "This sure is a treat."

Tears sprang to her eyes as Rosalee remembered the last time she gathered wild grapes. She must have been about seven. Aunt Bessie had taken her deep into the forest on a crisp October day. Rosalee couldn't shake the chill, no matter how fast she walked, and she wanted to go home the whole time. Even the thought of those sweet fruits and the jelly they could make wasn't enough to satisfy Rosalee that day, and she had complained to Bessie the whole time they walked. Bessie didn't respond but led her to a patch of woods with grapevines growing around all of the trees, twisting and climbing their way upward. Still silent, Bessie found a good stick on the ground and threw it high against the tree, where the dark fruits glistened like jewels in the autumnal sunlight.

After watching Bessie knock down several clumps of grapes, Rosalee picked up a stick and threw it at another tree. After a few attempts, she managed to break the vine, sending a cluster to the forest floor. She picked it up and ran to Bessie. "Look, Aunt Bessie! I can do it just like you!"

Bessie smiled and reached out her hand. Rosalee handed her the grapes, and Bessie pulled one off the stem and held it in front of Rosalee's lips. Seven-year-old Rosalee opened her mouth and Bessie tucked one in between her teeth. Rosalee rolled it around in her mouth for a moment, feeling the powder and dew on the skin, before squeezing it with her back teeth. The juice exploded onto her tongue and inside her cheek, coating almost her entire mouth with an intensely sweet and biting flavor unlike anything she had ever experienced. She closed her eyes, plunged into the singular, novel moment connecting her with every consciousness bearing the courage to face the enormity of existence.

When she opened her eyes, Bessie was smiling. "Now you understand, some things are worth suffering for."

Rosalee opened her eyes in that same forest to find Anna watching her. It occurred to Rosalee she ought to be embarrassed, but Anna's expression spoke of simple curiosity and tacit understanding. Rosalee finished her grapes as the sun filtered through the white willow branches, the flowers bloomed in defiance of impending winter, and Anna's blue eyes glittered like a stream.

The enduring pain and rare joys of her adult life hit Rosalee, and tears welled in her eyes. She did not want to burden a little girl with her troubles, but Rosalee's throat ached with tears and words unspoken, and Anna simply nodded as if she knew what Rosalee needed to say.

"Things haven't worked out like I thought—" she started, before losing all composure. She had thought she could tell a simple story of how she came to lie on the forest floor, seeking comfort from women who lay beneath leaves and roots, but instead she sobbed, hot tears turning her face red and dripping onto the immortal flowers.

Her words fell apart, and so Rosalee wept. The dead women were with her, though, and they painted the picture their beloved Rosalee could not speak: There she was, a girl who looked like her mother, but whose untamable spirit was fed with love for the wilderness, and by it. Next, a motherless child, robbed of the one who loved her most, becoming the caretaker before she was ready. Anna's eyes filled with tears, too, as she witnessed Rosalee's transformation into a defiant wife, and then a mother. The dead women told the story of an ever-shifting landscape, a treacherous river Rosalee must navigate to care for those around her and perhaps preserve what she treasured of her immutable self.

Somehow, Rosalee found herself with her arms around Anna, both of them crying, their heads resting on each other's shoulders. Their anguish filled the space beneath the willow's arms, and hidden roots pulled their sorrow into the ground, where it fed the heavenly flowers and earthworms alike.

Chapter 39

WINTER, 1938

December arrived without mercy, freezing the last of fall's lingering crops and frosting the inside of Rosalee's windows. When she awoke on that first winter day, which arrived a full three weeks before scheduled, Rosalee rushed to her sons' room to make sure they had not frozen in the night. Michael had already come to their room, though, and sat on the floor, stoking a fire in the boys' fireplace. Rosalee sighed and smiled at her brother. He was a man now, and had been for quite a while, but she knew he was always more prepared to grow up than she had been. *Because he didn't have a mother to love him,* she mused, but she regretted the thought as soon as it flitted through her mind.

Rosalee's appetite had returned after seeing Anna in the forest, and she ate so much through November, she was afraid they might run out of food or money before the baby came. Thoughts of Jimmy Adams and his warm brown eyes faded like color draining from the grasses and trees, leaving a sepia world to dominate until spring. December's first snow blanketed the world, and a second snow fell upon that one. The days darkened and clouded skies sank over the horizon until no one remembered the sun or its warmth.

Jabez and Ezra did chores outside with Michael every day, but the short days took their toll on everyone, and Rosalee looked for ways to cheer them. At night, she brought out a set of jacks with a rubber ball, which Samuel had brought Jabez from some city long ago, and pretended to care about losing, which made her boys eager to win. She sang songs to them as they fell asleep in bed, marveling at her own enthusiasm—she had not felt so lively in years.

Rosalee sent Michael to town with a twenty-dollar bill just before Christmas, with instructions to buy the boys a gift and replenish their dwindling supplies of flour, coffee, and salt. She knitted thick sweaters for the boys and men, even Joseph, though she imagined the needles piercing his skin with every stitch. For Bethany and the babies, she knitted soft hats from the prettiest wool yarn Michael could find in town.

Around suppertime on Christmas Day, Bethany and Joseph roared onto the farm in John's car, and the boys ran out to greet them, unbothered by the light snow falling onto their bare heads. Rosalee watched from the kitchen window and could tell Joseph had been drinking, as he staggered toward the house. Bethany stood by the car and looked at the ground until Joseph made his way up the steps and greeted the boys with too much enthusiasm, jostling with them through the door. He traipsed to the fireplace and fell into a chair, exclaiming how cold it was and how the boys had grown a foot since he'd seen them last.

Bethany tried to walk into the house without drawing attention to herself, but Rosalee pulled her aside right away. The skin around Bethany's right eye was yellow from a fading bruise. Around her left eye was darker, and Rosalee caught her breath when Bethany looked up at her with a bloodshot eye and swollen lip.

Rosalee's blood ran hot and she took a step toward Joseph, but Bethany reached out her hand and grabbed Rosalee's arm. The kitchen door opened and Michael came in from tending the pigs. He stopped to take off his shoes and put them outside the door, under the roof's overhang. Looking up at Rosalee, he started to apologize for the mess, but noticed Bethany's face and stopped talking. He glanced at Joseph, who sat with his back toward them, laughing and slurring as he talked to the boys about things that didn't fit together. Michael looked back at Bethany, who wiped her eyes and looked to the floor. Her belly protruded a little, not enough to see she was nearly five months pregnant. Rosalee grabbed Michael's wrist and shook her head. Michael held his gaze with her for a moment before walking off to his bedroom. As he passed Joseph and the boys, Joseph called out, "Merry Christmas, little brother! Come here and let's have a drink."

Michael muttered something under his breath.

"What's that, little brother?" Joseph's voice carried a challenge, and Rosalee calculated his strength against hers and Michael's, prepared to run to them if necessary. But Michael stopped and turned to look at Joseph over his shoulder. "I'll be right back." He shut the door behind him, and Rosalee held her breath as she tried to account for the guns her father had left behind.

The shotgun was in her bedroom, leaning inside the wardrobe next to dresses she had never worn off the farm. Michael had a shotgun, too, but she knew he wouldn't fire it in the house and scatter buckshot all over the walls. Her father was wearing a pistol when Samuel shot him. Where had it gone? In the back of her mind, she had assumed Joseph took it, or maybe Samuel hid it before he was arrested. But if Michael had it, or a different one she didn't know about, he could ruin everything in a misguided attempt to protect Bethany.

She walked toward the fireplace and put herself between Joseph and Michael's door. Rosalee tried to think of the right words to convince Michael to delay justice, but as he walked out of his room, she could only hold up her hands and stammer, "Wait—"

Michael read her face and knew what she left unsaid. He lifted his hands to show her the Christmas gifts he held.

"Do they have to wait, Rosalee? It *is* Christmas—let the boys open their presents."

Jabez and Ezra ran to him and grabbed their gifts, sat down on the floor, untied the twine, and tore the tissue paper concealing them. Jabez held up his Erector set for everyone to see, and Ezra showed off his Tinkertoys.

"Where'd you get that kind of money, little man? You ain't been snooping around, taking what ain't yours, have you?"

Rosalee bristled at the insult, but Michael kept his expression steady. "I did a little work in town this fall when Rosalee sent me for supplies."

"It'd been smarter to save that money for a rainy day," Joseph declared, as if he had saved any money himself.

Both Rosalee and Michael thought about what they wanted to say to him, and how he might respond to the truths they had each swallowed for so long. Jabez and Ezra played by the fire, quieter than before as they listened to the adults and absorbed the meaning behind what was said, and the silence. The air thickened and wrapped itself around Rosalee, pressing against her chest and throat, and she forced herself to take another breath, a new possible end.

"Here you go, husband." Bethany broke the silence and handed Joseph a jelly jar with whiskey in it. Joseph drank it down, then pushed himself out of the chair and refilled his glass in the kitchen. He staggered to the door, bumping into the table on his way to the back porch. He slammed the door behind him and relieved himself from the porch, everyone inside able to hear his hot urine as it landed on the ground. Bethany made a plate of food in silence and carried it outside for him, setting it next to his rocking chair. She came back inside and Rosalee's body relaxed and breathed with ease again. She and Bethany put supper on the table as Joseph sat outside, smoking and drinking, picking at his food, his mind adrift.

Rosalee passed out the gifts she had made, each wrapped in thin tissue. The boys pulled their sweaters on, and even Michael changed out of his button-down shirt, facing a corner as Bethany tried not to notice. Bethany's gift was tied with a pink ribbon from one of the packages Samuel had given Rosalee long ago. It had lost a bit of luster but still shone, unlike the cotton ties both women were more used to. She opened it and put the hat on, smiling for the first time since arriving there, and perhaps for the first time Rosalee had seen since not long after Bethany's wedding day.

A smoked ham served as the centerpiece of their Christmas feast, but Rosalee also made everyone's favorite dishes: chicken and dumplings, green beans she had canned, pickled squash, cornbread with butter, and fried apple pies. The boys ate in a hurry and ran back to their toys, building things they had never seen before, arguing over how tall the Empire State Building was. Rosalee, Michael, and Bethany ate in easy silence, each of them almost forgetting Joseph, but his occasional snore or grumble from the porch reminded them of his looming presence and intruded on their thoughts. Michael and Bethany stole glances at each other but tried to keep their eyes affixed to Rosalee when they spoke.

Joseph burst into the house as they finished eating. "Let's go, Bethany," he told her. "Time to get back to the house." Bethany looked at her plate and started to stand.

"Could she stay?" Rosalee asked. "I'm having some pains," she lied, resting her hands on her belly. "Baby might be coming soon."

Joseph shot a look toward Rosalee. "How do you expect me to eat if she's here taking care of you?"

Rosalee gestured at the food on the table. "We've got plenty. I'll send some home with you. You can have Christmas for a couple days." She smiled, thankful she had learned to hide her disdain so well.

Joseph looked hard at Michael. "Send her home in two days. She might not be much of a housewife, but she's got things to do."

After he left, Rosalee tried to get Bethany to talk, but the light had faded in the girl's eyes, and when she wasn't helping Rosalee in the kitchen, she sat by the fireplace, wrapped in a worn patchwork quilt.

Michael sat in the other chair, whittling horses and cows from cedar for the boys. After they ate dinner by lamplight, Bethany finally spoke.

"How bad are your pains?" she asked, nodding toward Rosalee's belly. "Do you need anything?"

"No, they've slowed down," she said in a rush, but Bethany and Michael saw the lie in Rosalee's eyes.

"When do you reckon you're due?" Bethany asked. Rosalee looked at her, and then at Michael.

"It'll be a while yet."

❀

Michael saddled up to take Bethany back to her house a couple of days later, along with most of the household's coffee, flour, and sugar. Rosalee checked to see how many bills were left in the coffee can and packed as many canned jars of food as she thought they could spare and Michael could carry on horseback. She also sent Bethany home with a quart of tea—her own blend of peppermint, rose hips, and raspberry leaf—and an unopened tin of Barbara's snuff.

"Don't linger there," Rosalee warned Michael when Bethany was out of earshot. He nodded and mounted his horse, not needing an explanation.

Rosalee tried to cheer the younger girl as they walked toward her horse. "I'll send Michael soon to ask Joseph to let you come back," she told Bethany. "I'll need help with the birth. Have you ever seen one?"

Bethany nodded. "I helped when some of my cousins were born."

"Good," Rosalee told her. "We should be able to handle it just fine."

Bethany furrowed her forehead in worry. The yellow bruise was gone now, and the darker one had lightened. Bethany had smiled several times the night before, sitting by the fire and watching Michael play with the boys. Rosalee wanted to tell her she would be okay back at home with Joseph, but she couldn't be sure it was true.

"I'll be praying for you," she told Bethany instead. "And you come here if you need to." Bethany nodded, the vacant expression returning to her eyes. "I'll send for you soon," Rosalee promised again. Bethany could see no end to her torment, though, and climbed onto her horse. Rosalee handed her a cotton sack laden with food and drink, and scoffed as she imagined Joseph accepting it all without question, already too worthless to feed his family himself.

Chapter 40

Michael returned to the farm several hours later, unhappy but unharmed. Winter deepened overnight, and the top two inches of well water froze, requiring him to bust it up with a shovel handle so Rosalee could draw icy water into the bucket for washing. Rosalee looked up to see the sky churn upon itself, and she knew in any other season, a tornado or thunderstorm would soon descend.

Once the snow started coming down, they thought it would never stop. The boys played in it at first, throwing snowballs and building makeshift forts. But the cold and damp seeped into the socks they wore on their hands, as well as the socks on their feet, so they came inside to strip by the fire and let their clothes dry while they huddled in blankets and drank warm milk.

The snow fell all night long and into the next day. At daybreak, Michael shoveled a path to the barns and trudged to tend the animals. Rosalee watched from the kitchen window and realized it was too late for him to ride to town and buy more food. Their horses would never make it, and whatever they had in the house would have to last until the snow melted. Evening came and the snow finally dwindled so a person could count the number of flakes falling outside. Over a foot of snow obscured the world, and the boys spent the next couple of days uncovering buckets and their favorite sticks, hollering to each other as if they had discovered oil just beneath the earth's surface.

Rosalee stayed up late with Michael on New Year's Eve, speaking little as they stared into the fire and watched possible futures unfolding for themselves. Michael stood up to refill his jelly jar with peach moonshine—*Don't drink too much*, Rosalee had implored—and looked outside at the sky. He grinned in return. "You know I never been real fond of this stuff. Reminds me too much of the medicine you always made me drink." Rosalee wanted to respond, but tears caught in her throat, and so she just smiled.

"Moon's up," he told her. "Happy New Year."

Rosalee accepted the jelly jar he offered her. "You too, little brother."

"Who you callin' little? I've already outgrown you," he replied. "If you measure up, at least. I don't think I'll outgrow you round-ways." He nodded to her belly and they both laughed.

"Well, I would hope not. You don't have much cause to grow any wider. Especially not before you've got a wife to feed you," she teased. They both fell quiet as their minds turned to Bethany and wondered how much worse things could be, stuck inside the house with Joseph.

Snow fell again the next day and the day after that, the temperatures dropping lower and lower each night. On the third day, Rosalee forbade the children to go outside, and Michael wrapped extra cloth around his face before facing the bitter air and walking to the barns.

He returned from his morning chores early, carrying a dead chicken by its feet, which he laid on the kitchen counter. Michael and Rosalee exchanged glances. "There's a pig, too. I'll have to drag it up here and try to butcher it by the meat house." He took a deep breath. "If the meat's not ruined, I'll cure it, but we're low on salt. Maybe I can take some over to them." He jerked his head toward Joseph's house.

"How about the rest of the animals?" Rosalee asked. "Do you think they're going to be alright?"

"They should be," Michael told her. "I think these froze because they wandered too far from their pens. I made sure everybody's bedding is good and deep." Michael hesitated before saying more. "It's awfully cold out there. I'll have to break up the ice on their drinking water a couple times a day."

Once again, he and Rosalee both thought about Joseph's house, and about the preparation required to keep animals alive and well in the cold Kentucky winters.

They didn't have to wonder for long. On the fourth day of January, Joseph forced the car through the snow and into Rosalee's yard, pushing snow over the front bumper. He revved the engine one more time before jumping out and didn't appear to notice the snow up to his knees. Bethany struggled out of the passenger side and held on to the car for a moment as she waited to see whether she would vomit or not. Joseph had already made it to the steps, though, and barged into the house without knocking the snow off his shoes.

"Goddamn farm is ruined," he announced to no one in particular. He walked to the shelf in Rosalee's kitchen and eyed her jars of liquor, some filled with plant matter tinting the clear liquor light brown or green. He chose a jar of plain moonshine and opened it up to take a swig. Rosalee had noticed he took a good bit of her father's moonshine and whiskey to his house when he moved, and though the men had stocked both houses in the past for drinking and medicine, Joseph didn't bring any to their house now. She wondered whether there would be any left to sell, with him in charge, and how much they might still have stashed in a barn. She realized while Samuel was too sure of himself, he *did* know how to do some things, but Joseph was both sure of himself and unable to do the things he claimed he could do. Even with as little experience as Rosalee had in the world, she knew that was an unfortunate combination.

Bethany made it to the door just as he sat at the kitchen table, moving slowly to balance her growing belly through the unpredictable snow. Rosalee helped her walk into the house and onto the wet kitchen floor, which was slick from the melting snow Joseph had tracked in.

"Dead. They're all dead," he told them. "How the hell could this happen? How's a man supposed to provide for his family"—he gestured at Bethany—"when hell's froze over and you can't keep nothing alive?"

Rosalee saw him clearly for the first time. He was a boy, not ready to handle a man's responsibilities, but sure of his right to enjoy the rewards. Driven by impulse and frustrated by life's consequences, he wanted pleasure alone and would not work to care for anything other than himself, so lasting pleasure would always elude him. And at this point, unless he found religion, he would wreak havoc on everyone and everything in his life until old age subdued him, or death took him.

Rosalee guided Bethany to a chair at the table across from Joseph and helped her ease into the seat. The girl's shoulders shook from the cold, and Rosalee retrieved Bethany's favorite quilt to cover her, the last one Barbara ever sewed. Looking down at Bethany's pregnant belly, she wondered whether the mother-to-be was getting enough to eat, or whether her fear of Joseph curbed her appetite.

"You can butcher them if they died from the cold," Rosalee offered, and Joseph scowled at her.

"Yeah, I know that, Rosie. I couldn't get out there for a couple days. The snow blocked me in. Something got ahold of most of them already, and there's no telling how long they've been laying there."

Rosalee heard the words he wasn't saying: he hadn't been to the barns or coop in days, or longer. He hadn't locked the doors at night. Everything he had been given was lost. She thought of her impulse to take her favorite animals with her, and how she had worried about leaving any of them. Overcome by heartache and anger, she didn't know which to feel first. But it didn't matter—she couldn't express either one. And there was Bethany to think about.

"We've got extra meat," Rosalee offered, with a glance toward Michael, who did not return her look but also did not furrow his brow in disapproval. "You all can take some with you for now, and Michael will bring some animals over when it warms up a little." She smiled at Bethany, who stared into the wood grain of the kitchen table as if watching the undoing of the world. "We'll keep that baby fed."

Joseph stood up, shoving his chair away from the table.

"Well, I don't need no goddamn charity." He glared at Rosalee, but his eyes could not hold steady and darted around her.

"Of course not, brother," she told him with a slight smile. "Family just takes care of each other. I know you'd do the same for me." They all knew it was a lie, but let it hang in the air, turning the idea over in their minds like a stranger's face not to be forgotten.

"I could really use Bethany's help here for a couple days," Rosalee thought to say. "This baby could come anytime now, and I've got more sewing to get done before it gets here." She rubbed her belly as Joseph eyed her.

"You don't look big enough to have a baby yet," he told her.

"That's right," Rosalee rushed to say. "Sometimes the McKenzie babies take longer. One of our cousins took all of ten months to have her first baby, and one of Mama's sisters was pregnant a full year before her second boy came along." She looked to Michael, and he met her eyes, looked at Joseph, and responded, "She's tellin' the truth. You can't be sure with the women in our family. The baby comes when it wants to and the Lord's willing."

Joseph scoffed, but his expression turned to disinterest. "Yeah, keep her here for a little bit. She's no use to me at the house, crying all the time." He looked at Bethany. "Get that over with while you're here, because we've got a lot of work to do when this snow melts."

Bethany nodded and stared at the table but then looked into his eyes to let him know she understood, and she would obey.

Joseph grabbed the last couple of biscuits out of the skillet where it sat on the cookstove, still warm from the embers of the morning fire.

He shot a look at Bethany and then at Rosalee before leaving, the door slamming shut behind him.

Michael and Rosalee saw the tears welling in Bethany's eyes, and sobs began to shake her thin frame before the sound could escape her throat.

"I'm going to check on the animals," Michael told Rosalee. She nodded and put her hands on Bethany's shoulders, careful not to startle her with an unexpected touch. She and Michael exchanged a look, Michael's eyes alight with righteous anger. He took a moment to collect himself and went back outside, into the wintry tomb.

Nearly a week passed before Joseph came back, and everyone in the house had grown so used to having Bethany there, it was hard to remember a time when she wasn't with them. The idea of Joseph's return flitted into Rosalee's mind a couple of times each day, but she wanted her new sister to stay with her, and so she allowed herself to ignore the inevitable, until it walked through the door with muddy boots and bloodshot eyes.

The air in the room changed, growing heavy with an unspoken dread that stole the light from Bethany's eyes and confused the boys, who had been playing cards with her and Michael by the fire. The fire itself flickered and jumped as if a cold wind had snatched the hot coals from beneath it, robbing it of all stability and sense.

"Get your things," Joseph commanded his wife, without greeting anyone, not remembering she had brought nothing with her.

Rosalee took the opportunity to escort Bethany to her bedroom and pack a few pieces of clothing into a sack to buy them time.

"I'm going to help you," she told her sister-in-law, knowing her options were so few, the window of opportunity so narrow, but unable to take on Joseph herself. Bethany stared into her eyes, but had gone somewhere else. Rosalee put her hands on Bethany's shoulders and whispered, "Hey, come back to me. I know you're scared, and have the right to be. Just try to stay strong for a little while longer."

Bethany returned from wherever her mind had flown to, and she attempted a smile. "I'll do my best, sister."

Chapter 41

Weeks went by and the bitter cold of February wrapped itself around the maple and walnut trees, freezing woody cells and the water within them. The cold reached deep into the forest floor and killed the ticks and other biting, burrowing creatures. Michael traveled back and forth between the two farmsteads, adding straw to the animals' beds to keep them alive, his face and head wrapped in layers of wool and cotton to keep frostbite at bay. If he resented having to care for the pigs and chickens he led over to Joseph's barns, he never said.

He came rushing across the fields on horseback one afternoon in late February, hollering for Rosalee as he approached the house. Jabez and Ezra were feeding the chickens meager scraps of cornbread and beans left over from dinner the night before, aiming pieces of food at the chicken's heads to see how many they could hit. When they heard Michael and saw the wild look in his eyes, Ezra dropped his scrap bucket and ran into the house to fetch his mother.

Rosalee rushed onto the porch, not wearing a coat or hat, and the air stung her eyes as it tried to freeze every bit of moisture it could find.

"Rosalee, you've got to come. It's Bethany, the baby—" Michael tried to put the right words together, but stumbled in his panic. Rosalee knew what he meant, though, and she yelled for the boys to come inside. She grabbed her coat and the first heavy piece of cloth she could find to wrap around her face. She stuffed clean cotton fabric into a sack and scanned the house for anything that might be useful: scissors, a needle and thread, some red raspberry leaf tonic, a quart of clear liquor to sterilize everything.

She had planned to give baby clothes to Bethany as soon as her own infant outgrew them, and she doubted Bethany had sewn much for her own child yet, if anything. She calculated the days and weeks—Bethany couldn't be any more than six months along. Rosalee let out a deep breath and ran into her bedroom to grab the smallest baby gown she could find, her hands shaking now.

She stopped to think of the baby in her belly and how dangerous this ride would be. One slip on the wintry trail, too much jostling—the risks were greater than any she had taken with previous pregnancies. But there was no other way, she determined. No time to take the wagon and no time to send Michael for the doctor in town. She had to go. She grabbed a prayer doll she had been working on but not yet finished, and she closed her eyes and wrapped the rest of the fabric around the doll's body, saying prayers for herself and for Bethany, hoping one doll would be enough for them both, just this time.

The boys stood next to the fireplace and watched as Rosalee threw the doll into the fire, whispering one last plea. She looked at the boys and told them, "You stay in the house and don't go outside for nothing. I mean it. We'll be back as soon as we can." She looked at Jabez. "You both know how to keep the fire going, but I want you to take care of it while I'm gone, you hear?" The seven-year-old nodded, proud of his new responsibility. Rosalee turned to Ezra. "You listen to your older brother, okay? There's plenty of soup beans on the stove if you all get hungry before I get back." She kissed Ezra's head and noticed his eyes glistening with tears.

She left the house and Jabez rolled his eyes at his younger brother. "You're such a baby." Ezra did not respond but wrapped himself in his favorite blanket and sat in his mother's chair to wait for her.

Outside, Rosalee found Michael had saddled her horse. He helped her onto it, mindful of her growing belly and the bulging flour sack containing all the help Bethany would have.

✣

They found Bethany on a quilt by the fireplace, pale as the ghosts in Bessie's stories of spurned lovers and unholy devotion. Sweat rolled down her forehead, not from the dim fire dying next to her, but from the convulsions racking her thin frame. Rosalee rushed to her, and only after she knelt next to Bethany did she notice the quilt was soaked with blood. She looked to Joseph, who sat in a chair next to the fireplace, his eyes empty and unfocused.

"How long has she been like this?" Rosalee asked.

The silence was broken only by Bethany's weak moans as Rosalee waited for him to answer. Joseph shrugged. "Sometime this morning, I reckon. Guess I won't be getting a son out of her this time around." He stood up without looking at the women and walked toward the door. As he passed Michael in the kitchen, he smirked and told him, "You best stay in here to help the women." He went outside, clamoring on the back porch as he started to make his way to the still in the woods.

Michael stood there shaking and met Rosalee's eyes, full of pleading. "Michael, get me some cloth and the tea. Pour a little moonshine over your hands before you touch anything." Her voice shook, too, and her mind tore loose with the thought that everyone was shaking now, together, all of them breaking together. She started to wonder whether they could mend each other if all of them were broken, and she filled with dread to see the baby coming much too early. Bethany moaned again and Rosalee snapped back into the present.

Throughout Bethany's labor, Michael sat at the kitchen table, staring out a window at the hard, gray sky except when Rosalee told him to bring her something else. Finally, three hours after their arrival, Bethany pushed with all the strength she had left, and Rosalee helped pull the baby from her. It was a girl, smaller than Rosalee's dolls, and Rosalee prayed for her to cry, but the baby was gone and had been for some time. Rosalee looked at Bethany, who had turned her head and stared into the last of the fire's embers.

"I know," Bethany whispered. "You don't have to say it."

Rosalee wrapped the baby in one of the quilts they had sewn and handed her to Bethany. Bethany held the baby but stared into the fireplace. Rosalee took a ragged breath.

"We've got to get the afterbirth now. I'll help you, but you've got to give a little push."

After it was all done, Rosalee washed Bethany with clean rags dipped in warm water, then wrapped her in cotton, Rosalee's touch more gentle than it had ever been with anyone before. Michael held the baby as Rosalee helped Bethany sit up and move onto a clean blanket, propping pillows behind her.

"Have you eaten anything today?"

Bethany answered after a pause, as if it took all of her strength to muster the word *no*.

Rosalee looked through the kitchen and found some biscuits on the stove. She slathered a bit of butter on one and brought it to Bethany, feeding her child-size morsels and putting the jar of tea to her lips to wash it down. Michael put the baby in the cradle and brought firewood from outside, bringing the flames back to life. After she ate half the biscuit, Bethany eased onto her side, her face warmed by the fire, and fell asleep.

Rosalee and Michael sat without speaking or looking at each other, until they heard Joseph's heavy feet on the porch again. They both tensed, waiting for him to fling the door open, but after a moment, they heard the car door slam instead, and the engine roared. They listened as he drove away toward town, and the sound of the motor faded.

"We can't wait too long to bury her," Michael told his sister. "And the ground is so hard, it'll be tough to dig a hole."

Rosalee looked at Bethany, who was lost in a deep, dreamless sleep born of exhaustion, and not from a sense of safety. She hadn't slept well for months now, so fearful were her days and nights with her husband.

"She won't be able to walk around 'til day after tomorrow, maybe longer." They both wondered when Joseph would come back, and what he would say if they buried his baby without him, or whether he would say anything at all.

"I think you should go do it now," Rosalee said. "Before it gets dark. I'll have to stay here with her and make sure she doesn't come down with a fever. You'll have to go back to take care of the boys and the animals."

Rosalee and Michael looked at each other, sharing the same fears about Joseph's return, both knowing there was no other choice. Michael sat for a few more minutes, the unspoken words passing between them, the future an unlit path. He stood up and wrapped himself once again to brace against the cold, and carried the infant outside, still wrapped in her quilt.

When he returned an hour later, Rosalee was cooking soup with ham and beans, and Bethany began to stir by the fireplace.

"Are you sure you want me to leave you all here?" Michael asked. "Maybe we could do something, I could get the wagon." He nodded toward Bethany.

"I wish we could," Rosalee said in a hushed voice. "It's just too much for her yet. And we don't know what happened." Michael understood what she wasn't saying: We don't know what happened to the baby, and the worst possibilities had occurred to them both.

Michael nodded. "I'll come back tomorrow and check on things." With a final glance toward Bethany, he left, and Rosalee prayed for Joseph to stay gone, maybe even forever. The sun went down as she and Bethany ate by the fire, neither of them speaking, while a barred owl sang its lament late into the night.

Chapter 42

The next morning, Rosalee helped Bethany change out of her sweat-soaked dress, revealing a purple-black bruise on her stomach, roughly the size of a man's fist. Rosalee's heart pounded, and she fought back the urge to vomit, staring at the bruise.

Bethany looked at it and up at Rosalee's face. There was nothing to say, and so much that needed to be said, but no real comfort to be found in the words they could share. She got Bethany into a clean gown and she lay on the bed, pillows behind her, while Rosalee brushed her hair.

"You've got the prettiest hair," Rosalee told her. "I could plait it for you, if you want."

Bethany shook her head. "He might not like it." Dread filled them both, as if thinking of Joseph might conjure his presence. Rosalee tried to hide her fear, hoping it would somehow help Bethany feel safer, but she wondered what either of them could do when he did return. She decided she would make a prayer doll, and with a startle, thought she might need to make more than one.

Her own husband had been gone so long by now, their life together almost didn't seem real. Had she once loved him, and had she shivered in ecstasy at his touch? Was it just a dream that she had worried over him in sleepless, jealous nights? Had she once feared him? The taste of blood, and the weight of his body flooded her memory, and she knew it was not a dream, but a nightmare on hold, and one she might not be able to leave by her will alone.

Her own baby would come in the next month or so, she knew. Jimmy's baby. The weight of that knowledge wound itself with the vision of Bethany's bruise, and Rosalee shook her head without meaning to, as if she could free herself from the threats growing around her.

Bethany ate a little food with Rosalee tending her as she would a child. Her skin had no color to it, and her bleeding had slowed but not stopped. She slept most of the day, and Rosalee couldn't be sure whether it was exhaustion or heartache affecting the young girl more. That afternoon, Rosalee heard sounds from the bedroom and went in to check on Bethany. She found the girl covered in sweat, talking in her sleep, speaking in fragments and phrases that made no sense to the awake world. Rosalee laid the back of her hand on Bethany's forehead and jerked it away, so hot was the girl's skin.

Bethany had tangled herself in the bedding, and her gown was wrapped around her in a mess. Rosalee pulled the blanket away and fixed Bethany's gown and sheet, careful not to awaken her. She found a clean rag to dip into the cool water sitting in the wash basin, and dabbed the wet cloth along Bethany's temples and neck, lost in thought about whether she could get Bethany to eat or drink anything.

Michael arrived to feed the animals and check on his sister and sister-in-law, and before he made it to the porch, the sound of a car engine rumbled somewhere just out of sight. Rosalee had stepped out to greet Michael, and they realized they had little time to speak before Joseph would arrive.

"I need my coneflower medicine," Rosalee said in a rush. "And more clean rags. And the bloodroot. The names are written—"

"I know where they are, don't worry," Michael interrupted. "What else? What does she need? Is she okay?" He blushed a little then, his pale cheeks betraying the care he felt for Bethany.

A Woman in Time

Rosalee hesitated. She considered telling him about the bruise, and how it had probably hurt the baby, and there was no telling what other damage Joseph had inflicted upon Bethany. But Rosalee didn't want to find out what it would take to lose Michael to anger or grief, or find out how he would handle either one, now that he was no longer a child. And then Rosalee would have no one, and there would be no saving any of their broken selves.

"That's all," she told him. "But can you get it and come right back? She can't wait."

"What about him?" Michael asked in a low voice as Joseph slung the car into the driveway, spraying melting snow and mud all around.

"I'll be fine," Rosalee told him, hoping it was true.

Michael nodded and climbed onto his horse, holding a hand up to greet Joseph as he rode back home.

Rosalee had turned around and was about to enter the house when Joseph opened the car door and called out to her, "Where's everybody going in such a hurry?"

Rosalee wanted to ignore him, but she knew how little it took for a Carter man to lose his temper. She turned back to look at him as she spoke. "Michael's going to get me some more medicine for Bethany. She's got a fever."

Joseph chuckled, and Rosalee noticed his unshaven face and bleary eyes. It looked like he might not have slept at all the night before. He walked to the porch and stood a couple of feet away from Rosalee, the hot, sour smell of liquor emanating from his pores. She tried not to gag when he spoke again, his breath reeking of stale cigarette smoke and whiskey and remnants of everything he had eaten over the past two days.

"So, your little brother's coming back here?"

Rosalee nodded, her stomach tightening with fear. She laid her hands on her growing belly.

Joseph looked down at her hands and ran his eyes over her belly and the rest of her before looking at her face. He laughed and walked over to the edge of the porch, where he unzipped his pants and urinated onto the ground, the odor reaching Rosalee's nose in another assault to the senses. She started to walk inside and he called over his shoulder, "Make sure you fix something good for my supper tonight. I haven't had a decent meal in too long."

Rosalee burned with indignation, but said she would. From inside the house, she heard Joseph stumble around the back porch, tools and empty bottles clattering as he searched for something in the growing mess. He disappeared into the woods, heading to the still, and Rosalee let herself breathe once again. She hoped he would be too drunk to do much of anything when he returned, and he would pass out in a chair after eating his supper.

Michael returned with the supplies after Rosalee cut up a chicken and started a pot of dumplings. She had recognized the chicken as she pulled out its feathers—it was one of her favorite laying hens, and they had left it for Joseph. Found on the ground, frozen and not yet claimed by other animals, it was the first of the dead animals she and Michael would butcher, salvaging all they could. How many eggs had she eaten from this hen, Rosalee wondered. Too many to count. And how many chicks had she hatched? Something about those questions unloosed a flood of tears, but when Michael entered the house, Rosalee dried them in a hurry and thought she would have to revisit that sorrow some other time.

"You okay?" he asked.

"Yeah, just cutting some onions for supper and they're burning my eyes." He could tell it was a lie, and she saw he wasn't going to let her answer go unchallenged. "Are the boys alright?"

Michael nodded. "They're fine. I hate to leave you all here. Do you think she could move yet? What if I take the wagon real slow?"

Rosalee shook her head. "She can't get out of bed right now. Just moving her to the wagon might be too much."

"I know you know what's best," he responded, "but as soon as we can get you all out of here, we're doing it, okay?" Rosalee nodded and reached for her brother, surprising them both. He hesitated but embraced her, and any lingering strain between them fell away. Michael pulled back to smile at his sister. "I better go and tend to those boys of yours before Jabez makes Ezra do all his chores. I'll be back tomorrow."

Rosalee nodded again, knowing she would cry if she tried to speak, so she smiled and hoped it was enough to tell her brother everything she couldn't put into words.

Once the dumplings were finished cooking, Rosalee moved the pot to the back of the stove to keep them warm and went to check on Bethany. She found her awake, staring out the window at the sugar maple Rosalee had watched from that same position so many times before. For now, the limbs were bare and carried no visible promise of life slumbering within or below, no promise of spring or any respite from an endless winter.

Rosalee brushed the younger woman's hair from her face, and found her skin still hot to the touch. Bethany turned to look at her and Rosalee asked, "How you feeling, little sister?"

She looked back outside before answering, "I'll be okay."

Rosalee picked up Bethany's hand and clasped it between hers. "Whatever you're feeling, you can say it when you're ready. I'm here for you, no matter what." She brought a jelly jar to Bethany's lips, and Bethany drank the medicine without reacting to the bitter taste. She took the sip of water Rosalee offered, and turned her face back toward the window.

Bethany grimaced as the maple branches creaked and waved against an impossibly blue sky. "There's not much to say. It's probably better this way. Except he wants a boy and won't want to wait to have it."

Rosalee sat back as Bethany's words sank in. She knew what this would mean for Bethany's weak body, and she knew Bethany was right: Joseph would insist on getting his wife pregnant again, whether she was ready for it or able to withstand it. What would matter least of all was how she felt about his touch.

She tried to think of the right thing to say, and once again searched her mind for a memory with Mama or Bessie that could help now, but there was nothing. She tried to think of something, anything to comfort Bethany, but Bethany fell back to sleep before Rosalee could speak. Rosalee let go of Bethany's hand, sliding her own out from underneath so as not to disturb her. She sat and listened to Bethany's breathing for a few minutes, remembering her own sleepless nights in that room, the tortured mornings after those nights, and the way she could hardly pull herself out of that very bed after giving birth to her children.

None of it made sense anymore, and for the first time, she felt a flash of anger that her mother had left her at such a young age, and that Aunt Bessie had done the same. She recalled her father's resentment, which had taken up more and more space in their home, like an uninvited guest, and how she had carried the invisible mantle after the grown women had passed, pulling their little family back together. But her father had come home with another woman to take her mother's place, without once considering what his children needed. The good life they had for a short time, he had destroyed, and invited more pain into their lives than Rosalee could have imagined possible.

She thought about the few tender moments she had shared with Barbara, and wondered where the cruelty in her sons had come from—was it from her, or maybe from their dead father? Maybe most men were like them, but some hid it better. Rosalee thought of her own boys and the cruelty they might be capable of, how it might be something unknown to her still, but lurking within either or both of them.

A sound in the kitchen pulled Rosalee's attention back to the present. It was Joseph, and she heard him take the lid off the dumplings.

From the slurping sound and silverware clattering on the stove, she figured he must have tasted the dumpling straight out of the pot.

"Rosie!" he called out. "Rosie! Come here and get me some of these dumplings." Rosalee wanted to stay in the bedroom with Bethany and as far away from him as possible, but she knew he wasn't going to stop yelling for her and would wake Bethany.

She went into the kitchen, straight toward the dish cabinets, and got out a bowl for him as he watched her movements from a kitchen chair. He kept watching as she ladled dumplings and broth into the bowl, picked up his spoon, and set them in front of him.

"Be a sweetheart and get me a drink. Water'll do for now." He watched her fill a pint jar for him from a bucket of drinking water, the corners of his mouth curled in a half smile. After she set the jar in front of him, she tried to walk back to the bedroom. "Nah, stay in here, Rosie—keep me company. You must want to talk to someone who's got some sense after being with her all day." He jerked his head toward the bedroom where Bethany slept.

Rosalee returned to the table, her steps slow and deliberate as everything inside her fought against moving closer to him. She sat as far away as she could, and then hopped back up to clean the few dishes she had left in the sink. She could feel Joseph watching her, and she realized he wasn't making a sound, so he must no longer be eating.

Her hands began to shake as she washed a fork for the third time, and she smelled the whiskey oozing from his pores before she felt his breath on her neck. She tried to turn around, soapy fork in hand, but he pressed himself up against her, holding her wrists and pushing her pregnant belly into the cast iron sink.

"Hey, take it easy, Rosie. You don't have to fight me all the time," he slurred into her ear. "I know you must be lonely with my brother gone. Be a good girl and I'll take care of you when he's not here." He let go of one wrist to unbutton his pants, and Rosalee spun around, stabbing the soapy fork into his arm, thinking only of Bethany and not what he was trying to do to her, or what he could do.

"What the hell? Dammit, you uppity bitch!" Joseph let go of her other wrist and slapped her face with his open hand. He then pulled the fork from his arm and threw it on the floor. Rosalee put her hand to the place where he slapped her, as tears leaked from that eye.

Joseph laughed. "You are a wildcat, aren't you? That's okay—we can play rough." Rosalee looked to her left and right, searching for a knife, a jar, anything to hit him with. The only thing she could reach was a kitchen rag, and she grabbed it, desperate for something to change the fate she knew she was about to suffer.

"When you gonna have that baby, Rosie? It's been an awful long time. You sure it's my brother's?"

Rosalee's heart pounded in her ears and she tried to keep her breath steady, but the sun was going down and the house was sinking into shadows. Joseph's hand flew out to grab her hair and pull her head backward. Before she could say anything, he shoved his tongue into her mouth and she could taste the whiskey, the cigarettes, and the dumplings he had just eaten. He kept pulling her head back farther and used his other hand to pull at the front of her dress, trying to untie it.

Just as Joseph was about to rip her dress open, Samuel and the sheriff walked through the door.

"What in the hell is going on here?" Samuel demanded. Joseph let go of Rosalee, and she collapsed to the floor on her knees, sobbing.

"Ah, didn't expect you back so soon, brother." Joseph wiped his mouth with the back of his hand.

"So you think you can help yourself to my wife, is that it?"

Through the tears streaming down her face, Rosalee saw Samuel gesture at her and Joseph put his hands in his pockets, like they were talking about buying a farm animal.

The sheriff spoke up. "I don't want any trouble out of you all over this, you hear?" He looked at Rosalee, still on the floor. "I'm sure it's not what it looks like. I'll take my leave, and you be in touch with me early next week for that delivery," he told Samuel.

Samuel nodded, still looking at Joseph. "I'll have it ready," he replied. The sheriff turned around and left, and as the sound of his car faded into the distance, Rosalee wished she could die now—anything other than being left with these two men, waiting to see who would end up controlling her.

Chapter 43

W hat the hell are you doing here, Rosalee? The sheriff took me to the house and Michael said you was here. Why ain't you at home, where you belong?" Samuel still stared at Joseph, refusing to look in his wife's direction. Rosalee tried to steady herself and stand, but she was shaking too hard to find her balance.

"I came here—" Her voice broke, and she took a few shallow breaths before she could speak again. "Bethany, his wife, she lost the baby. I've been tending her." She stole a glance at Joseph, who returned his brother's stare without emotion.

"What's the matter, little brother? You can't take care of your own woman, so you think you need mine?" Samuel took a step toward Joseph, his fists clenched by his side. "I saw the way you all acted at the jail." He shot a look to Rosalee. "You sure were friendly to him."

Rosalee thought about what she had done and said in the jail, and why, but now it didn't seem like such a good idea after all. The bruise on Bethany's belly came back to mind, and she wrapped her arms around her own belly, scared in a new way, a fear she hadn't known was possible before now.

"I didn't mean anything by it," she tried to say, but she could only whisper. Joseph stood there, smirking.

"Why ain't you had the baby, Rosalee?" Samuel asked. He was too calm in his asking, and Rosalee knew the worst was yet to come.

"Whose baby is it? I reckon not mine—it's a couple months late for that."

"The McKenzie women—" she stammered, trying to repeat the lie she had told Joseph. Samuel's eyes, she noticed, were not the gray color she had long ago come to recognize as a sign of his anger. Instead, they were the color of slate from the creek bed, so dark the iris and pupil blended together. She forgot what she was trying to tell him, her thoughts lost in the dark pools.

"Don't give me a line of shit, Rosalee. I know what happened while I was gone."

Samuel threw his fist into Joseph's jaw, dislocating it and loosening two of Joseph's teeth. Taken by surprise, Joseph put his hand to his face before drawing his own fist, but Samuel tackled him before the younger brother could take aim. Rosalee let out a yelp as Joseph's head hit her leg. Rosalee crawled away from them and pushed herself onto her feet near the bedroom, leaving the brothers to wrestle on the kitchen floor, throwing their fists with as much power as the years of drunken indulgence would allow.

Just then, she heard Bethany call out, "Rosalee? What's wrong?"

Samuel and Joseph stood still for a moment, and Samuel looked at Rosalee. She hastened to the bedroom and pushed the door closed in the dark, wondering whether she should barricade it. She leaned her back against the wall, noticing the moonlight on Bethany's face and how it lit the room as if it were some holy place. From the kitchen, she heard Samuel tell Joseph, "Fight me like a man."

Joseph grumbled something in return, and the front door slammed shut once, then twice. Rosalee climbed into the bed next to Bethany and cradled her head, still damp with fevered sweat, as they listened to shouting outside. The first gunshot sounded, and the second. A lost voice called for his mother, and then there was silence.

Samuel sat on the front porch until the first rays of dawn reached over the hills and poured into the holler. If it had been any other man, on any other night, he would have died from the cold. Rosalee had fallen into a fitful sleep with Bethany, neither of them certain of who had survived the fight, or what exactly had happened in the darkness. Rosalee awoke first and went outside to find her husband sitting on the porch, a drink in hand, staring at his brother's body as it grew stiff from an endless chill.

She walked around to the side of the house and steadied herself on the porch rail before vomiting onto the ground below.

When Michael arrived later in the morning, he found Samuel next to the fireplace. "Everything alright?" he asked, but Samuel didn't respond. Rosalee heard his voice and called out, "Michael." He walked to the bedroom and pushed the door open to find Bethany and Rosalee huddled together on the bed. Rosalee's eyes were dark from lack of sleep, while Bethany looked stronger than before, but still so pale as to be nearly translucent.

"What's going on?" he asked.

Rosalee stared at him, unable to find the words at first. "Didn't you see him?" she asked after Michael began to grow impatient.

"Yes, of course, I saw Samuel. He's by the fireplace." Michael lowered his voice. "Is everything okay? Did he say something? Or . . ." he trailed off, glancing at Bethany before returning his gaze to Rosalee. "Where's Joseph?" he asked, not wanting to know the answer.

Rosalee turned her head to look out the window, while Bethany's gaze drifted across Michael's face, as if she couldn't see him or anything else.

"Rosalee. Tell me what on earth is going on."

She turned back to face him and nodded her head toward the wall separating them from the living room where Samuel sat. "They had a fight," she said, her voice breaking.

The meaning behind her words sank in, and Michael took a step backward. "Where's Joseph?" he asked. "Did he go to jail or something?"

Rosalee shook her head and tears slid down her cheeks, a torrent of relief and shock unloosed. She leaned her head onto Bethany's shoulder and wept without making a sound. As the unspoken truth dawned on him, Michael turned to look into the room where Samuel still sat, his eyes turned to stone so the firelight wouldn't reflect in them. Michael shivered and looked back to the women.

"We need to go."

Rosalee hesitated, and then stood and packed as many of Bethany's things as she could wrap her mind around. She picked up the baby gown she had brought with her, and looked at Bethany's face. Her eyes were fixed at some point in front of the wall. Perhaps she saw something in the air itself no one else could see, and nothing visible mattered so much as the space between dust motes floating in the waning sun of winter.

Rosalee dropped the baby gown onto the floor and gathered the cotton sacks she had filled with Bethany's clothes and the supplies that remained. She nodded to Michael, and he approached the bed with care, wrapping the blanket Bethany lay on around her arms. Bethany's eyes did not move even as he lifted her and carried her like a child out of the bedroom, through the house, and to the wagon he had driven there, just in case she could be moved.

Samuel's eyes also remained fixed, intent on some flame that would never cast light into his vision.

Chapter 44

Spring, 1939

The first days of March transformed the Kentucky landscape with such fervor, a visitor would have mistaken the land for a hospitable place. The redbuds boasted their purple glory, while yellow daffodils sang across garden beds and spilled into ditches and graveyards. Rosalee knew without seeing them that the wild lilies and trillium had exploded in the forest, intent to usher in an early spring. Almost all the signs of their treacherous winter had disappeared into the sodden ground.

The boys grumbled about sleeping on the floor, but their home felt complete with Bethany there. They pleaded with Rosalee to have a fourth bedroom built, and she shushed them, but set the idea aside to think on later. The thought of Samuel's return came to Rosalee's mind several times a day, puncturing the daydream of their simple lives together, and she wished beyond all other wishes that something could change what she knew was yet to come. Bethany's body had just recovered from all it had been subjected to, while Rosalee's belly had grown and stretched with the passion of this early spring. And then, two weeks after he arrived with the sheriff, Samuel returned home.

Rosalee heard the car before she saw it, and for less than a breath's worth of time, she thought it was Jimmy Adams coming back to see her, to claim his child and family. She looked up from the laundry she was hanging, careful not to lift too much or move too fast. The car still bore the mud splatters from Joseph's last drive. Rosalee kept pinning laundry to the line, but the music of the spring birds hardened, their voices no longer a chorus but a warning.

Samuel didn't look at her as he parked the car and entered the house. Rosalee heard Jabez and Ezra holler with delight as they greeted their father and threw their arms around him. She carried the empty basket into the house, her stomach once again filled with dread.

Rosalee served everyone supper that evening, the table fuller than it had ever been before in her memory. Bethany was able to sit on a makeshift cushion—just like Barbara had once made for Rosalee—and eat most of her meal with them, even if her gaze remained fixed on something no one else could see. Jabez and Ezra lapped up their father's attention like starved dogs, asking him questions about jail that Samuel answered with his familiar grin, his slate eyes untouched by the lamplight around them.

Michael and Rosalee ate without speaking or smiling. Outside, where the sun had warmed the farm with such cheer, thick clouds gathered as if to counter the unexpected early spring. A hush fell over the farm and invaded the house and the minds of everyone in it.

After supper, Rosalee coaxed the boys to bed, sending them to sleep on Michael's floor or perhaps at the foot of his bed, if he was willing to share the space. Rosalee then helped Bethany to bed, and the two women wanted to whisper to one another, to offer comfort or condolences, but they knew it was better to be quiet. This understanding passed between them in the light of a single candle that was somehow supposed to illuminate their paths. Rosalee smiled at Bethany, a wildflower whose beauty was her only defense against cruelty and decay. She leaned over and kissed Bethany's forehead before pinching the flame from the candlewick.

When she came out of the bedroom, she found Samuel in the kitchen, pulling jars from the shelves. He examined each by holding it in front of the lamplight, looking at the color imbued into it. He scoffed and shook his head at the fine whiskey he found ruined by roots and flowers Rosalee had stuffed into the bottles. He found one still clear, untainted by a woman's notions and whims, and poured himself a generous drink. Rosalee saw the familiar pistol on the side of his hip once more. Outside the kitchen window, the last of the green sky disappeared, and the world plunged into darkness.

Rosalee sat by the fire, where Michael was watching the light and shadows play against the backdrop of stone. Samuel walked over and stood for a moment, drink in hand, as if to survey the scene. He had hardly spoken except with the children, and Rosalee's dread gave way to acceptance. He would do whatever he chose, and there was nothing she could do to change that. It was too late for prayers or dolls or songs. Whether Samuel waited until Michael had gone to bed, or perhaps even waited until Rosalee was asleep, he would punish her, and there was little room to survive it.

She imagined herself buried next to her mama and aunt, her only daughter still inside her, forever cradled and never knowing the harsh touch of the world. Rosalee smiled and regretted only that she couldn't tell her brother where to bury her. The wind began to whistle outside, low at first, like a widow singing church hymns.

She looked at Samuel, knowing she should be careful, but too tired to pretend anymore, too tired to sneak glances and hide every last thing. She noticed the changes in his face for the first time since his unexpected arrival at Joseph's house, which had once been home to Samuel and Rosalee when they were newlyweds and young parents. The faint lines across his forehead and around his mouth had deepened, and the last of his boyish looks had abandoned him. Samuel was still handsome, to be sure, but the darkness that had once been hidden was now made visible, etched into the lines in his face, imbued in the veils over his eyes.

They sat in silence as the fire died down, each of them lost in a labyrinth of the merciless past. Samuel refilled his glass once, and then twice. Each time, Rosalee considered leaving the room when his back was turned, but she knew he would see that as an invitation for rage. As he emptied the jar of clear whiskey, his face grew red and his body seemed looser, even while sitting in the chair. The wind picked up outside and rattled the wooden shutters, and Samuel smiled at his wife.

"Well, Rosie, it sure has been a long time since I got to be home. Of course, this wasn't home when I left"—he gestured around the room—"but I reckon it'll do." Rosalee waited for him to continue, and Samuel let out a sigh. "You're probably sore at me for what I did to your daddy." He looked at his drink as if to understand it better, and took another swig. "But seems we're even, when you figure in what happened between you and my brother while I was locked up."

"Now, Samuel—" Michael started to speak.

"Don't start with me, boy," Samuel said to him. "This is between me and my wife, and I don't need your nose in my business. Why don't you go to bed like the other kids." It was a command, not a question, and both Michael and Rosalee weighed the threat in Samuel's voice against the damage he could do with them awake, asleep, or in any state at all.

Lightning hit a tree outside, splitting it with a thunderous crack. Rosalee and Michael jumped, while Samuel scowled at the window, as if the storm had interrupted him. Michael started to respond to Samuel, but Rosalee spoke up first.

"You'd better go to bed, in case the storm wakes the boys up. They'll feel better with you in there." Michael looked at her, pressed his lips together, and pushed himself out of his chair. He cast one last glance toward Rosalee before shutting his bedroom door.

The rain began to pound on the tin roof. Rosalee turned to Samuel, ready now for whatever would come next. She ached for her unborn daughter, longed to hold the girl she now understood she would never meet.

Samuel stood up and the wind howled now, flinging hail against the glass windows, which cracked from impact and the shifting pressure. Rosalee closed her eyes, bracing for his touch, but Samuel went to the kitchen once more, this time grabbing the last Mason jar from the pantry. It was the color of ripe strawberries—Barbara's tonic that was not meant for Rosalee. Too drunk to care about the color or the meddling of women, Samuel poured himself another drink and lifted it to his mouth before Rosalee could find the words to speak.

"Looks like you all've had a great time while I've been gone," he laughed, though Rosalee recognized the warning in his voice. "Drank an awful lot of whiskey—there'd better be some left in the barn." Rosalee stood, frozen, waiting for him to continue. "Ain't no matter. I'll be back at it in no time. Looks like I'll have to teach you a lesson, though." He glared at her as best he could, his eyes losing focus.

He sat down in a kitchen chair, his head heavy and full, and tried to finish his drink. Rosalee watched from beside the fireplace, still ready for his wrath. Samuel coughed as he swallowed the last of his mother's tonic, and then wiped his mouth on his arm. He stood up and took a step toward Rosalee before a look of surprise crossed his face. Rosalee also stood, not sure whether to walk toward him or farther away, and Samuel laughed a little. Before he could do anything else, confusion took hold and Samuel looked around, as if he had forgotten what he was doing.

Thunder and lightning cracked again, and though no one was there to see it, the wind tore the roof from Joseph's house and flung it on top of the shallow grave where he lay cold. The wind flew through the house where Rosalee had given birth and suffered her husband, and it pulled timbers from nails as cracks ran through the stone mortar of the fireplace. The walls groaned and then crumbled, shattering every piece of glass and splintering each board, until only the unworn baby gown remained intact, still on the floor where Rosalee had dropped it.

Rosalee's childhood home creaked and moaned under the storm, and Samuel fell further into delirium, his mind a storm, his thoughts a broken house. Rosalee sat by the fire, all of her tears far away, and everyone awoke at once, not knowing why. Phantoms flew as Samuel forced his body to stand from the chair, mumbled something about needing to piss, and stumbled out the door.

EPILOGUE

Rosalee visited the woods one more time before her daughter was born, despite Michael's concern about her going off by herself. Things would be different this time, she knew, but she was still surprised at the changes she discovered.

The storm had torn down tree after tree, so Rosalee had to find a different way to enter the forest. Her foot-worn path was gone, and the landscape made anew. She climbed over fallen pines and cedars in the wetter part of the forest, searching through a maze of destruction for those landmarks she had depended on for so long now. The sun climbed overhead, and Rosalee's stomach rumbled with hunger. She realized she was wandering without aim, and resigned herself to going home and returning sometime after the baby was born.

As she turned to search for her way back, the sun glimmered off something beneath a broken branch. Rosalee walked closer and found a dead oak branch on top of the spring. The tin cup sat on the rock shelf undisturbed, catching the light. She tried to pull the branch, but it was heavier than it looked, and she paused to think about what she could do with the baby so close to birth.

"Mama says it ain't safe to be lifting too much when you've got a baby on the way." Rosalee dropped the branch and spun around, startled even though she recognized the voice. Anna stood with her basket about twenty feet away.

She gave a little laugh and responded, "You're right—I mean, she's right. I ought to know better." Rosalee smoothed the front of her dress and brushed off pieces of bark sticking to it. "You out here gathering again, Anna?"

Anna nodded, her blue eyes deeper than they had ever been before, but Rosalee noticed nothing else had changed since they last saw each other. "Got to keep the medicine jars full." Rosalee's mind raced over the questions she wanted to ask Anna and the different bits of news she could share with the girl. Before she could say anything, Anna walked away, and Rosalee decided to follow her.

When Anna stopped, she had reached a familiar opening in the canopy, and Rosalee caught up a moment later to find her staring at the white willow. Rosalee couldn't see any missing limbs or other storm damage, but the tree no longer radiated like it did before. The hanging branches had just begun to bud, bringing a hint of life to the otherwise bare woodland body. Rosalee looked for traces of the mysterious flowers that had carpeted the forest floor, but only found decaying leaves and unopened trilliums.

She looked at Anna, who stood watching Rosalee, as if she was waiting for Rosalee to finish some necessary task. Rosalee walked into the carpet of bloomless ginger, which had grown over the limestone marking Mary Ann's grave. She pushed the leaves aside, and thought she would come back often to clear the lush plants so they wouldn't hide her mother's grave forever.

She was struck by the finality of her mother's departure, and by the senseless losses mounting around her. No longer was she the child of someone—she could only be the mother, and perhaps someday, the grandmother. She might become someone's aunt, and she may even be a wife again, after the proper mourning time had passed. But the sweetness of childhood was long gone.

A rustling sound interrupted Rosalee's grief, and she turned to find a doe standing where Anna had been. The deer's belly was swollen with life. *We look just alike,* Rosalee thought with a smile. As they looked into each other's eyes, the doe bleated her long, low call to a yearling Rosalee could not see, and walked away, disappearing into the forest.

ACKNOWLEDGMENTS

I have so many people to thank for helping bring this story to life. I wrote a large portion of it during 2020, stuck in a small apartment with my daughter. I am eternally grateful for her patience, kindness, and resilience, as well as the lighthearted moments we shared dancing, laughing at *The Office*, and eating more than enough Chipotle. Thank you, sweet girl, for being there and for all you are.

Thank you to my son, Aubrey, who is a constant light in my life, in his sister's life, and in the lives of so many others. As you have grown into adulthood, you continue to teach me so much about motherhood, and I think the world of you. Becoming a mother was the best thing that could have happened to me, and you are a blessing.

To Steve McCallum, thank you for your love and kindness, your discernment, and your generosity. Your careful attention to this book helped push it to where it needed to be, and I am forever grateful to you.

I am especially thankful for Carla Gover and all our conversations about life in Eastern Kentucky and my depictions of it, as well as for her being a wonderful art friend.

I am grateful for my mother, who has shown a great amount of support as I write stories, some of which include parts of her own story. Your graciousness amazes me, and I appreciate it more than I can express.

Thank you to my Granny Conn—Delores Ann McKenzie—who taught me about strength and love. And thank you to the other McKenzie women who reached out after my memoir was first published. Your support was a great surprise, and I am uplifted just to know you love and accept me. I hope you find this story a worthy tribute to our family name.

A lot of emotional and physical effort went into writing this book. I am forever thankful for the friendship of Dr. Jennifer See and Paul See, who welcomed us and provided support in a challenging time. You all have been amazing, and we love you.

Barbara Roberts and Maria Wright were generous with their time and attention, reading multiple drafts and discussing this story with me as it evolved. Your friendship means a lot to me, and I am thankful for your keen insights as avid readers. To Ellen Mitchell, Kari Major, and Angela Anderson—thank you for being here together through our journeys. I count myself lucky to have you as friends.

So much of my journey as an author was made possible because of Lois Giancola Papania and the friendship that developed from that first life-changing appointment. I am forever grateful for your support and how you believed in me when I needed it most.

Thank you to Rachel Smith for your work as a neurofeedback therapist, for helping me understand how I have been impacted by trauma, and for helping me free myself from some of those impacts. My work with you has deepened my gratitude for life and for opportunities to heal.

Writing this book involved a lot of knowledge I had gleaned over the years or just thought to be true, but God is in the details, as many brilliant minds have observed. I appreciated having Andrew Bentley read this story for accuracy in the plant medicine references; Rachel Kennedy for historic architecture and other historic information; and Candace Robinson for her expertise in childbirth (for more reasons than one).

I am grateful to the entire team at Little A for believing in this story. Carmen Johnson was gracious to move this project forward, while Heather Lazarre, as an editing consultant, lent her incredible skills to shape and improve the story. Laura Van der Veer provided invaluable support and editorial input, and I am most grateful to have such a group of women rally behind this book. My thanks also to Hafizah Geter, my first editor, for the work we were able to do together and for helping make this book possible. Emma Reh and Laura Whittemore provided invaluable editing services, helping this manuscript become the best it could be—thank you.

Thank you again to my agent, Adriann Zurhellen, for coming to the conference where we first met. Thank you for listening, giving advice, and going to bat for me.

Finally, thank you to the many women and men in my family who, whether I met them in person or not, helped shape me and bring our story to this point. You all have been incredibly strong, and I hope I have made you proud.

ABOUT THE AUTHOR

Photo © 2019 Erica Chambers Photography

Bobi Conn is the author of the memoir *In the Shadow of the Valley*. Born in Morehead, Kentucky, and raised in a nearby holler, Bobi developed a deep connection with the land and her Appalachian roots. She obtained her bachelor's degree at Berea College, the first school in the American South to integrate racially and to teach men and women in the same classrooms. She attended graduate school, where she earned a master's degree in English with an emphasis in creative writing. In addition to writing, Bobi loves playing pool, telling jokes, cooking, being in the woods, attempting to grow a garden, and spending time with her incredible children.